DISNEY MASTERS

DONALD DUCK: UNCLE SCROOGE'S MONEY ROCKET

by Luciano Bottaro

Publisher: GARY GROTH
Senior Editor: J. MICHAEL CATRON
Archival Editor: DAVID GERSTEIN
Designer: KEELI McCARTHY
Production: PAUL BARESH
Associate Publisher: ERIC REYNOLDS

Fantagraphics Books, Inc.
7563 Lake City Way NE
Seattle WA 98115
(800) 657-1100

Thanks to Gareth Bentall, Avi Kool, R.J. Casey, and Sean David Williams.

Visit us at fantagraphics.com. Follow us on Twitter at @fantagraphics
and on Facebook at facebook.com/fantagraphics.

First printing: August 2018
ISBN 978-1-68396-109-3
Printed in The Republic of Korea
Library of Congress Control Number: 2017956971

The stories in this volume were originally published in Italy, and appear in English here for the first time.
"Uncle Scrooge's Money Rocket" ("Paperino e il razzo interplanetario") in *Topolino* #230-232,
March 10, March 25, and April 10, 1960 (I TL 230-BP)
Untitled illustration on page 76 in *Tesori Disney* #7, July 2010
"The Return of Rebo" ("Paperino e il ritorno di Rebo") in *Topolino* #2049, March 7, 1995 (I TL 2049-1)
"TV Trickery" ("Zio Paperone e il telescrocco") in *Topolino* #397, July 7, 1963 (I TL 397-A)

These stories were created during an earlier time and may include cartoon violence, historically dated content, or gags that depict smoking, drinking, gunplay, or ethnic stereotypes. We present them here with their original flaws with a caution to the reader that they reflect a bygone era.

Front cover illustration by Marco Gervasio, color by Stefano Intini.
Back cover illustration by Luciano Bottaro, color by Christos Kentrotis.

TITLES IN THIS SERIES

Mickey Mouse: The Delta Dimension (Romano Scarpa) (*Disney Masters* Vol. 1)
Donald Duck: Uncle Scrooge's Money Rocket (Luciano Bottaro) (*Disney Masters* Vol. 2)

COMING SOON

Mickey Mouse: The Case of the Vanishing Bandit (Paul Murry) (*Disney Masters* Vol. 3)
Donald Duck: The Great Survival Test (Daan Jippes and Freddy Milton) (*Disney Masters* Vol. 4)

ALSO AVAILABLE

Walt Disney's Donald Duck: "The Lost Peg Leg Mine" (Carl Barks)
Walt Disney Uncle Scrooge and Donald Duck: "The Three Caballeros Ride Again!" (Don Rosa)
The Return of Snow White and the Seven Dwarfs (Romano Scarpa)

WALT DISNEY
Donald Duck

Uncle Scrooge's
MONEY ROCKET

FANTAGRAPHICS BOOKS

SEATTLE

CONTENTS

All comics stories illustrated by Luciano Bottaro

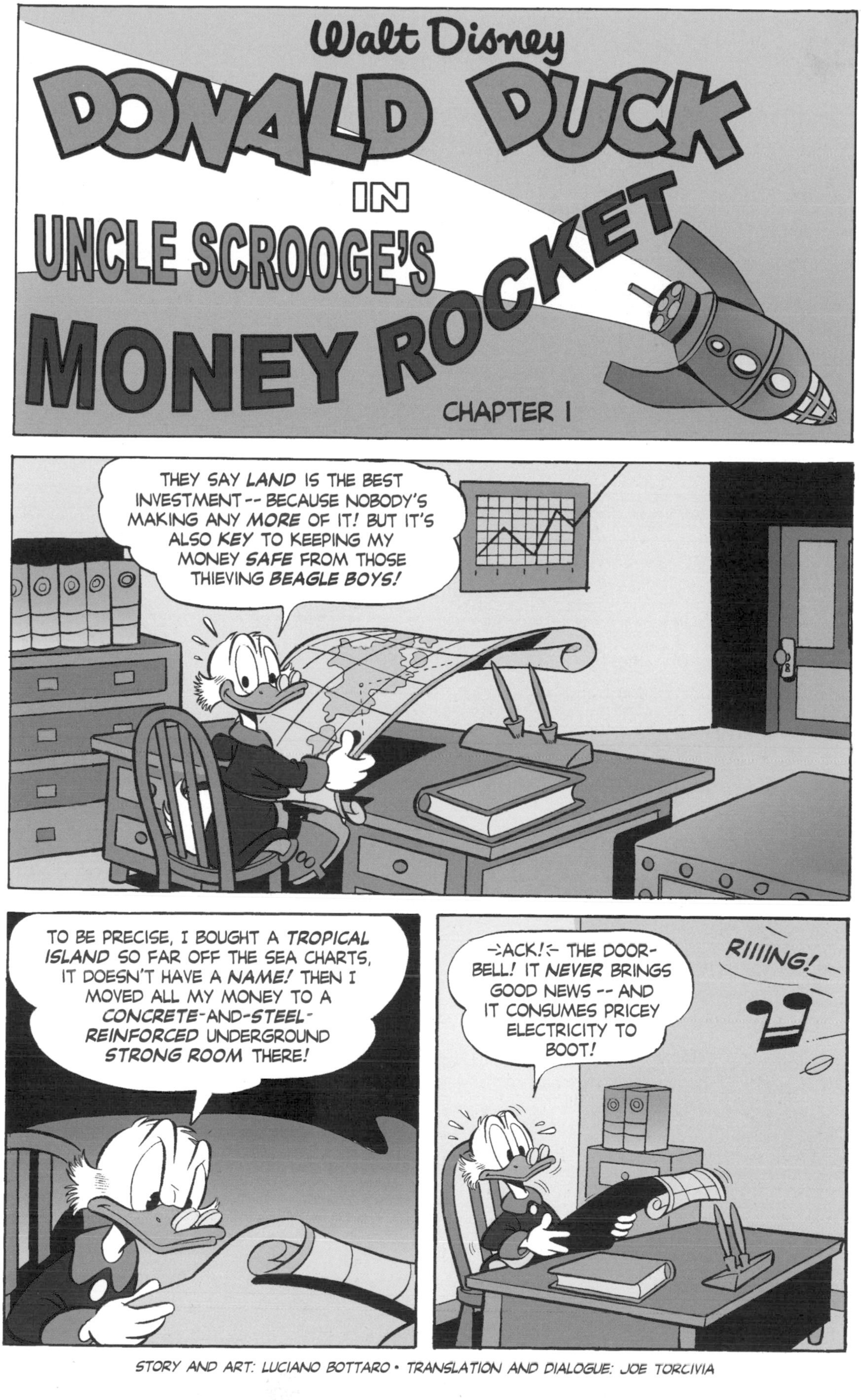
Walt Disney
DONALD DUCK
IN
UNCLE SCROOGE'S
MONEY ROCKET
CHAPTER 1
THEY SAY LAND IS THE BEST INVESTMENT -- BECAUSE NOBODY'S MAKING ANY MORE OF IT! BUT IT'S ALSO KEY TO KEEPING MY MONEY SAFE FROM THOSE THIEVING BEAGLE BOYS!
TO BE PRECISE, I BOUGHT A TROPICAL ISLAND SO FAR OFF THE SEA CHARTS, IT DOESN'T HAVE A NAME! THEN I MOVED ALL MY MONEY TO A CONCRETE-AND-STEEL-REINFORCED UNDERGROUND STRONG ROOM THERE!
RIIIING!
ACK! THE DOORBELL! IT NEVER BRINGS GOOD NEWS -- AND IT CONSUMES PRICEY ELECTRICITY TO BOOT!

STORY AND ART: LUCIANO BOTTARO • TRANSLATION AND DIALOGUE: JOE TORCIVIA

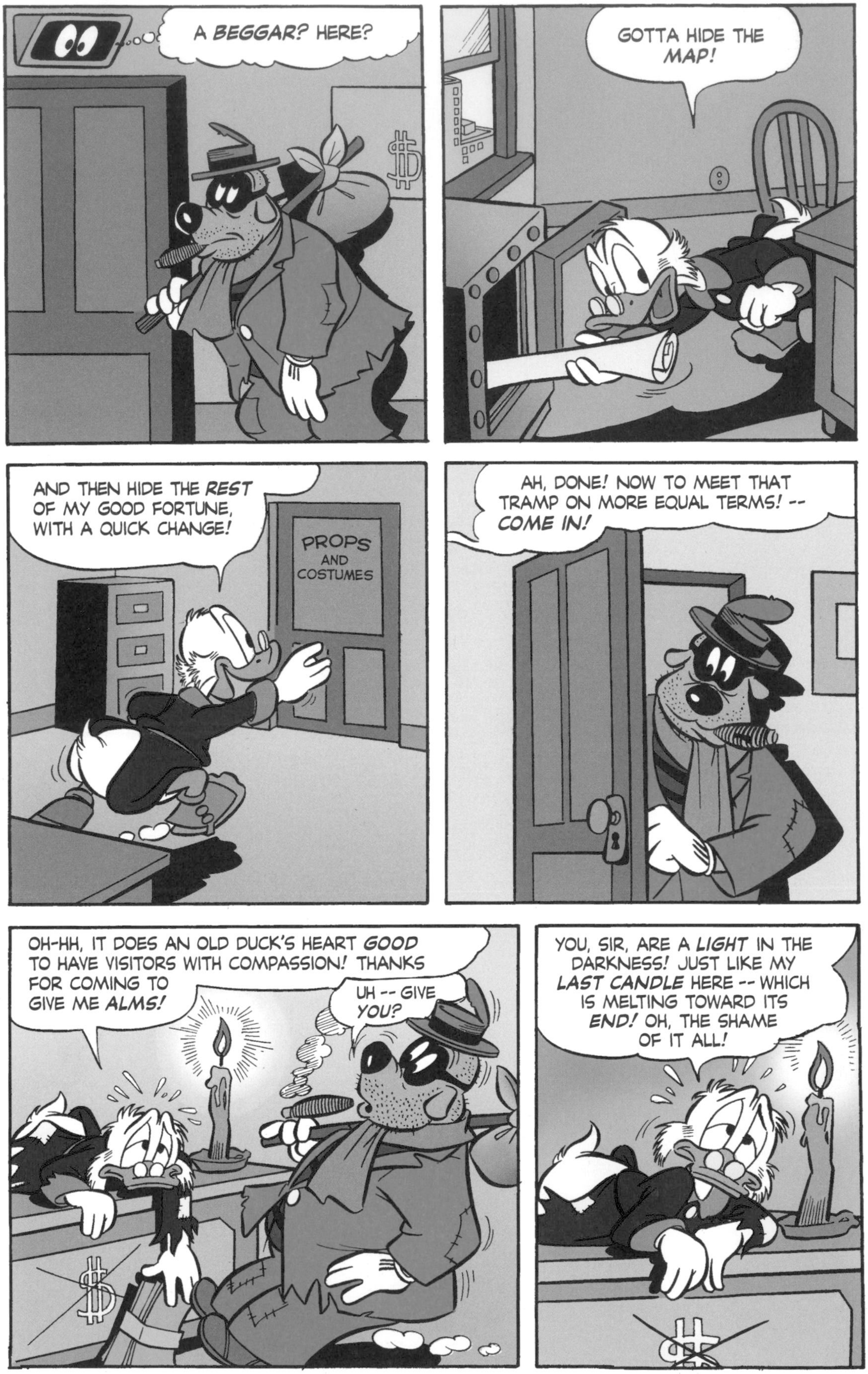
A BEGGAR? HERE?
GOTTA HIDE THE MAP!
AND THEN HIDE THE REST OF MY GOOD FORTUNE, WITH A QUICK CHANGE!
PROPS AND COSTUMES
AH, DONE! NOW TO MEET THAT TRAMP ON MORE EQUAL TERMS! -- COME IN!
OH-HH, IT DOES AN OLD DUCK'S HEART GOOD TO HAVE VISITORS WITH COMPASSION! THANKS FOR COMING TO GIVE ME ALMS!
UH -- GIVE YOU?
YOU, SIR, ARE A LIGHT IN THE DARKNESS! JUST LIKE MY LAST CANDLE HERE -- WHICH IS MELTING TOWARD ITS END! OH, THE SHAME OF IT ALL!

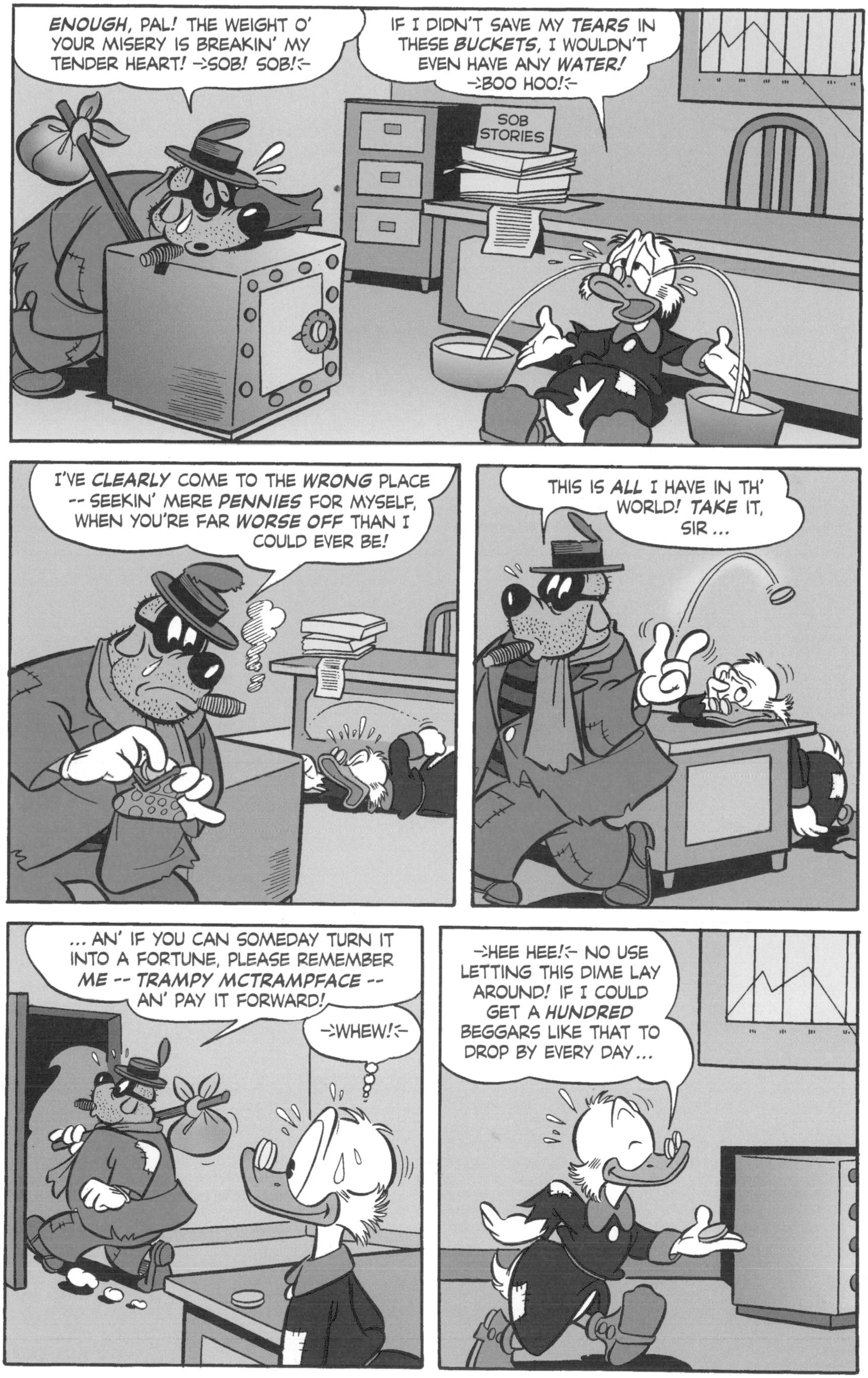
ENOUGH, PAL! THE WEIGHT O' YOUR MISERY IS BREAKIN' MY TENDER HEART! –SOB! SOB!–
IF I DIDN'T SAVE MY TEARS IN THESE BUCKETS, I WOULDN'T EVEN HAVE ANY WATER! –BOO HOO!–
SOB STORIES
I'VE CLEARLY COME TO THE WRONG PLACE -- SEEKIN' MERE PENNIES FOR MYSELF, WHEN YOU'RE FAR WORSE OFF THAN I COULD EVER BE!
THIS IS ALL I HAVE IN TH' WORLD! TAKE IT, SIR ...
... AN' IF YOU CAN SOMEDAY TURN IT INTO A FORTUNE, PLEASE REMEMBER ME -- TRAMPY MCTRAMPFACE -- AN' PAY IT FORWARD!
–WHEW!–
–HEE HEE!– NO USE LETTING THIS DIME LAY AROUND! IF I COULD GET A HUNDRED BEGGARS LIKE THAT TO DROP BY EVERY DAY ...

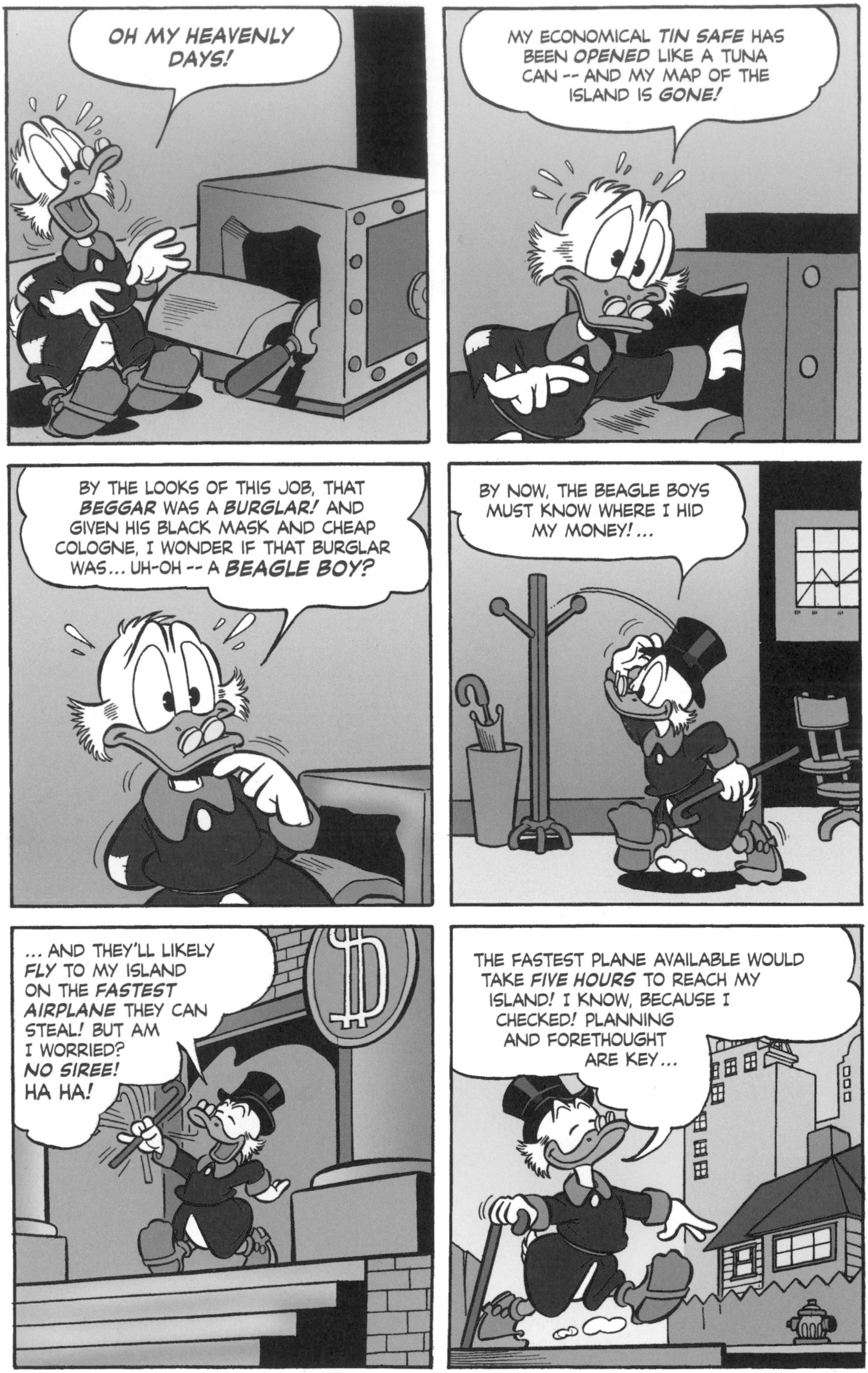
OH MY HEAVENLY DAYS!
MY ECONOMICAL TIN SAFE HAS BEEN OPENED LIKE A TUNA CAN -- AND MY MAP OF THE ISLAND IS GONE!
BY THE LOOKS OF THIS JOB, THAT BEGGAR WAS A BURGLAR! AND GIVEN HIS BLACK MASK AND CHEAP COLOGNE, I WONDER IF THAT BURGLAR WAS... UH-OH -- A BEAGLE BOY?
BY NOW, THE BEAGLE BOYS MUST KNOW WHERE I HID MY MONEY!...
... AND THEY'LL LIKELY FLY TO MY ISLAND ON THE FASTEST AIRPLANE THEY CAN STEAL! BUT AM I WORRIED? NO SIREE! HA HA!
THE FASTEST PLANE AVAILABLE WOULD TAKE FIVE HOURS TO REACH MY ISLAND! I KNOW, BECAUSE I CHECKED! PLANNING AND FORETHOUGHT ARE KEY...

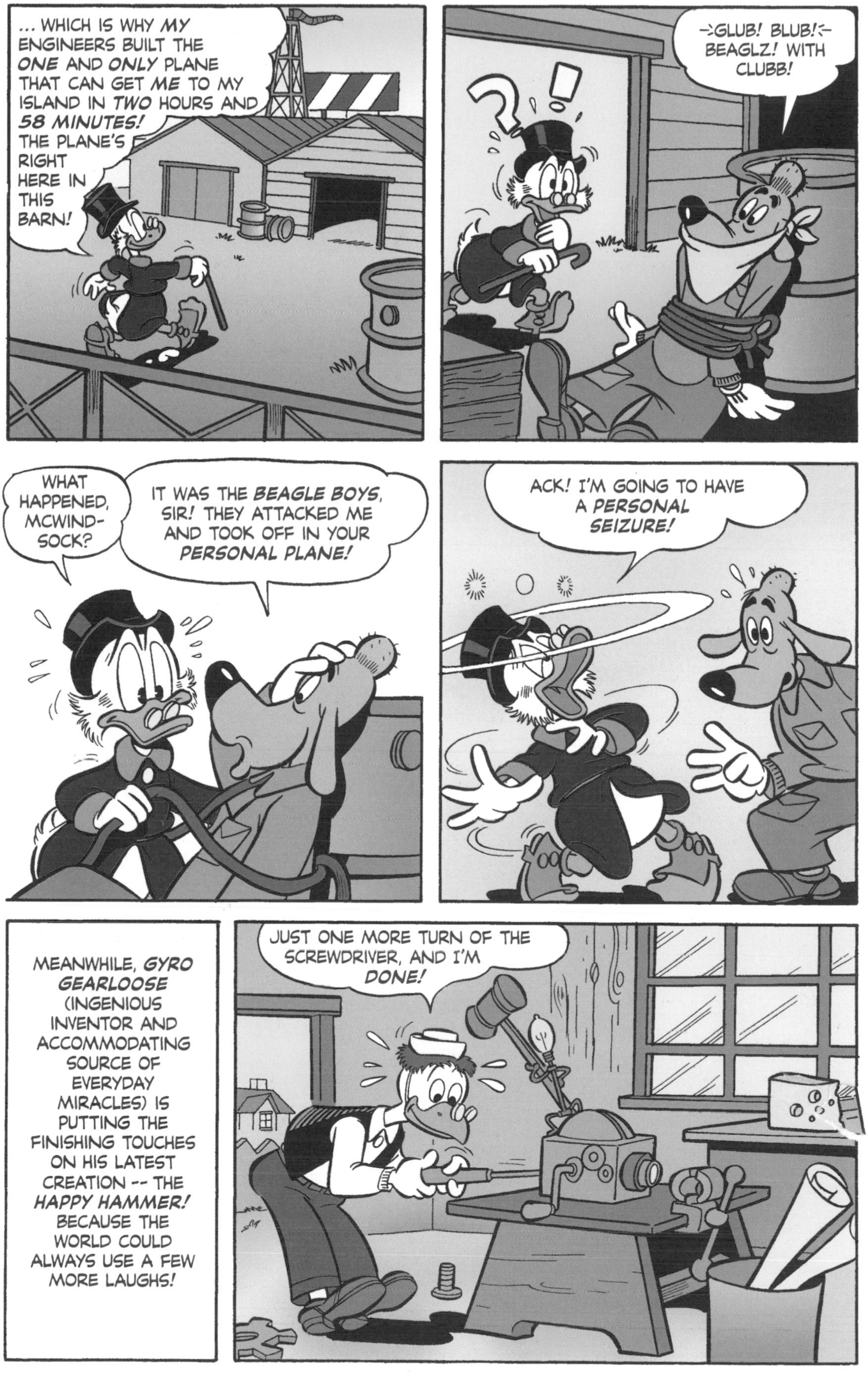
... WHICH IS WHY MY ENGINEERS BUILT THE ONE AND ONLY PLANE THAT CAN GET ME TO MY ISLAND IN TWO HOURS AND 58 MINUTES! THE PLANE'S RIGHT HERE IN THIS BARN!
-GLUB! BLUB!- BEAGLZ! WITH CLUBB!
WHAT HAPPENED, MCWIND-SOCK?
IT WAS THE BEAGLE BOYS, SIR! THEY ATTACKED ME AND TOOK OFF IN YOUR PERSONAL PLANE!
ACK! I'M GOING TO HAVE A PERSONAL SEIZURE!
MEANWHILE, GYRO GEARLOOSE (INGENIOUS INVENTOR AND ACCOMMODATING SOURCE OF EVERYDAY MIRACLES) IS PUTTING THE FINISHING TOUCHES ON HIS LATEST CREATION -- THE HAPPY HAMMER! BECAUSE THE WORLD COULD ALWAYS USE A FEW MORE LAUGHS!
JUST ONE MORE TURN OF THE SCREWDRIVER, AND I'M DONE!

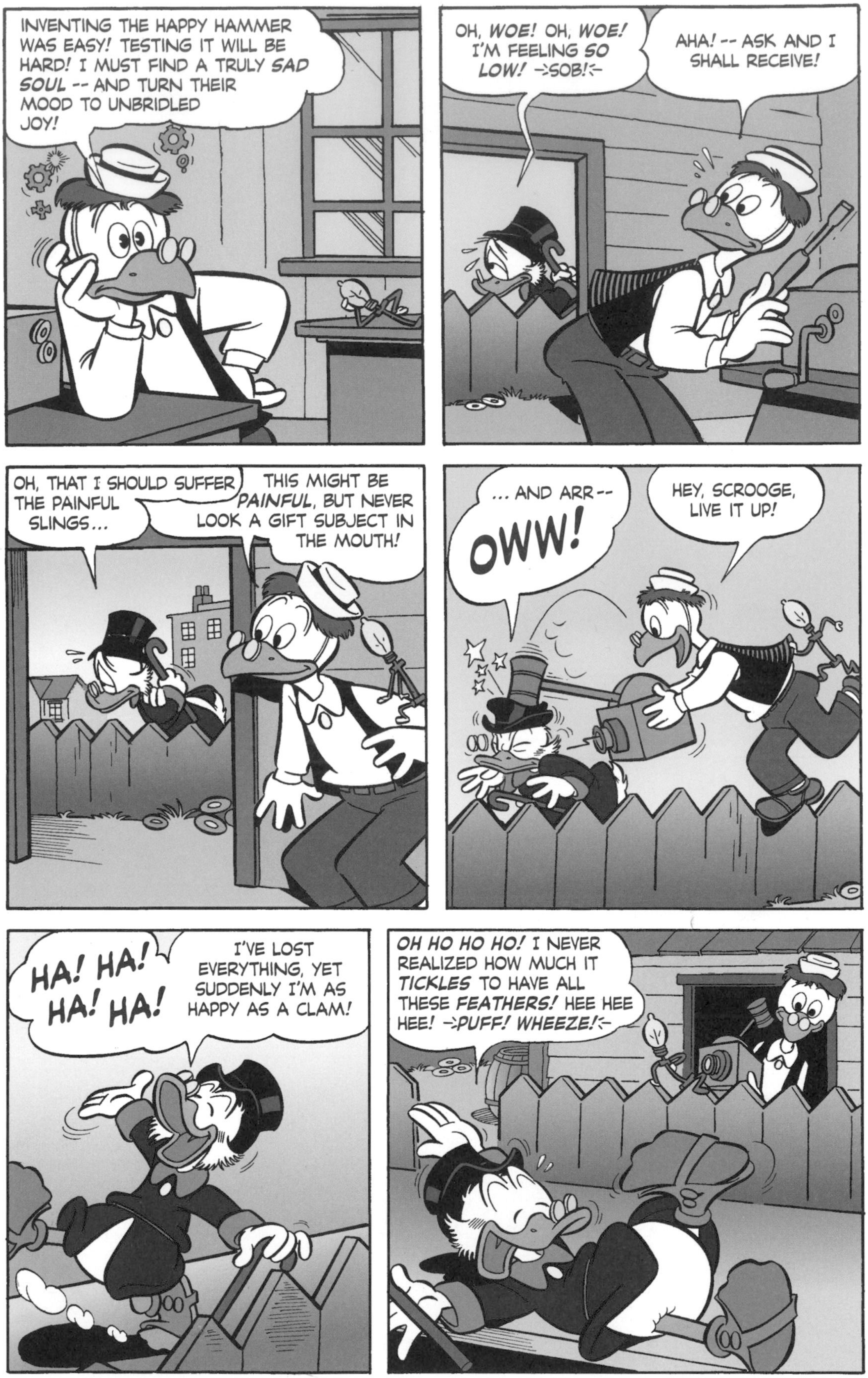

INVENTING THE HAPPY HAMMER WAS EASY! TESTING IT WILL BE HARD! I MUST FIND A TRULY SAD SOUL -- AND TURN THEIR MOOD TO UNBRIDLED JOY!
OH, WOE! OH, WOE! I'M FEELING SO LOW! -SOB!-
AHA! -- ASK AND I SHALL RECEIVE!
OH, THAT I SHOULD SUFFER THE PAINFUL SLINGS...
THIS MIGHT BE PAINFUL, BUT NEVER LOOK A GIFT SUBJECT IN THE MOUTH!
... AND ARR--
OWW!
HEY, SCROOGE, LIVE IT UP!
HA! HA! HA! HA!
I'VE LOST EVERYTHING, YET SUDDENLY I'M AS HAPPY AS A CLAM!
OH HO HO HO! I NEVER REALIZED HOW MUCH IT TICKLES TO HAVE ALL THESE FEATHERS! HEE HEE HEE! -PUFF! WHEEZE!-

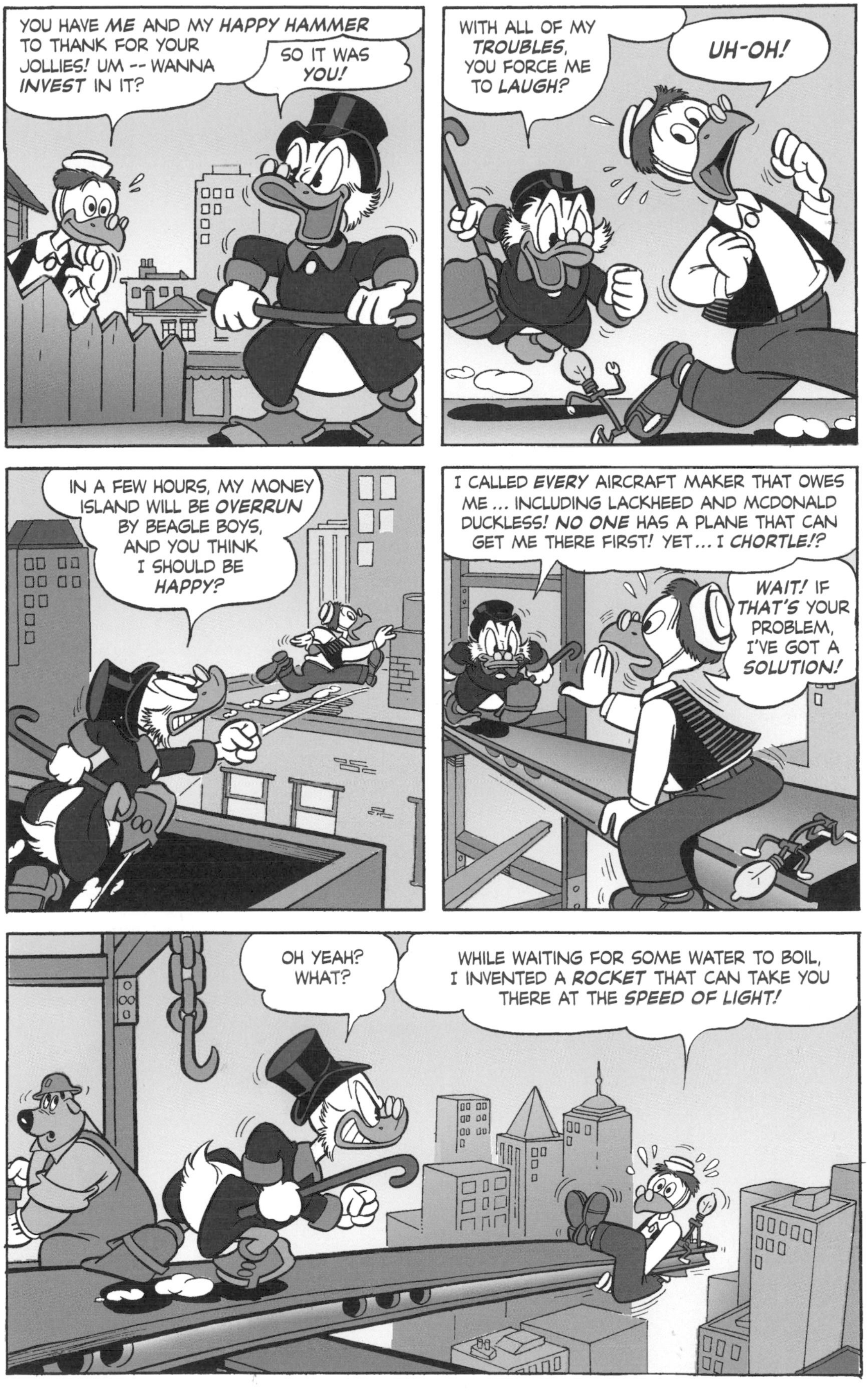
YOU HAVE ME AND MY HAPPY HAMMER TO THANK FOR YOUR JOLLIES! UM -- WANNA INVEST IN IT?
SO IT WAS YOU!
WITH ALL OF MY TROUBLES, YOU FORCE ME TO LAUGH?
UH-OH!
IN A FEW HOURS, MY MONEY ISLAND WILL BE OVERRUN BY BEAGLE BOYS, AND YOU THINK I SHOULD BE HAPPY?
I CALLED EVERY AIRCRAFT MAKER THAT OWES ME ... INCLUDING LACKHEED AND MCDONALD DUCKLESS! NO ONE HAS A PLANE THAT CAN GET ME THERE FIRST! YET ... I CHORTLE!?
WAIT! IF THAT'S YOUR PROBLEM, I'VE GOT A SOLUTION!
OH YEAH? WHAT?
WHILE WAITING FOR SOME WATER TO BOIL, I INVENTED A ROCKET THAT CAN TAKE YOU THERE AT THE SPEED OF LIGHT!

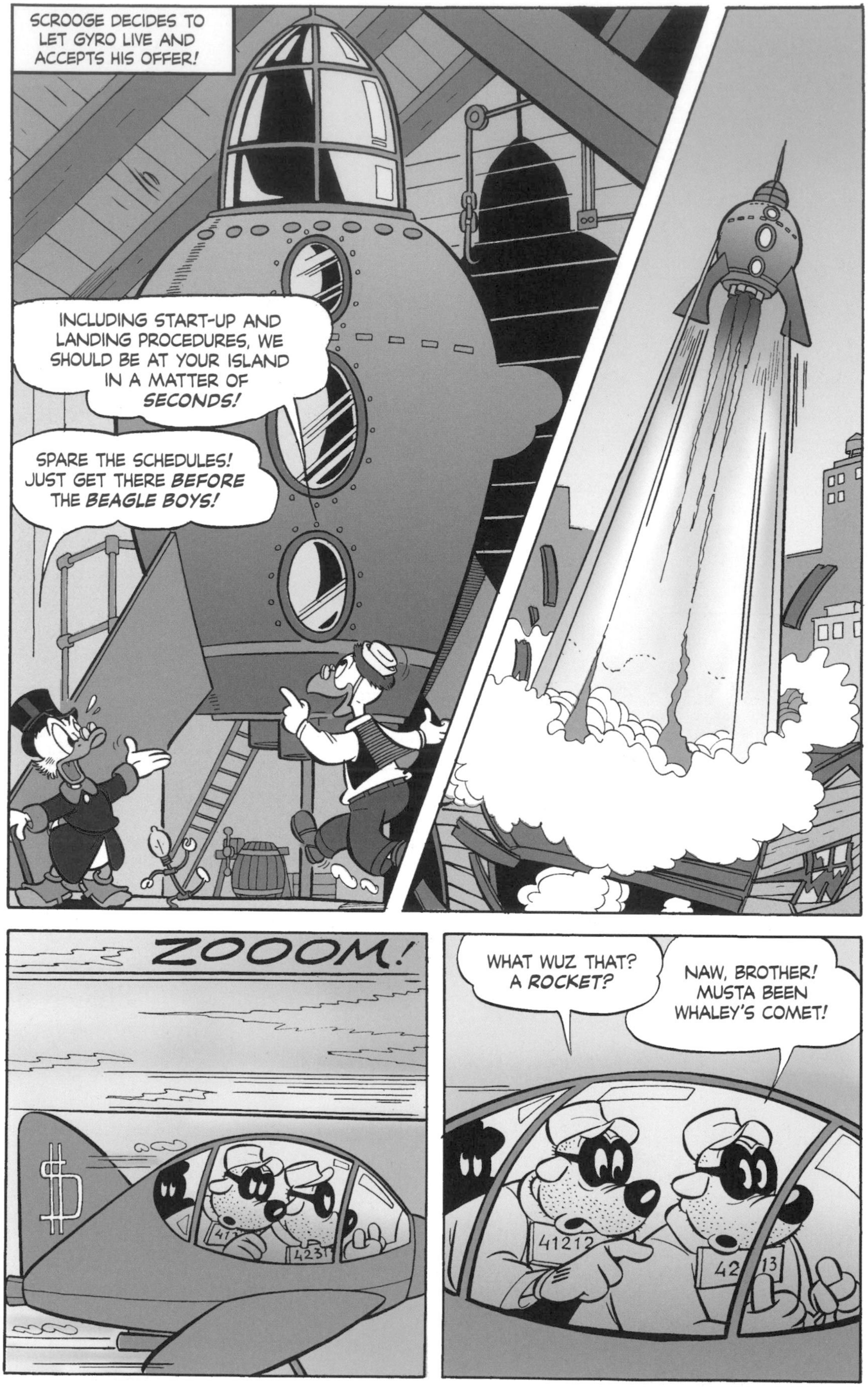
SCROOGE DECIDES TO LET GYRO LIVE AND ACCEPTS HIS OFFER!
INCLUDING START-UP AND LANDING PROCEDURES, WE SHOULD BE AT YOUR ISLAND IN A MATTER OF SECONDS!
SPARE THE SCHEDULES! JUST GET THERE BEFORE THE BEAGLE BOYS!
ZOOOM!
WHAT WUZ THAT? A ROCKET?
NAW, BROTHER! MUSTA BEEN WHALEY'S COMET!
41212
42 13

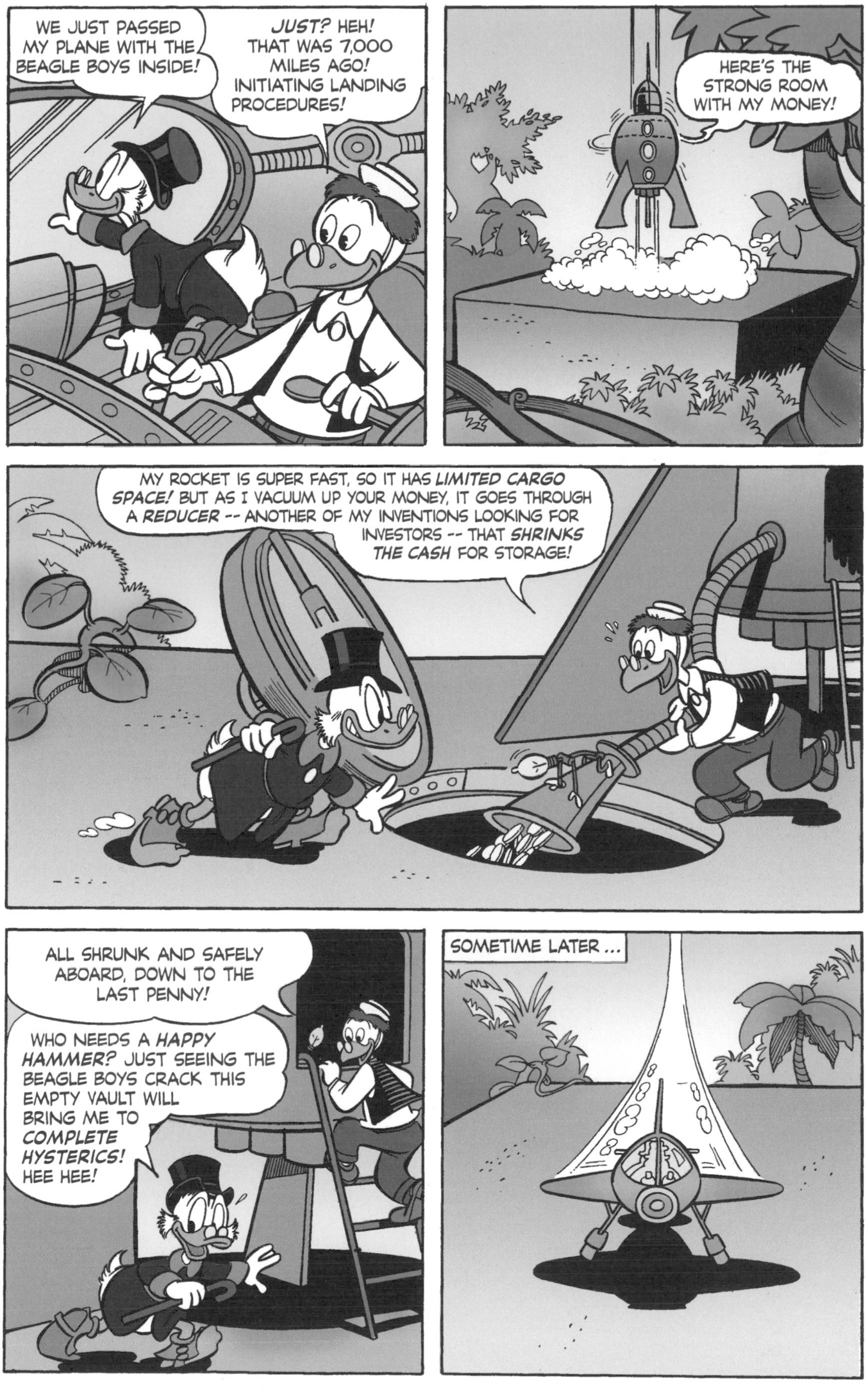
WE JUST PASSED MY PLANE WITH THE BEAGLE BOYS INSIDE!
JUST? HEH! THAT WAS 7,000 MILES AGO! INITIATING LANDING PROCEDURES!
HERE'S THE STRONG ROOM WITH MY MONEY!
MY ROCKET IS SUPER FAST, SO IT HAS LIMITED CARGO SPACE! BUT AS I VACUUM UP YOUR MONEY, IT GOES THROUGH A REDUCER -- ANOTHER OF MY INVENTIONS LOOKING FOR INVESTORS -- THAT SHRINKS THE CASH FOR STORAGE!
ALL SHRUNK AND SAFELY ABOARD, DOWN TO THE LAST PENNY!
WHO NEEDS A HAPPY HAMMER? JUST SEEING THE BEAGLE BOYS CRACK THIS EMPTY VAULT WILL BRING ME TO COMPLETE HYSTERICS! HEE HEE!
SOMETIME LATER ...

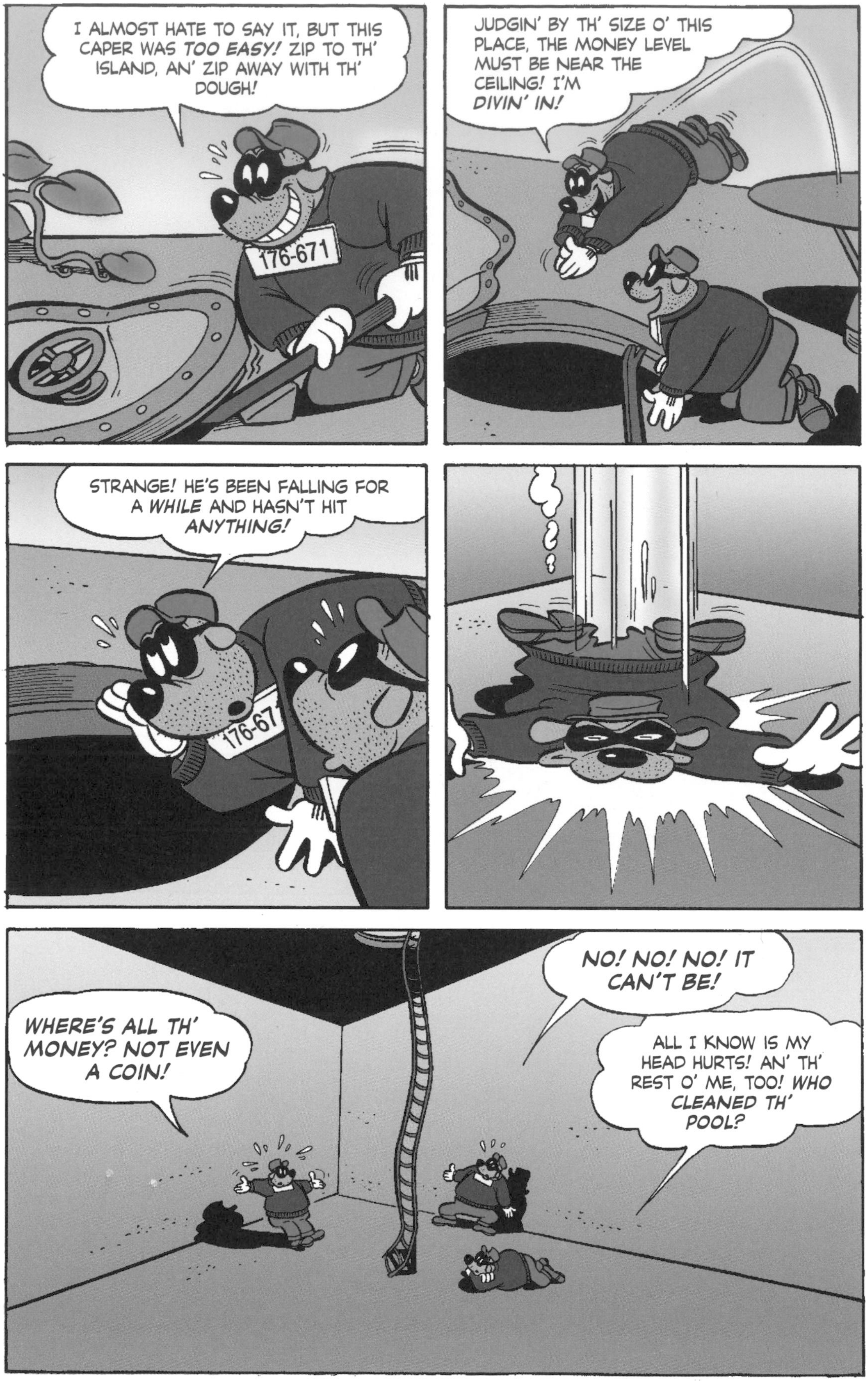
I ALMOST HATE TO SAY IT, BUT THIS CAPER WAS *TOO EASY!* ZIP TO TH' ISLAND, AN' ZIP AWAY WITH TH' DOUGH!
176-671
JUDGIN' BY TH' SIZE O' THIS PLACE, THE MONEY LEVEL MUST BE NEAR THE CEILING! I'M *DIVIN' IN!*
STRANGE! HE'S BEEN FALLING FOR A *WHILE* AND HASN'T HIT *ANYTHING!*
WHERE'S ALL TH' MONEY? NOT EVEN A COIN!
NO! NO! NO! IT CAN'T BE!
ALL I KNOW IS MY HEAD HURTS! AN' TH' REST O' ME, TOO! *WHO CLEANED TH' POOL?*

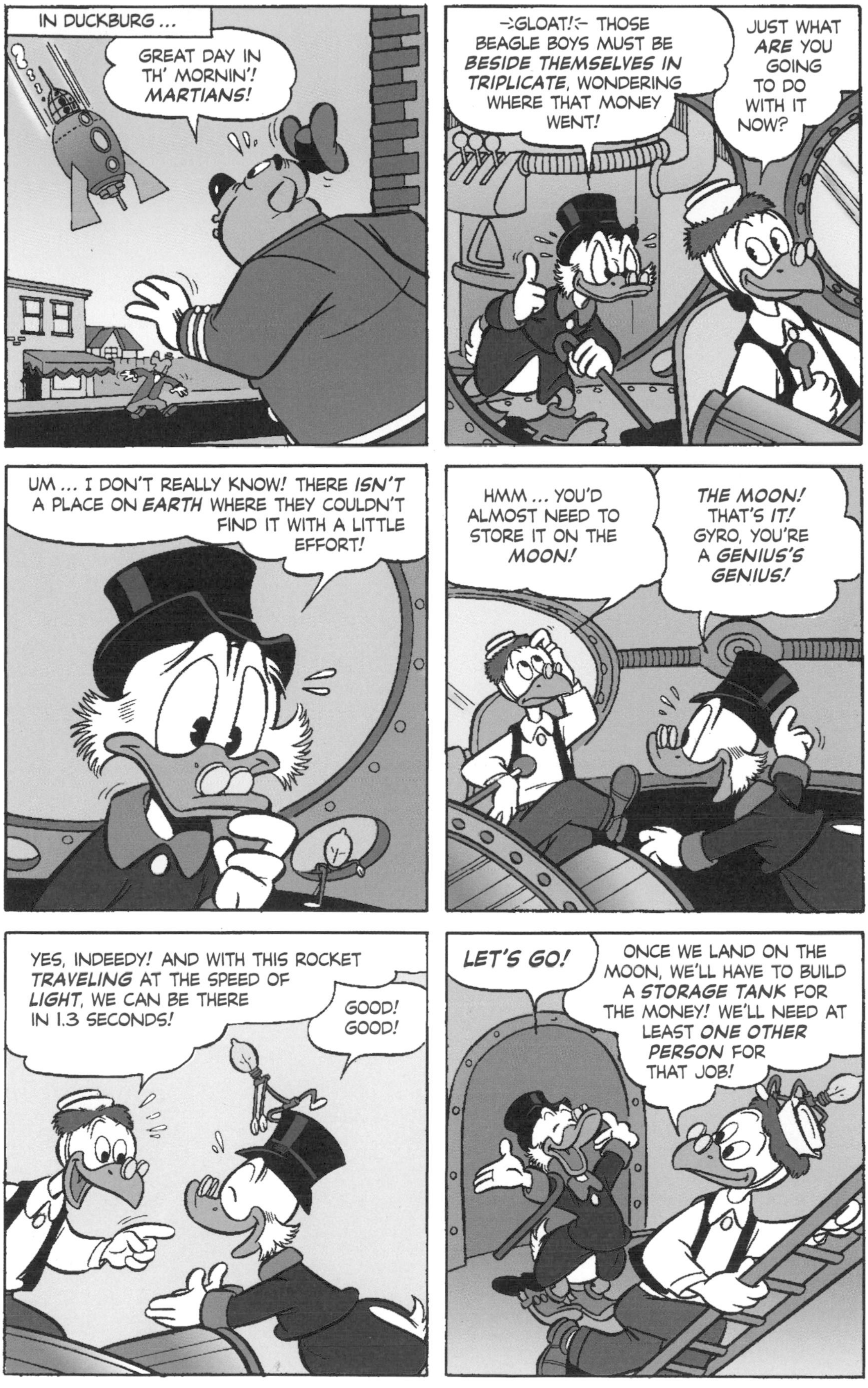
IN DUCKBURG ...
GREAT DAY IN TH' MORNIN'! MARTIANS!
~GLOAT!~ THOSE BEAGLE BOYS MUST BE BESIDE THEMSELVES IN TRIPLICATE, WONDERING WHERE THAT MONEY WENT!
JUST WHAT ARE YOU GOING TO DO WITH IT NOW?
UM ... I DON'T REALLY KNOW! THERE ISN'T A PLACE ON EARTH WHERE THEY COULDN'T FIND IT WITH A LITTLE EFFORT!
HMM ... YOU'D ALMOST NEED TO STORE IT ON THE MOON!
THE MOON! THAT'S IT! GYRO, YOU'RE A GENIUS'S GENIUS!
YES, INDEEDY! AND WITH THIS ROCKET TRAVELING AT THE SPEED OF LIGHT, WE CAN BE THERE IN 1.3 SECONDS!
GOOD! GOOD!
LET'S GO!
ONCE WE LAND ON THE MOON, WE'LL HAVE TO BUILD A STORAGE TANK FOR THE MONEY! WE'LL NEED AT LEAST ONE OTHER PERSON FOR THAT JOB!

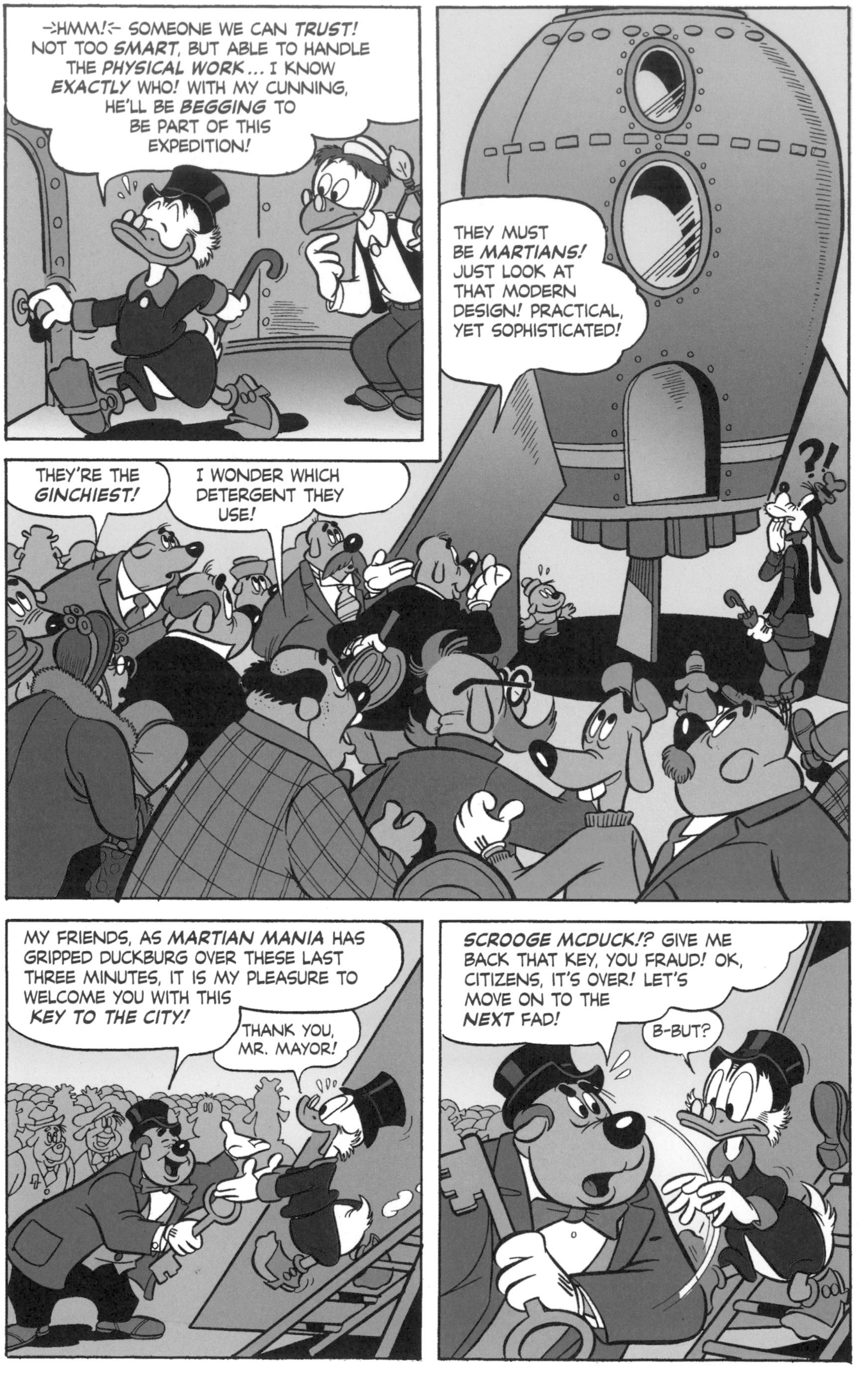
-HMM!- SOMEONE WE CAN TRUST! NOT TOO SMART, BUT ABLE TO HANDLE THE PHYSICAL WORK... I KNOW EXACTLY WHO! WITH MY CUNNING, HE'LL BE BEGGING TO BE PART OF THIS EXPEDITION!
THEY MUST BE MARTIANS! JUST LOOK AT THAT MODERN DESIGN! PRACTICAL, YET SOPHISTICATED!
THEY'RE THE GINCHIEST!
I WONDER WHICH DETERGENT THEY USE!
?!
MY FRIENDS, AS MARTIAN MANIA HAS GRIPPED DUCKBURG OVER THESE LAST THREE MINUTES, IT IS MY PLEASURE TO WELCOME YOU WITH THIS KEY TO THE CITY!
THANK YOU, MR. MAYOR!
SCROOGE MCDUCK!? GIVE ME BACK THAT KEY, YOU FRAUD! OK, CITIZENS, IT'S OVER! LET'S MOVE ON TO THE NEXT FAD!
B-BUT?

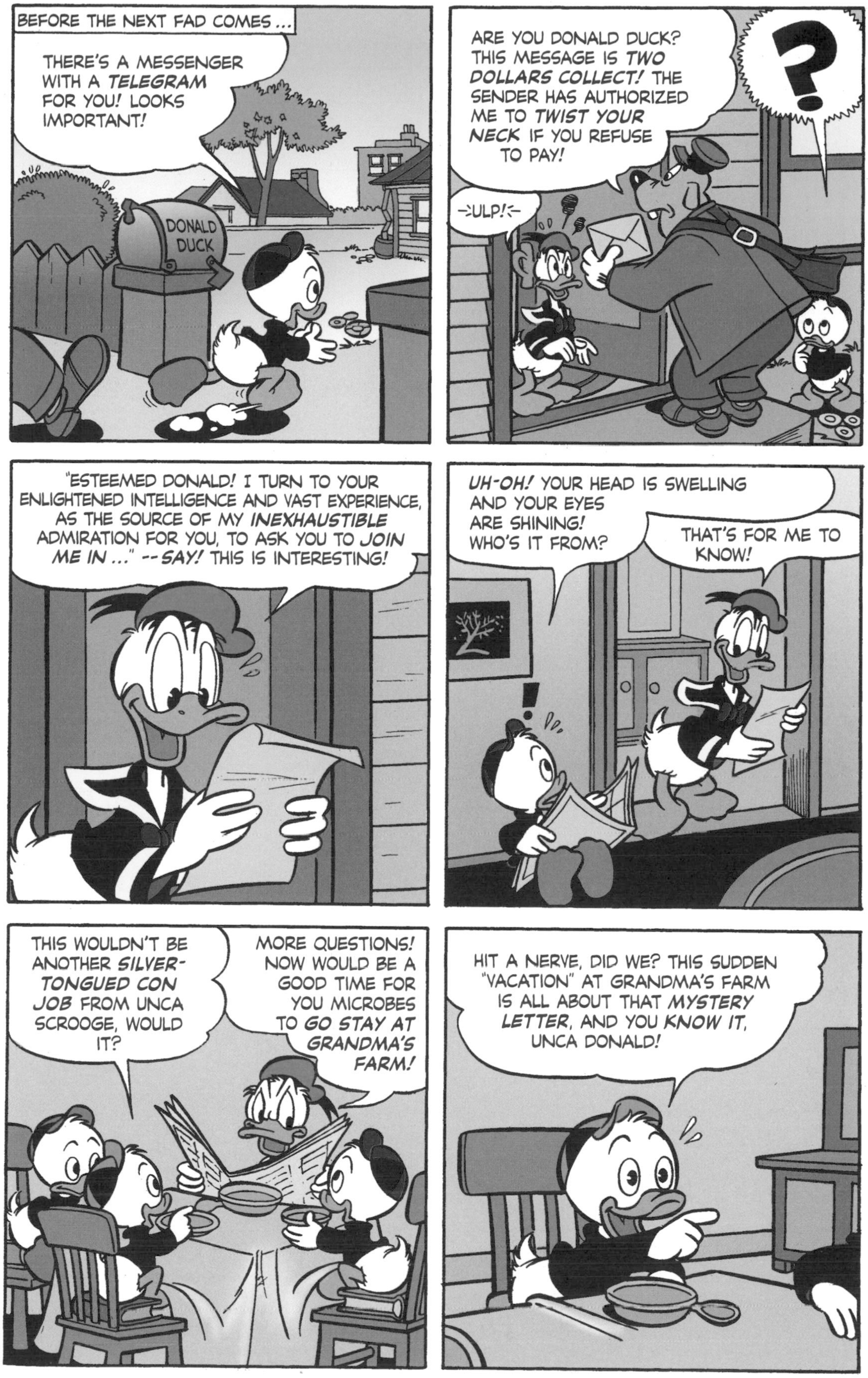

BEFORE THE NEXT FAD COMES ...
THERE'S A MESSENGER WITH A TELEGRAM FOR YOU! LOOKS IMPORTANT!
DONALD DUCK
ARE YOU DONALD DUCK? THIS MESSAGE IS TWO DOLLARS COLLECT! THE SENDER HAS AUTHORIZED ME TO TWIST YOUR NECK IF YOU REFUSE TO PAY!
?
ULP!
"ESTEEMED DONALD! I TURN TO YOUR ENLIGHTENED INTELLIGENCE AND VAST EXPERIENCE, AS THE SOURCE OF MY INEXHAUSTIBLE ADMIRATION FOR YOU, TO ASK YOU TO JOIN ME IN ..." --SAY! THIS IS INTERESTING!
UH-OH! YOUR HEAD IS SWELLING AND YOUR EYES ARE SHINING! WHO'S IT FROM?
THAT'S FOR ME TO KNOW!
!
THIS WOULDN'T BE ANOTHER SILVER-TONGUED CON JOB FROM UNCA SCROOGE, WOULD IT?
MORE QUESTIONS! NOW WOULD BE A GOOD TIME FOR YOU MICROBES TO GO STAY AT GRANDMA'S FARM!
HIT A NERVE, DID WE? THIS SUDDEN "VACATION" AT GRANDMA'S FARM IS ALL ABOUT THAT MYSTERY LETTER, AND YOU KNOW IT, UNCA DONALD!

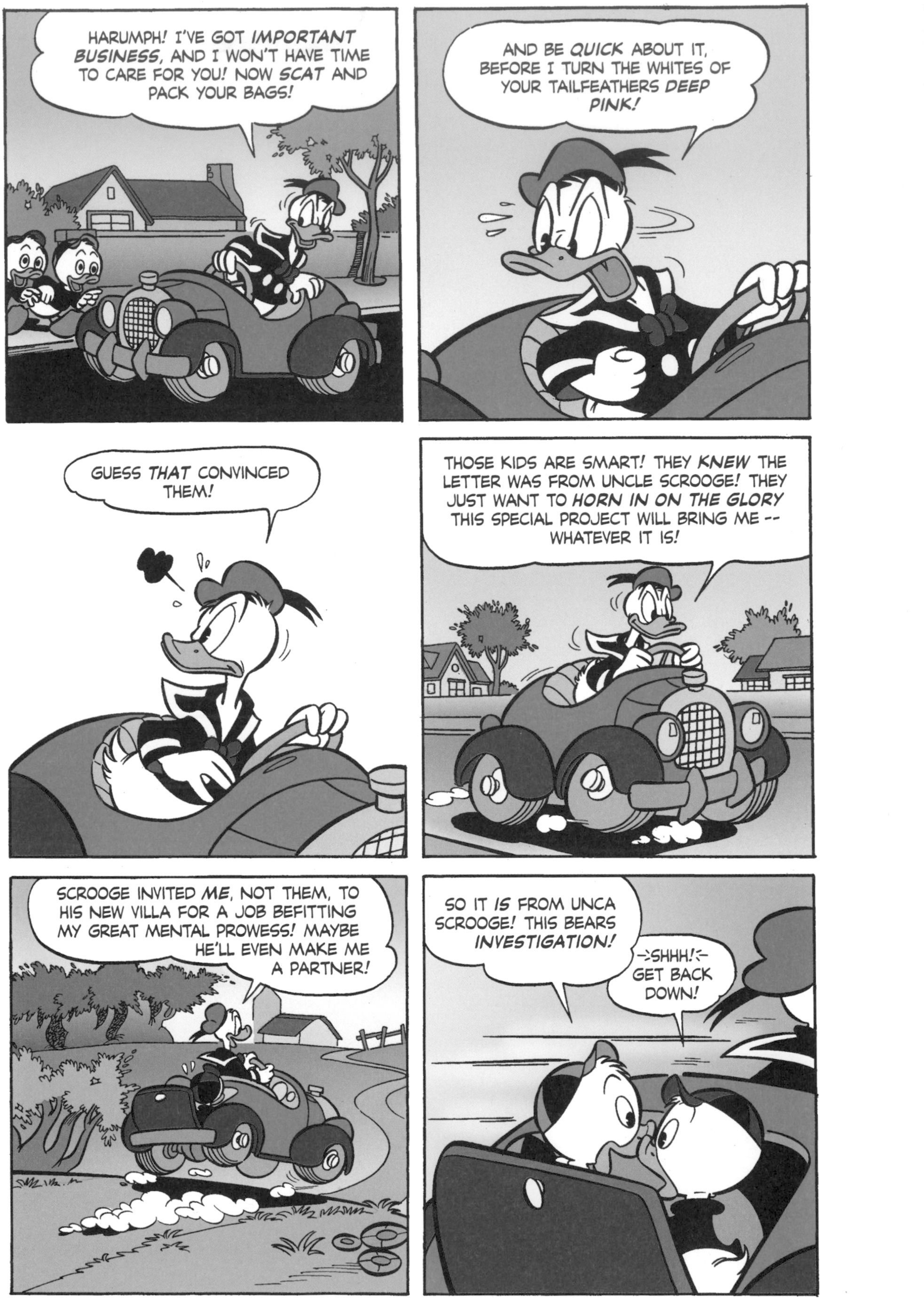
HARUMPH! I'VE GOT IMPORTANT BUSINESS, AND I WON'T HAVE TIME TO CARE FOR YOU! NOW SCAT AND PACK YOUR BAGS!
AND BE QUICK ABOUT IT, BEFORE I TURN THE WHITES OF YOUR TAILFEATHERS DEEP PINK!
GUESS THAT CONVINCED THEM!
THOSE KIDS ARE SMART! THEY KNEW THE LETTER WAS FROM UNCLE SCROOGE! THEY JUST WANT TO HORN IN ON THE GLORY THIS SPECIAL PROJECT WILL BRING ME -- WHATEVER IT IS!
SCROOGE INVITED ME, NOT THEM, TO HIS NEW VILLA FOR A JOB BEFITTING MY GREAT MENTAL PROWESS! MAYBE HE'LL EVEN MAKE ME A PARTNER!
SO IT IS FROM UNCA SCROOGE! THIS BEARS INVESTIGATION!
SHHH! GET BACK DOWN!

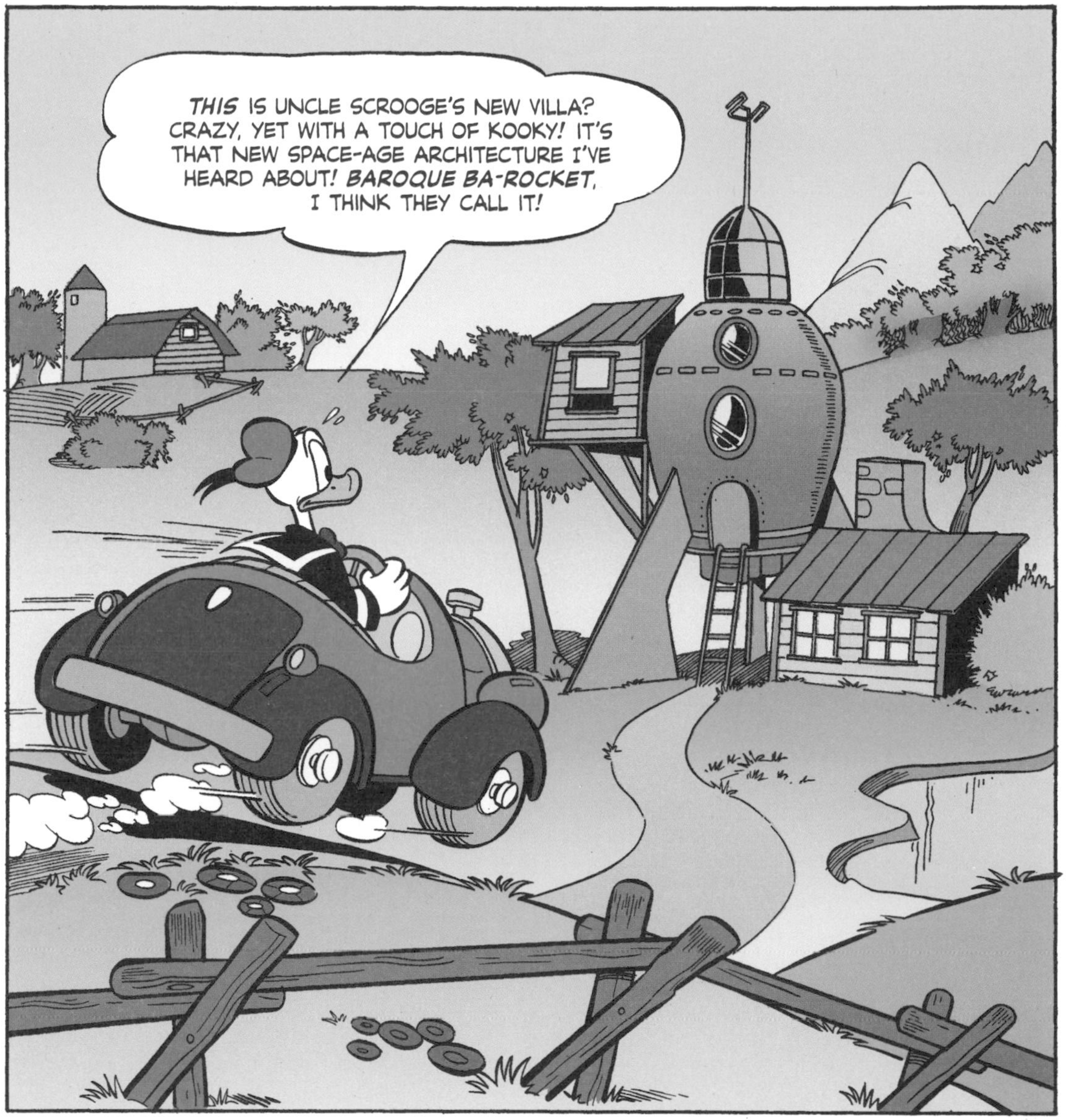
THIS IS UNCLE SCROOGE'S NEW VILLA? CRAZY, YET WITH A TOUCH OF KOOKY! IT'S THAT NEW SPACE-AGE ARCHITECTURE I'VE HEARD ABOUT! BAROQUE BA-ROCKET, I THINK THEY CALL IT!

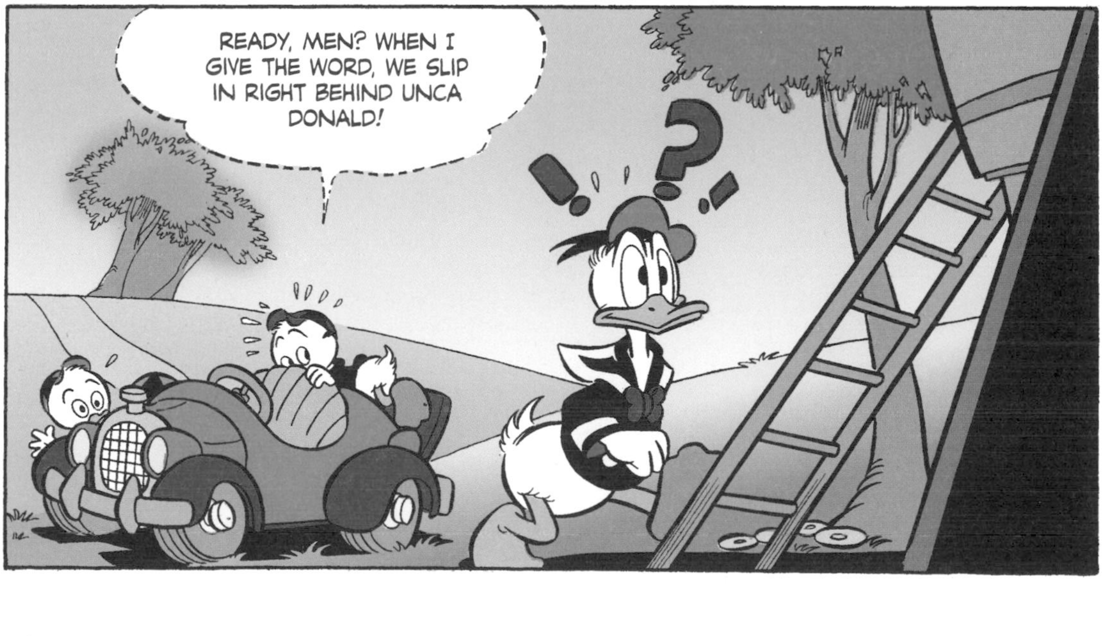
READY, MEN? WHEN I GIVE THE WORD, WE SLIP IN RIGHT BEHIND UNCA DONALD!

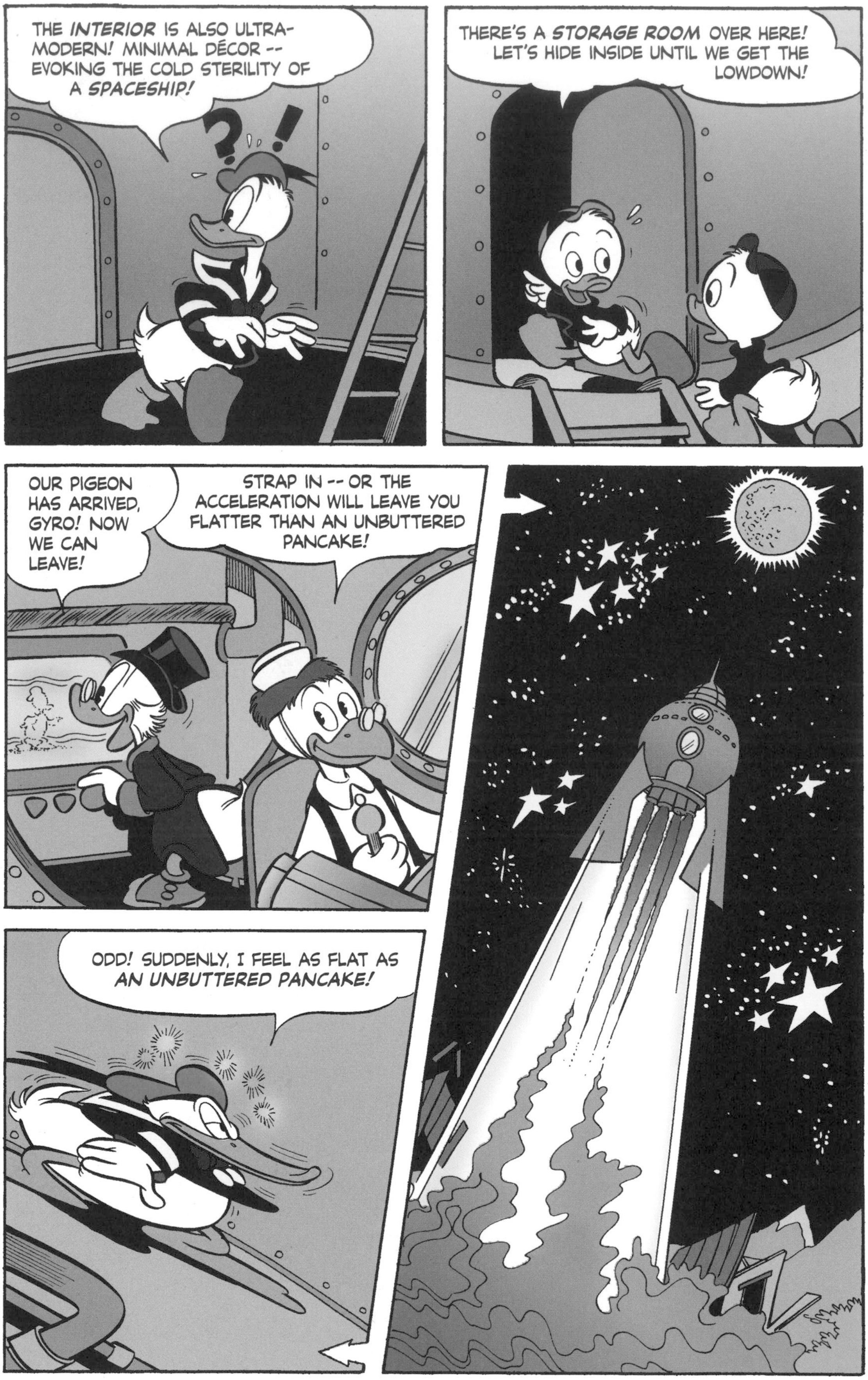
THE *INTERIOR* IS ALSO ULTRA-MODERN! MINIMAL DÉCOR -- EVOKING THE COLD STERILITY OF A *SPACESHIP!*
?!
THERE'S A *STORAGE ROOM* OVER HERE! LET'S HIDE INSIDE UNTIL WE GET THE LOWDOWN!
OUR PIGEON HAS ARRIVED, GYRO! NOW WE CAN LEAVE!
STRAP IN -- OR THE ACCELERATION WILL LEAVE YOU FLATTER THAN AN UNBUTTERED PANCAKE!
ODD! SUDDENLY, I FEEL AS FLAT AS *AN UNBUTTERED PANCAKE!*

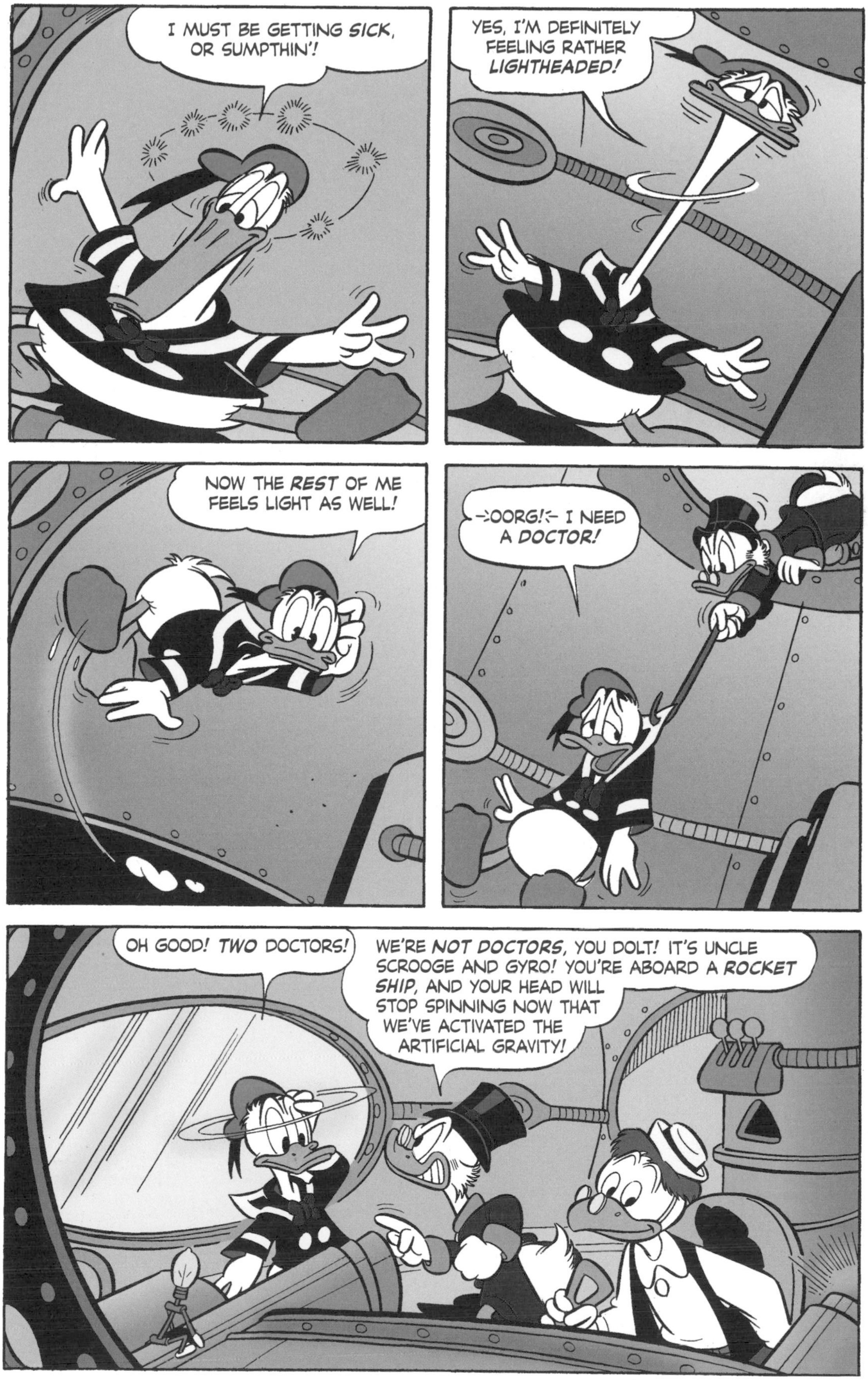
I MUST BE GETTING SICK, OR SUMPTHIN'!
YES, I'M DEFINITELY FEELING RATHER LIGHTHEADED!
NOW THE REST OF ME FEELS LIGHT AS WELL!
OORG! I NEED A DOCTOR!
OH GOOD! TWO DOCTORS!
WE'RE NOT DOCTORS, YOU DOLT! IT'S UNCLE SCROOGE AND GYRO! YOU'RE ABOARD A ROCKET SHIP, AND YOUR HEAD WILL STOP SPINNING NOW THAT WE'VE ACTIVATED THE ARTIFICIAL GRAVITY!

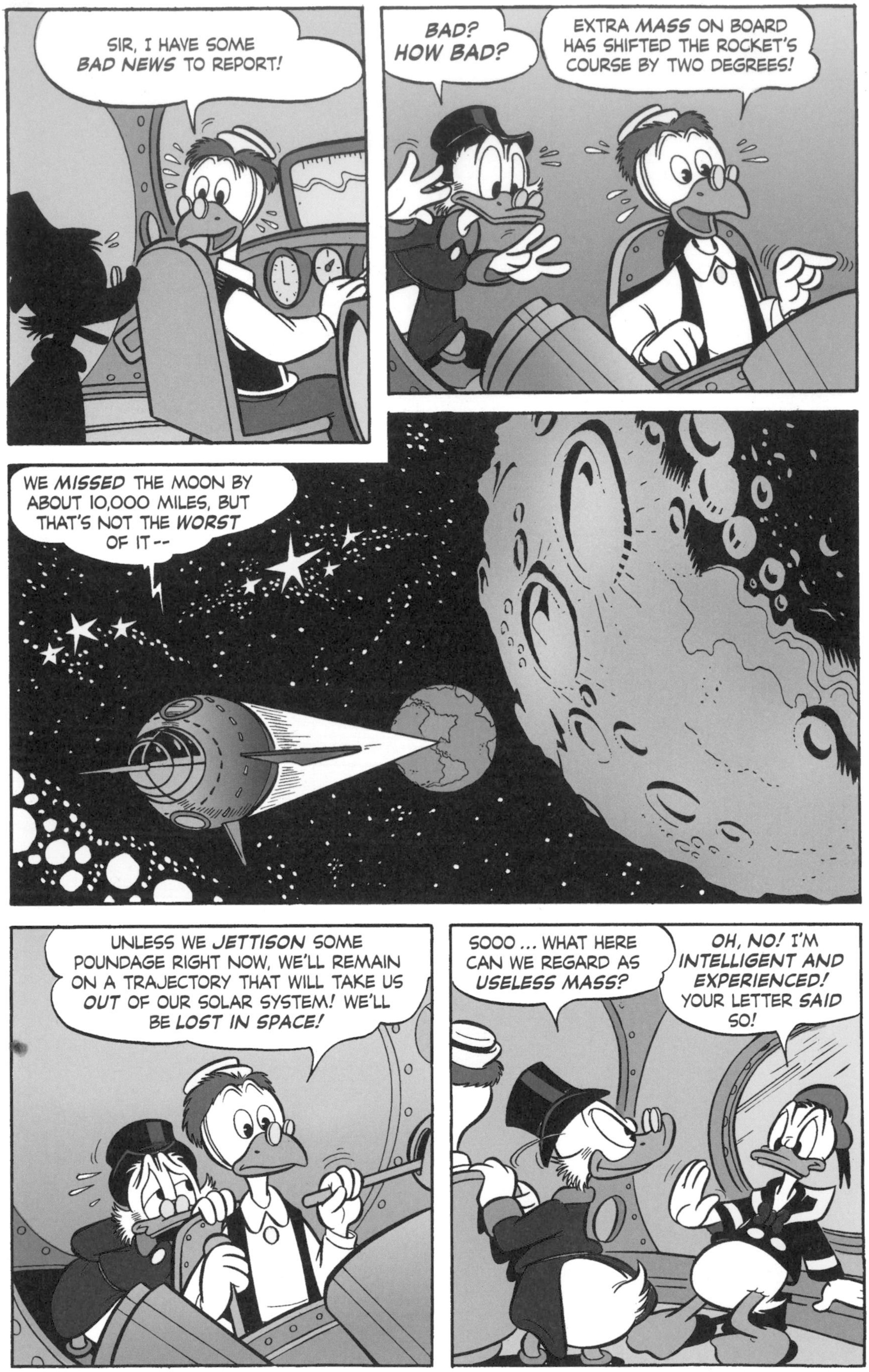
SIR, I HAVE SOME BAD NEWS TO REPORT!
BAD? HOW BAD?
EXTRA MASS ON BOARD HAS SHIFTED THE ROCKET'S COURSE BY TWO DEGREES!
WE MISSED THE MOON BY ABOUT 10,000 MILES, BUT THAT'S NOT THE WORST OF IT --
UNLESS WE JETTISON SOME POUNDAGE RIGHT NOW, WE'LL REMAIN ON A TRAJECTORY THAT WILL TAKE US OUT OF OUR SOLAR SYSTEM! WE'LL BE LOST IN SPACE!
SOOO ... WHAT HERE CAN WE REGARD AS USELESS MASS?
OH, NO! I'M INTELLIGENT AND EXPERIENCED! YOUR LETTER SAID SO!

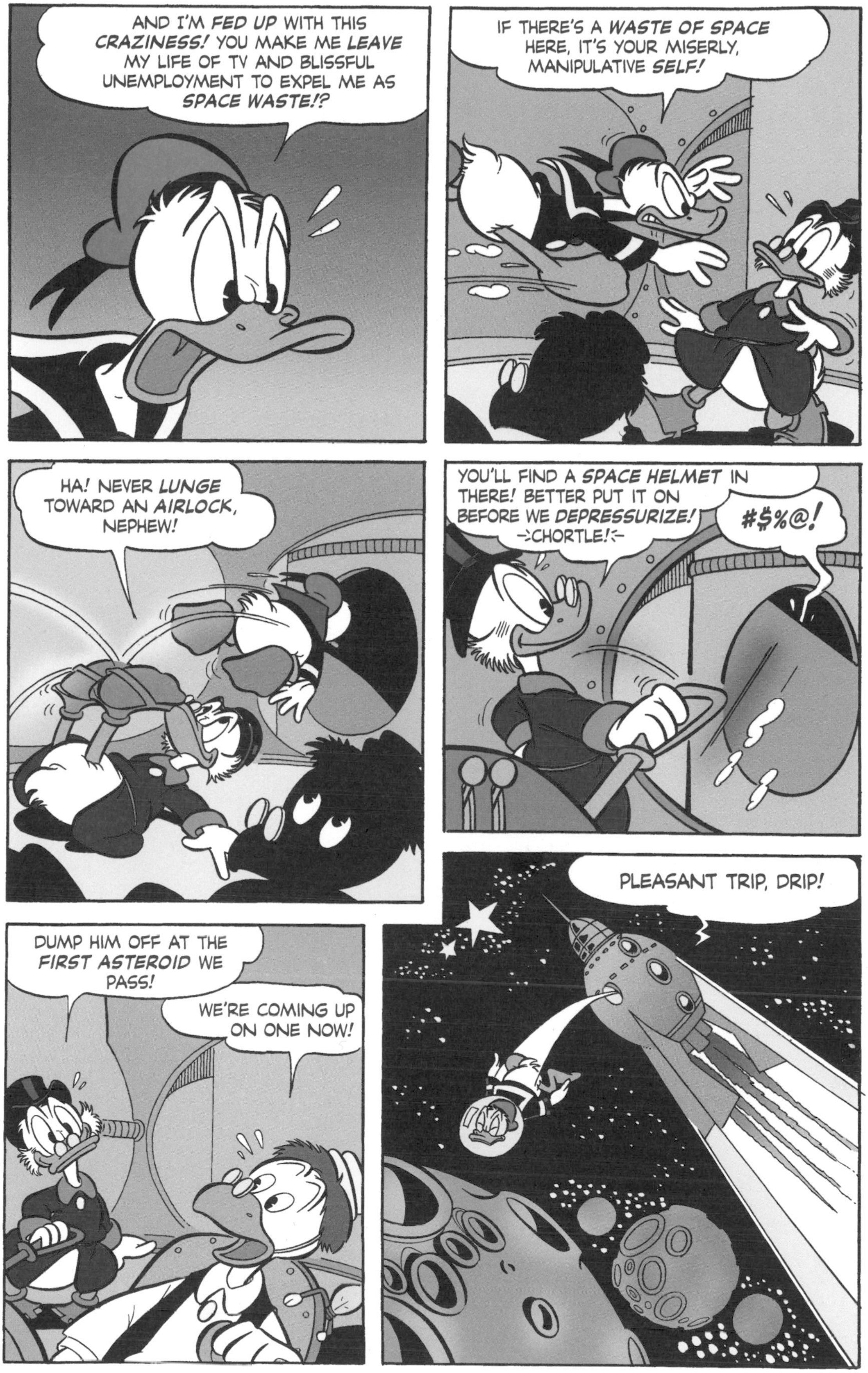
AND I'M FED UP WITH THIS CRAZINESS! YOU MAKE ME LEAVE MY LIFE OF TV AND BLISSFUL UNEMPLOYMENT TO EXPEL ME AS SPACE WASTE!?
IF THERE'S A WASTE OF SPACE HERE, IT'S YOUR MISERLY, MANIPULATIVE SELF!
HA! NEVER LUNGE TOWARD AN AIRLOCK, NEPHEW!
YOU'LL FIND A SPACE HELMET IN THERE! BETTER PUT IT ON BEFORE WE DEPRESSURIZE! CHORTLE!
#$%@!
DUMP HIM OFF AT THE FIRST ASTEROID WE PASS!
WE'RE COMING UP ON ONE NOW!
PLEASANT TRIP, DRIP!

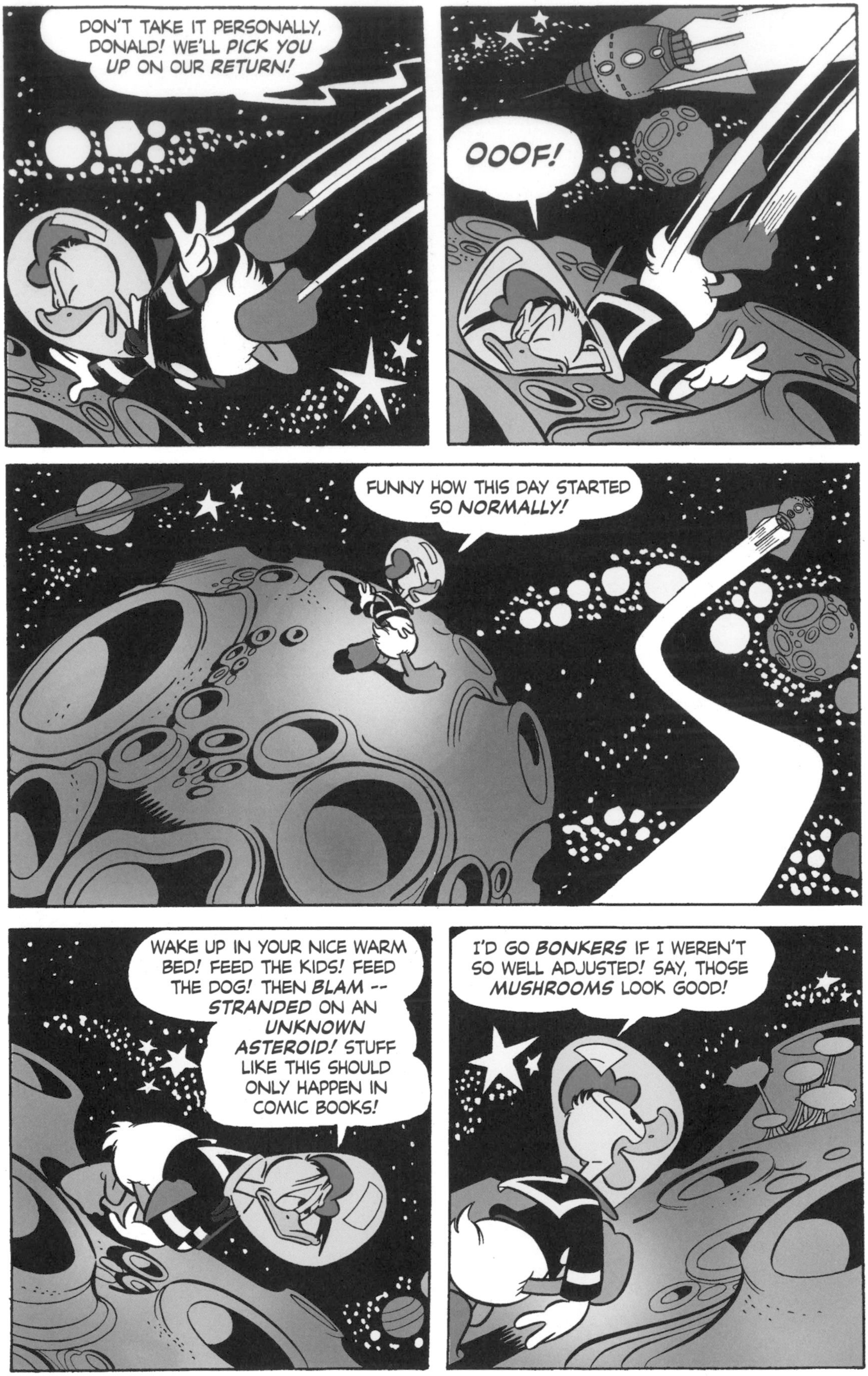

DON'T TAKE IT PERSONALLY, DONALD! WE'LL PICK YOU UP ON OUR RETURN!
OOOF!
FUNNY HOW THIS DAY STARTED SO NORMALLY!
WAKE UP IN YOUR NICE WARM BED! FEED THE KIDS! FEED THE DOG! THEN BLAM -- STRANDED ON AN UNKNOWN ASTEROID! STUFF LIKE THIS SHOULD ONLY HAPPEN IN COMIC BOOKS!
I'D GO BONKERS IF I WEREN'T SO WELL ADJUSTED! SAY, THOSE MUSHROOMS LOOK GOOD!

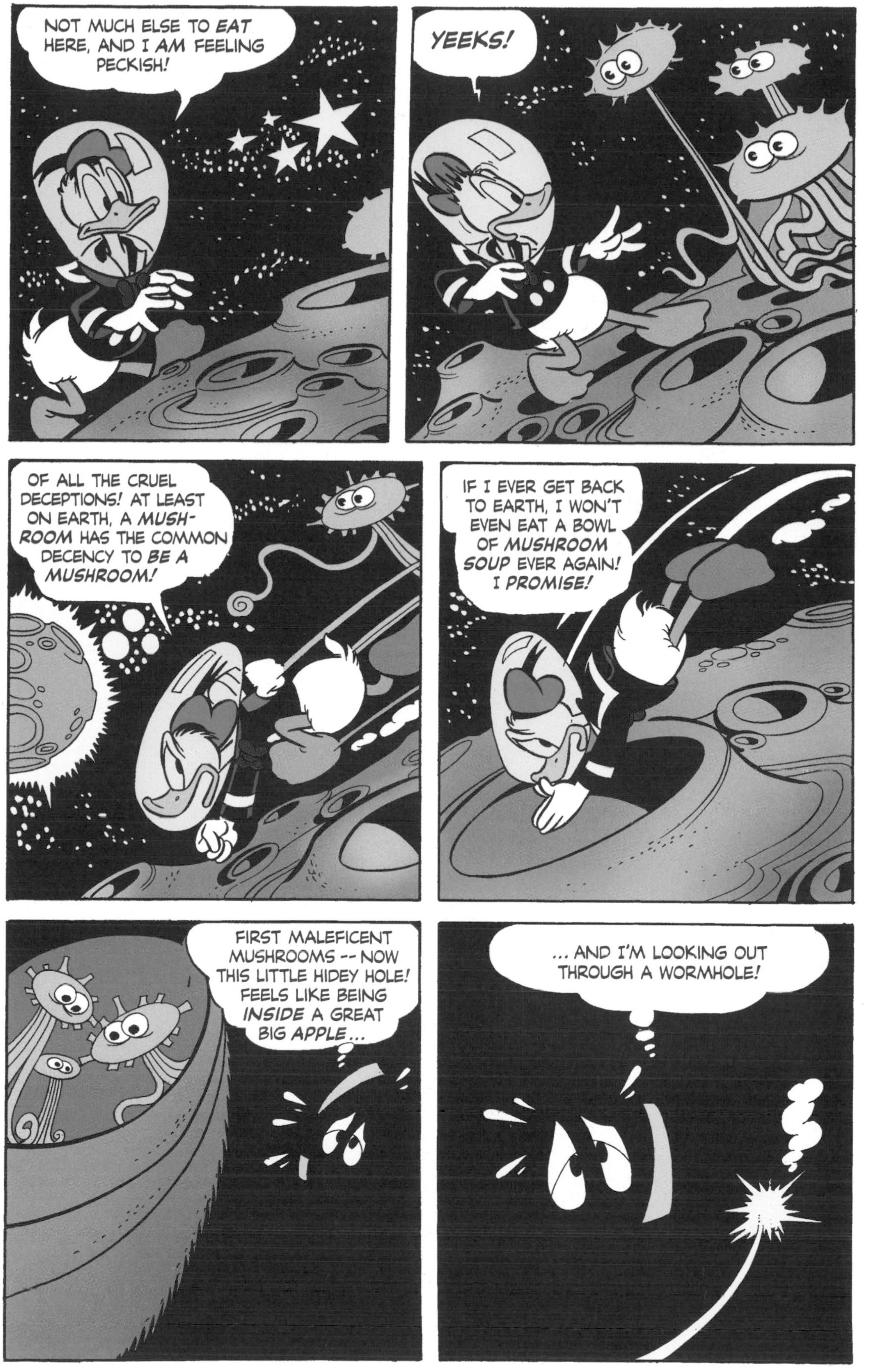

NOT MUCH ELSE TO EAT HERE, AND I AM FEELING PECKISH!
YEEKS!
OF ALL THE CRUEL DECEPTIONS! AT LEAST ON EARTH, A MUSH-ROOM HAS THE COMMON DECENCY TO BE A MUSHROOM!
IF I EVER GET BACK TO EARTH, I WON'T EVEN EAT A BOWL OF MUSHROOM SOUP EVER AGAIN! I PROMISE!
FIRST MALEFICENT MUSHROOMS -- NOW THIS LITTLE HIDEY HOLE! FEELS LIKE BEING INSIDE A GREAT BIG APPLE...
... AND I'M LOOKING OUT THROUGH A WORMHOLE!

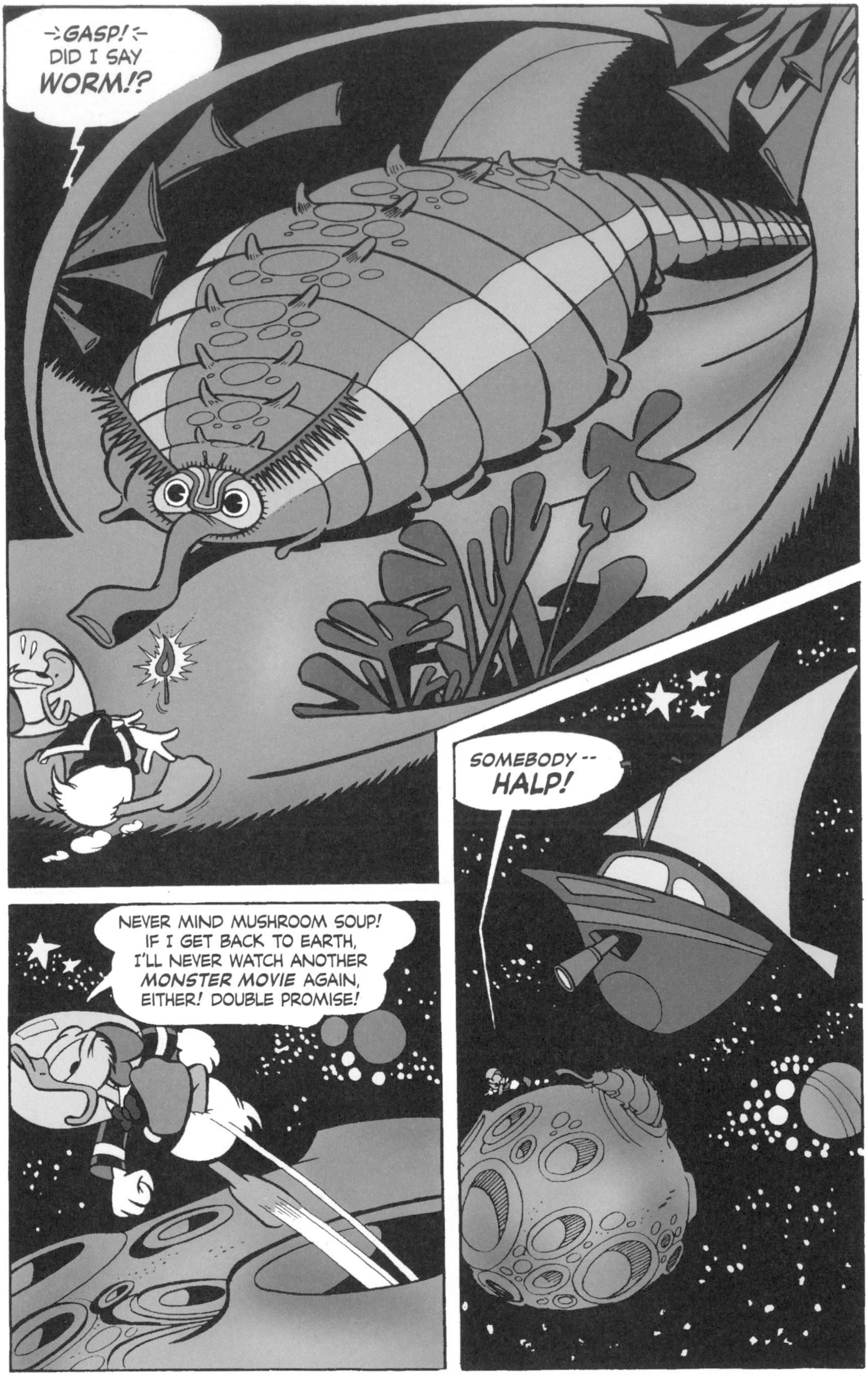

-GASP!- DID I SAY WORM!?
SOMEBODY -- HALP!
NEVER MIND MUSHROOM SOUP! IF I GET BACK TO EARTH, I'LL NEVER WATCH ANOTHER MONSTER MOVIE AGAIN, EITHER! DOUBLE PROMISE!

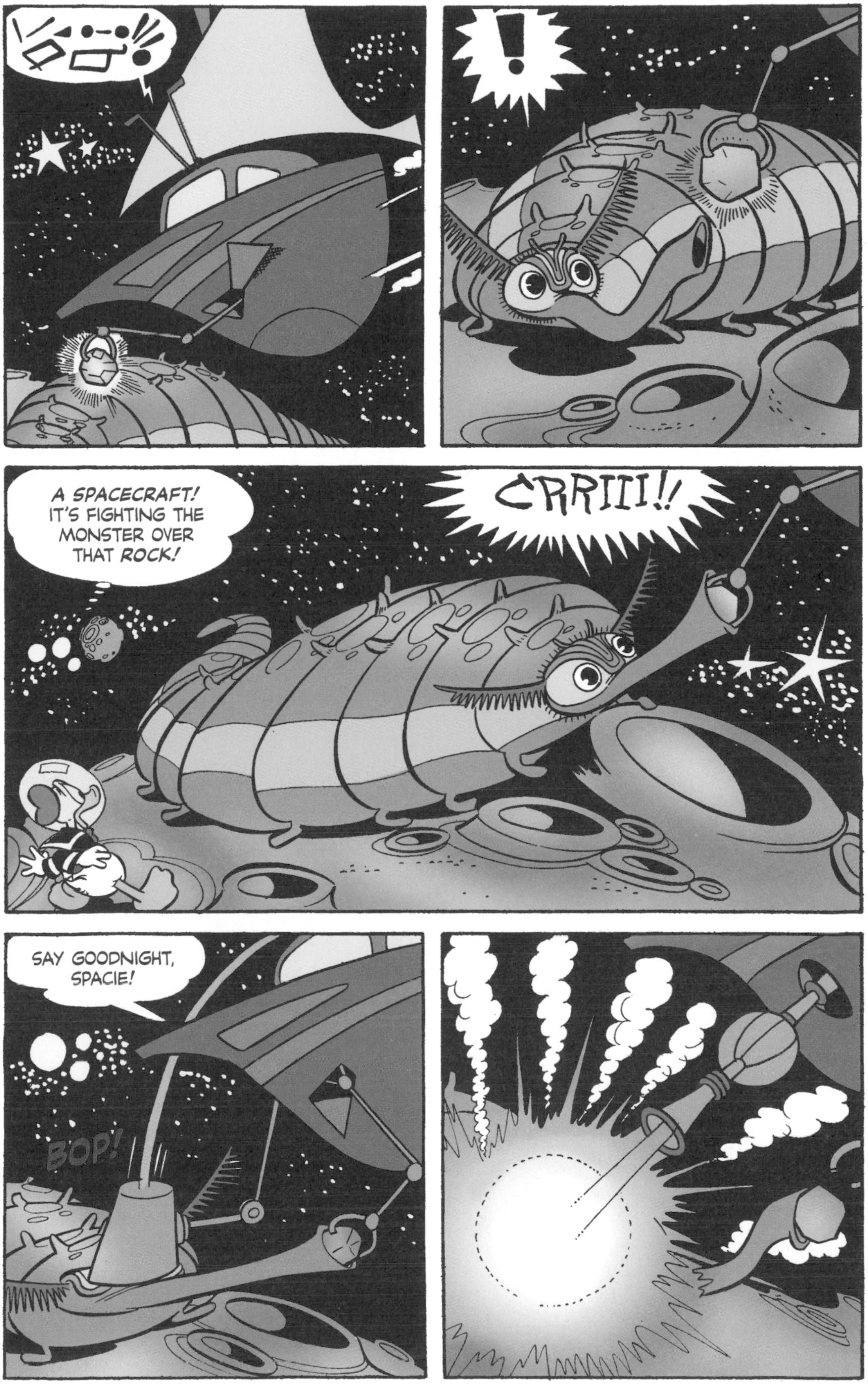
!
A SPACECRAFT! IT'S FIGHTING THE MONSTER OVER THAT ROCK!
CRRIII!!
SAY GOODNIGHT, SPACIE!
BOP!

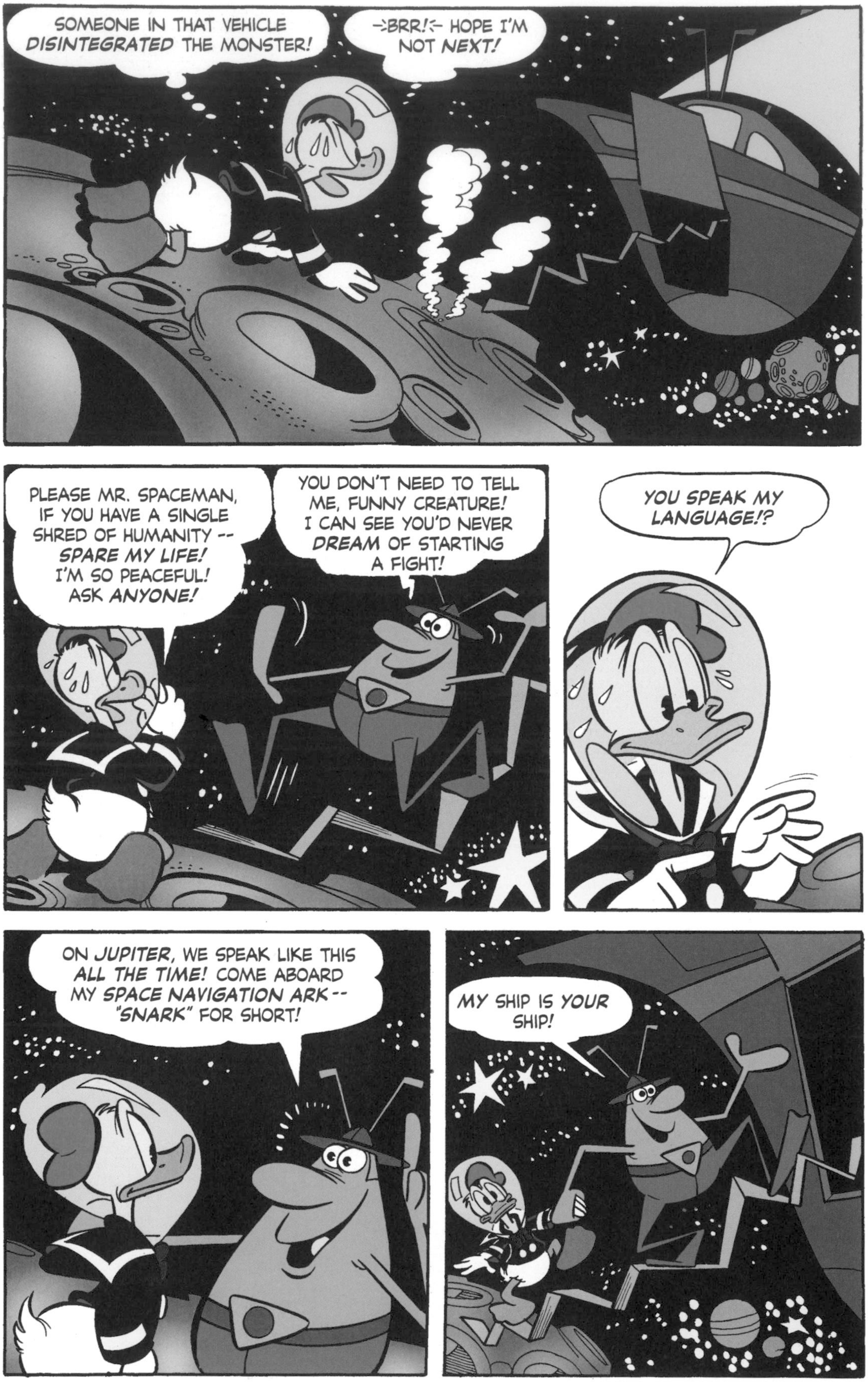
SOMEONE IN THAT VEHICLE DISINTEGRATED THE MONSTER!
–BRR!– HOPE I'M NOT NEXT!
PLEASE MR. SPACEMAN, IF YOU HAVE A SINGLE SHRED OF HUMANITY -- SPARE MY LIFE! I'M SO PEACEFUL! ASK ANYONE!
YOU DON'T NEED TO TELL ME, FUNNY CREATURE! I CAN SEE YOU'D NEVER DREAM OF STARTING A FIGHT!
YOU SPEAK MY LANGUAGE!?
ON JUPITER, WE SPEAK LIKE THIS ALL THE TIME! COME ABOARD MY SPACE NAVIGATION ARK -- "SNARK" FOR SHORT!
MY SHIP IS YOUR SHIP!

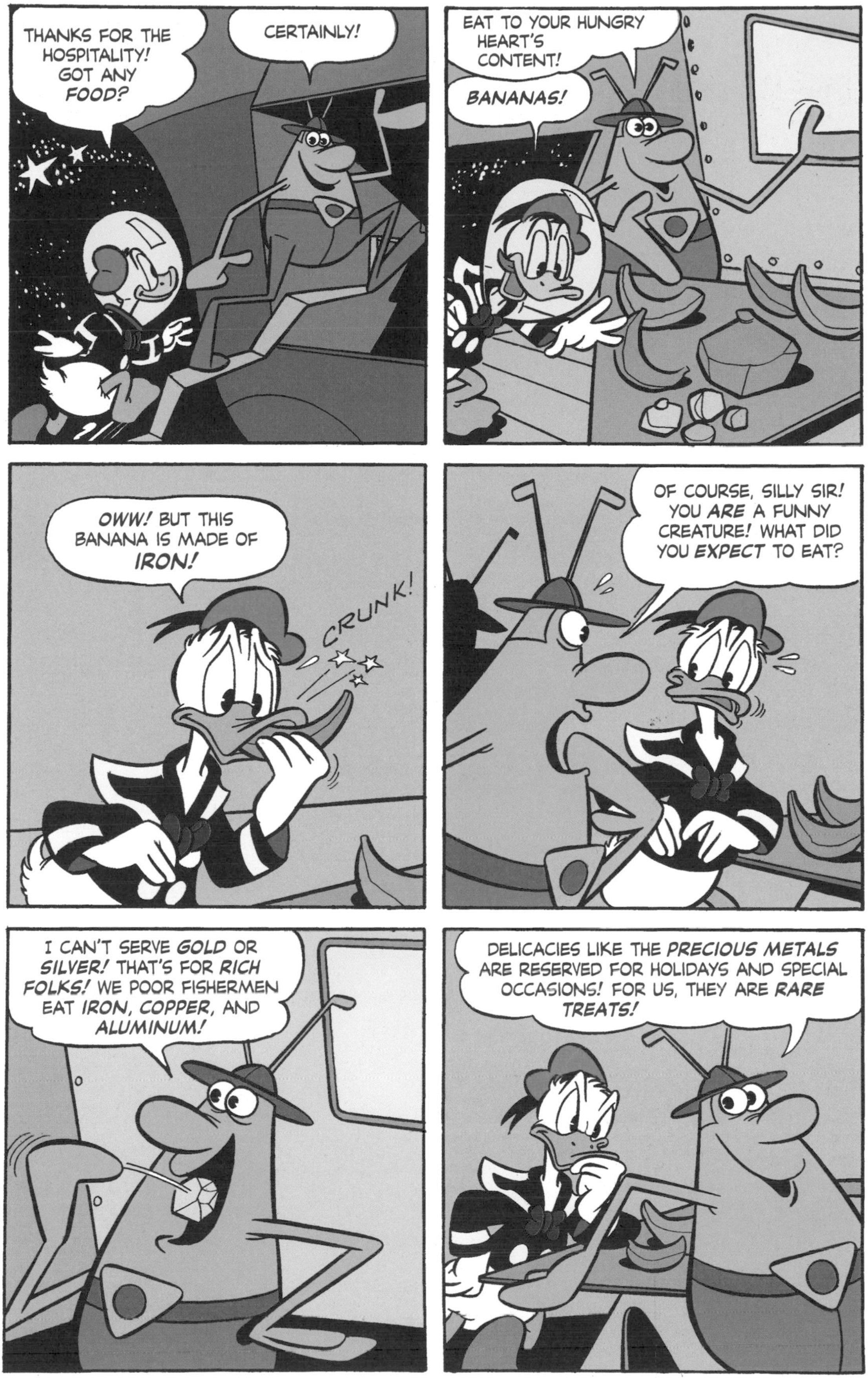
THANKS FOR THE HOSPITALITY! GOT ANY FOOD?
CERTAINLY!
EAT TO YOUR HUNGRY HEART'S CONTENT!
BANANAS!
OWW! BUT THIS BANANA IS MADE OF IRON!
CRUNK!
OF COURSE, SILLY SIR! YOU ARE A FUNNY CREATURE! WHAT DID YOU EXPECT TO EAT?
I CAN'T SERVE GOLD OR SILVER! THAT'S FOR RICH FOLKS! WE POOR FISHERMEN EAT IRON, COPPER, AND ALUMINUM!
DELICACIES LIKE THE PRECIOUS METALS ARE RESERVED FOR HOLIDAYS AND SPECIAL OCCASIONS! FOR US, THEY ARE RARE TREATS!

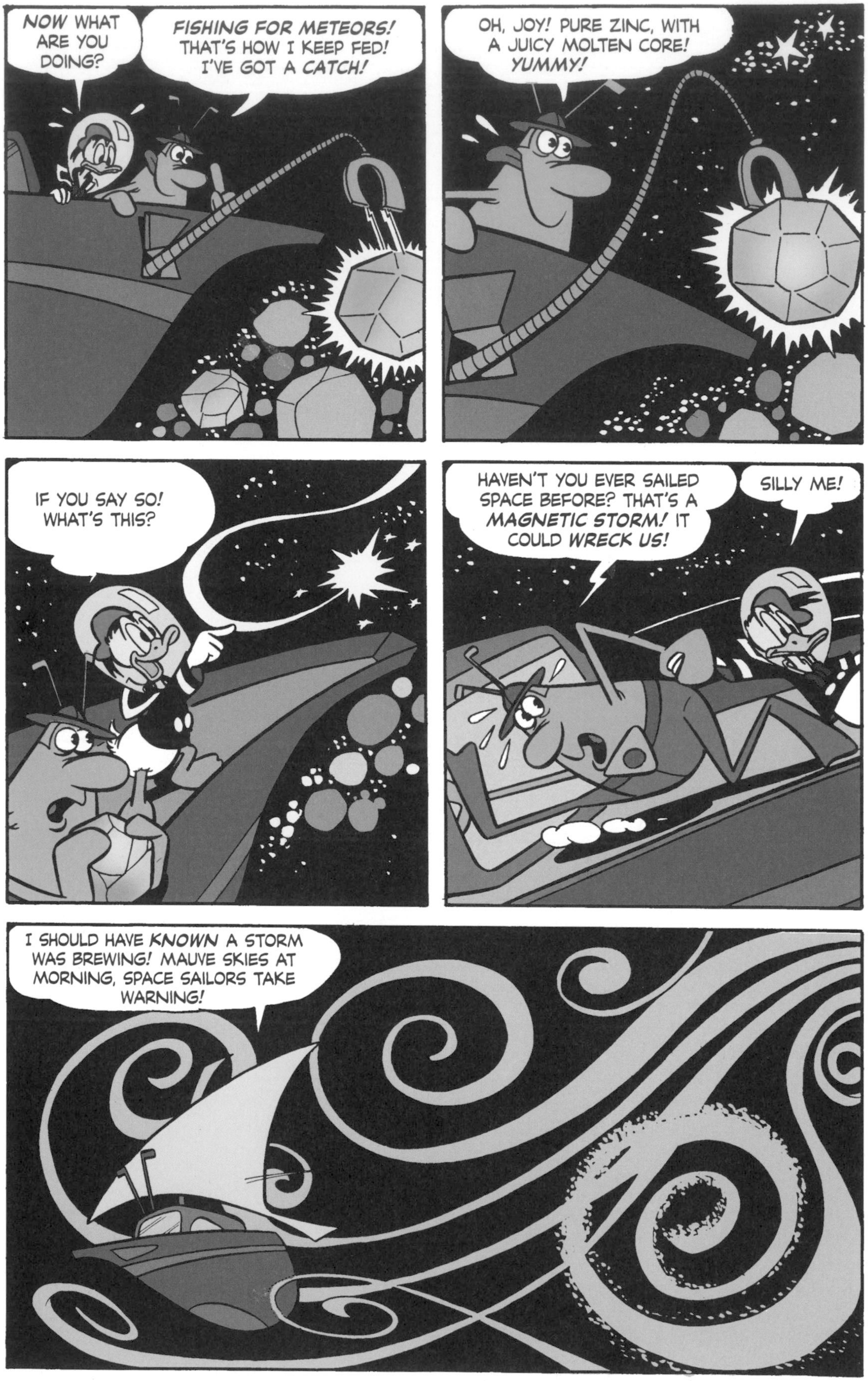

NOW WHAT ARE YOU DOING?
FISHING FOR METEORS! THAT'S HOW I KEEP FED! I'VE GOT A CATCH!
OH, JOY! PURE ZINC, WITH A JUICY MOLTEN CORE! YUMMY!
IF YOU SAY SO! WHAT'S THIS?
HAVEN'T YOU EVER SAILED SPACE BEFORE? THAT'S A MAGNETIC STORM! IT COULD WRECK US!
SILLY ME!
I SHOULD HAVE KNOWN A STORM WAS BREWING! MAUVE SKIES AT MORNING, SPACE SAILORS TAKE WARNING!

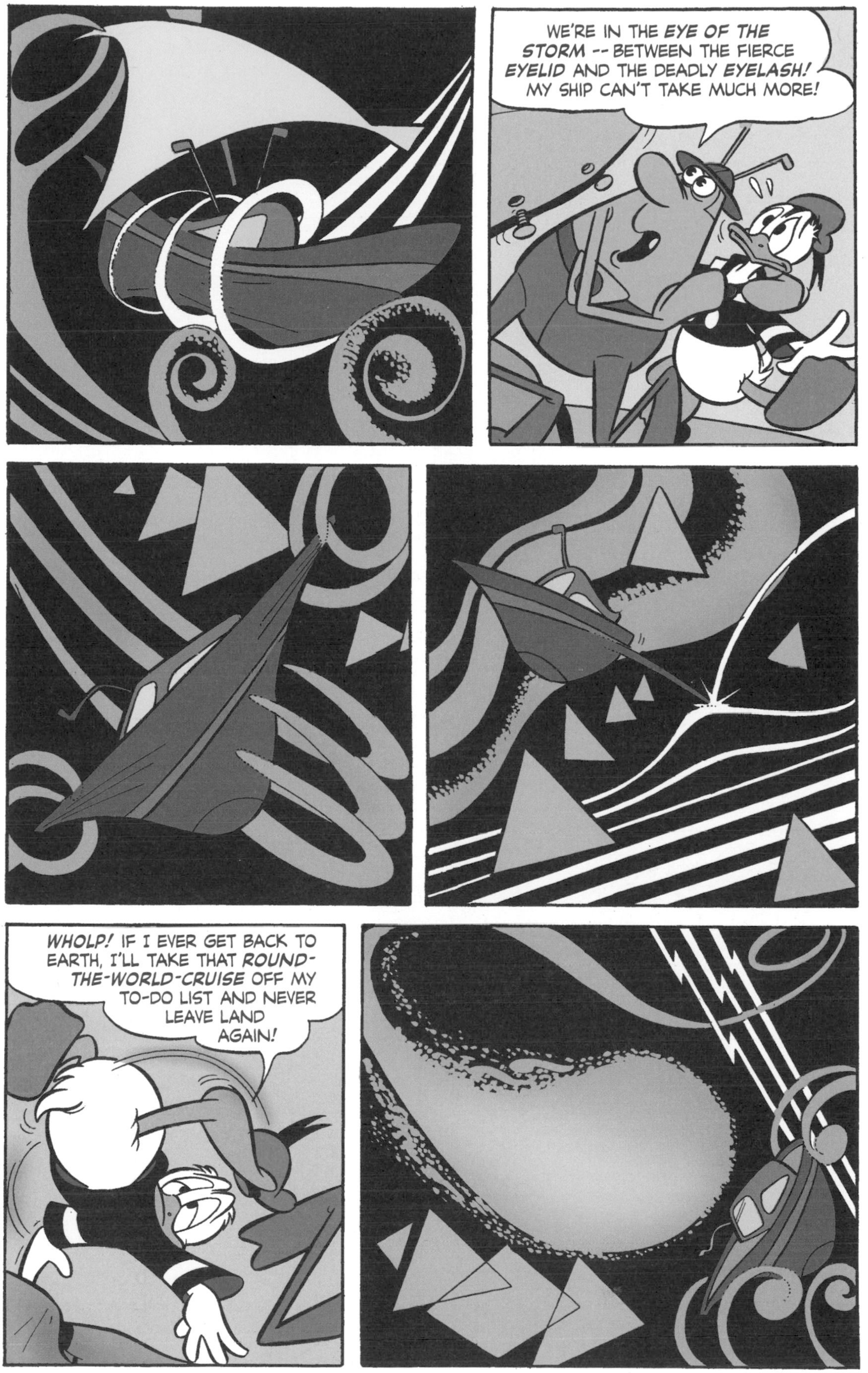
WE'RE IN THE *EYE OF THE STORM* -- BETWEEN THE FIERCE *EYELID* AND THE DEADLY *EYELASH!* MY SHIP CAN'T TAKE MUCH MORE!
WHOLP! IF I EVER GET BACK TO EARTH, I'LL TAKE THAT *ROUND-THE-WORLD-CRUISE* OFF MY TO-DO LIST AND NEVER LEAVE LAND AGAIN!

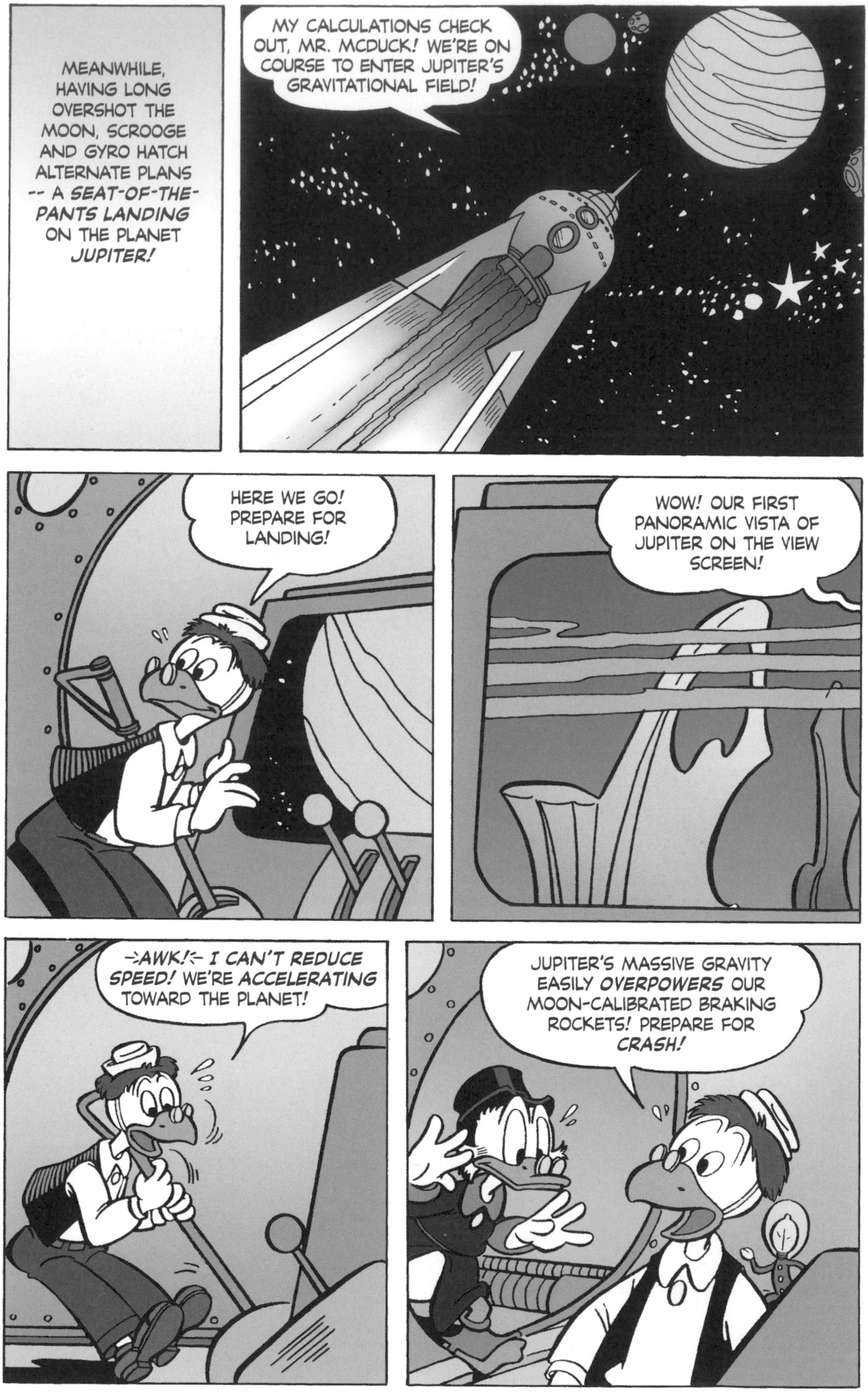
MEANWHILE, HAVING LONG OVERSHOT THE MOON, SCROOGE AND GYRO HATCH ALTERNATE PLANS -- A SEAT-OF-THE-PANTS LANDING ON THE PLANET JUPITER!
MY CALCULATIONS CHECK OUT, MR. MCDUCK! WE'RE ON COURSE TO ENTER JUPITER'S GRAVITATIONAL FIELD!
HERE WE GO! PREPARE FOR LANDING!
WOW! OUR FIRST PANORAMIC VISTA OF JUPITER ON THE VIEW SCREEN!
—AWK!— I CAN'T REDUCE SPEED! WE'RE ACCELERATING TOWARD THE PLANET!
JUPITER'S MASSIVE GRAVITY EASILY OVERPOWERS OUR MOON-CALIBRATED BRAKING ROCKETS! PREPARE FOR CRASH!

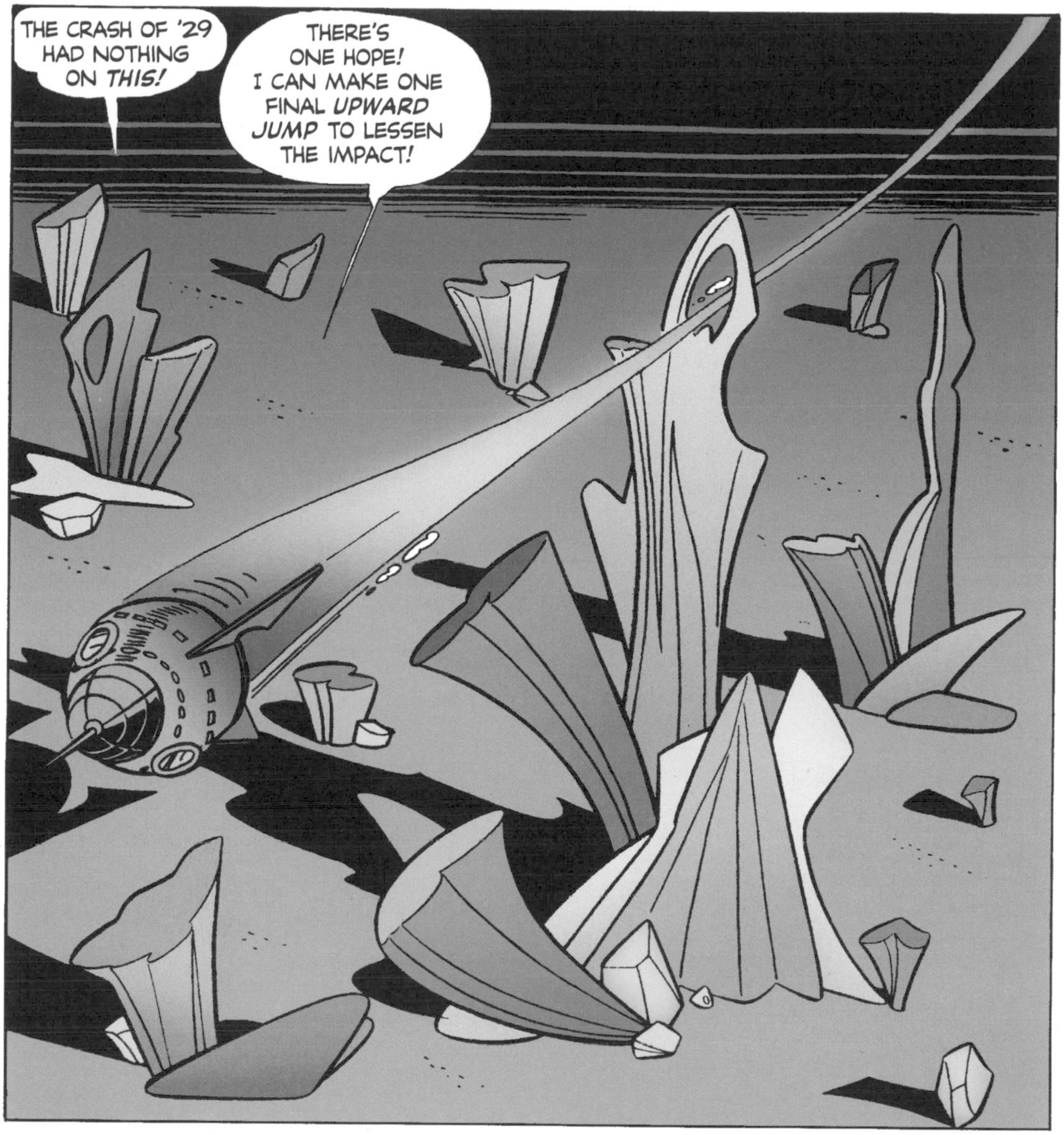
THE CRASH OF '29 HAD NOTHING ON *THIS!*
THERE'S ONE HOPE! I CAN MAKE ONE FINAL *UPWARD JUMP* TO LESSEN THE IMPACT!

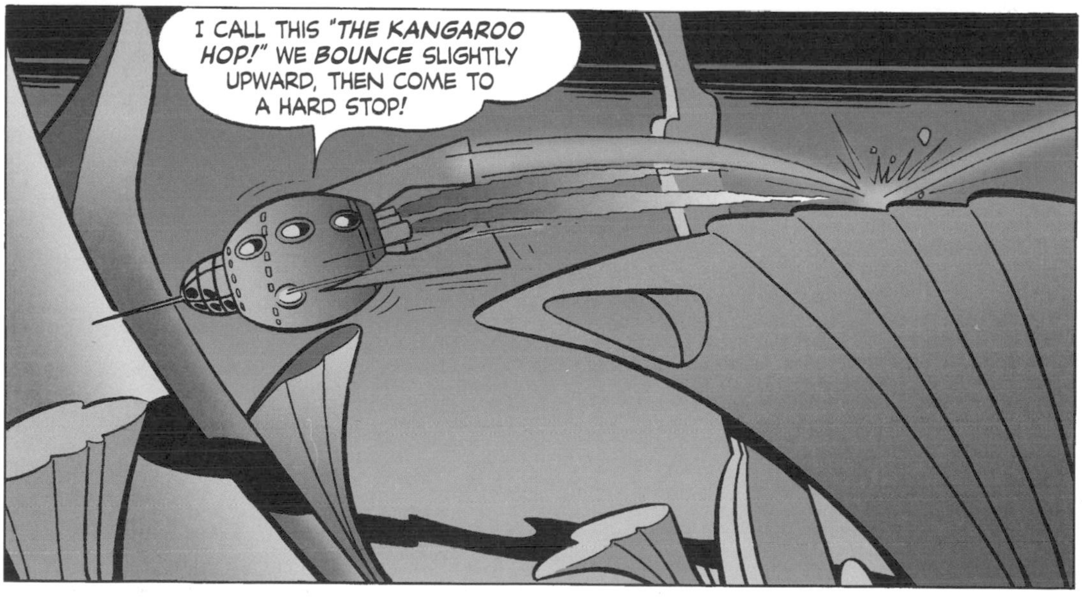
I CALL THIS *"THE KANGAROO HOP!"* WE *BOUNCE* SLIGHTLY UPWARD, THEN COME TO A HARD STOP!

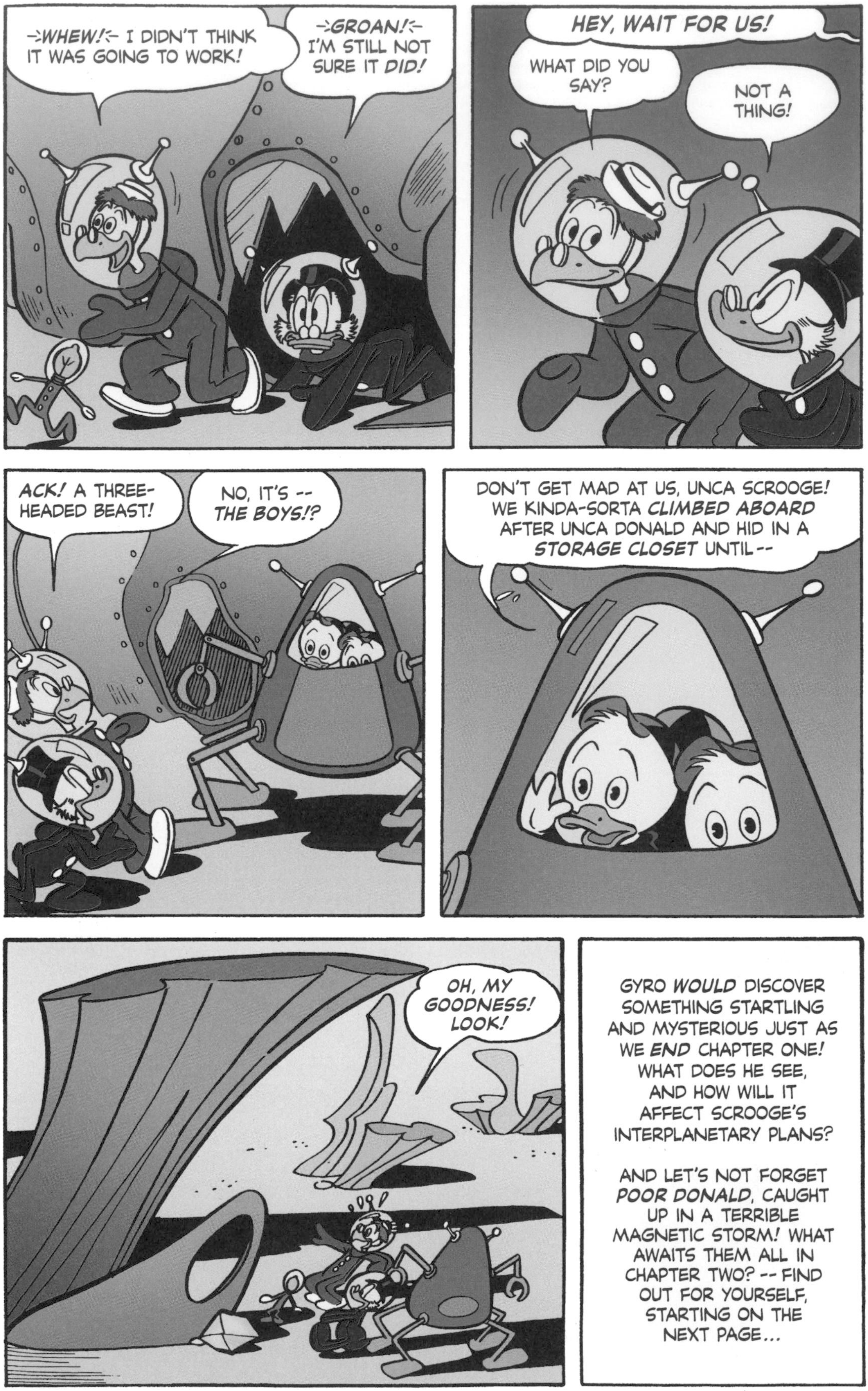
-WHEW!- I DIDN'T THINK IT WAS GOING TO WORK!
-GROAN!- I'M STILL NOT SURE IT DID!
HEY, WAIT FOR US!
WHAT DID YOU SAY?
NOT A THING!
ACK! A THREE-HEADED BEAST!
NO, IT'S -- THE BOYS!?
DON'T GET MAD AT US, UNCA SCROOGE! WE KINDA-SORTA CLIMBED ABOARD AFTER UNCA DONALD AND HID IN A STORAGE CLOSET UNTIL--
OH, MY GOODNESS! LOOK!
GYRO WOULD DISCOVER SOMETHING STARTLING AND MYSTERIOUS JUST AS WE END CHAPTER ONE! WHAT DOES HE SEE, AND HOW WILL IT AFFECT SCROOGE'S INTERPLANETARY PLANS?
AND LET'S NOT FORGET POOR DONALD, CAUGHT UP IN A TERRIBLE MAGNETIC STORM! WHAT AWAITS THEM ALL IN CHAPTER TWO? -- FIND OUT FOR YOURSELF, STARTING ON THE NEXT PAGE...

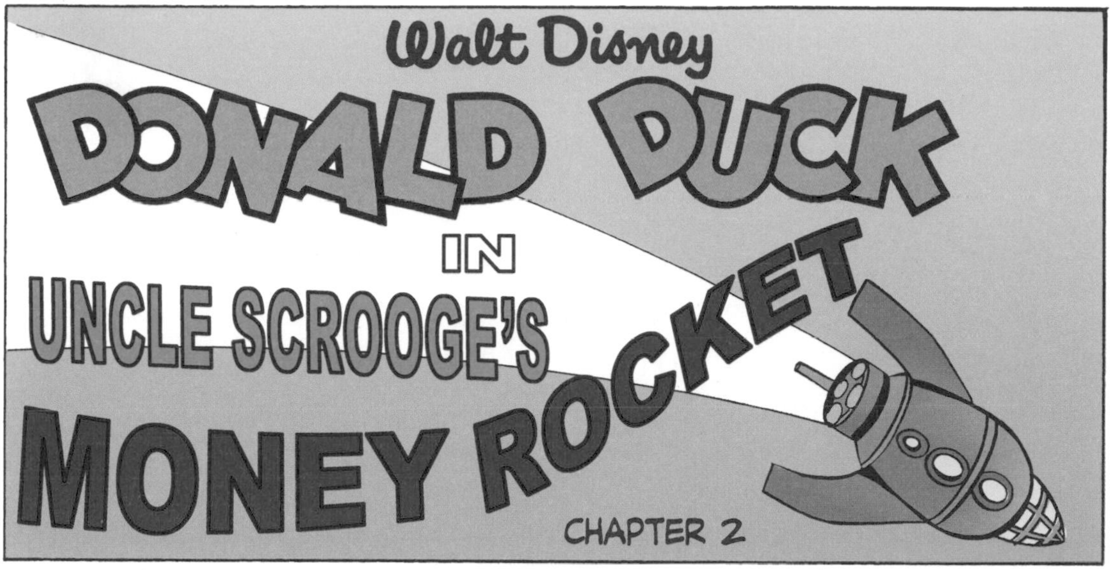
Walt Disney
DONALD DUCK
IN
UNCLE SCROOGE'S
MONEY ROCKET
CHAPTER 2

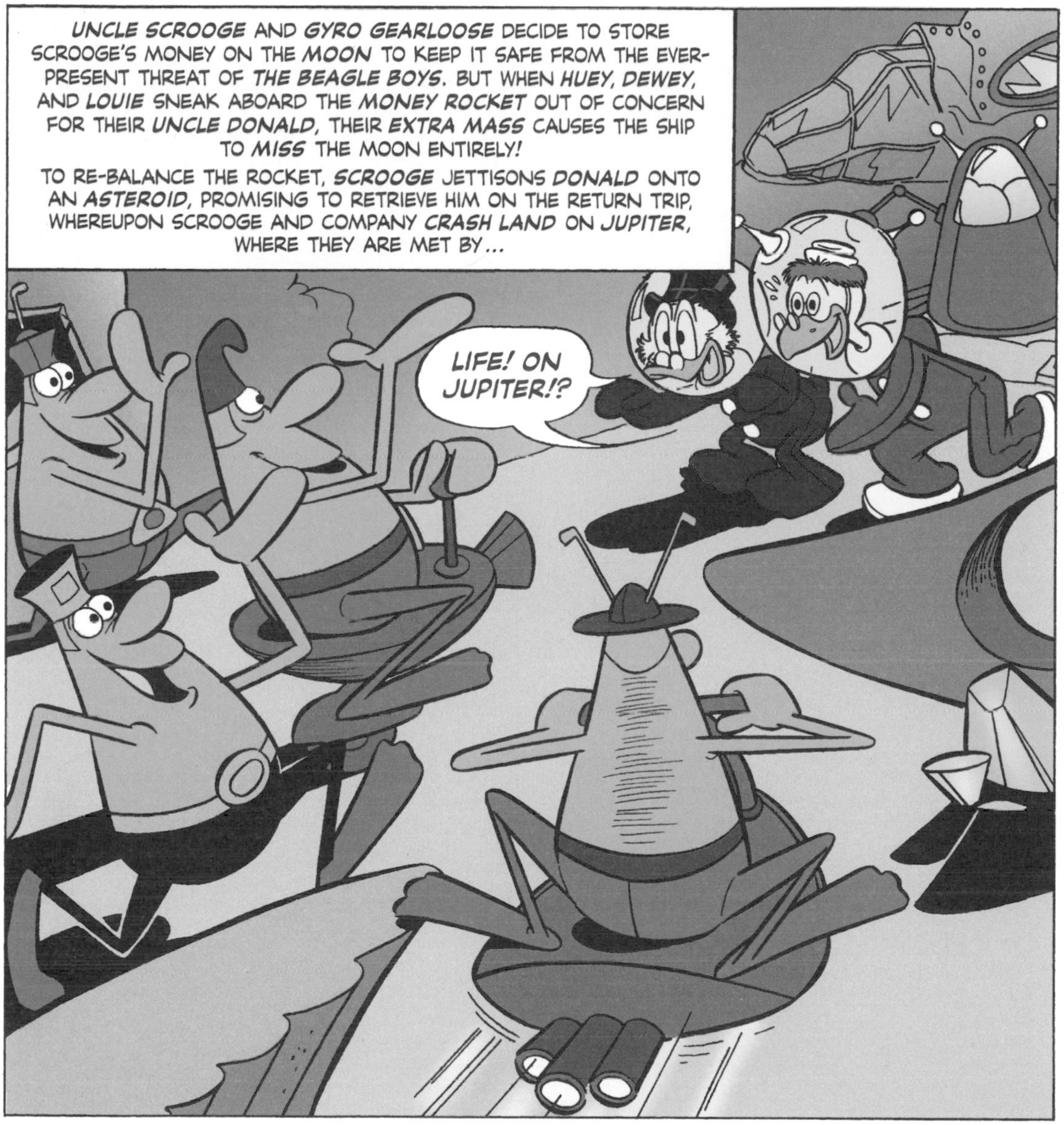
UNCLE SCROOGE AND GYRO GEARLOOSE DECIDE TO STORE SCROOGE'S MONEY ON THE MOON TO KEEP IT SAFE FROM THE EVER-PRESENT THREAT OF THE BEAGLE BOYS. BUT WHEN HUEY, DEWEY, AND LOUIE SNEAK ABOARD THE MONEY ROCKET OUT OF CONCERN FOR THEIR UNCLE DONALD, THEIR EXTRA MASS CAUSES THE SHIP TO MISS THE MOON ENTIRELY!
TO RE-BALANCE THE ROCKET, SCROOGE JETTISONS DONALD ONTO AN ASTEROID, PROMISING TO RETRIEVE HIM ON THE RETURN TRIP, WHEREUPON SCROOGE AND COMPANY CRASH LAND ON JUPITER, WHERE THEY ARE MET BY...
LIFE! ON JUPITER!?

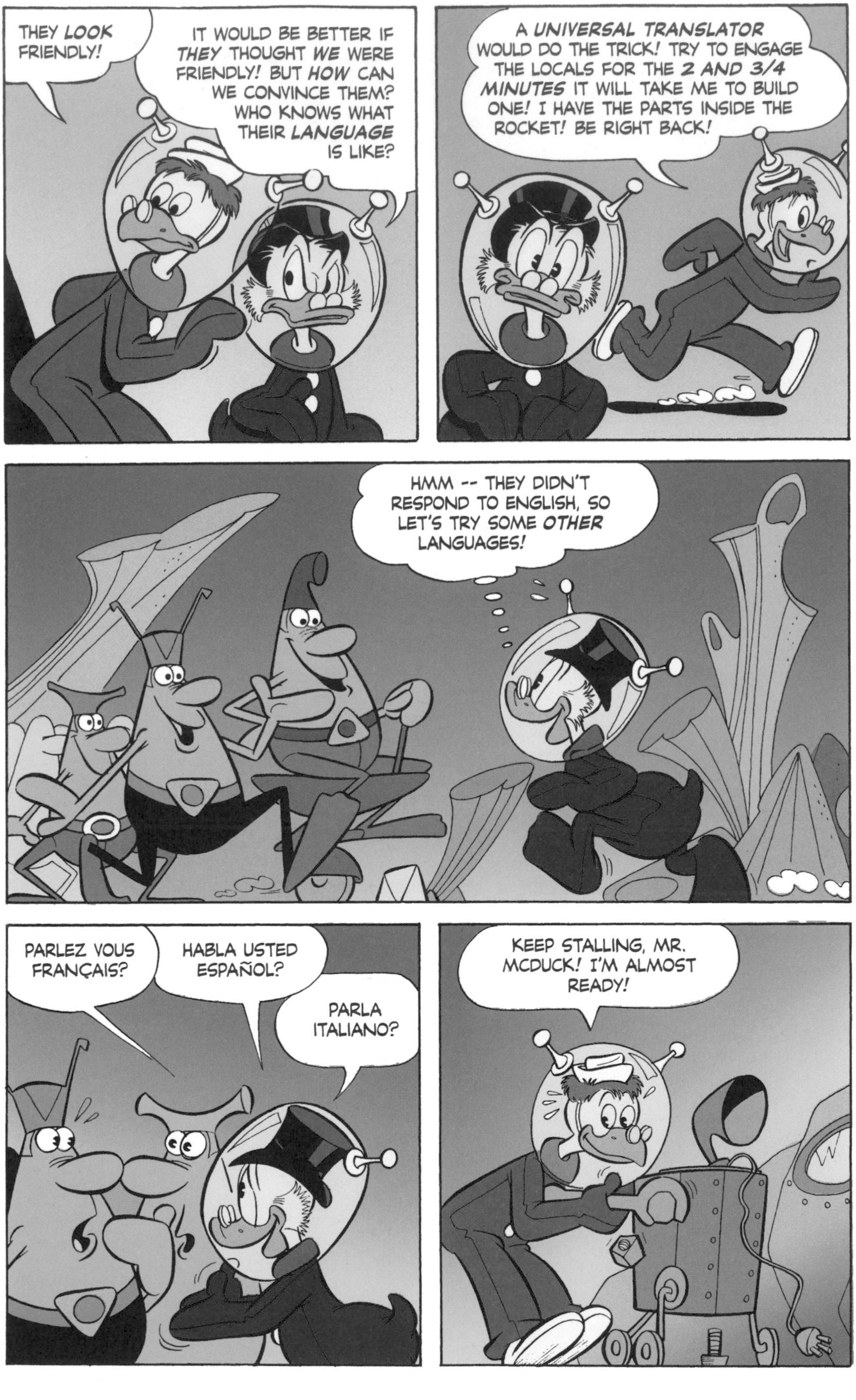
THEY LOOK FRIENDLY!
IT WOULD BE BETTER IF THEY THOUGHT WE WERE FRIENDLY! BUT HOW CAN WE CONVINCE THEM? WHO KNOWS WHAT THEIR LANGUAGE IS LIKE?
A UNIVERSAL TRANSLATOR WOULD DO THE TRICK! TRY TO ENGAGE THE LOCALS FOR THE 2 AND 3/4 MINUTES IT WILL TAKE ME TO BUILD ONE! I HAVE THE PARTS INSIDE THE ROCKET! BE RIGHT BACK!
HMM -- THEY DIDN'T RESPOND TO ENGLISH, SO LET'S TRY SOME OTHER LANGUAGES!
PARLEZ VOUS FRANÇAIS?
HABLA USTED ESPAÑOL?
PARLA ITALIANO?
KEEP STALLING, MR. MCDUCK! I'M ALMOST READY!

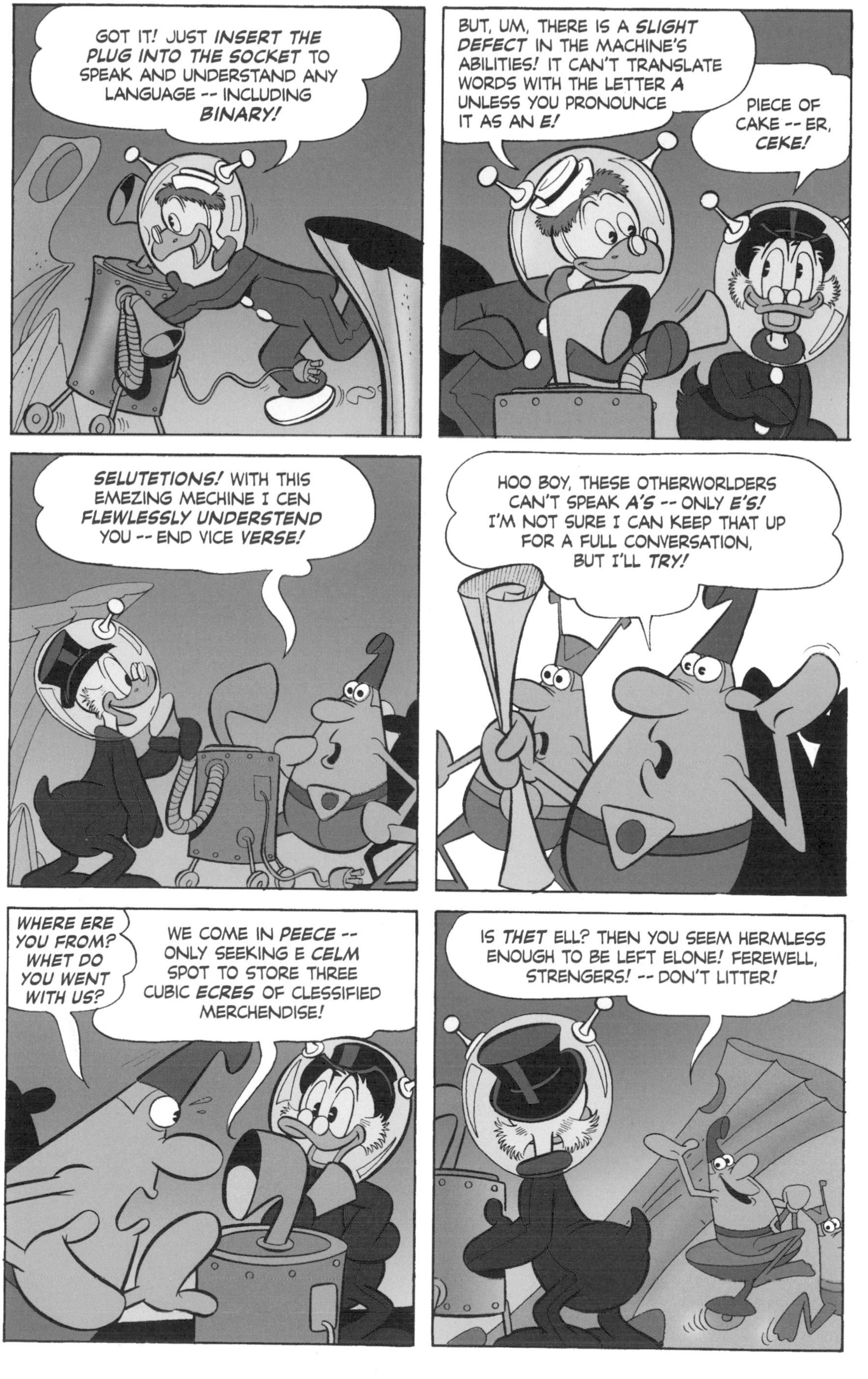
GOT IT! JUST INSERT THE PLUG INTO THE SOCKET TO SPEAK AND UNDERSTAND ANY LANGUAGE -- INCLUDING BINARY!
BUT, UM, THERE IS A SLIGHT DEFECT IN THE MACHINE'S ABILITIES! IT CAN'T TRANSLATE WORDS WITH THE LETTER A UNLESS YOU PRONOUNCE IT AS AN E!
PIECE OF CAKE -- ER, CEKE!
SELUTETIONS! WITH THIS EMEZING MECHINE I CEN FLEWLESSLY UNDERSTEND YOU -- END VICE VERSE!
HOO BOY, THESE OTHERWORLDERS CAN'T SPEAK A'S -- ONLY E'S! I'M NOT SURE I CAN KEEP THAT UP FOR A FULL CONVERSATION, BUT I'LL TRY!
WHERE ERE YOU FROM? WHET DO YOU WENT WITH US?
WE COME IN PEECE -- ONLY SEEKING E CELM SPOT TO STORE THREE CUBIC ECRES OF CLESSIFIED MERCHENDISE!
IS THET ELL? THEN YOU SEEM HERMLESS ENOUGH TO BE LEFT ELONE! FEREWELL, STRENGERS! -- DON'T LITTER!

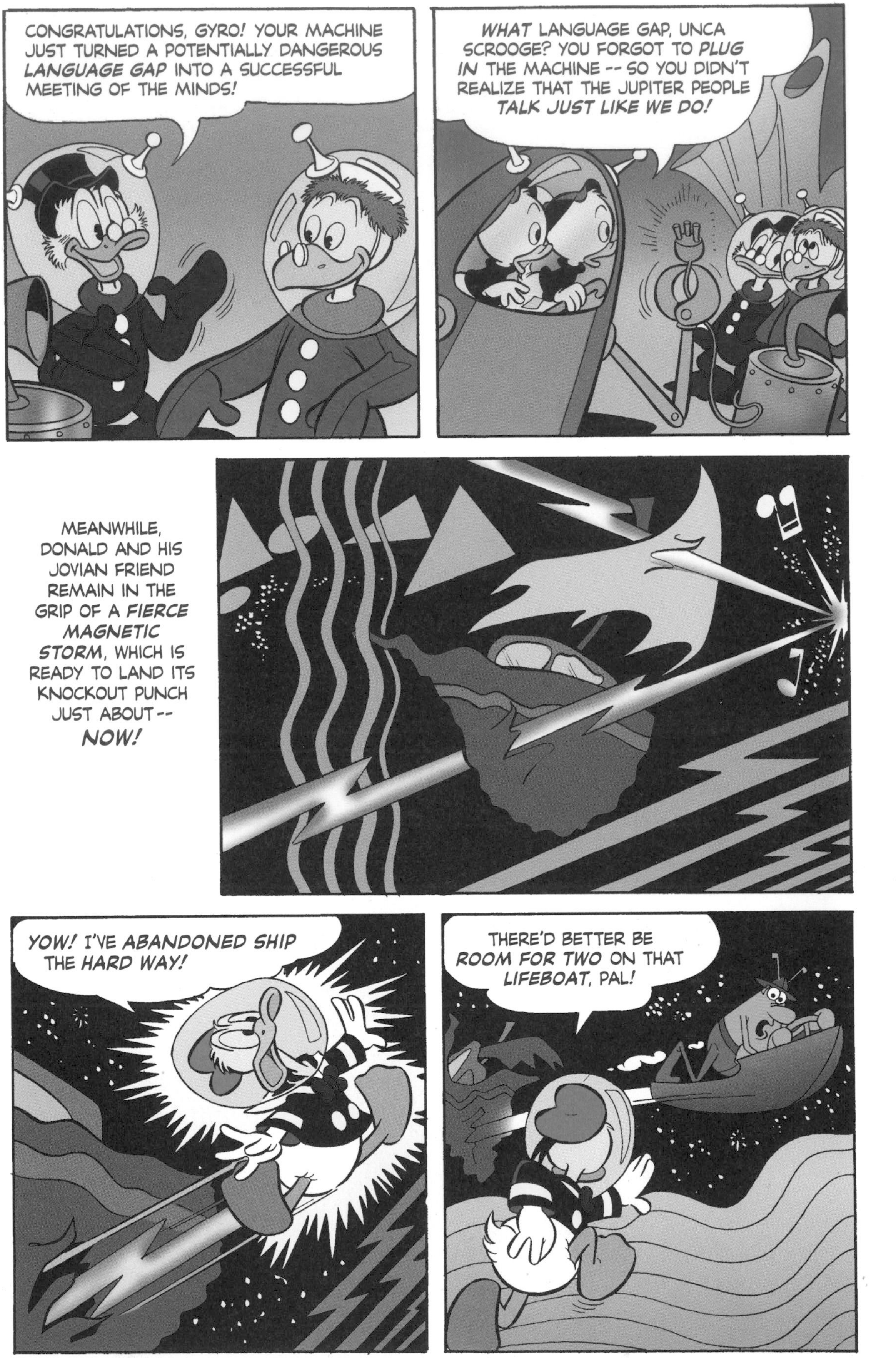
CONGRATULATIONS, GYRO! YOUR MACHINE JUST TURNED A POTENTIALLY DANGEROUS LANGUAGE GAP INTO A SUCCESSFUL MEETING OF THE MINDS!
WHAT LANGUAGE GAP, UNCA SCROOGE? YOU FORGOT TO PLUG IN THE MACHINE -- SO YOU DIDN'T REALIZE THAT THE JUPITER PEOPLE TALK JUST LIKE WE DO!
MEANWHILE, DONALD AND HIS JOVIAN FRIEND REMAIN IN THE GRIP OF A FIERCE MAGNETIC STORM, WHICH IS READY TO LAND ITS KNOCKOUT PUNCH JUST ABOUT -- NOW!
YOW! I'VE ABANDONED SHIP THE HARD WAY!
THERE'D BETTER BE ROOM FOR TWO ON THAT LIFEBOAT, PAL!

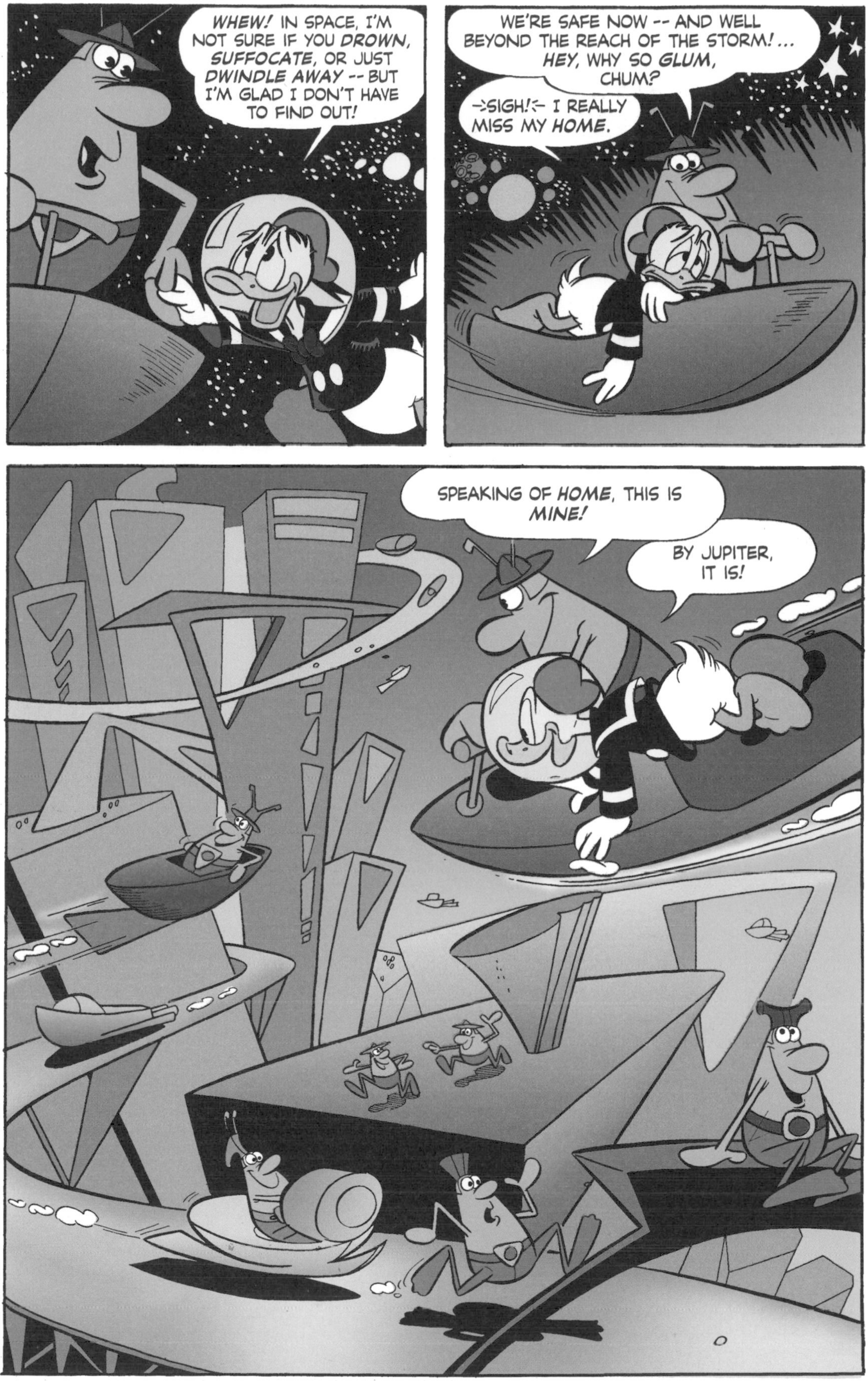
WHEW! IN SPACE, I'M NOT SURE IF YOU DROWN, SUFFOCATE, OR JUST DWINDLE AWAY -- BUT I'M GLAD I DON'T HAVE TO FIND OUT!
WE'RE SAFE NOW -- AND WELL BEYOND THE REACH OF THE STORM! ... HEY, WHY SO GLUM, CHUM?
→SIGH!← I REALLY MISS MY HOME.
SPEAKING OF HOME, THIS IS MINE!
BY JUPITER, IT IS!

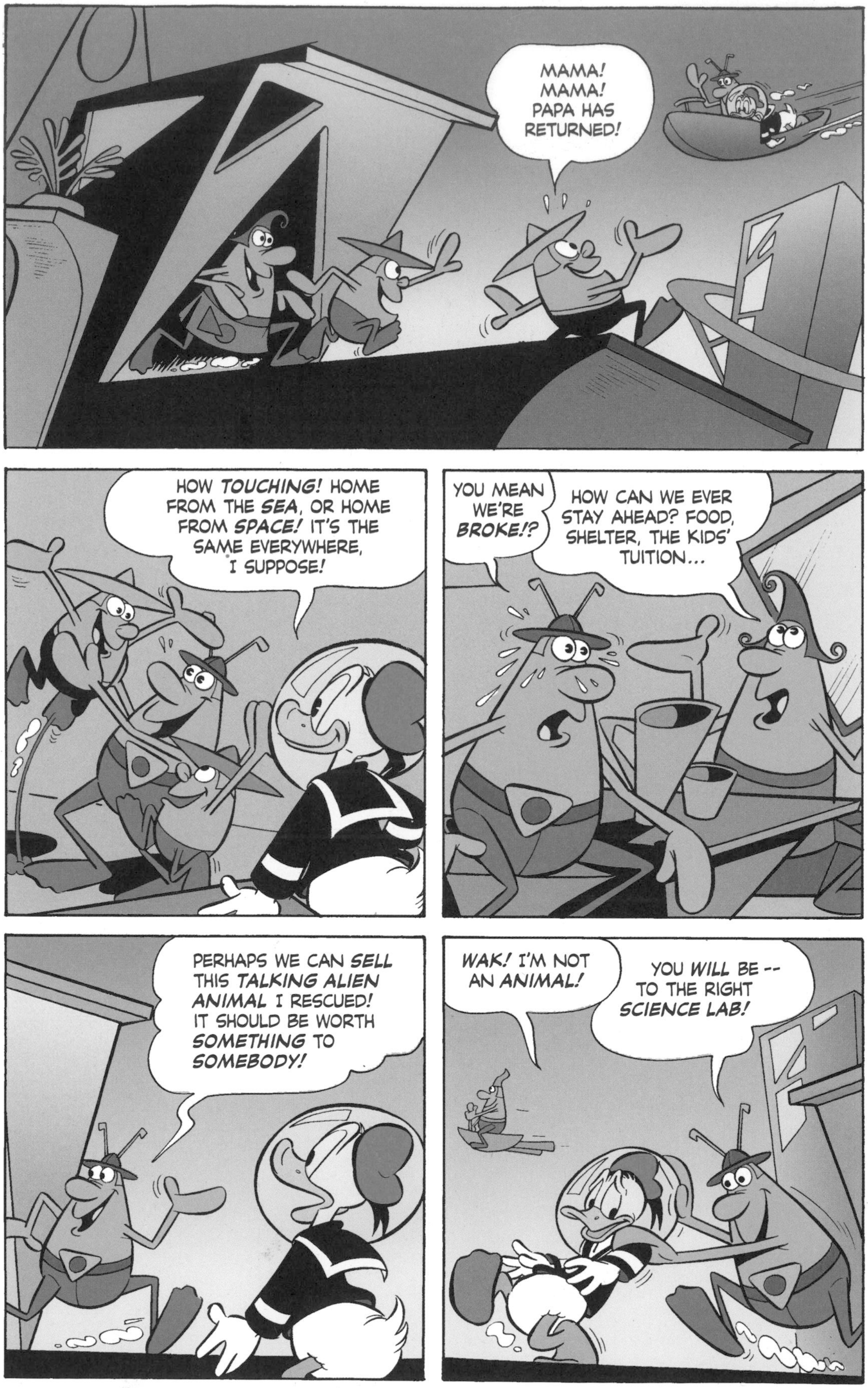
MAMA! MAMA! PAPA HAS RETURNED!
HOW TOUCHING! HOME FROM THE SEA, OR HOME FROM SPACE! IT'S THE SAME EVERYWHERE, I SUPPOSE!
YOU MEAN WE'RE BROKE!?
HOW CAN WE EVER STAY AHEAD? FOOD, SHELTER, THE KIDS' TUITION...
PERHAPS WE CAN SELL THIS TALKING ALIEN ANIMAL I RESCUED! IT SHOULD BE WORTH SOMETHING TO SOMEBODY!
WAK! I'M NOT AN ANIMAL!
YOU WILL BE -- TO THE RIGHT SCIENCE LAB!

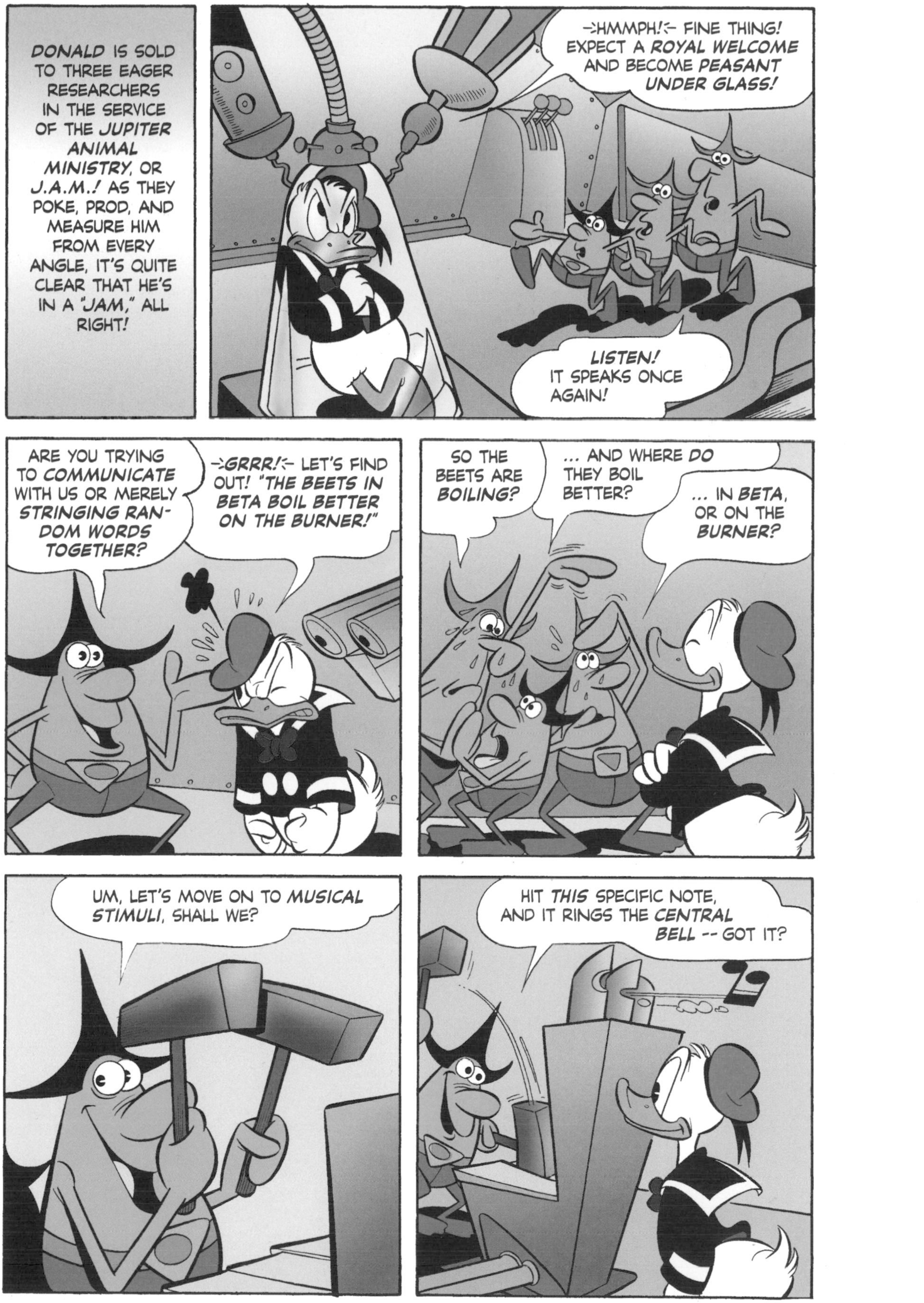
DONALD IS SOLD TO THREE EAGER RESEARCHERS IN THE SERVICE OF THE JUPITER ANIMAL MINISTRY, OR J.A.M.! AS THEY POKE, PROD, AND MEASURE HIM FROM EVERY ANGLE, IT'S QUITE CLEAR THAT HE'S IN A "JAM," ALL RIGHT!
-HMMPH!- FINE THING! EXPECT A ROYAL WELCOME AND BECOME PEASANT UNDER GLASS!
LISTEN! IT SPEAKS ONCE AGAIN!
ARE YOU TRYING TO COMMUNICATE WITH US OR MERELY STRINGING RANDOM WORDS TOGETHER?
-GRRR!- LET'S FIND OUT! "THE BEETS IN BETA BOIL BETTER ON THE BURNER!"
SO THE BEETS ARE BOILING?
... AND WHERE DO THEY BOIL BETTER?
... IN BETA, OR ON THE BURNER?
UM, LET'S MOVE ON TO MUSICAL STIMULI, SHALL WE?
HIT THIS SPECIFIC NOTE, AND IT RINGS THE CENTRAL BELL -- GOT IT?

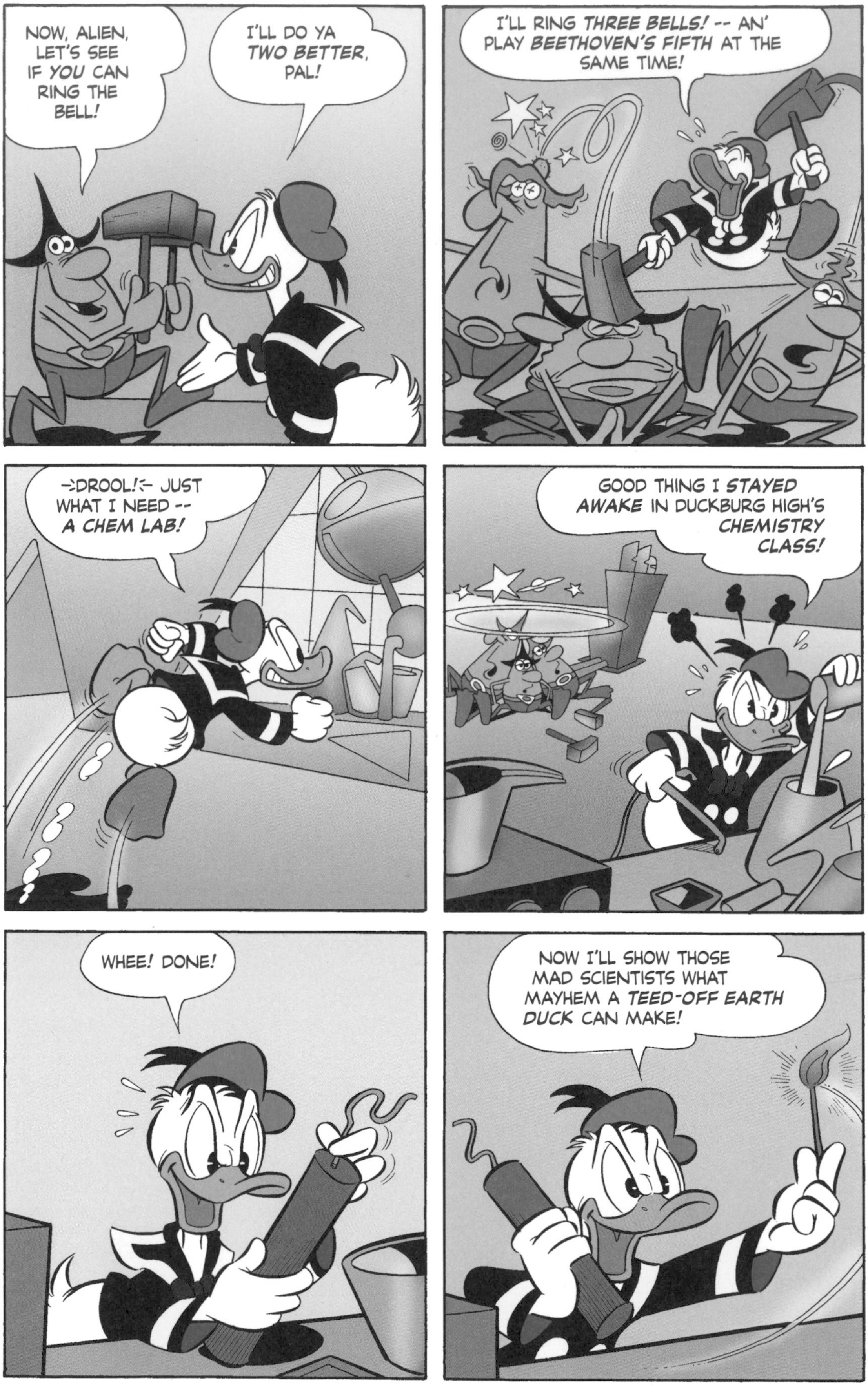
NOW, ALIEN, LET'S SEE IF YOU CAN RING THE BELL!
I'LL DO YA TWO BETTER, PAL!
I'LL RING THREE BELLS! -- AN' PLAY BEETHOVEN'S FIFTH AT THE SAME TIME!
DROOL! JUST WHAT I NEED -- A CHEM LAB!
GOOD THING I STAYED AWAKE IN DUCKBURG HIGH'S CHEMISTRY CLASS!
WHEE! DONE!
NOW I'LL SHOW THOSE MAD SCIENTISTS WHAT MAYHEM A TEED-OFF EARTH DUCK CAN MAKE!

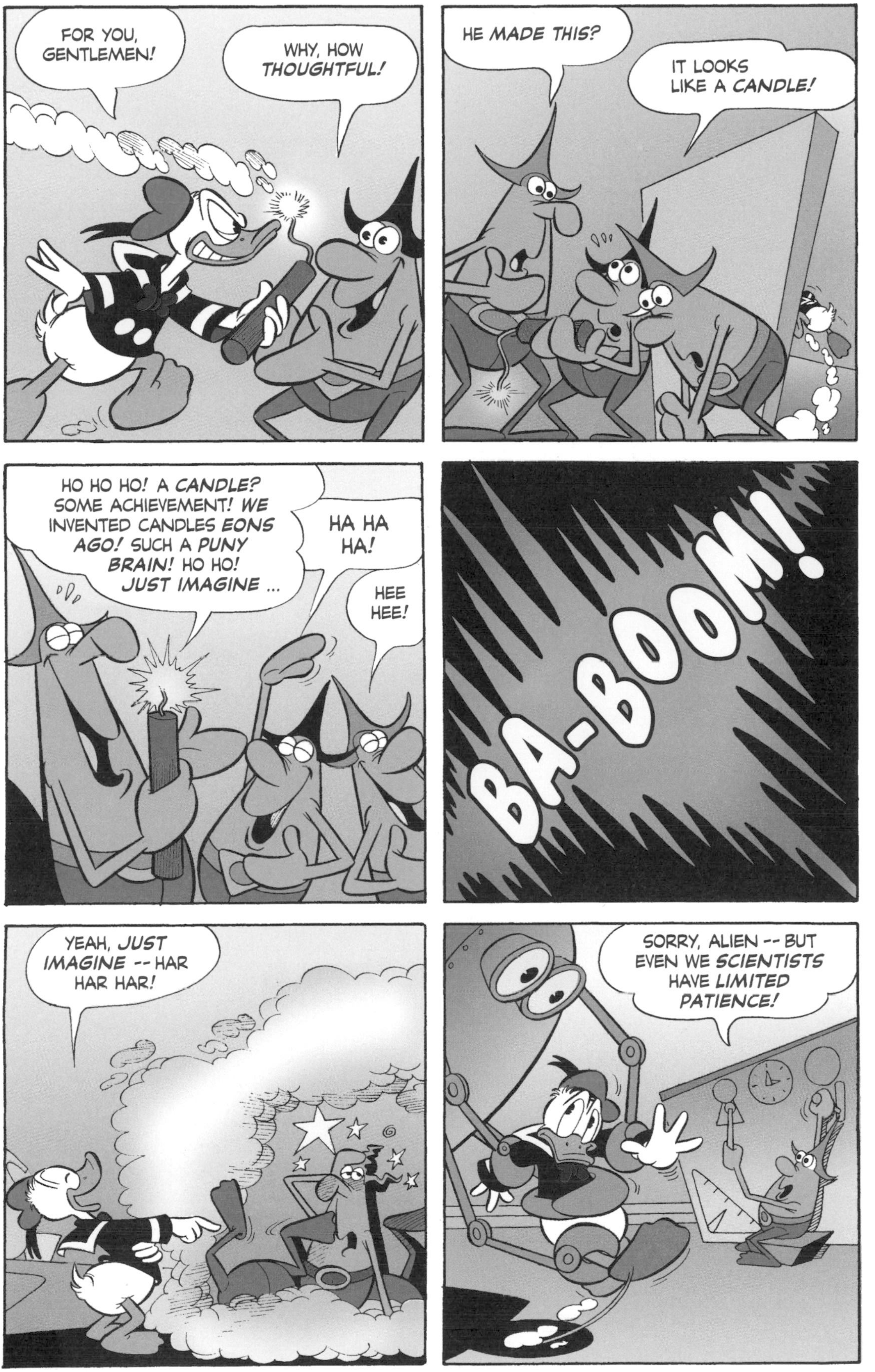
FOR YOU, GENTLEMEN!
WHY, HOW THOUGHTFUL!
HE MADE THIS?
IT LOOKS LIKE A CANDLE!
HO HO HO! A CANDLE? SOME ACHIEVEMENT! WE INVENTED CANDLES EONS AGO! SUCH A PUNY BRAIN! HO HO! JUST IMAGINE ...
HA HA HA!
HEE HEE!
BA-BOOM!
YEAH, JUST IMAGINE -- HAR HAR HAR!
SORRY, ALIEN -- BUT EVEN WE SCIENTISTS HAVE LIMITED PATIENCE!

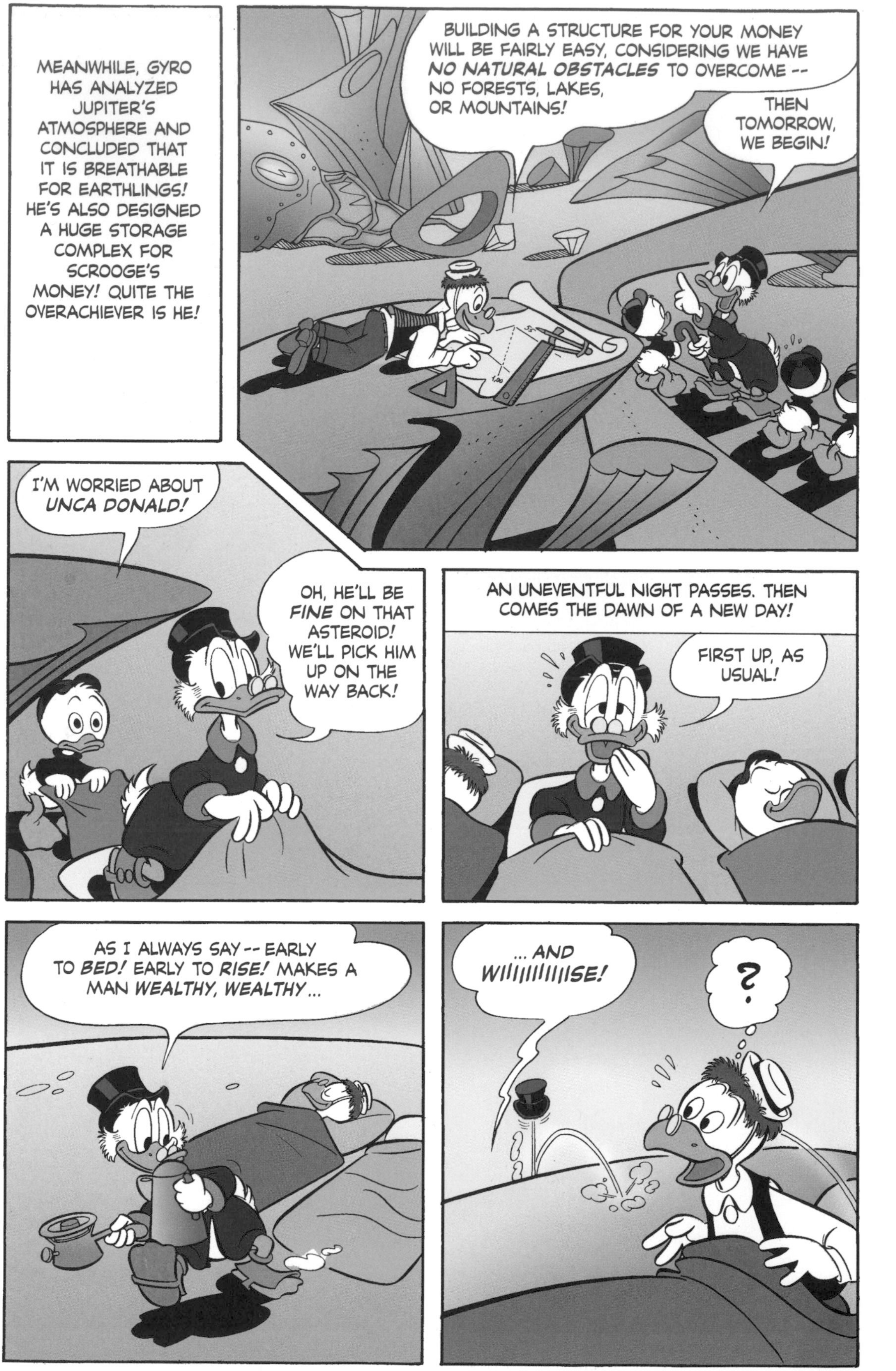
MEANWHILE, GYRO HAS ANALYZED JUPITER'S ATMOSPHERE AND CONCLUDED THAT IT IS BREATHABLE FOR EARTHLINGS! HE'S ALSO DESIGNED A HUGE STORAGE COMPLEX FOR SCROOGE'S MONEY! QUITE THE OVERACHIEVER IS HE!
BUILDING A STRUCTURE FOR YOUR MONEY WILL BE FAIRLY EASY, CONSIDERING WE HAVE NO NATURAL OBSTACLES TO OVERCOME -- NO FORESTS, LAKES, OR MOUNTAINS!
THEN TOMORROW, WE BEGIN!
I'M WORRIED ABOUT UNCA DONALD!
OH, HE'LL BE FINE ON THAT ASTEROID! WE'LL PICK HIM UP ON THE WAY BACK!
AN UNEVENTFUL NIGHT PASSES. THEN COMES THE DAWN OF A NEW DAY!
FIRST UP, AS USUAL!
AS I ALWAYS SAY -- EARLY TO BED! EARLY TO RISE! MAKES A MAN WEALTHY, WEALTHY...
... AND WIIIIIIIIIISE!
?

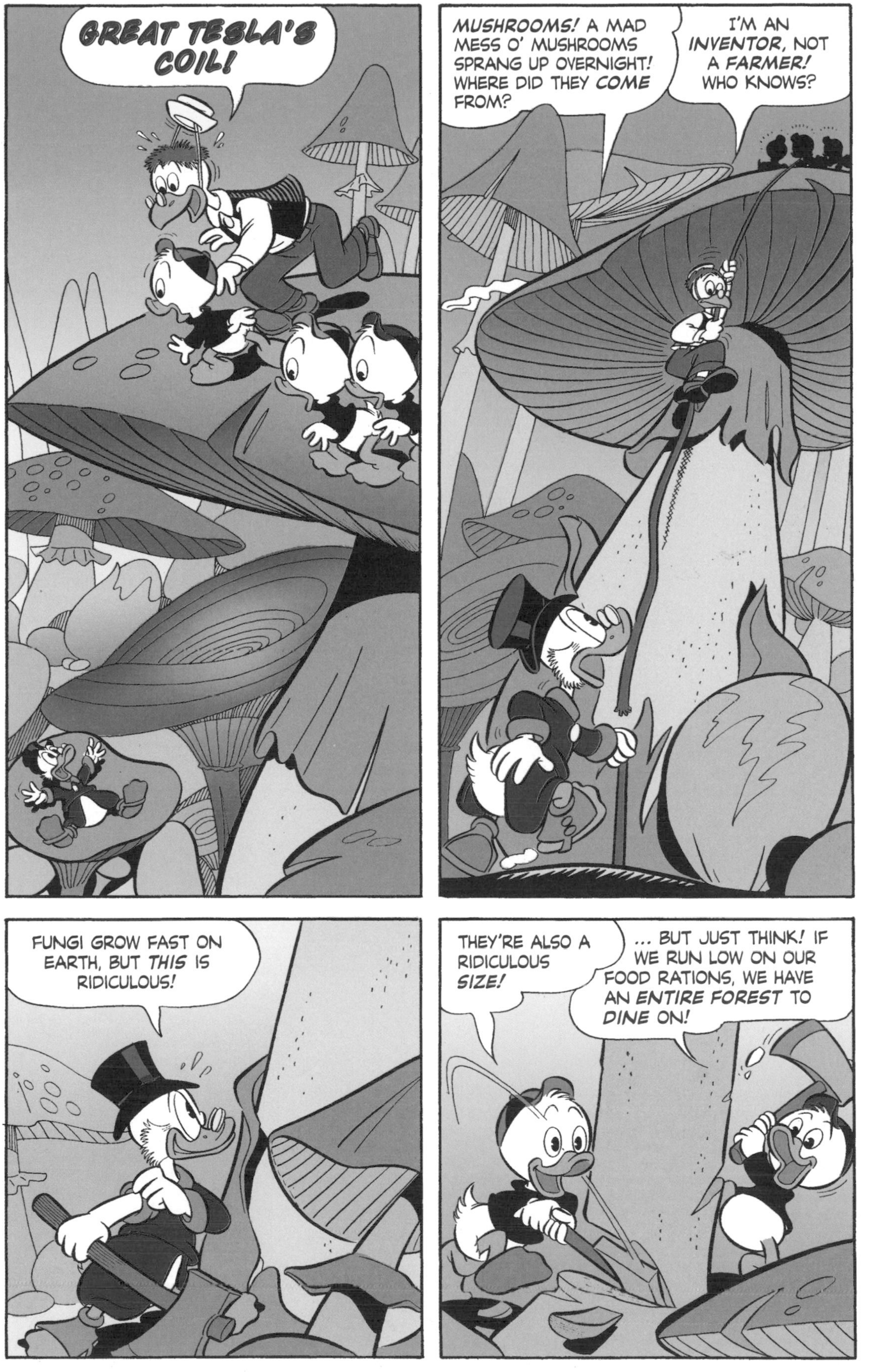
GREAT TESLA'S COIL!
MUSHROOMS! A MAD MESS O' MUSHROOMS SPRANG UP OVERNIGHT! WHERE DID THEY COME FROM?
I'M AN INVENTOR, NOT A FARMER! WHO KNOWS?
FUNGI GROW FAST ON EARTH, BUT THIS IS RIDICULOUS!
THEY'RE ALSO A RIDICULOUS SIZE!
... BUT JUST THINK! IF WE RUN LOW ON OUR FOOD RATIONS, WE HAVE AN ENTIRE FOREST TO DINE ON!

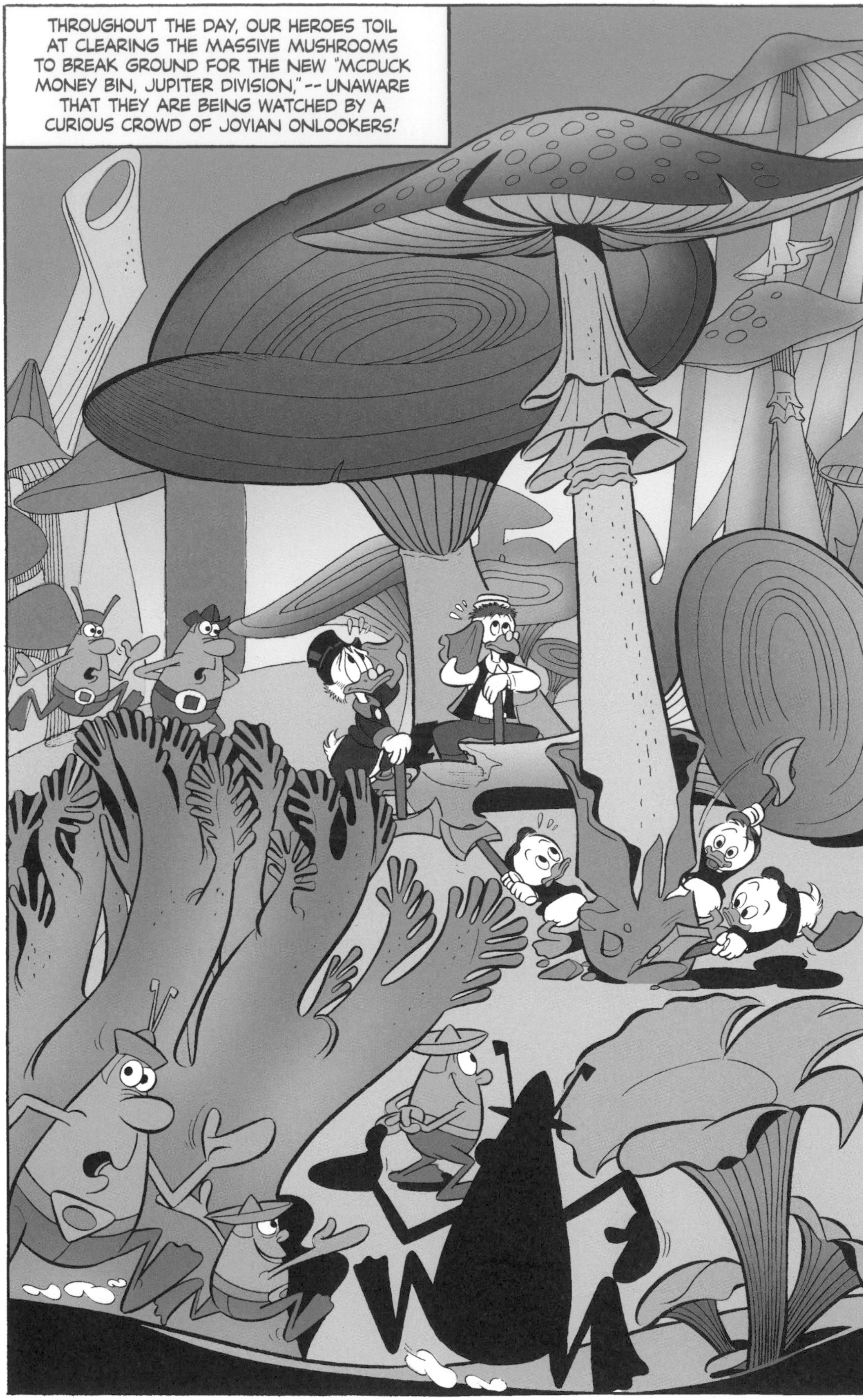
THROUGHOUT THE DAY, OUR HEROES TOIL AT CLEARING THE MASSIVE MUSHROOMS TO BREAK GROUND FOR THE NEW "MCDUCK MONEY BIN, JUPITER DIVISION," -- UNAWARE THAT THEY ARE BEING WATCHED BY A CURIOUS CROWD OF JOVIAN ONLOOKERS!

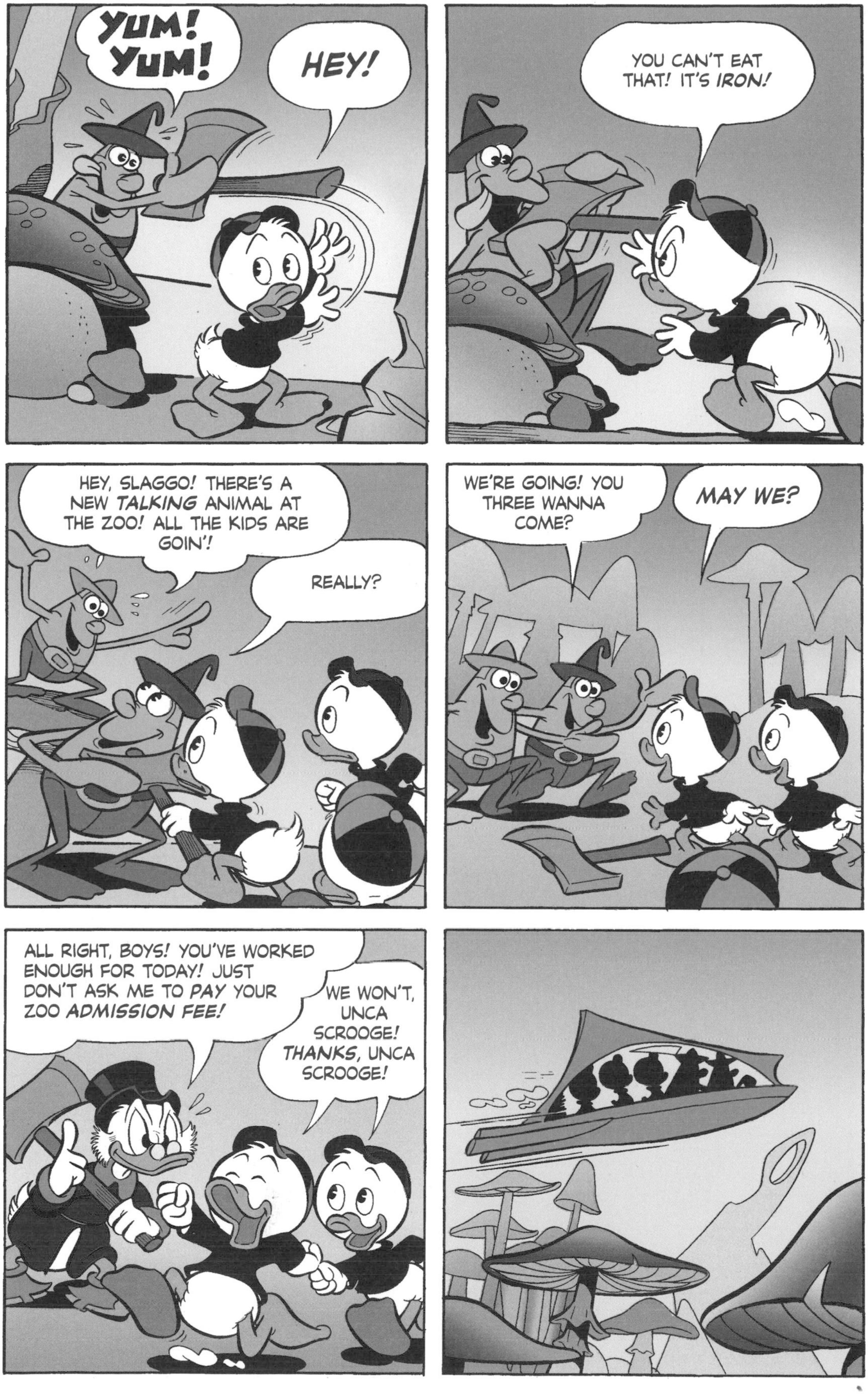
YUM! YUM!
HEY!
YOU CAN'T EAT THAT! IT'S IRON!
HEY, SLAGGO! THERE'S A NEW TALKING ANIMAL AT THE ZOO! ALL THE KIDS ARE GOIN'!
REALLY?
WE'RE GOING! YOU THREE WANNA COME?
MAY WE?
ALL RIGHT, BOYS! YOU'VE WORKED ENOUGH FOR TODAY! JUST DON'T ASK ME TO PAY YOUR ZOO ADMISSION FEE!
WE WON'T, UNCA SCROOGE! THANKS, UNCA SCROOGE!

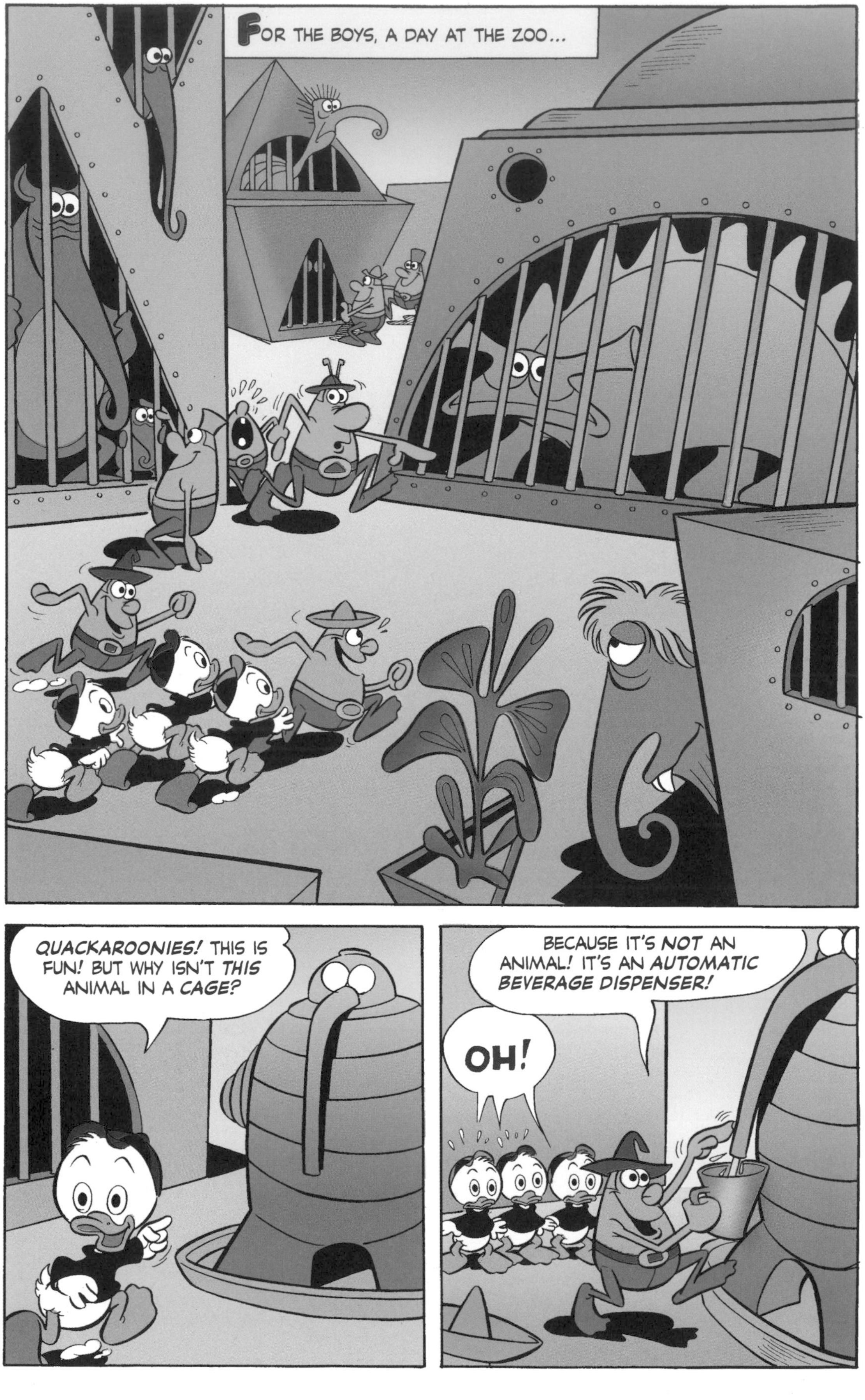
FOR THE BOYS, A DAY AT THE ZOO...
QUACKAROONIES! THIS IS FUN! BUT WHY ISN'T THIS ANIMAL IN A CAGE?
BECAUSE IT'S NOT AN ANIMAL! IT'S AN AUTOMATIC BEVERAGE DISPENSER!
OH!

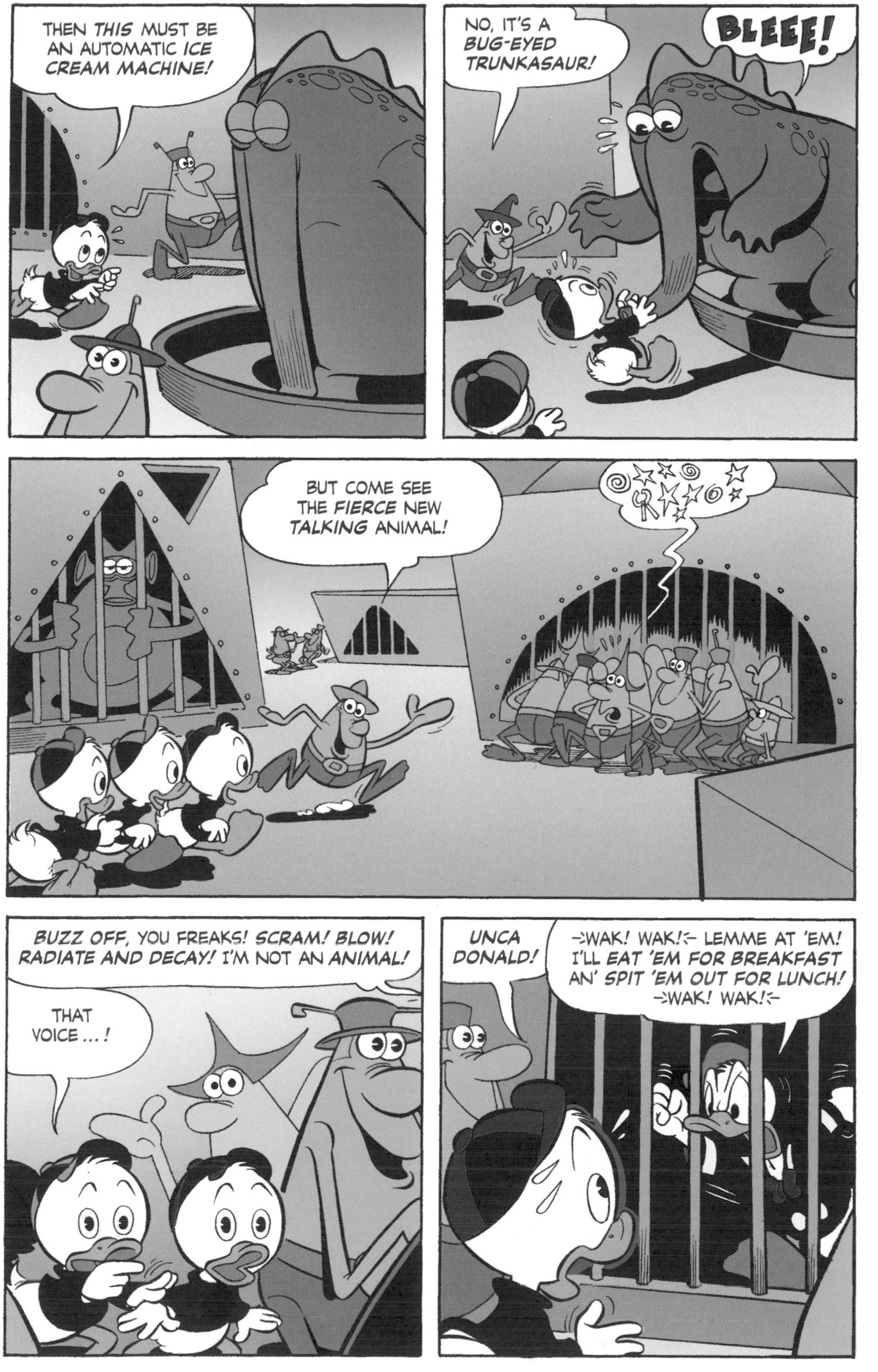
THEN THIS MUST BE AN AUTOMATIC ICE CREAM MACHINE!
NO, IT'S A BUG-EYED TRUNKASAUR!
BLEEE!
BUT COME SEE THE FIERCE NEW TALKING ANIMAL!
BUZZ OFF, YOU FREAKS! SCRAM! BLOW! RADIATE AND DECAY! I'M NOT AN ANIMAL!
THAT VOICE ...!
UNCA DONALD!
-WAK! WAK!- LEMME AT 'EM! I'LL EAT 'EM FOR BREAKFAST AN' SPIT 'EM OUT FOR LUNCH! -WAK! WAK!-

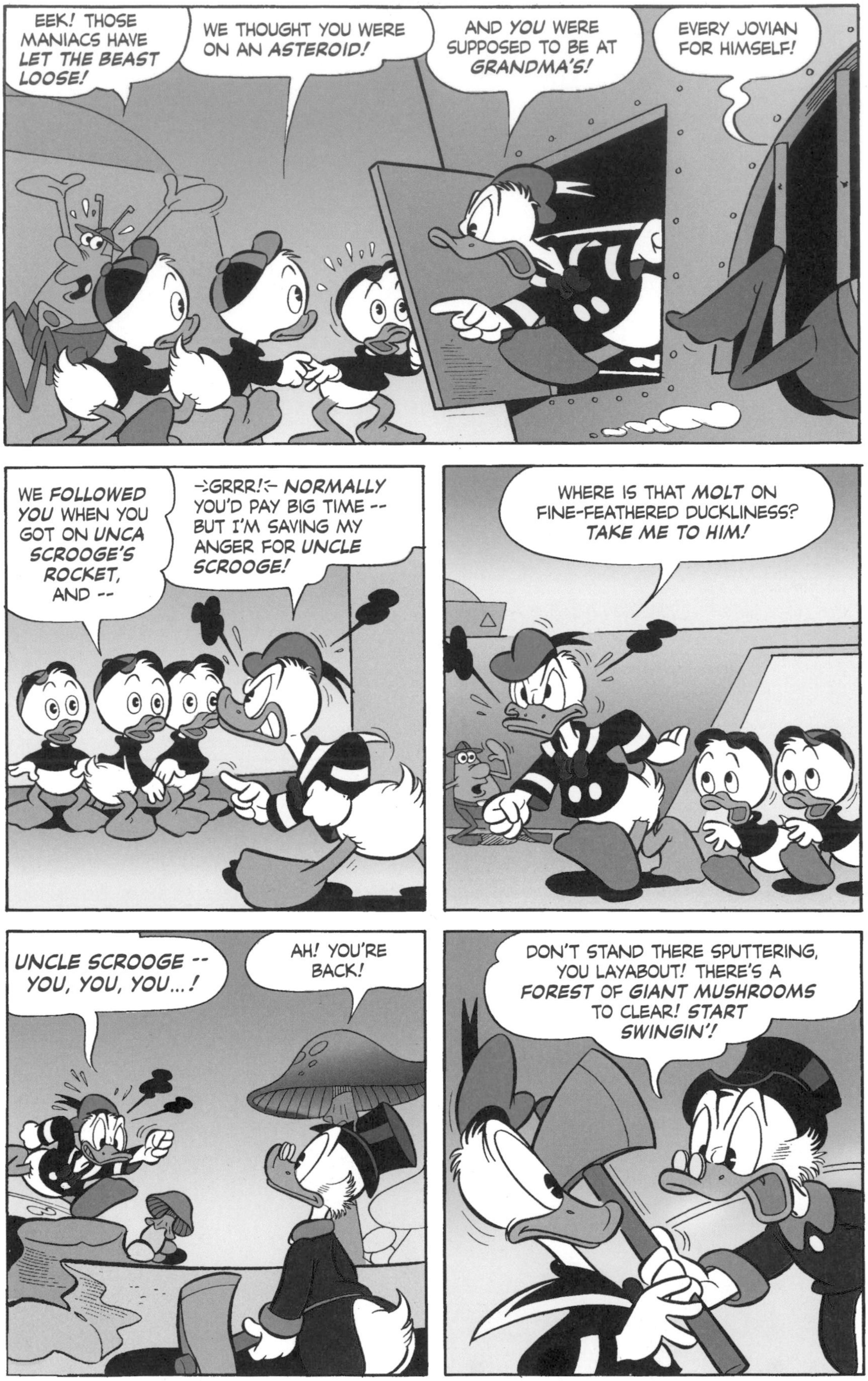
EEK! THOSE MANIACS HAVE LET THE BEAST LOOSE!
WE THOUGHT YOU WERE ON AN ASTEROID!
AND YOU WERE SUPPOSED TO BE AT GRANDMA'S!
EVERY JOVIAN FOR HIMSELF!
WE FOLLOWED YOU WHEN YOU GOT ON UNCA SCROOGE'S ROCKET, AND --
-GRRR!- NORMALLY YOU'D PAY BIG TIME -- BUT I'M SAVING MY ANGER FOR UNCLE SCROOGE!
WHERE IS THAT MOLT ON FINE-FEATHERED DUCKLINESS? TAKE ME TO HIM!
UNCLE SCROOGE -- YOU, YOU, YOU...!
AH! YOU'RE BACK!
DON'T STAND THERE SPUTTERING, YOU LAYABOUT! THERE'S A FOREST OF GIANT MUSHROOMS TO CLEAR! START SWINGIN'!

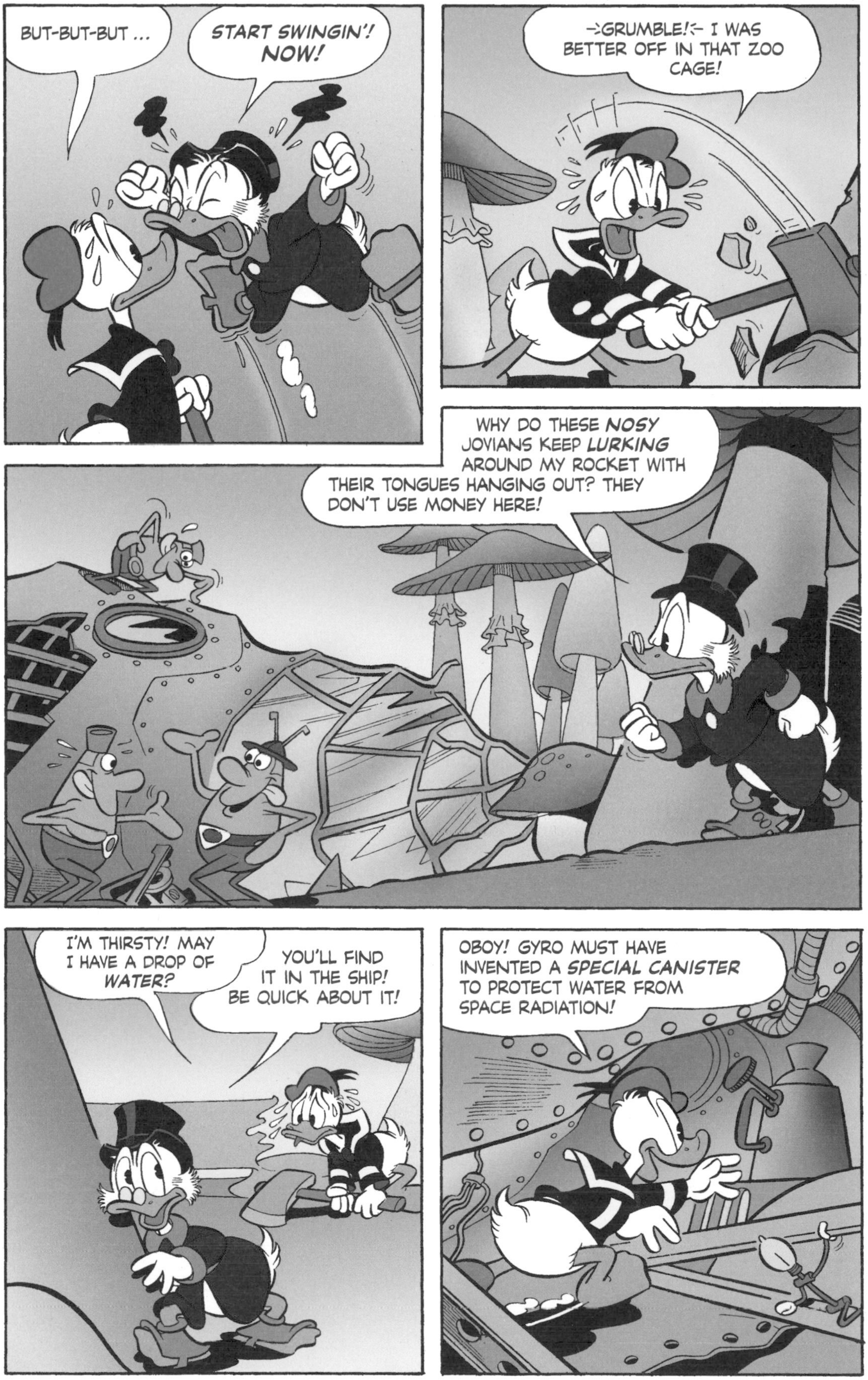
BUT-BUT-BUT ...
START SWINGIN'! NOW!
-GRUMBLE!- I WAS BETTER OFF IN THAT ZOO CAGE!
WHY DO THESE NOSY JOVIANS KEEP LURKING AROUND MY ROCKET WITH THEIR TONGUES HANGING OUT? THEY DON'T USE MONEY HERE!
I'M THIRSTY! MAY I HAVE A DROP OF WATER?
YOU'LL FIND IT IN THE SHIP! BE QUICK ABOUT IT!
OBOY! GYRO MUST HAVE INVENTED A SPECIAL CANISTER TO PROTECT WATER FROM SPACE RADIATION!

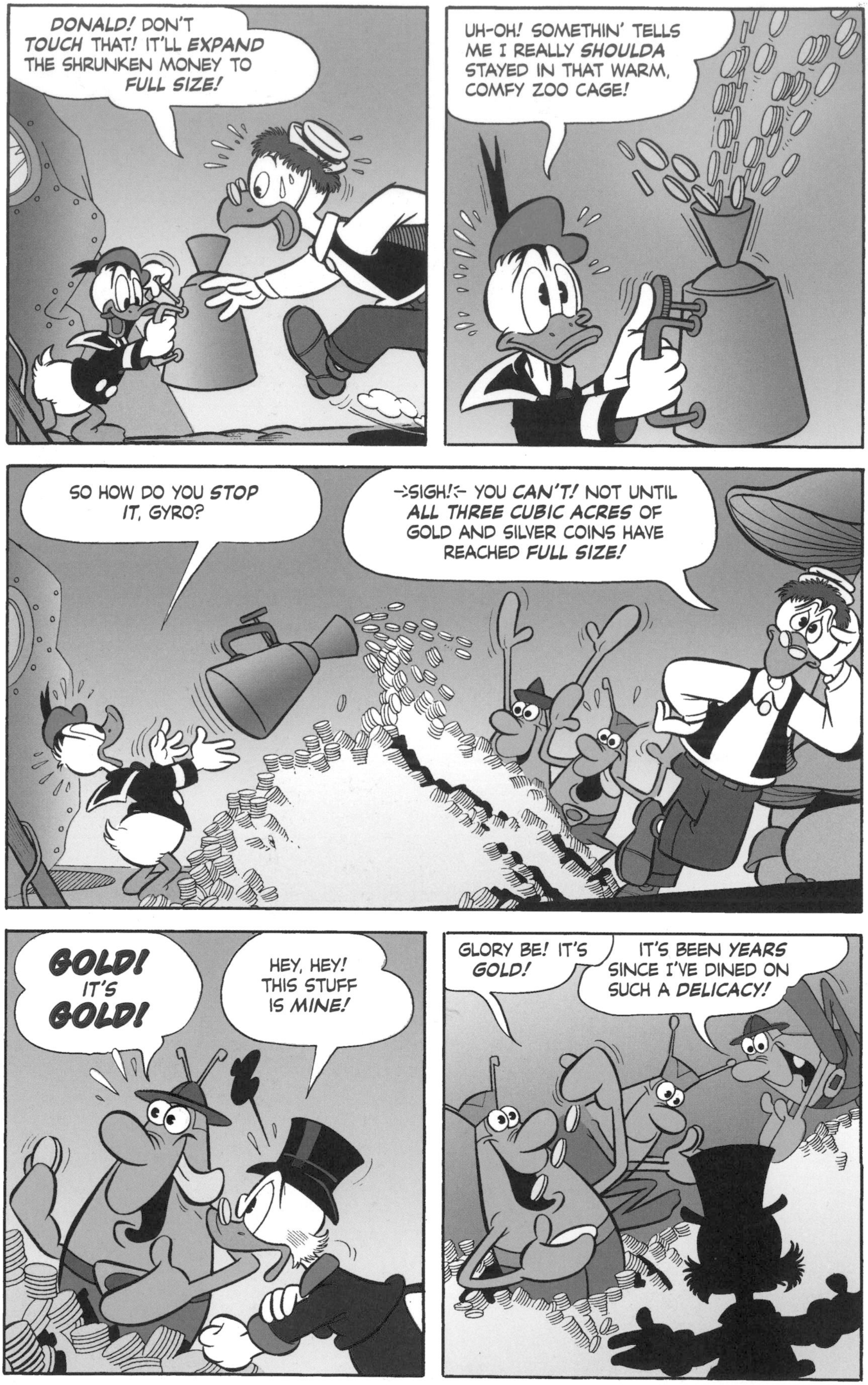
DONALD! DON'T TOUCH THAT! IT'LL EXPAND THE SHRUNKEN MONEY TO FULL SIZE!
UH-OH! SOMETHIN' TELLS ME I REALLY SHOULDA STAYED IN THAT WARM, COMFY ZOO CAGE!
SO HOW DO YOU STOP IT, GYRO?
-SIGH!- YOU CAN'T! NOT UNTIL ALL THREE CUBIC ACRES OF GOLD AND SILVER COINS HAVE REACHED FULL SIZE!
GOLD! IT'S GOLD!
HEY, HEY! THIS STUFF IS MINE!
GLORY BE! IT'S GOLD!
IT'S BEEN YEARS SINCE I'VE DINED ON SUCH A DELICACY!

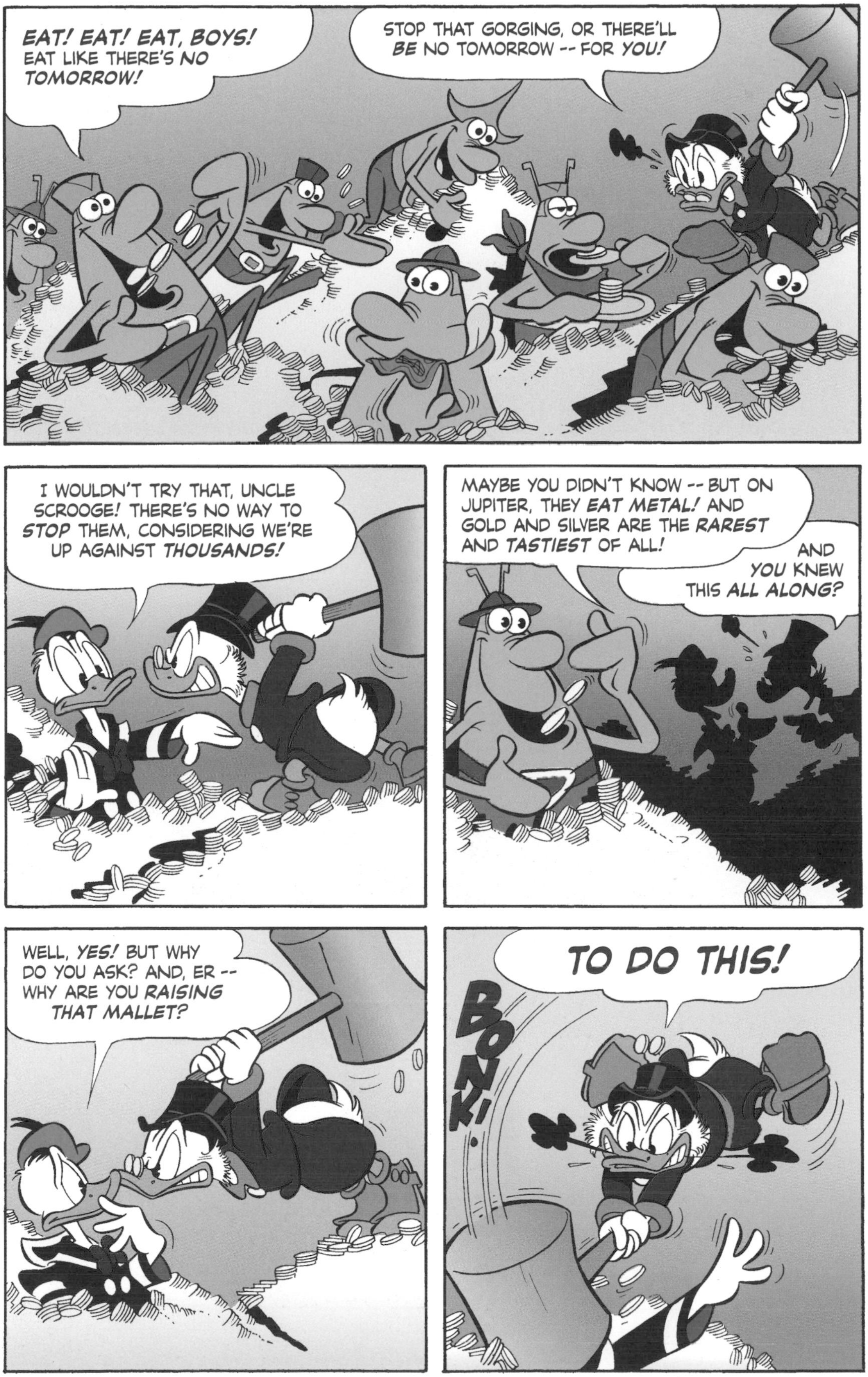
EAT! EAT! EAT, BOYS! EAT LIKE THERE'S NO TOMORROW!
STOP THAT GORGING, OR THERE'LL BE NO TOMORROW -- FOR YOU!
I WOULDN'T TRY THAT, UNCLE SCROOGE! THERE'S NO WAY TO STOP THEM, CONSIDERING WE'RE UP AGAINST THOUSANDS!
MAYBE YOU DIDN'T KNOW -- BUT ON JUPITER, THEY EAT METAL! AND GOLD AND SILVER ARE THE RAREST AND TASTIEST OF ALL!
AND YOU KNEW THIS ALL ALONG?
WELL, YES! BUT WHY DO YOU ASK? AND, ER -- WHY ARE YOU RAISING THAT MALLET?
TO DO THIS!
BONK!

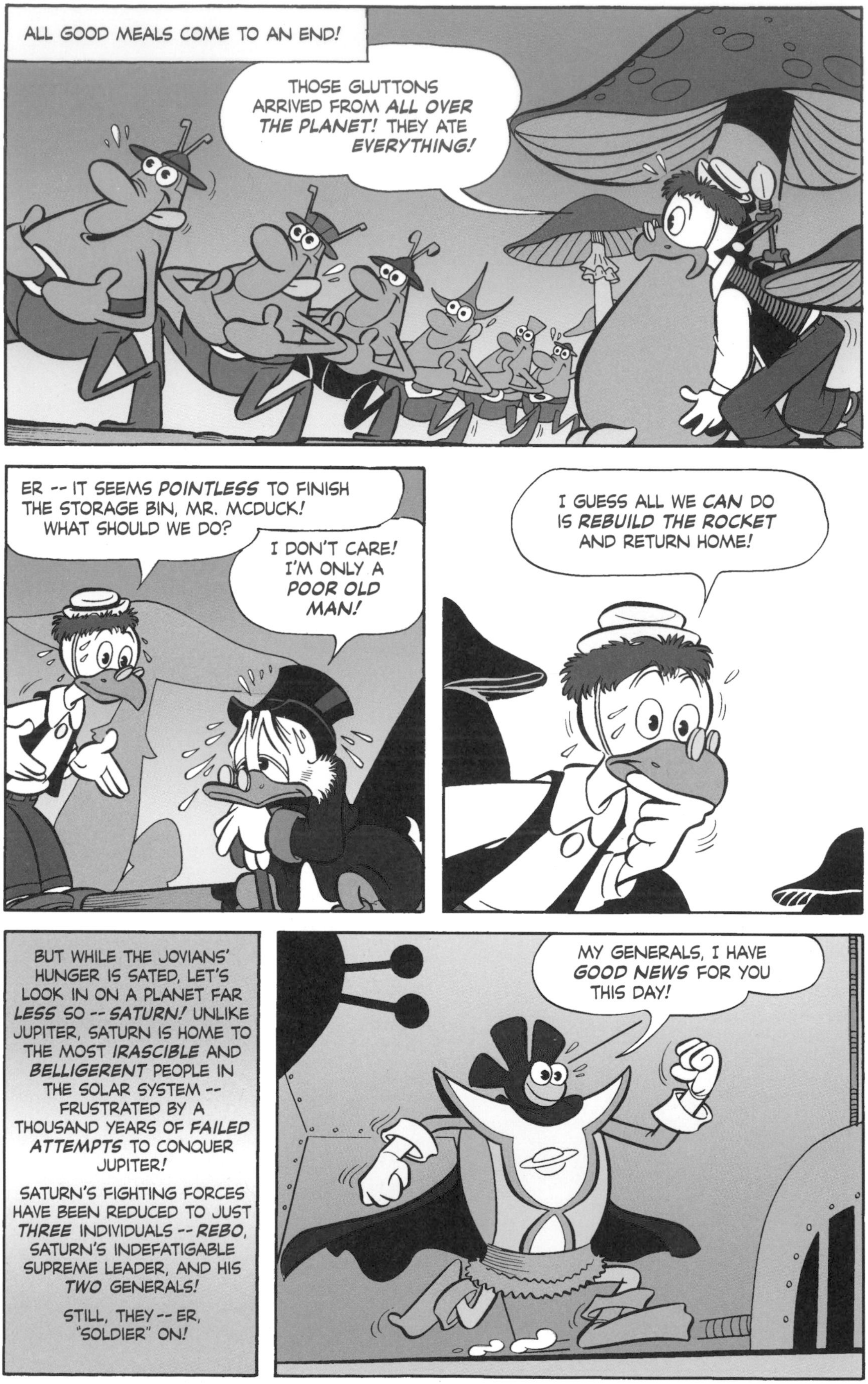

ALL GOOD MEALS COME TO AN END!
THOSE GLUTTONS ARRIVED FROM ALL OVER THE PLANET! THEY ATE EVERYTHING!
ER -- IT SEEMS POINTLESS TO FINISH THE STORAGE BIN, MR. MCDUCK! WHAT SHOULD WE DO?
I DON'T CARE! I'M ONLY A POOR OLD MAN!
I GUESS ALL WE CAN DO IS REBUILD THE ROCKET AND RETURN HOME!
BUT WHILE THE JOVIANS' HUNGER IS SATED, LET'S LOOK IN ON A PLANET FAR LESS SO -- SATURN! UNLIKE JUPITER, SATURN IS HOME TO THE MOST IRASCIBLE AND BELLIGERENT PEOPLE IN THE SOLAR SYSTEM -- FRUSTRATED BY A THOUSAND YEARS OF FAILED ATTEMPTS TO CONQUER JUPITER!
SATURN'S FIGHTING FORCES HAVE BEEN REDUCED TO JUST THREE INDIVIDUALS -- REBO, SATURN'S INDEFATIGABLE SUPREME LEADER, AND HIS TWO GENERALS!
STILL, THEY -- ER, "SOLDIER" ON!
MY GENERALS, I HAVE GOOD NEWS FOR YOU THIS DAY!

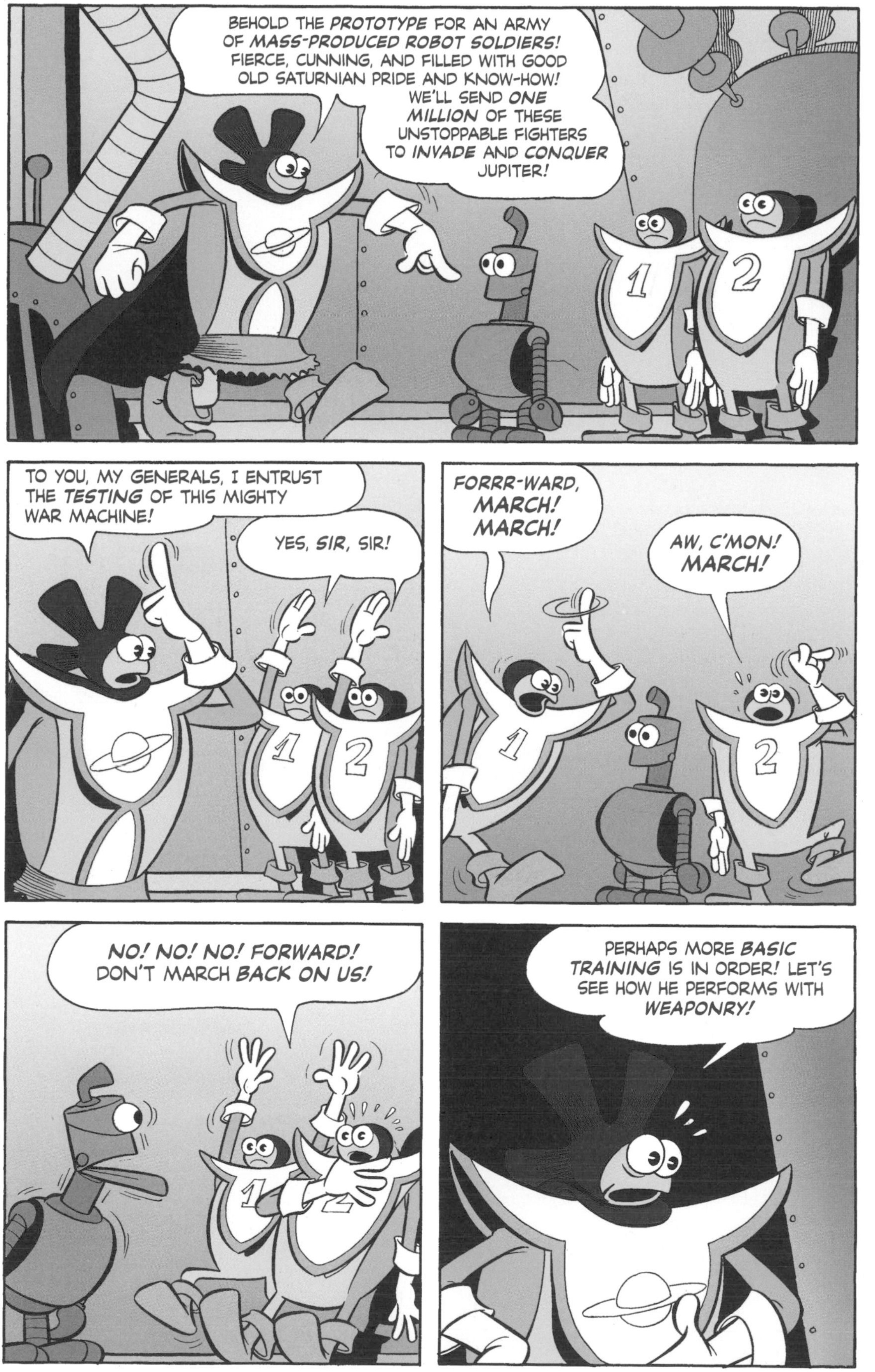
BEHOLD THE PROTOTYPE FOR AN ARMY OF MASS-PRODUCED ROBOT SOLDIERS! FIERCE, CUNNING, AND FILLED WITH GOOD OLD SATURNIAN PRIDE AND KNOW-HOW!
WE'LL SEND ONE MILLION OF THESE UNSTOPPABLE FIGHTERS TO INVADE AND CONQUER JUPITER!
TO YOU, MY GENERALS, I ENTRUST THE TESTING OF THIS MIGHTY WAR MACHINE!
YES, SIR, SIR!
FORRR-WARD, MARCH! MARCH!
AW, C'MON! MARCH!
NO! NO! NO! FORWARD! DON'T MARCH BACK ON US!
PERHAPS MORE BASIC TRAINING IS IN ORDER! LET'S SEE HOW HE PERFORMS WITH WEAPONRY!

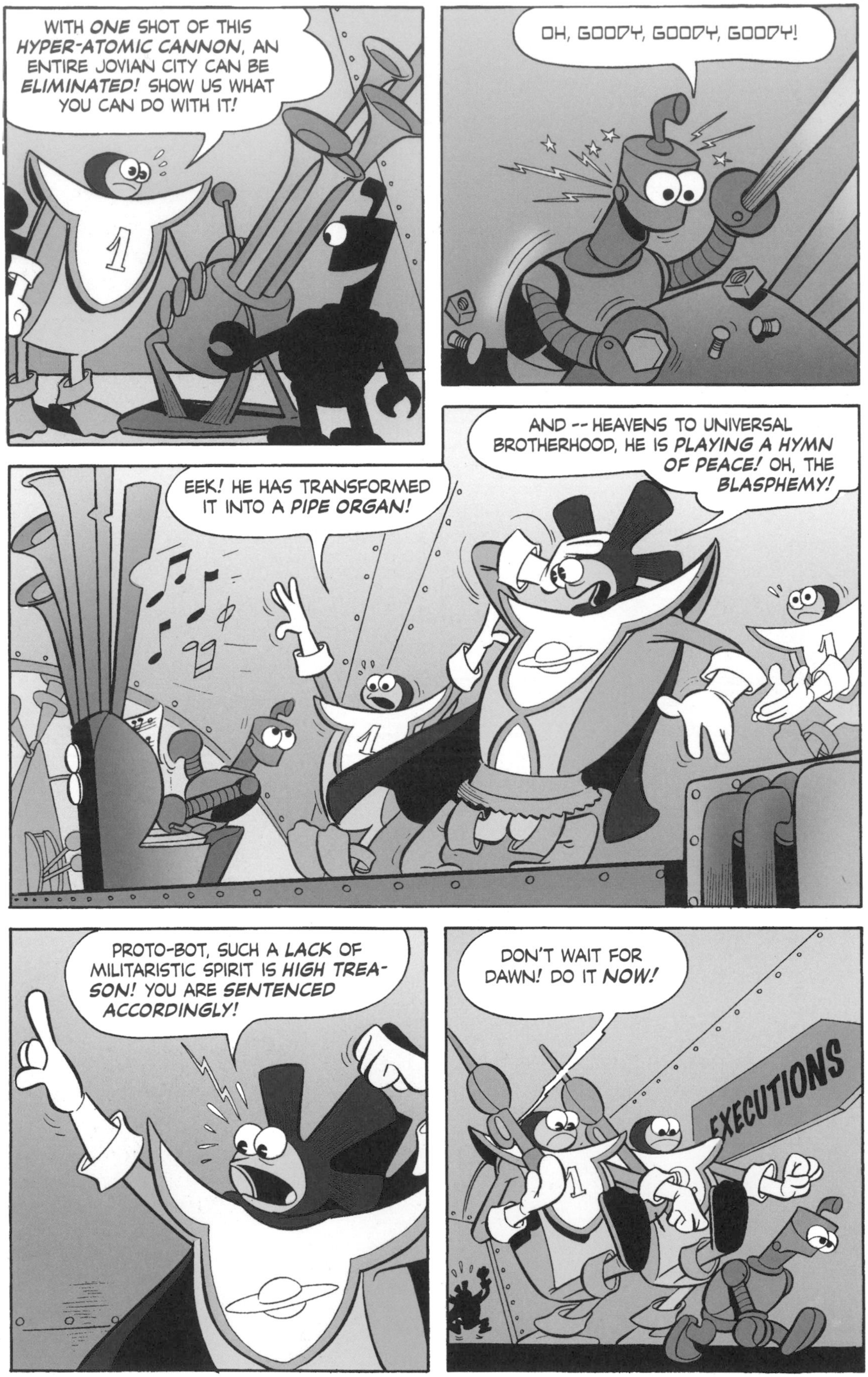
WITH ONE SHOT OF THIS HYPER-ATOMIC CANNON, AN ENTIRE JOVIAN CITY CAN BE ELIMINATED! SHOW US WHAT YOU CAN DO WITH IT!
OH, GOODY, GOODY, GOODY!
EEK! HE HAS TRANSFORMED IT INTO A PIPE ORGAN!
AND -- HEAVENS TO UNIVERSAL BROTHERHOOD, HE IS PLAYING A HYMN OF PEACE! OH, THE BLASPHEMY!
PROTO-BOT, SUCH A LACK OF MILITARISTIC SPIRIT IS HIGH TREASON! YOU ARE SENTENCED ACCORDINGLY!
DON'T WAIT FOR DAWN! DO IT NOW!
EXECUTIONS

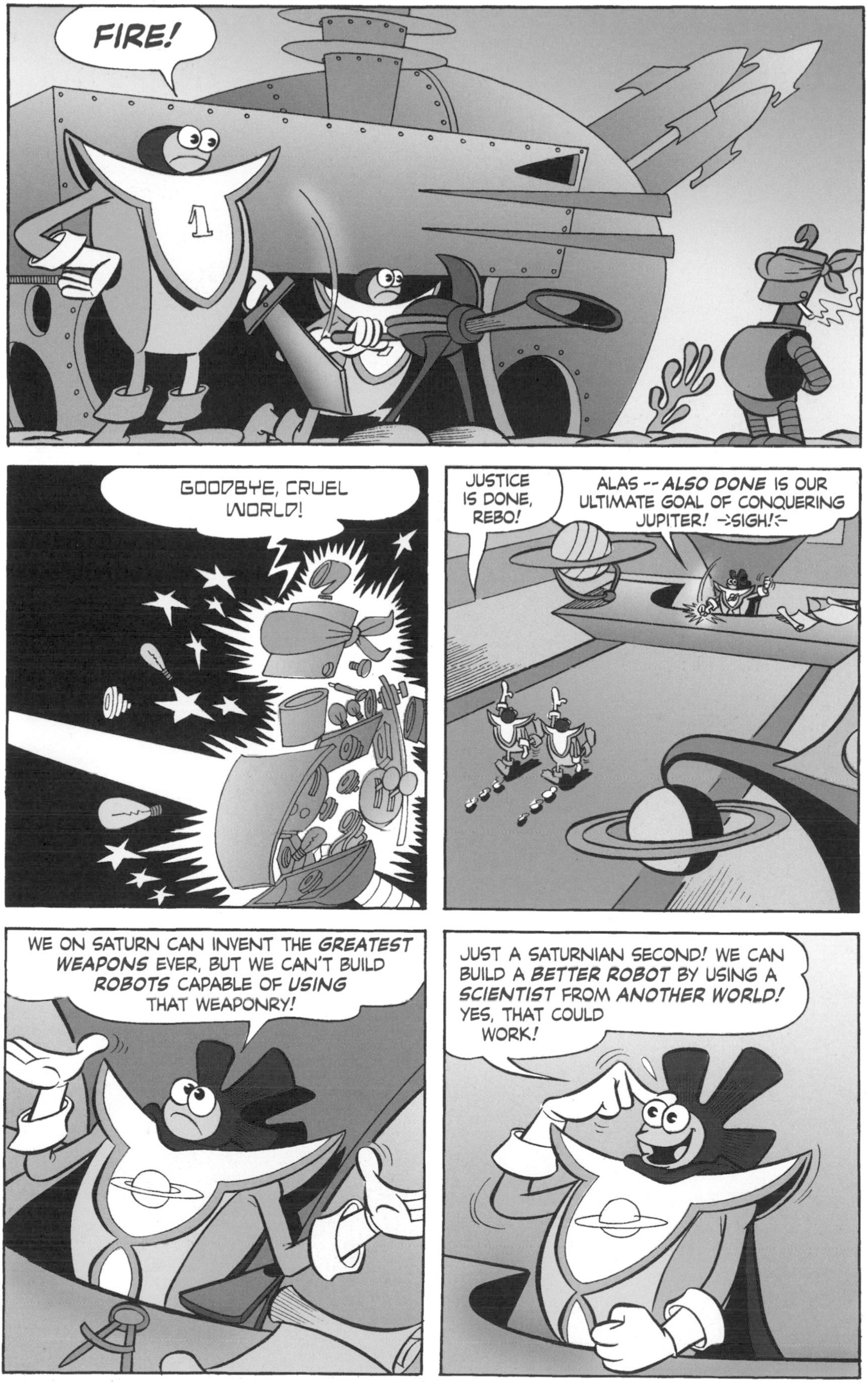
FIRE!
GOODBYE, CRUEL WORLD!
JUSTICE IS DONE, REBO!
ALAS -- ALSO DONE IS OUR ULTIMATE GOAL OF CONQUERING JUPITER! -SIGH!-
WE ON SATURN CAN INVENT THE GREATEST WEAPONS EVER, BUT WE CAN'T BUILD ROBOTS CAPABLE OF USING THAT WEAPONRY!
JUST A SATURNIAN SECOND! WE CAN BUILD A BETTER ROBOT BY USING A SCIENTIST FROM ANOTHER WORLD! YES, THAT COULD WORK!

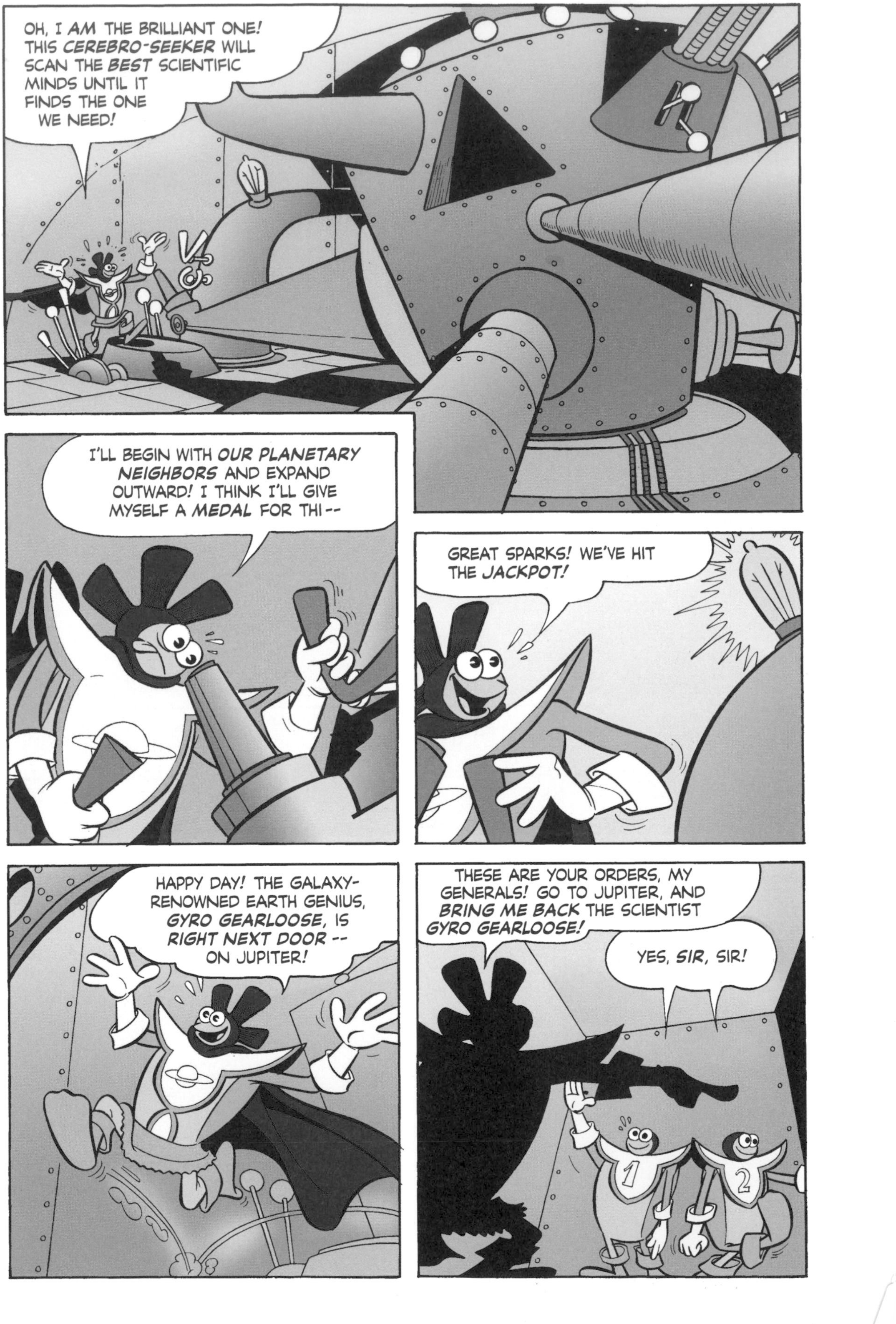
OH, I AM THE BRILLIANT ONE! THIS CEREBRO-SEEKER WILL SCAN THE BEST SCIENTIFIC MINDS UNTIL IT FINDS THE ONE WE NEED!
I'LL BEGIN WITH OUR PLANETARY NEIGHBORS AND EXPAND OUTWARD! I THINK I'LL GIVE MYSELF A MEDAL FOR THI--
GREAT SPARKS! WE'VE HIT THE JACKPOT!
HAPPY DAY! THE GALAXY-RENOWNED EARTH GENIUS, GYRO GEARLOOSE, IS RIGHT NEXT DOOR -- ON JUPITER!
THESE ARE YOUR ORDERS, MY GENERALS! GO TO JUPITER, AND BRING ME BACK THE SCIENTIST GYRO GEARLOOSE!
YES, SIR, SIR!

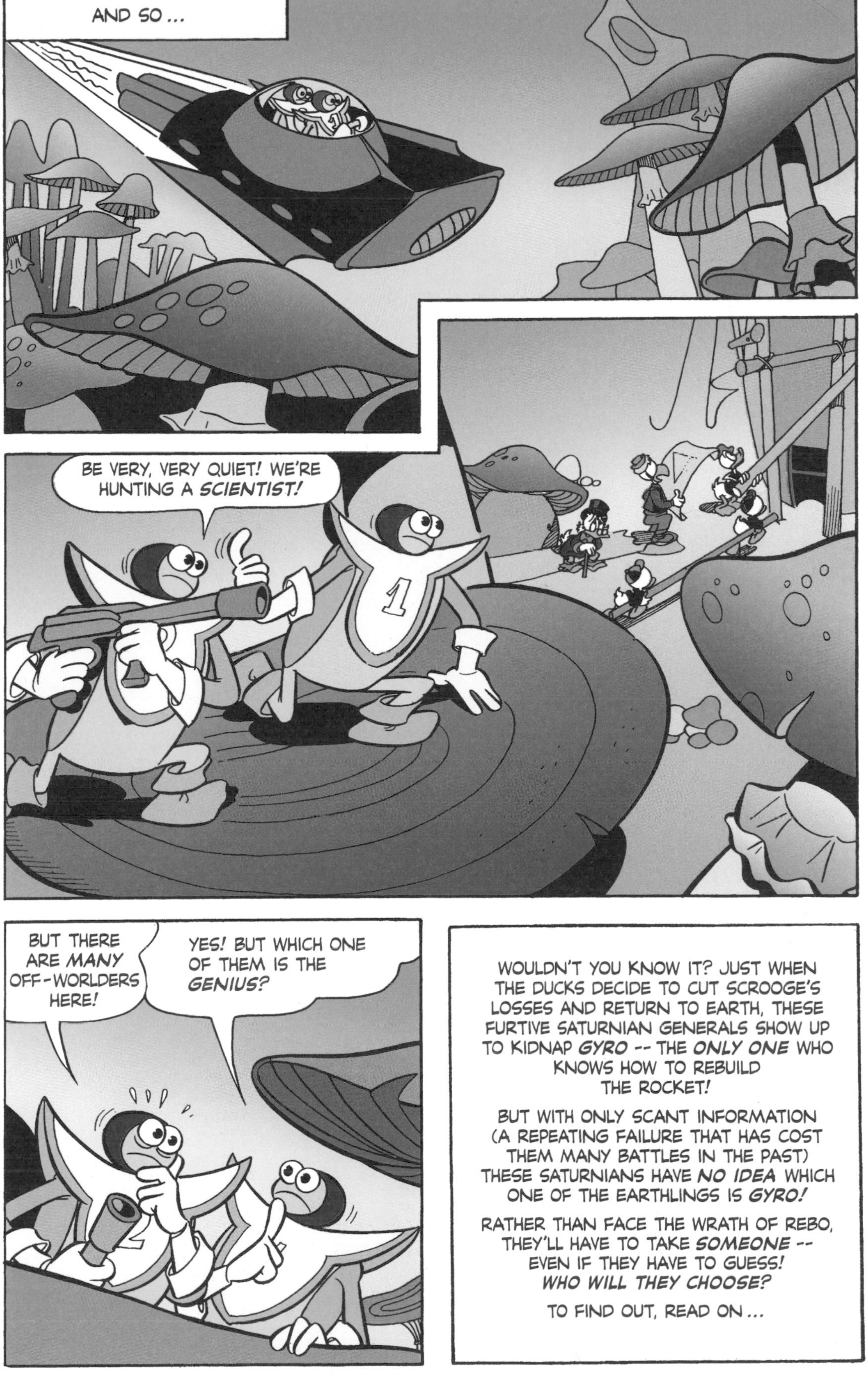
AND SO ...
BE VERY, VERY QUIET! WE'RE HUNTING A *SCIENTIST!*
BUT THERE ARE *MANY* OFF-WORLDERS HERE!
YES! BUT WHICH ONE OF THEM IS THE *GENIUS?*
WOULDN'T YOU KNOW IT? JUST WHEN THE DUCKS DECIDE TO CUT SCROOGE'S LOSSES AND RETURN TO EARTH, THESE FURTIVE SATURNIAN GENERALS SHOW UP TO KIDNAP *GYRO* -- THE *ONLY ONE* WHO KNOWS HOW TO REBUILD THE ROCKET!
BUT WITH ONLY SCANT INFORMATION (A REPEATING FAILURE THAT HAS COST THEM MANY BATTLES IN THE PAST) THESE SATURNIANS HAVE *NO IDEA* WHICH ONE OF THE EARTHLINGS IS *GYRO!*
RATHER THAN FACE THE WRATH OF REBO, THEY'LL HAVE TO TAKE *SOMEONE* -- EVEN IF THEY HAVE TO GUESS! *WHO WILL THEY CHOOSE?*
TO FIND OUT, READ ON ...

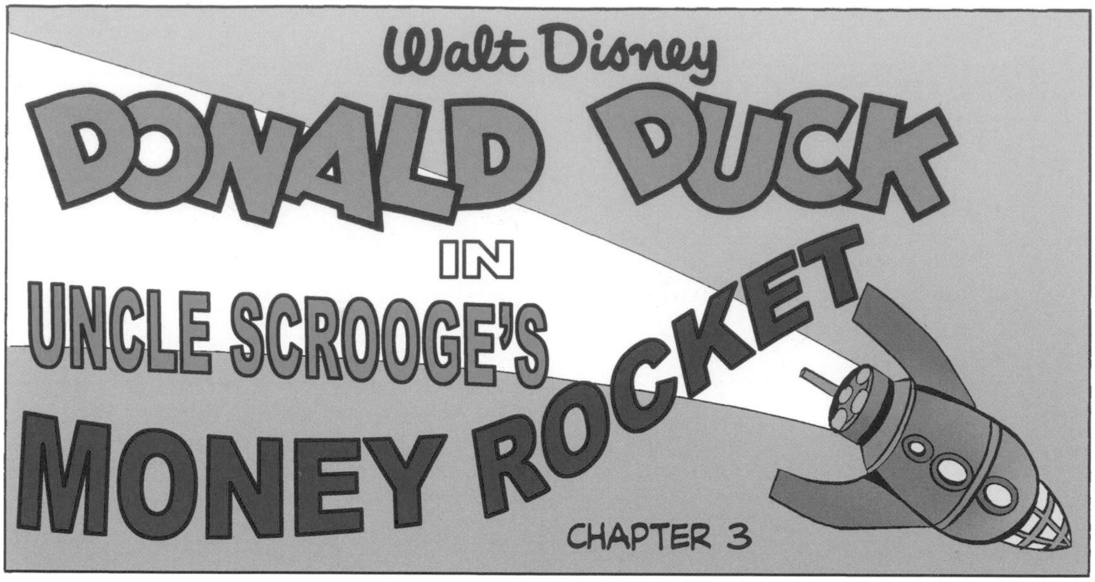
Walt Disney
DONALD DUCK
IN
UNCLE SCROOGE'S
MONEY ROCKET
CHAPTER 3

UNCLE SCROOGE, FEARFUL THAT HIS MONEY IS UNSAFE ON EARTH, ROCKETS IT TO *JUPITER*, WHERE RAVENOUS *METAL-EATING* DENIZENS HAVE *CONSUMED* HIS COINS! ONE PLANET OVER, THREE *WARLIKE SATURNIANS* -- WHO HAVE NO TROOPS -- PLAN TO CONQUER JUPITER WITH *ROBOTS* TO BE DESIGNED BY *GYRO GEARLOOSE!* BUT FIRST THEY HAVE TO KIDNAP HIM! THE HITCH? THE SATURNIANS CAN'T TELL *GYRO* FROM A ROCKET TUBE -- SO THEY'LL JUST HAVE TO *GUESS!* AND LOOK WHO'S COMING BY!

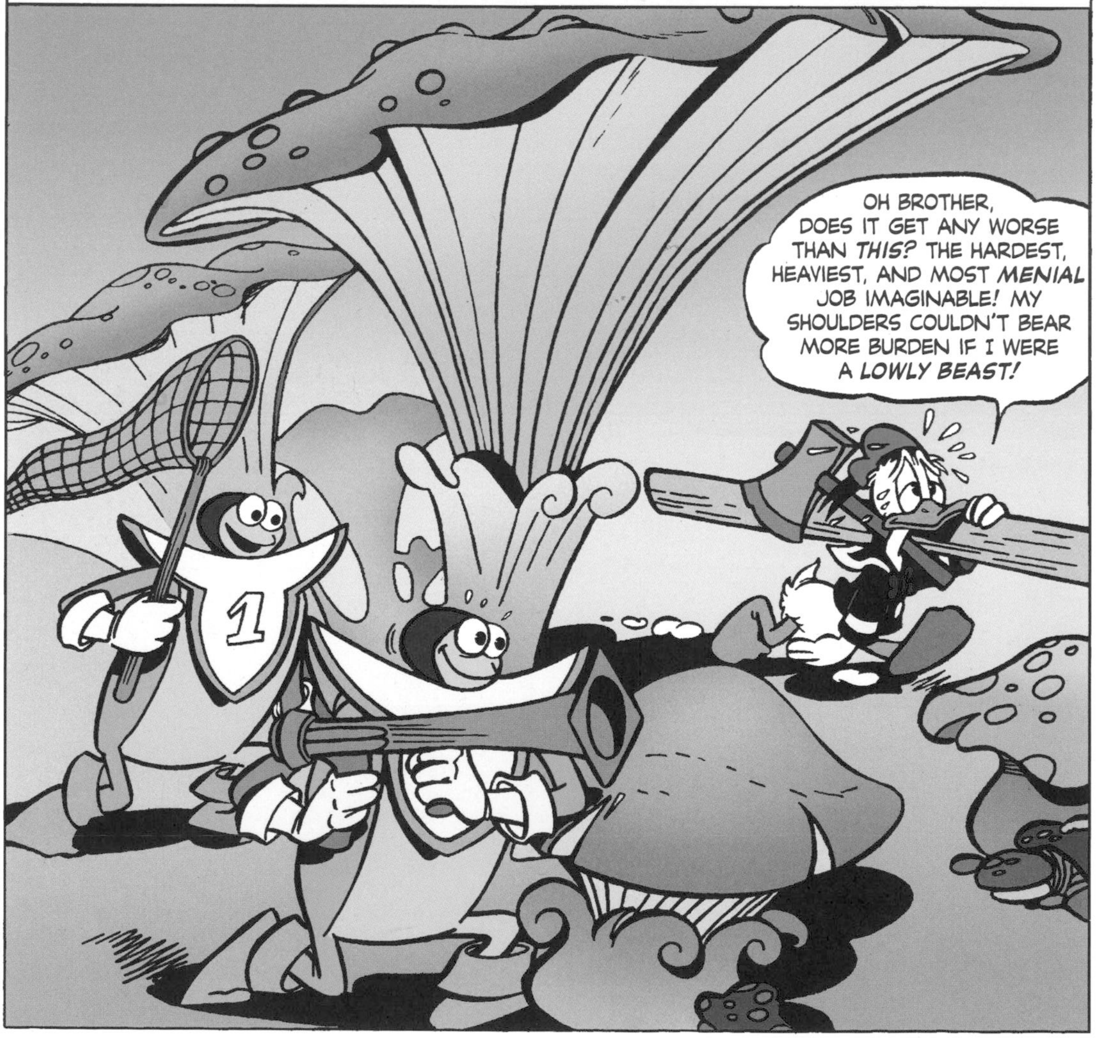
OH BROTHER, DOES IT GET ANY WORSE THAN THIS? THE HARDEST, HEAVIEST, AND MOST MENIAL JOB IMAGINABLE! MY SHOULDERS COULDN'T BEAR MORE BURDEN IF I WERE A LOWLY BEAST!
1

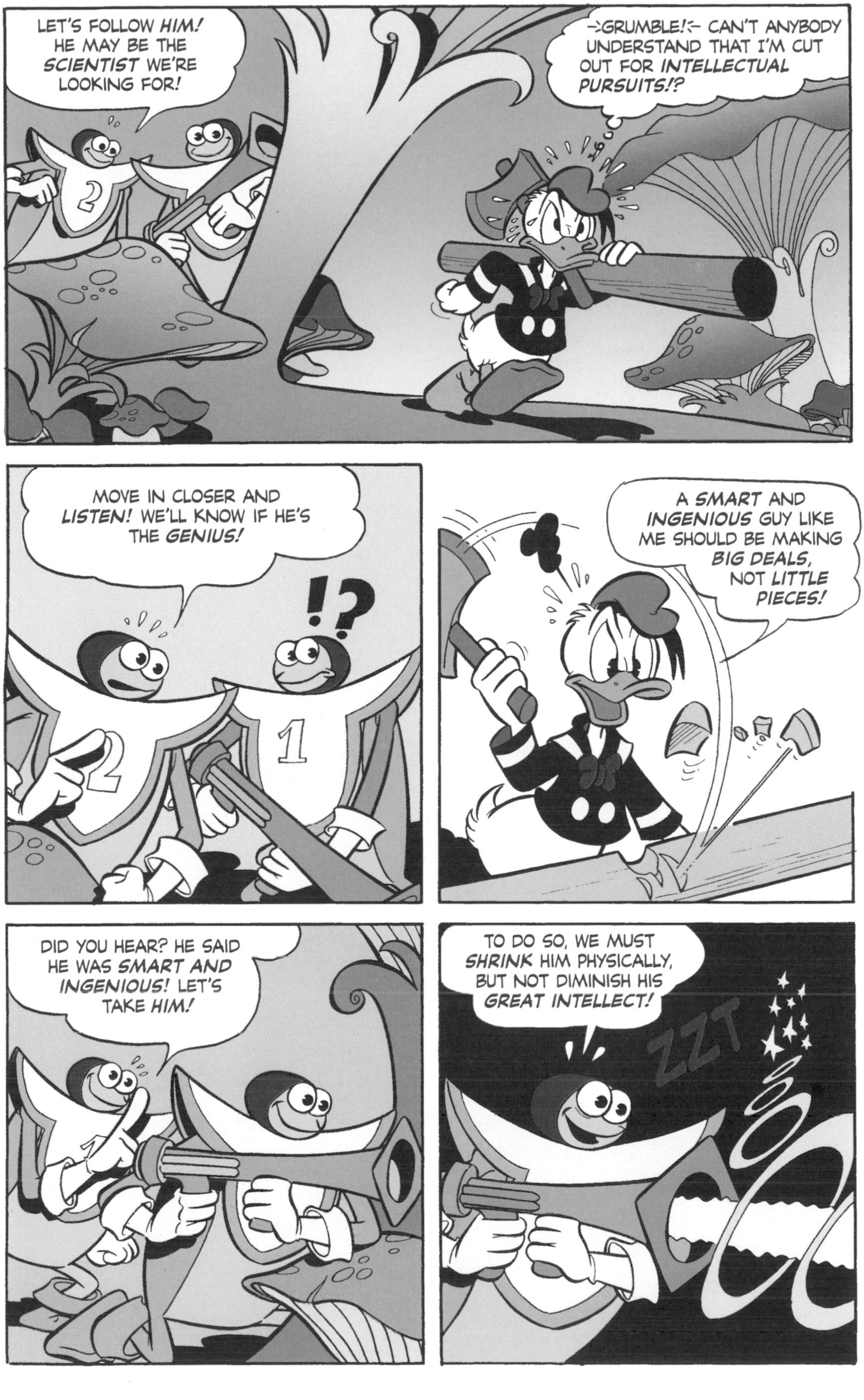
LET'S FOLLOW HIM! HE MAY BE THE SCIENTIST WE'RE LOOKING FOR!
–GRUMBLE!– CAN'T ANYBODY UNDERSTAND THAT I'M CUT OUT FOR INTELLECTUAL PURSUITS!?
MOVE IN CLOSER AND LISTEN! WE'LL KNOW IF HE'S THE GENIUS!
!?
A SMART AND INGENIOUS GUY LIKE ME SHOULD BE MAKING BIG DEALS, NOT LITTLE PIECES!
DID YOU HEAR? HE SAID HE WAS SMART AND INGENIOUS! LET'S TAKE HIM!
TO DO SO, WE MUST SHRINK HIM PHYSICALLY, BUT NOT DIMINISH HIS GREAT INTELLECT!
ZZT

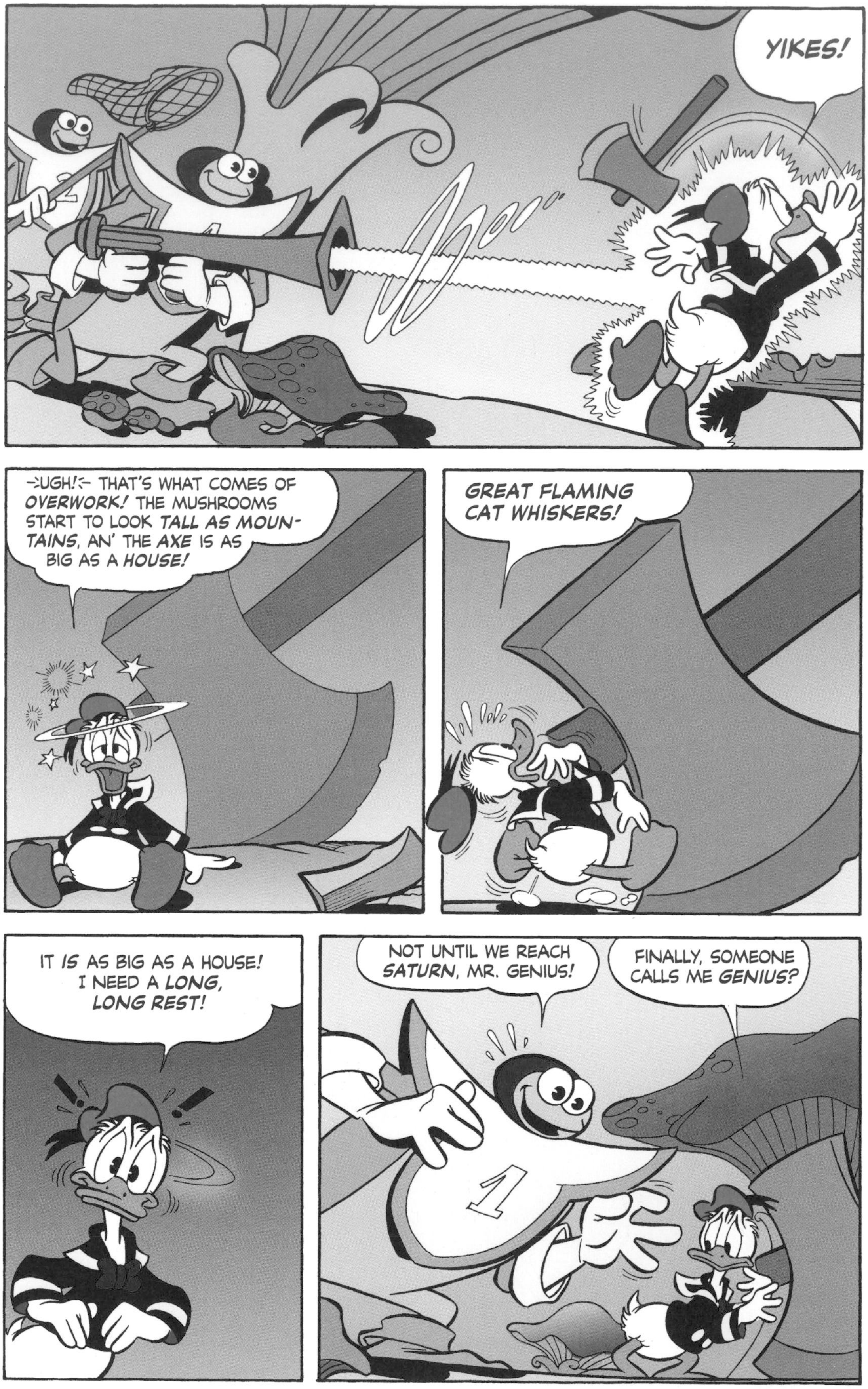
YIKES!
–UGH!– THAT'S WHAT COMES OF OVERWORK! THE MUSHROOMS START TO LOOK TALL AS MOUNTAINS, AN' THE AXE IS AS BIG AS A HOUSE!
GREAT FLAMING CAT WHISKERS!
IT IS AS BIG AS A HOUSE! I NEED A LONG, LONG REST!
NOT UNTIL WE REACH SATURN, MR. GENIUS!
FINALLY, SOMEONE CALLS ME GENIUS?

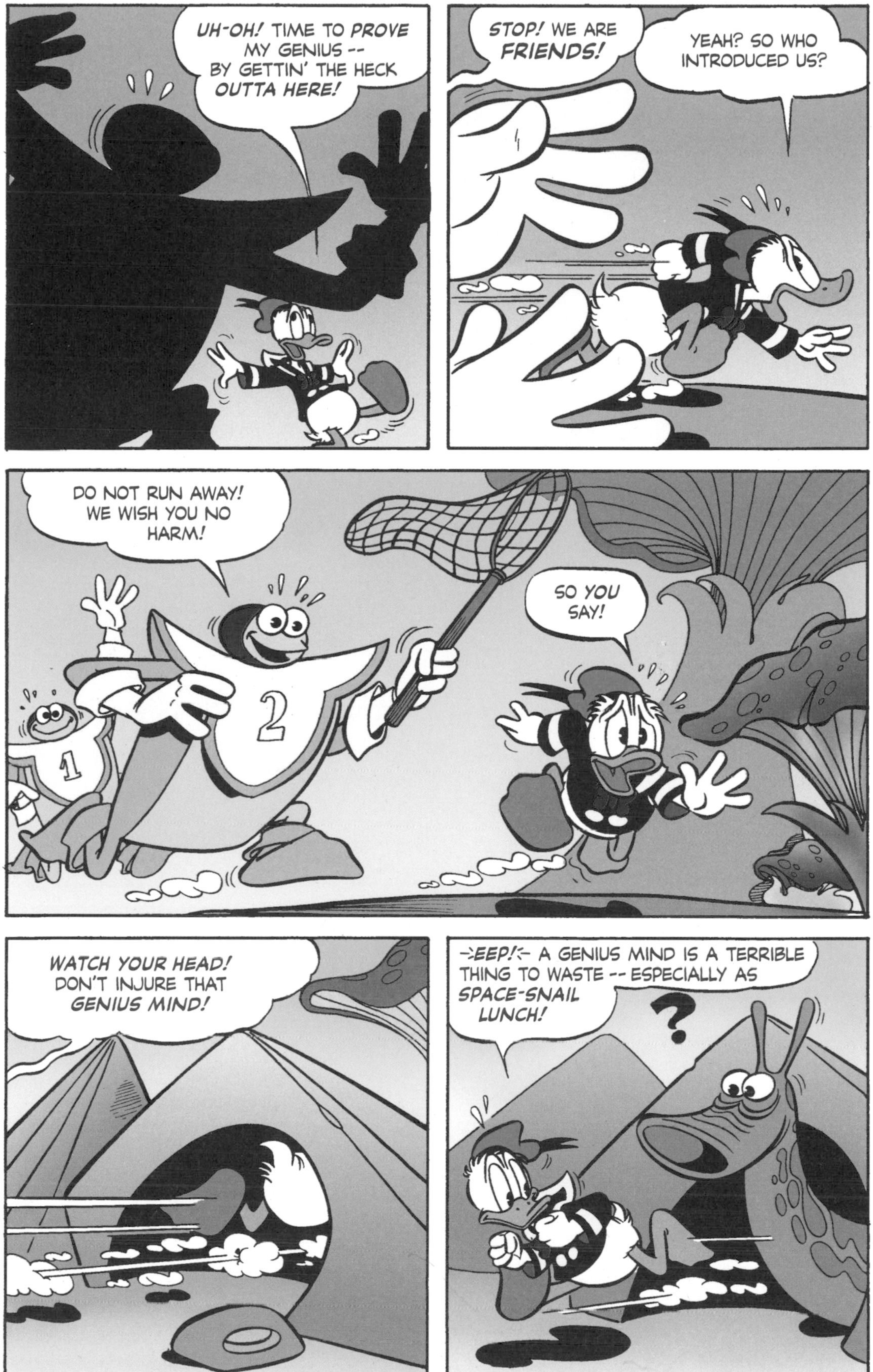
UH-OH! TIME TO PROVE MY GENIUS -- BY GETTIN' THE HECK OUTTA HERE!
STOP! WE ARE FRIENDS!
YEAH? SO WHO INTRODUCED US?
DO NOT RUN AWAY! WE WISH YOU NO HARM!
SO YOU SAY!
2
1
WATCH YOUR HEAD! DON'T INJURE THAT GENIUS MIND!
-EEP!- A GENIUS MIND IS A TERRIBLE THING TO WASTE -- ESPECIALLY AS SPACE-SNAIL LUNCH!
?

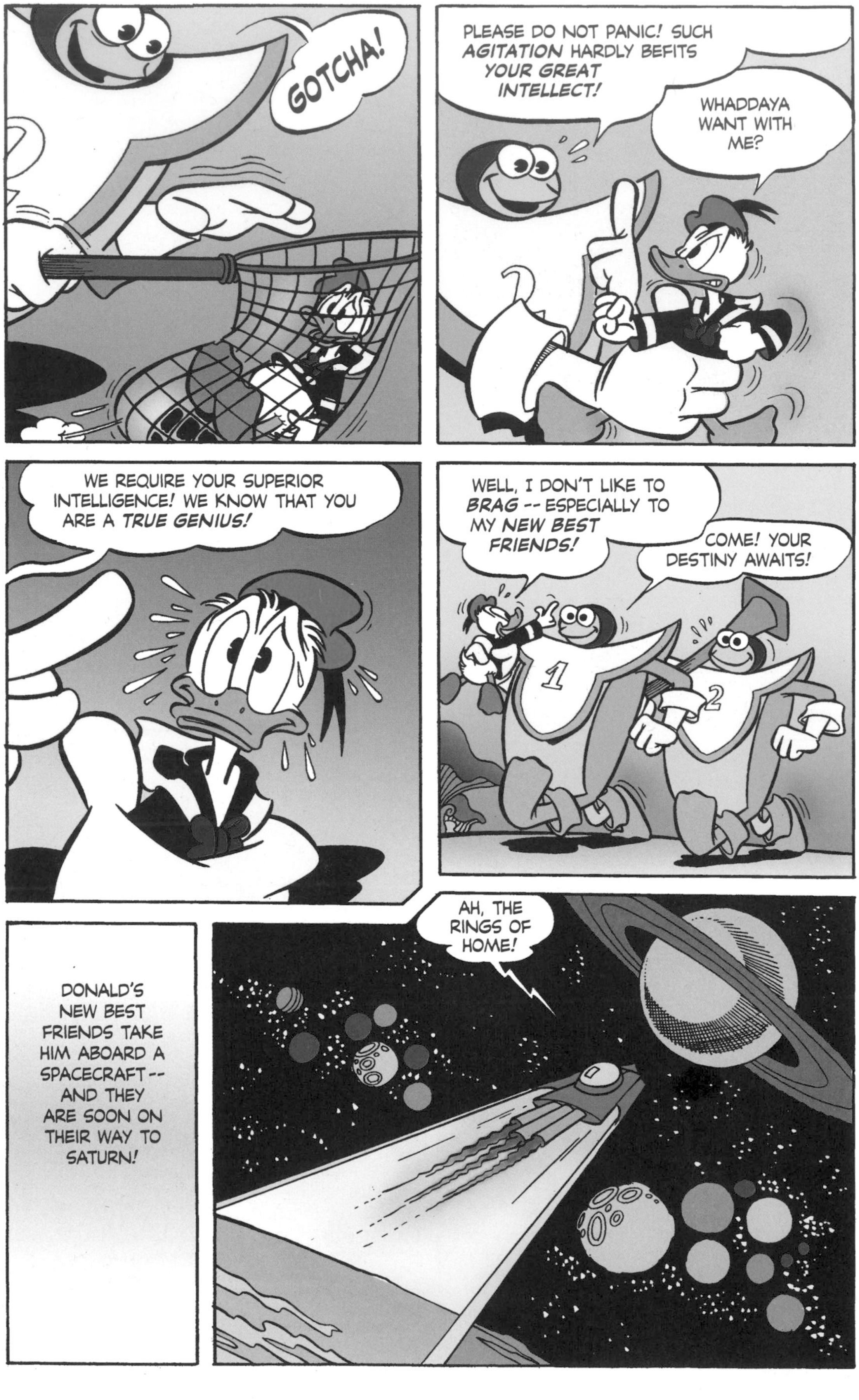
GOTCHA!
PLEASE DO NOT PANIC! SUCH AGITATION HARDLY BEFITS YOUR GREAT INTELLECT!
WHADDAYA WANT WITH ME?
WE REQUIRE YOUR SUPERIOR INTELLIGENCE! WE KNOW THAT YOU ARE A TRUE GENIUS!
WELL, I DON'T LIKE TO BRAG -- ESPECIALLY TO MY NEW BEST FRIENDS!
COME! YOUR DESTINY AWAITS!
1
2
DONALD'S NEW BEST FRIENDS TAKE HIM ABOARD A SPACECRAFT -- AND THEY ARE SOON ON THEIR WAY TO SATURN!
AH, THE RINGS OF HOME!

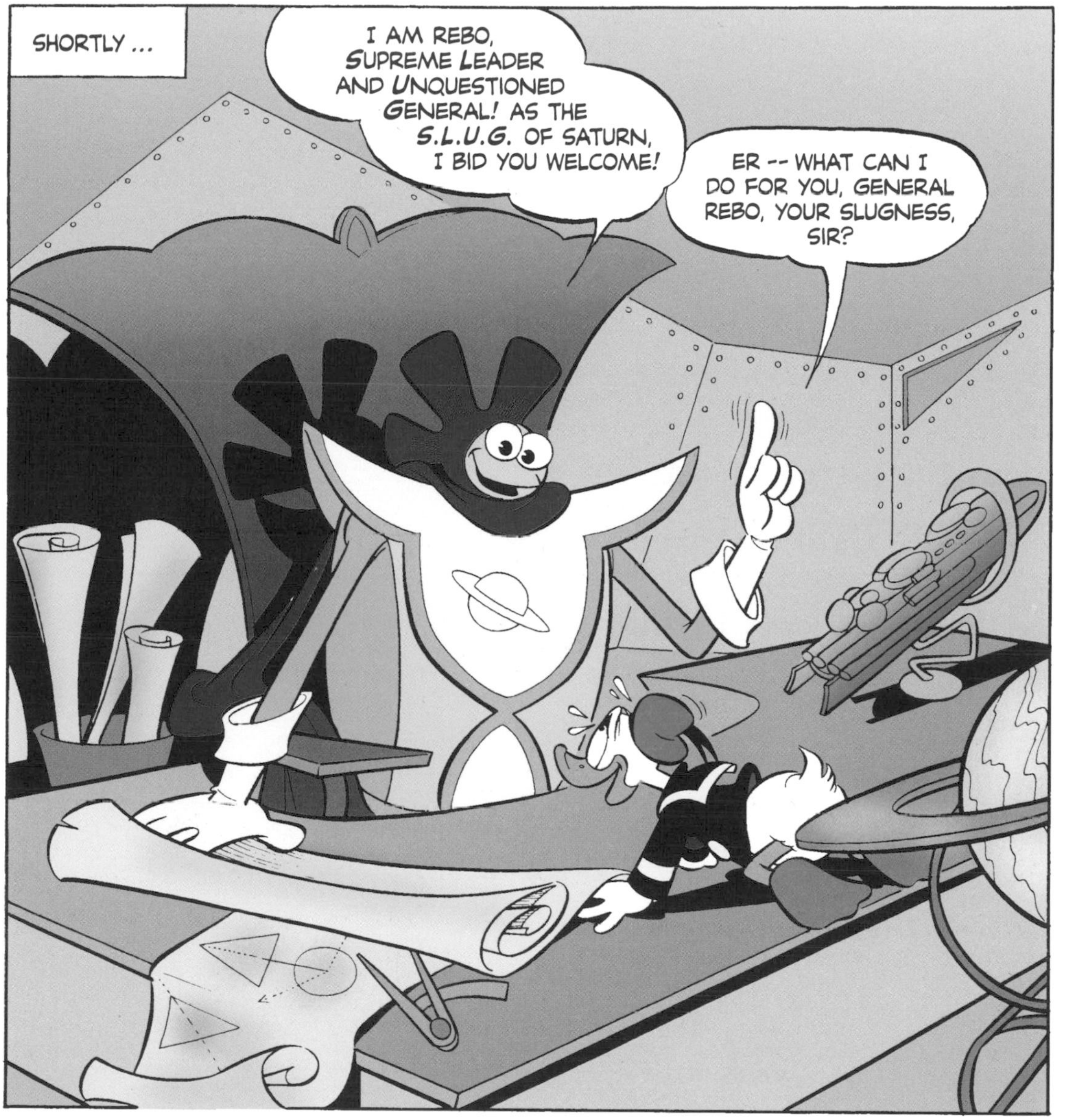
SHORTLY ...
I AM REBO, SUPREME LEADER AND UNQUESTIONED GENERAL! AS THE S.L.U.G. OF SATURN, I BID YOU WELCOME!
ER -- WHAT CAN I DO FOR YOU, GENERAL REBO, YOUR SLUGNESS, SIR?

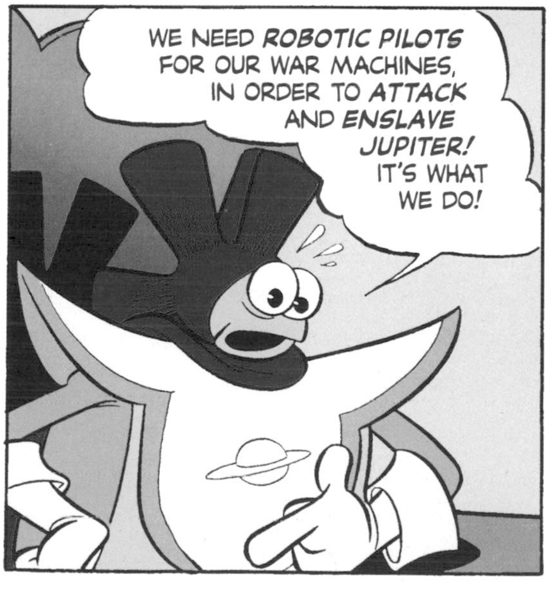
WE NEED ROBOTIC PILOTS FOR OUR WAR MACHINES, IN ORDER TO ATTACK AND ENSLAVE JUPITER! IT'S WHAT WE DO!

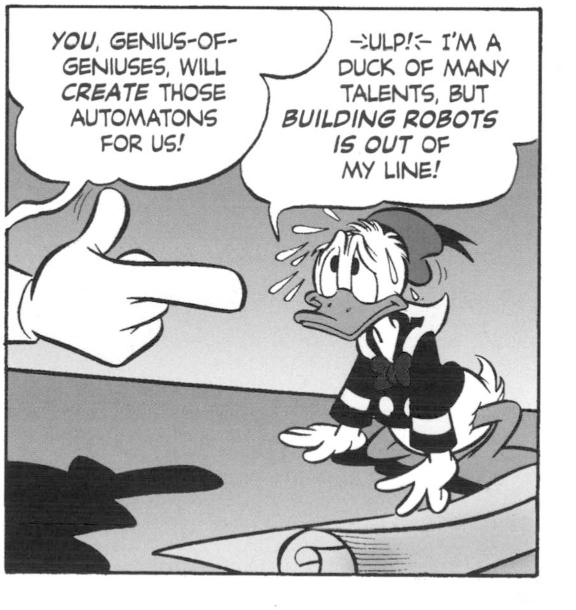
YOU, GENIUS-OF-GENIUSES, WILL CREATE THOSE AUTOMATONS FOR US!
-ULP!- I'M A DUCK OF MANY TALENTS, BUT BUILDING ROBOTS IS OUT OF MY LINE!

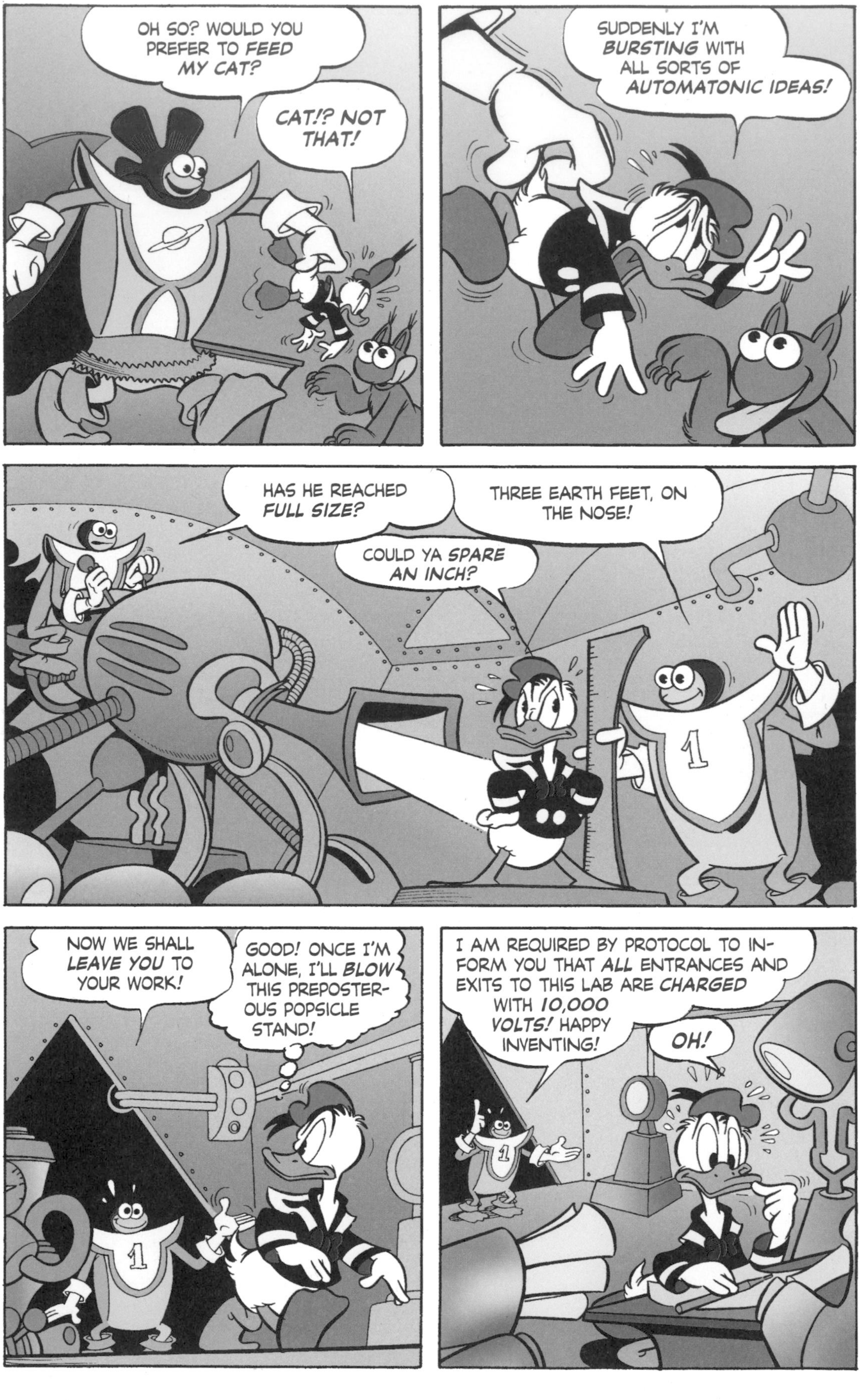
OH SO? WOULD YOU PREFER TO FEED MY CAT?
CAT!? NOT THAT!
SUDDENLY I'M BURSTING WITH ALL SORTS OF AUTOMATONIC IDEAS!
HAS HE REACHED FULL SIZE?
THREE EARTH FEET, ON THE NOSE!
COULD YA SPARE AN INCH?
NOW WE SHALL LEAVE YOU TO YOUR WORK!
GOOD! ONCE I'M ALONE, I'LL BLOW THIS PREPOSTER-OUS POPSICLE STAND!
I AM REQUIRED BY PROTOCOL TO IN-FORM YOU THAT ALL ENTRANCES AND EXITS TO THIS LAB ARE CHARGED WITH 10,000 VOLTS! HAPPY INVENTING!
OH!

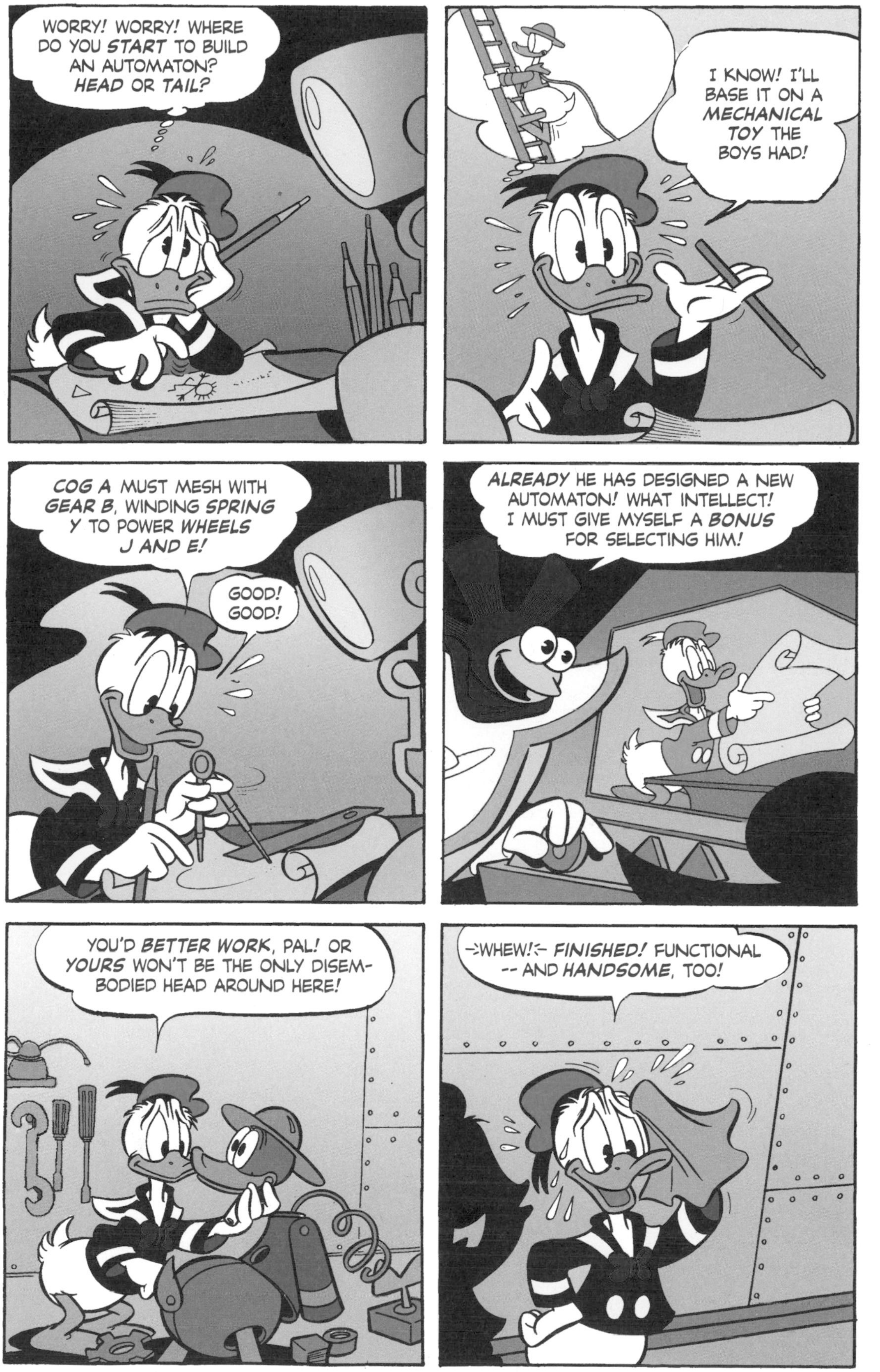
WORRY! WORRY! WHERE DO YOU START TO BUILD AN AUTOMATON? HEAD OR TAIL?
I KNOW! I'LL BASE IT ON A MECHANICAL TOY THE BOYS HAD!
COG A MUST MESH WITH GEAR B, WINDING SPRING Y TO POWER WHEELS J AND E!
GOOD! GOOD!
ALREADY HE HAS DESIGNED A NEW AUTOMATON! WHAT INTELLECT! I MUST GIVE MYSELF A BONUS FOR SELECTING HIM!
YOU'D BETTER WORK, PAL! OR YOURS WON'T BE THE ONLY DISEMBODIED HEAD AROUND HERE!
-WHEW!- FINISHED! FUNCTIONAL -- AND HANDSOME, TOO!

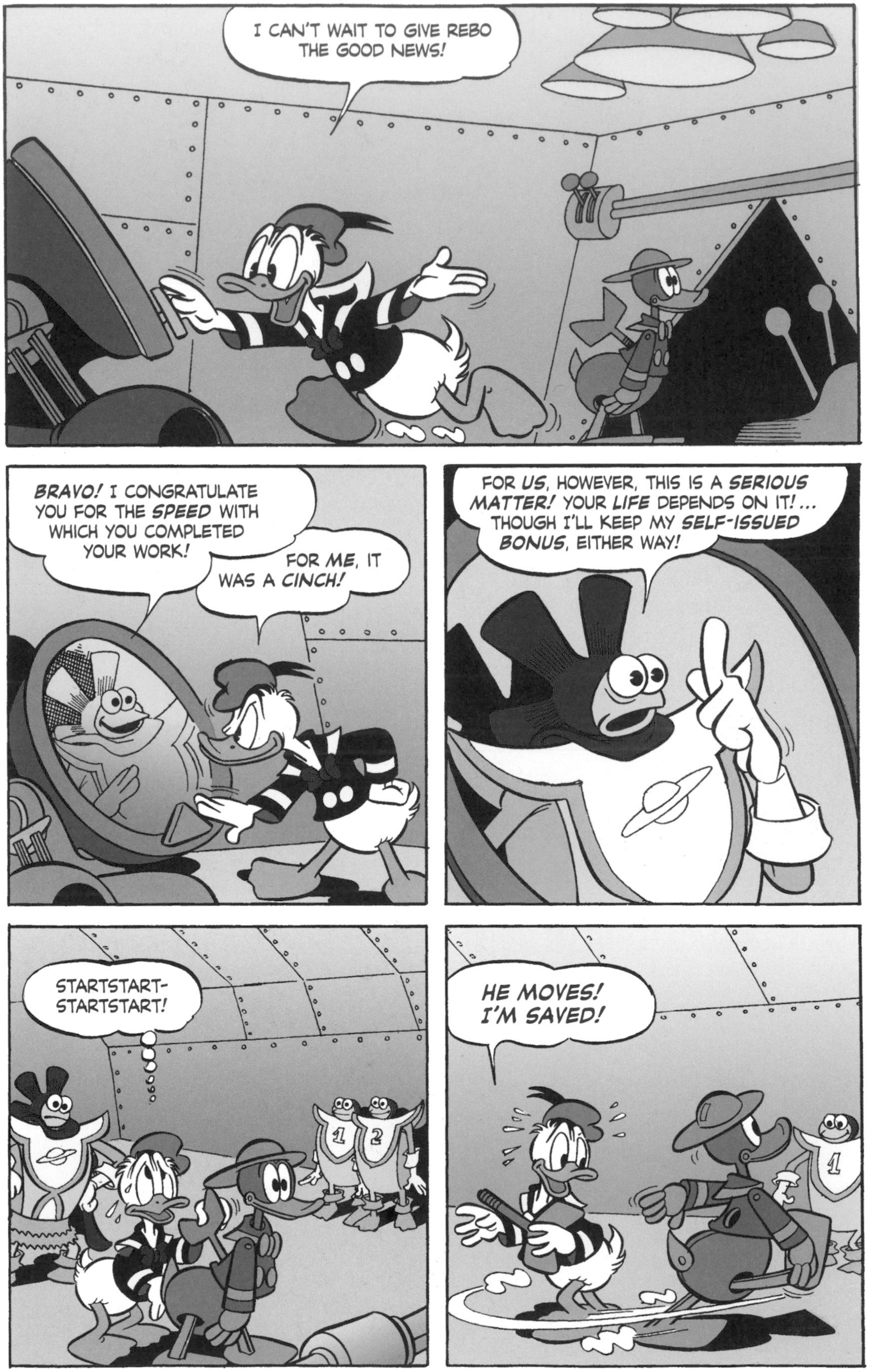
I CAN'T WAIT TO GIVE REBO THE GOOD NEWS!
BRAVO! I CONGRATULATE YOU FOR THE SPEED WITH WHICH YOU COMPLETED YOUR WORK!
FOR ME, IT WAS A CINCH!
FOR US, HOWEVER, THIS IS A SERIOUS MATTER! YOUR LIFE DEPENDS ON IT! ... THOUGH I'LL KEEP MY SELF-ISSUED BONUS, EITHER WAY!
STARTSTART-STARTSTART!
HE MOVES! I'M SAVED!

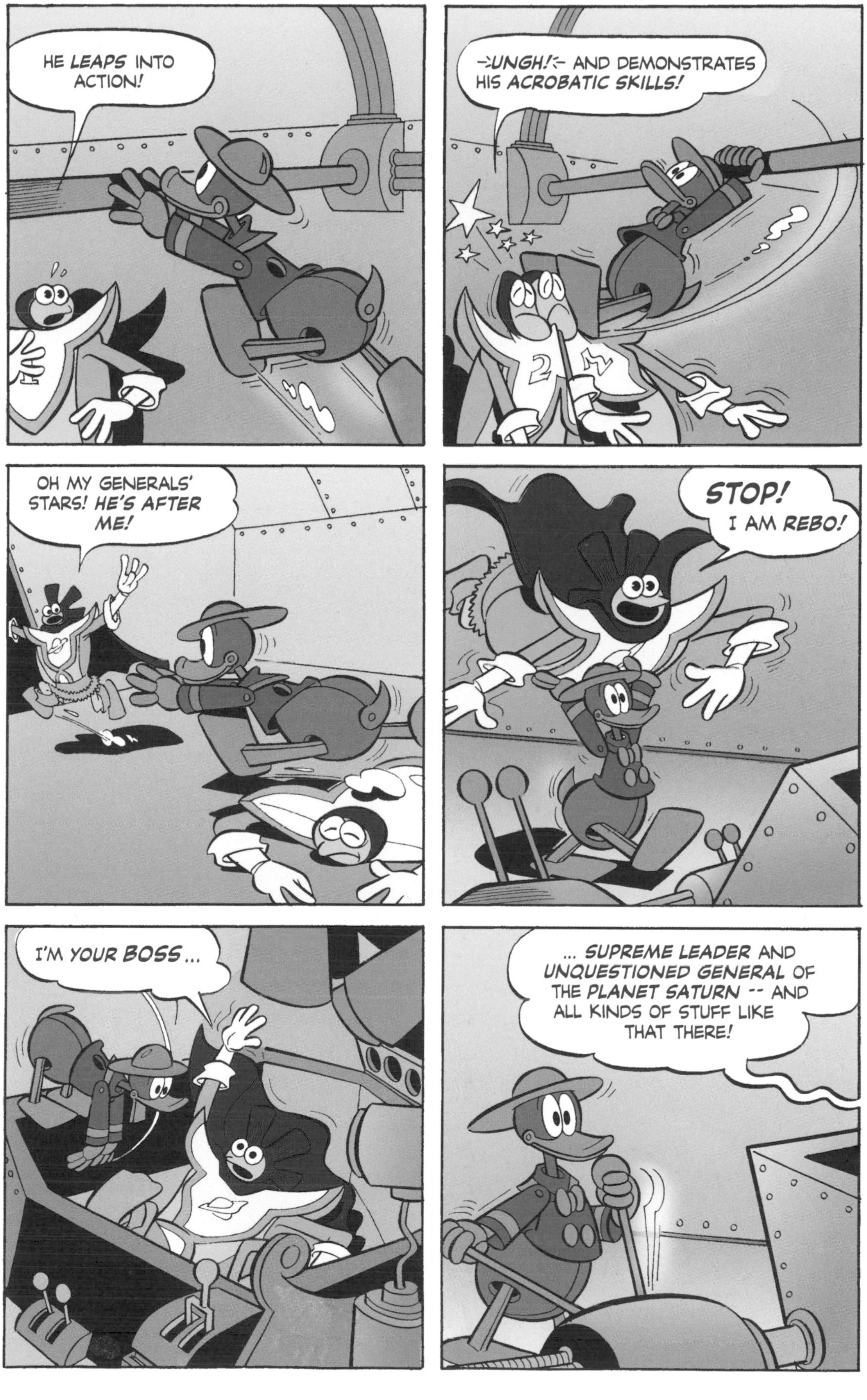

HE LEAPS INTO ACTION!
-UNGH!- AND DEMONSTRATES HIS ACROBATIC SKILLS!
OH MY GENERALS' STARS! HE'S AFTER ME!
STOP! I AM REBO!
I'M YOUR BOSS...
... SUPREME LEADER AND UNQUESTIONED GENERAL OF THE PLANET SATURN -- AND ALL KINDS OF STUFF LIKE THAT THERE!

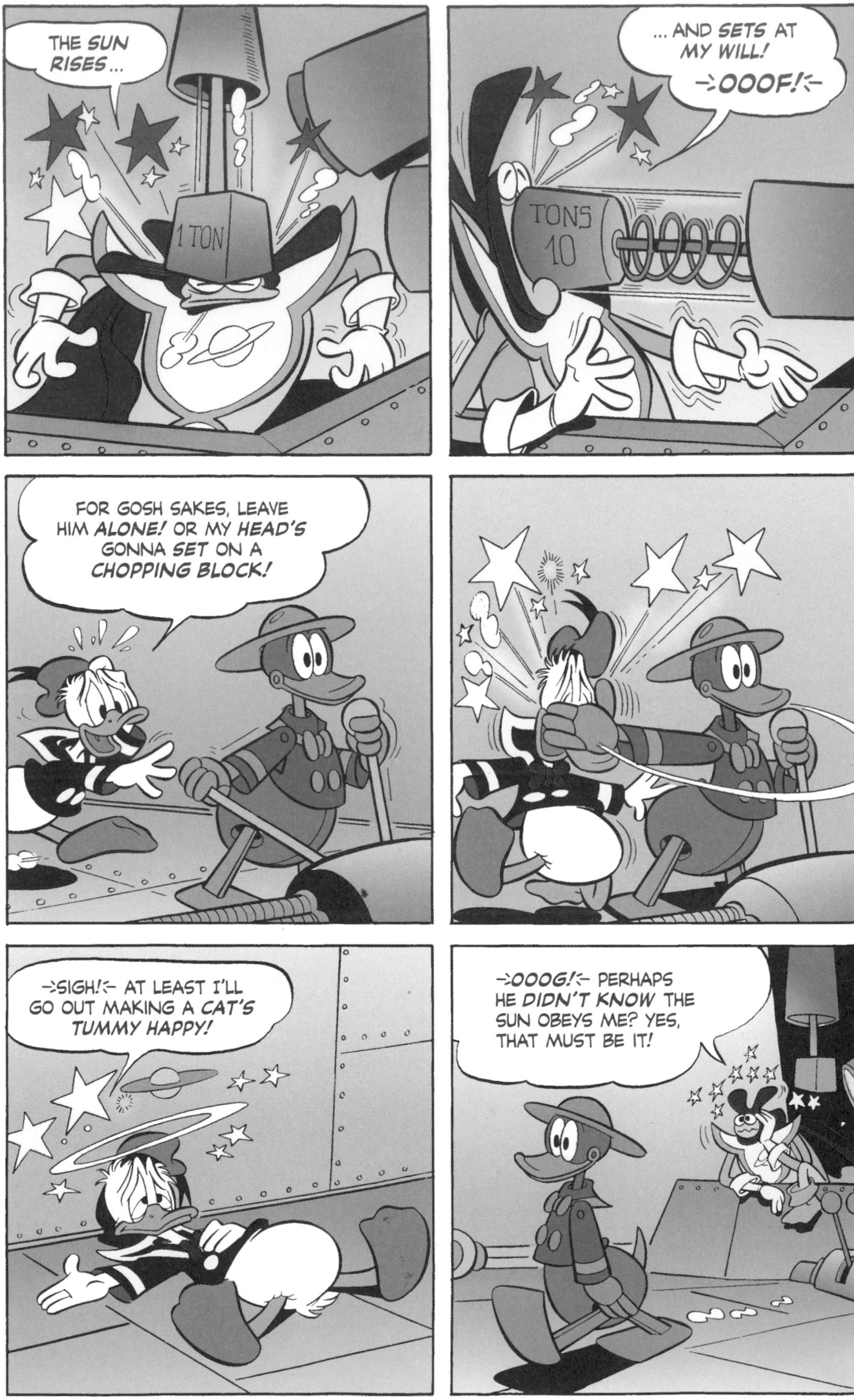
THE SUN RISES...
1 TON
... AND SETS AT MY WILL!
-OOOF!-
TONS 10
FOR GOSH SAKES, LEAVE HIM ALONE! OR MY HEAD'S GONNA SET ON A CHOPPING BLOCK!
-SIGH!- AT LEAST I'LL GO OUT MAKING A CAT'S TUMMY HAPPY!
-OOOG!- PERHAPS HE DIDN'T KNOW THE SUN OBEYS ME? YES, THAT MUST BE IT!

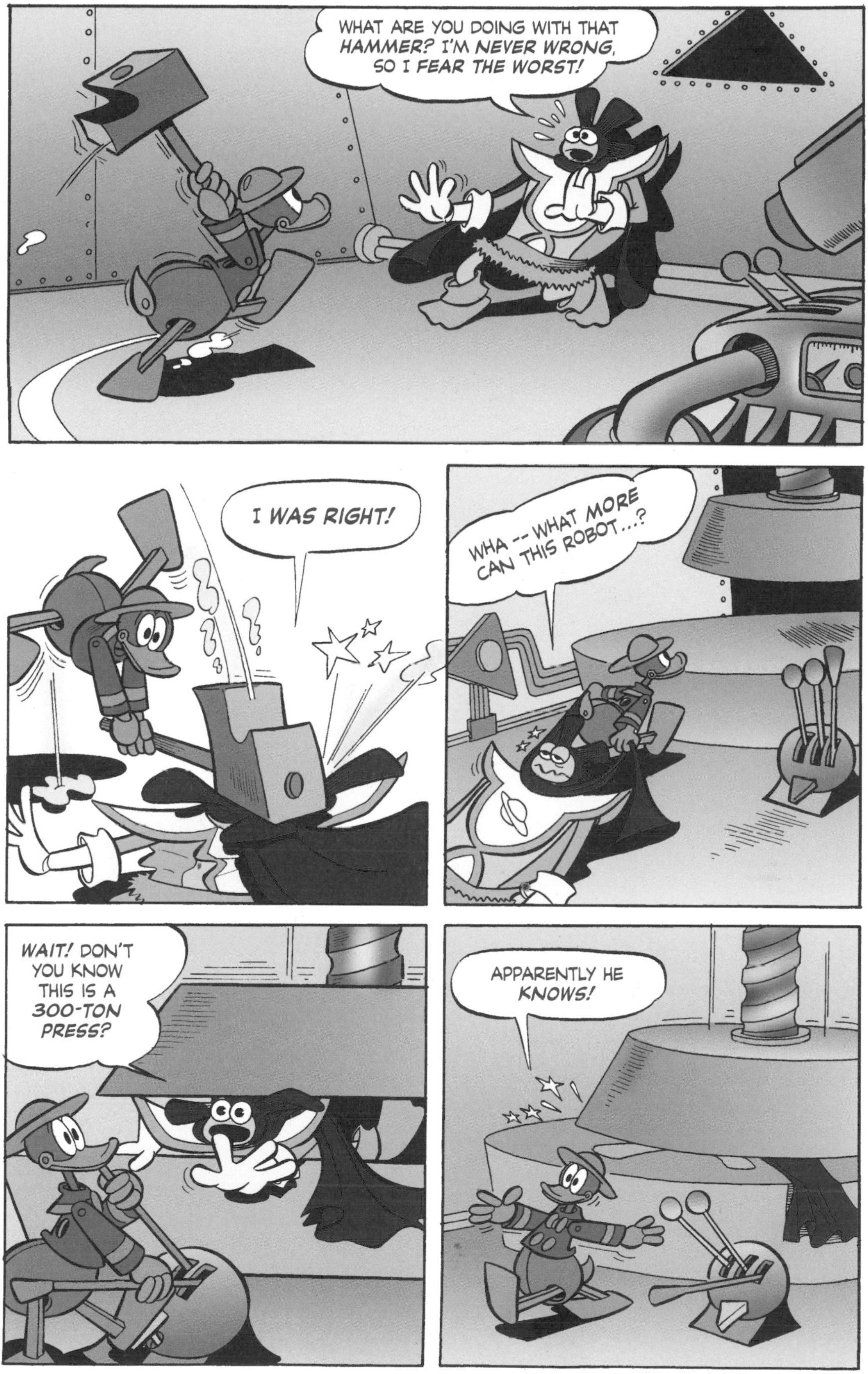

WHAT ARE YOU DOING WITH THAT HAMMER? I'M NEVER WRONG, SO I FEAR THE WORST!
I WAS RIGHT!
WHA -- WHAT MORE CAN THIS ROBOT...?
WAIT! DON'T YOU KNOW THIS IS A 300-TON PRESS?
APPARENTLY HE KNOWS!

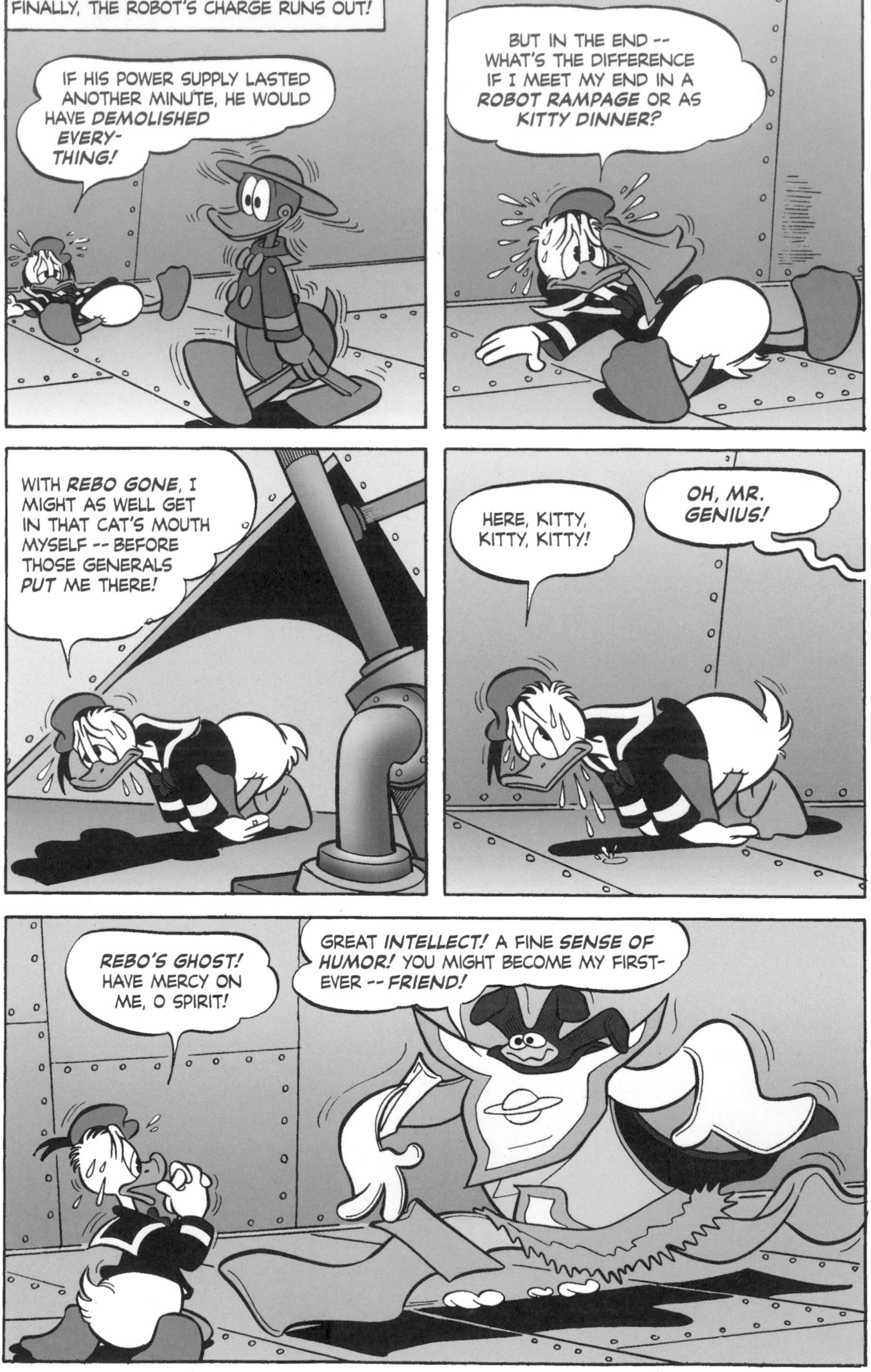
FINALLY, THE ROBOT'S CHARGE RUNS OUT!
IF HIS POWER SUPPLY LASTED ANOTHER MINUTE, HE WOULD HAVE *DEMOLISHED EVERY-THING!*
BUT IN THE END -- WHAT'S THE DIFFERENCE IF I MEET MY END IN A *ROBOT RAMPAGE* OR AS *KITTY DINNER?*
WITH *REBO GONE*, I MIGHT AS WELL GET IN THAT CAT'S MOUTH MYSELF -- BEFORE THOSE GENERALS *PUT* ME THERE!
HERE, KITTY, KITTY, KITTY!
OH, MR. GENIUS!
REBO'S GHOST! HAVE MERCY ON ME, O SPIRIT!
GREAT *INTELLECT!* A FINE *SENSE OF HUMOR!* YOU MIGHT BECOME MY FIRST-EVER -- *FRIEND!*

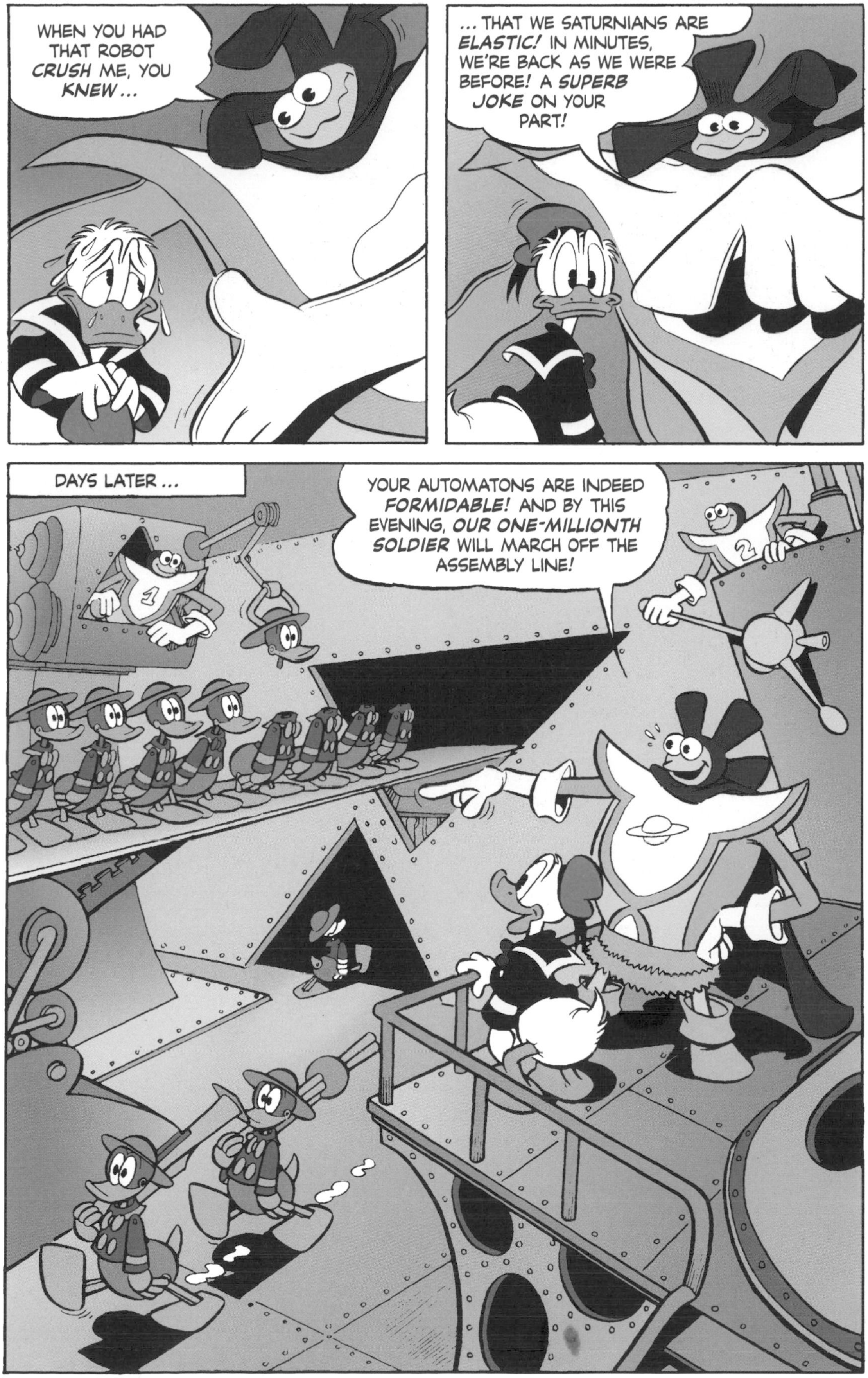
WHEN YOU HAD THAT ROBOT CRUSH ME, YOU KNEW...
... THAT WE SATURNIANS ARE ELASTIC! IN MINUTES, WE'RE BACK AS WE WERE BEFORE! A SUPERB JOKE ON YOUR PART!
DAYS LATER...
YOUR AUTOMATONS ARE INDEED FORMIDABLE! AND BY THIS EVENING, OUR ONE-MILLIONTH SOLDIER WILL MARCH OFF THE ASSEMBLY LINE!

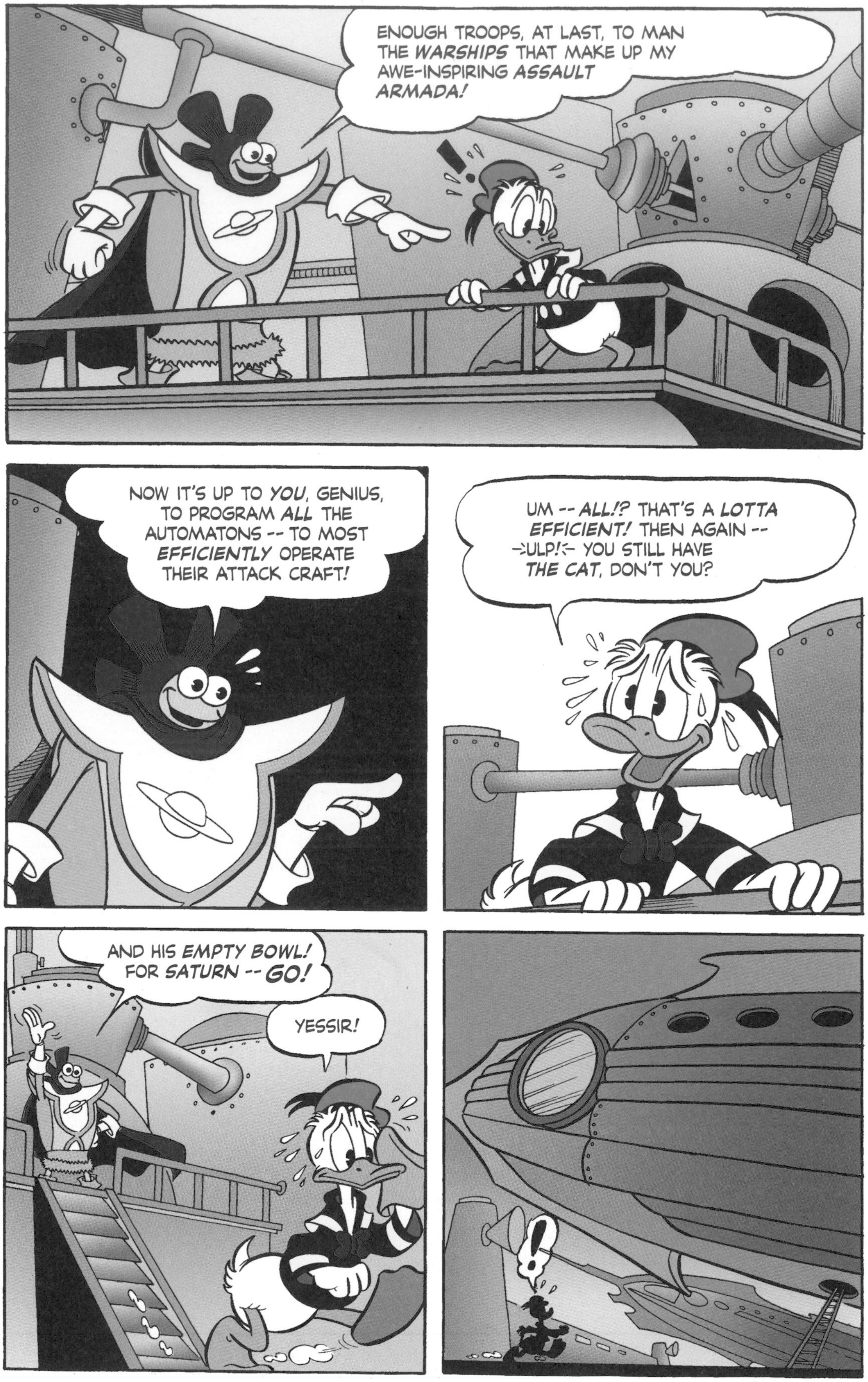
ENOUGH TROOPS, AT LAST, TO MAN THE WARSHIPS THAT MAKE UP MY AWE-INSPIRING ASSAULT ARMADA!
!
NOW IT'S UP TO YOU, GENIUS, TO PROGRAM ALL THE AUTOMATONS -- TO MOST EFFICIENTLY OPERATE THEIR ATTACK CRAFT!
UM -- ALL!? THAT'S A LOTTA EFFICIENT! THEN AGAIN -- -ULP!- YOU STILL HAVE THE CAT, DON'T YOU?
AND HIS EMPTY BOWL! FOR SATURN -- GO!
YESSIR!
!

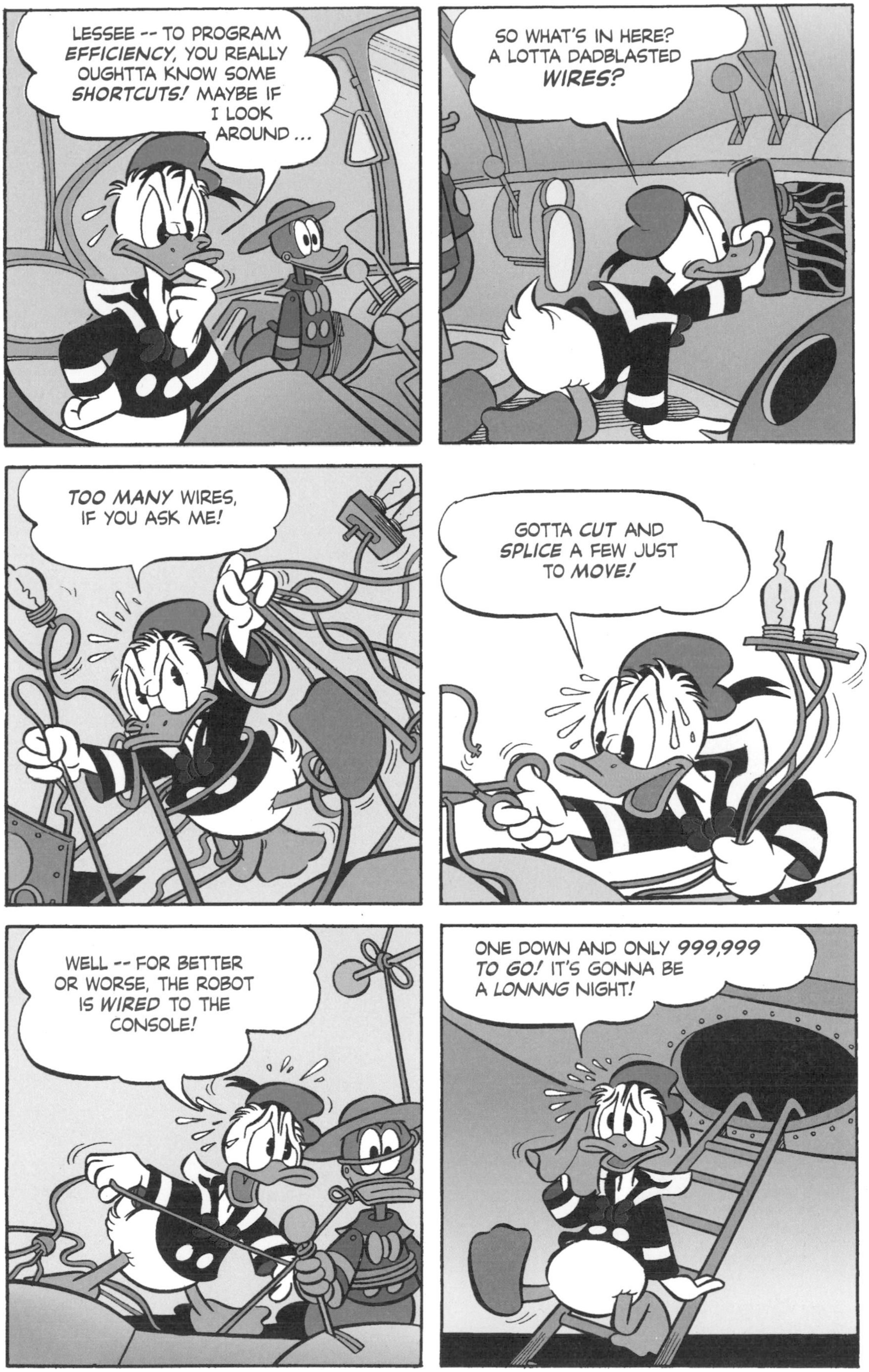
LESSEE -- TO PROGRAM EFFICIENCY, YOU REALLY OUGHTTA KNOW SOME SHORTCUTS! MAYBE IF I LOOK AROUND ...
SO WHAT'S IN HERE? A LOTTA DADBLASTED WIRES?
TOO MANY WIRES, IF YOU ASK ME!
GOTTA CUT AND SPLICE A FEW JUST TO MOVE!
WELL -- FOR BETTER OR WORSE, THE ROBOT IS WIRED TO THE CONSOLE!
ONE DOWN AND ONLY 999,999 TO GO! IT'S GONNA BE A LONNNG NIGHT!

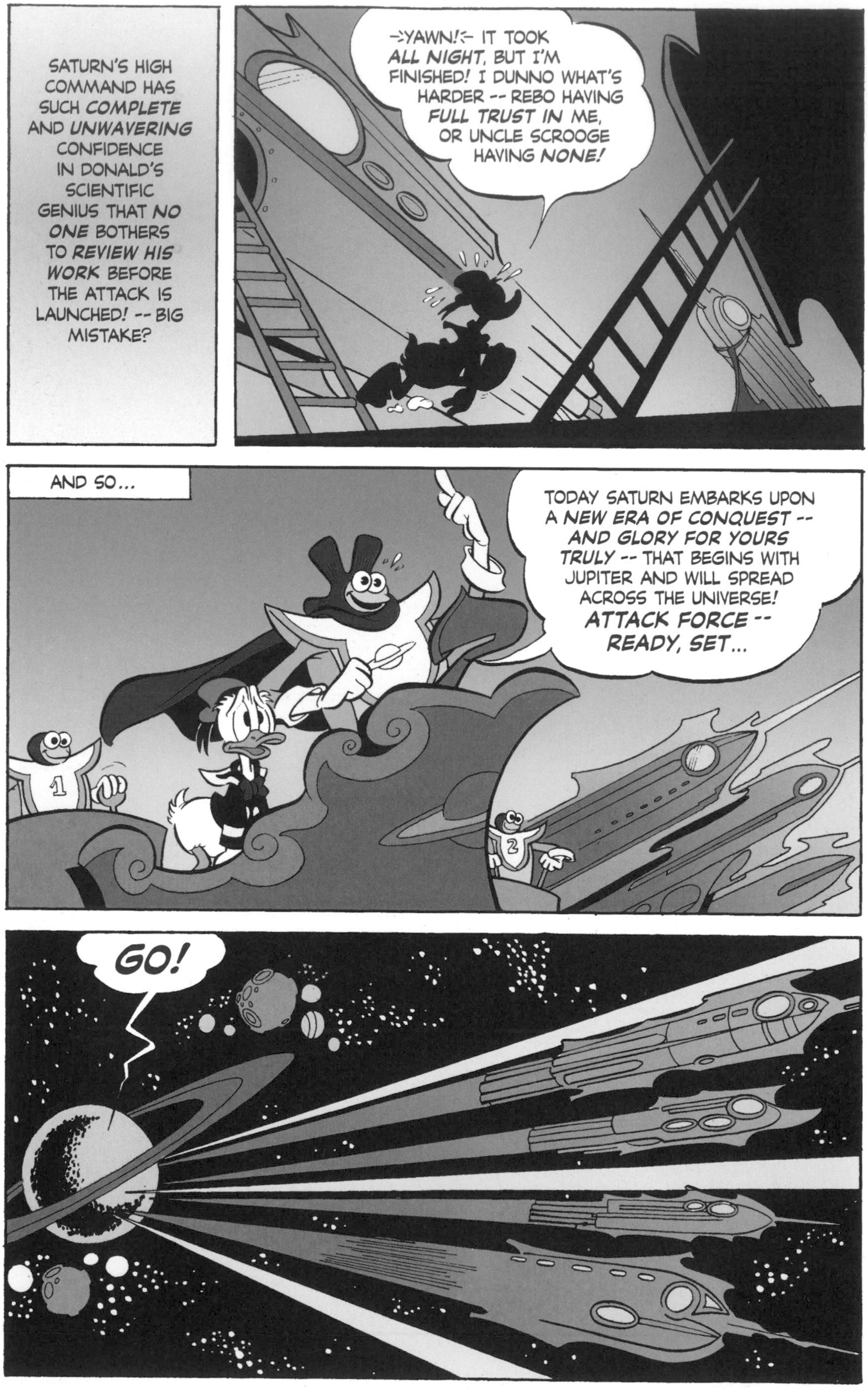
SATURN'S HIGH COMMAND HAS SUCH COMPLETE AND UNWAVERING CONFIDENCE IN DONALD'S SCIENTIFIC GENIUS THAT NO ONE BOTHERS TO REVIEW HIS WORK BEFORE THE ATTACK IS LAUNCHED! -- BIG MISTAKE?
-YAWN!- IT TOOK ALL NIGHT, BUT I'M FINISHED! I DUNNO WHAT'S HARDER -- REBO HAVING FULL TRUST IN ME, OR UNCLE SCROOGE HAVING NONE!
AND SO...
TODAY SATURN EMBARKS UPON A NEW ERA OF CONQUEST -- AND GLORY FOR YOURS TRULY -- THAT BEGINS WITH JUPITER AND WILL SPREAD ACROSS THE UNIVERSE! ATTACK FORCE -- READY, SET...
1
2
GO!

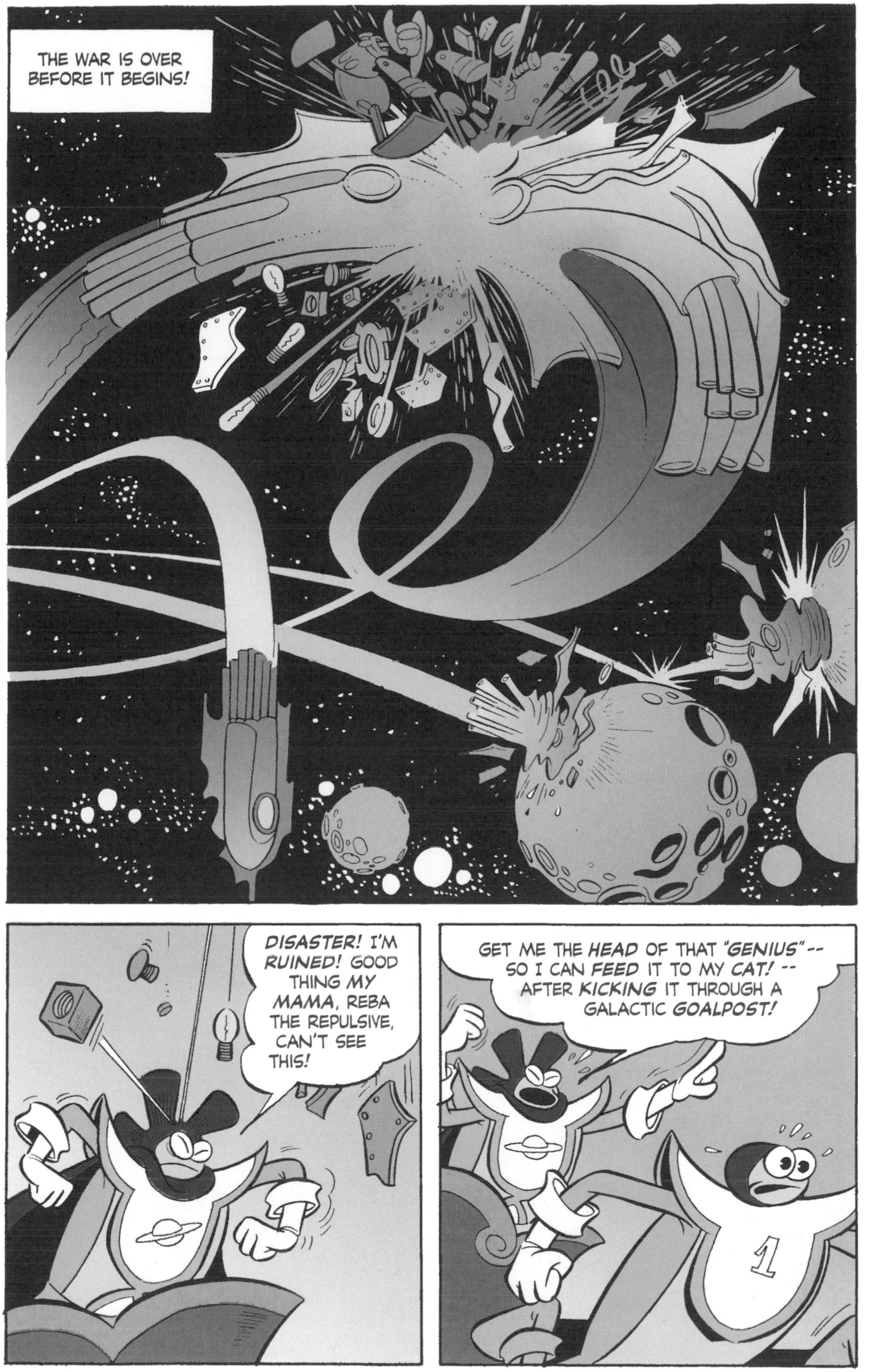
THE WAR IS OVER BEFORE IT BEGINS!
DISASTER! I'M RUINED! GOOD THING MY MAMA, REBA THE REPULSIVE, CAN'T SEE THIS!
GET ME THE HEAD OF THAT "GENIUS" -- SO I CAN FEED IT TO MY CAT! -- AFTER KICKING IT THROUGH A GALACTIC GOALPOST!

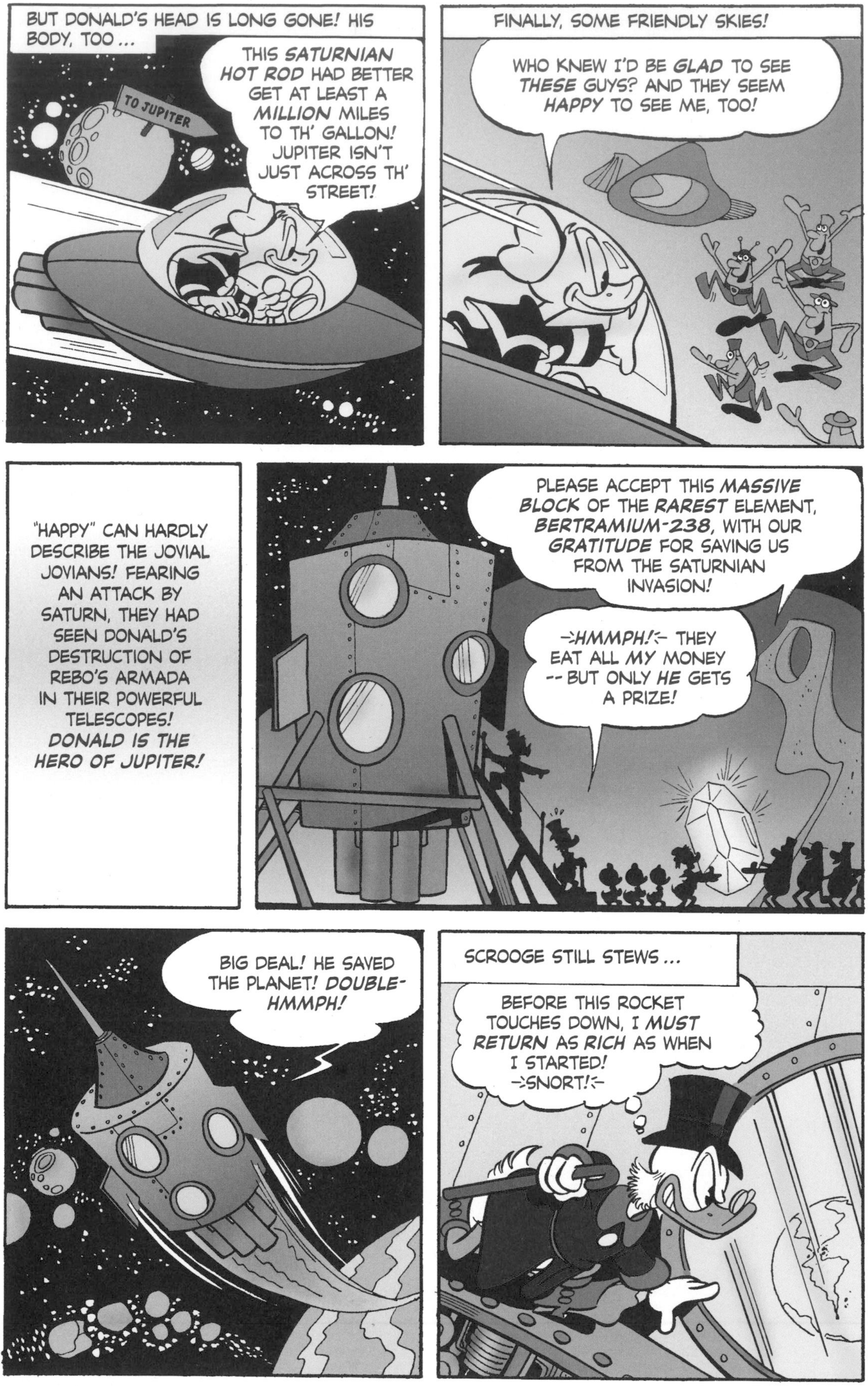
BUT DONALD'S HEAD IS LONG GONE! HIS BODY, TOO ...
THIS SATURNIAN HOT ROD HAD BETTER GET AT LEAST A MILLION MILES TO TH' GALLON! JUPITER ISN'T JUST ACROSS TH' STREET!
TO JUPITER
FINALLY, SOME FRIENDLY SKIES!
WHO KNEW I'D BE GLAD TO SEE THESE GUYS? AND THEY SEEM HAPPY TO SEE ME, TOO!
"HAPPY" CAN HARDLY DESCRIBE THE JOVIAL JOVIANS! FEARING AN ATTACK BY SATURN, THEY HAD SEEN DONALD'S DESTRUCTION OF REBO'S ARMADA IN THEIR POWERFUL TELESCOPES! DONALD IS THE HERO OF JUPITER!
PLEASE ACCEPT THIS MASSIVE BLOCK OF THE RAREST ELEMENT, BERTRAMIUM-238, WITH OUR GRATITUDE FOR SAVING US FROM THE SATURNIAN INVASION!
HMMPH! THEY EAT ALL MY MONEY -- BUT ONLY HE GETS A PRIZE!
BIG DEAL! HE SAVED THE PLANET! DOUBLE-HMMPH!
SCROOGE STILL STEWS ...
BEFORE THIS ROCKET TOUCHES DOWN, I MUST RETURN AS RICH AS WHEN I STARTED! SNORT!

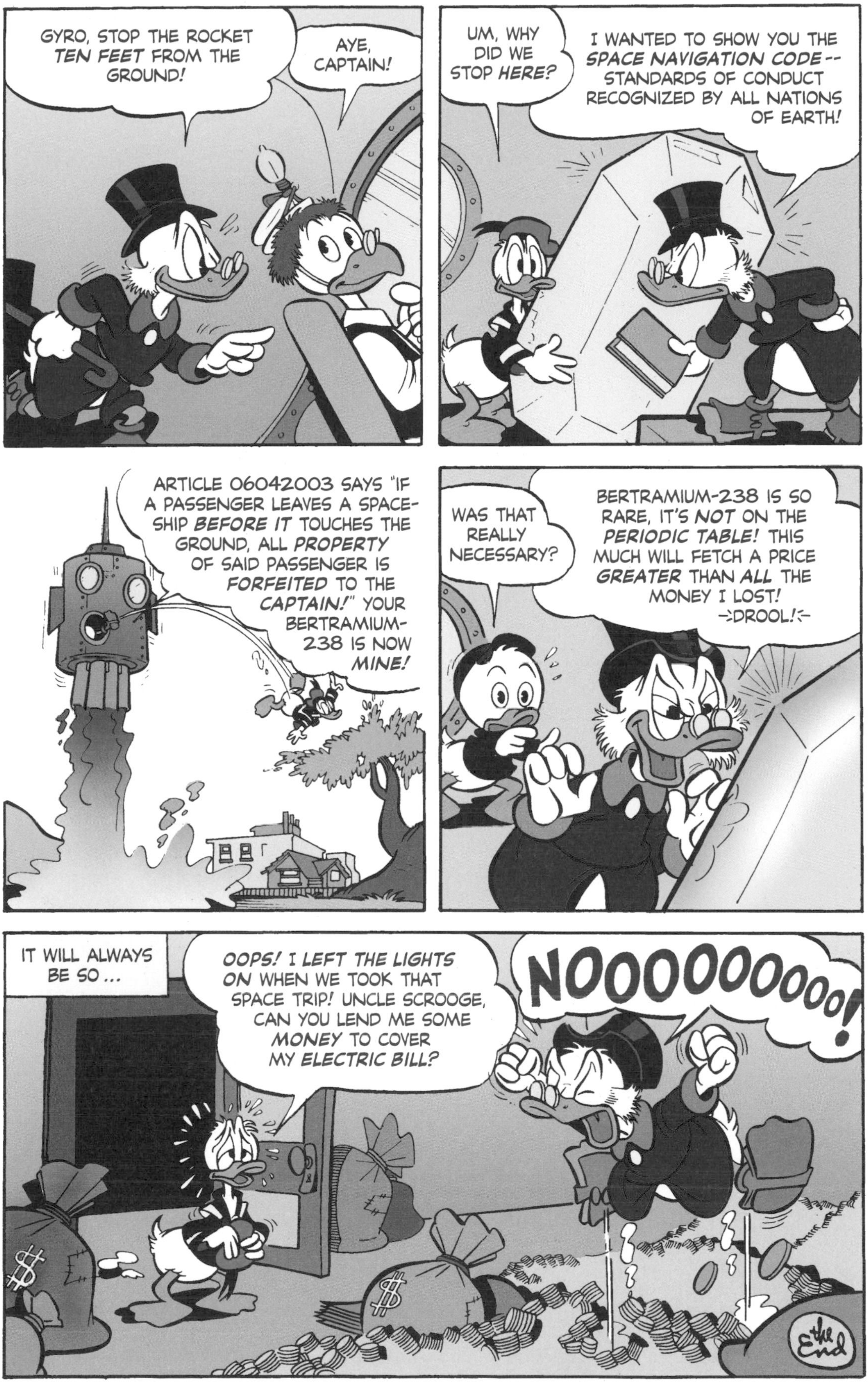

GYRO, STOP THE ROCKET TEN FEET FROM THE GROUND!
AYE, CAPTAIN!
UM, WHY DID WE STOP HERE?
I WANTED TO SHOW YOU THE SPACE NAVIGATION CODE -- STANDARDS OF CONDUCT RECOGNIZED BY ALL NATIONS OF EARTH!
ARTICLE 06042003 SAYS "IF A PASSENGER LEAVES A SPACESHIP BEFORE IT TOUCHES THE GROUND, ALL PROPERTY OF SAID PASSENGER IS FORFEITED TO THE CAPTAIN!" YOUR BERTRAMIUM-238 IS NOW MINE!
WAS THAT REALLY NECESSARY?
BERTRAMIUM-238 IS SO RARE, IT'S NOT ON THE PERIODIC TABLE! THIS MUCH WILL FETCH A PRICE GREATER THAN ALL THE MONEY I LOST!
DROOL!
IT WILL ALWAYS BE SO ...
OOPS! I LEFT THE LIGHTS ON WHEN WE TOOK THAT SPACE TRIP! UNCLE SCROOGE, CAN YOU LEND ME SOME MONEY TO COVER MY ELECTRIC BILL?
NOOOOOOOOoo!
the End

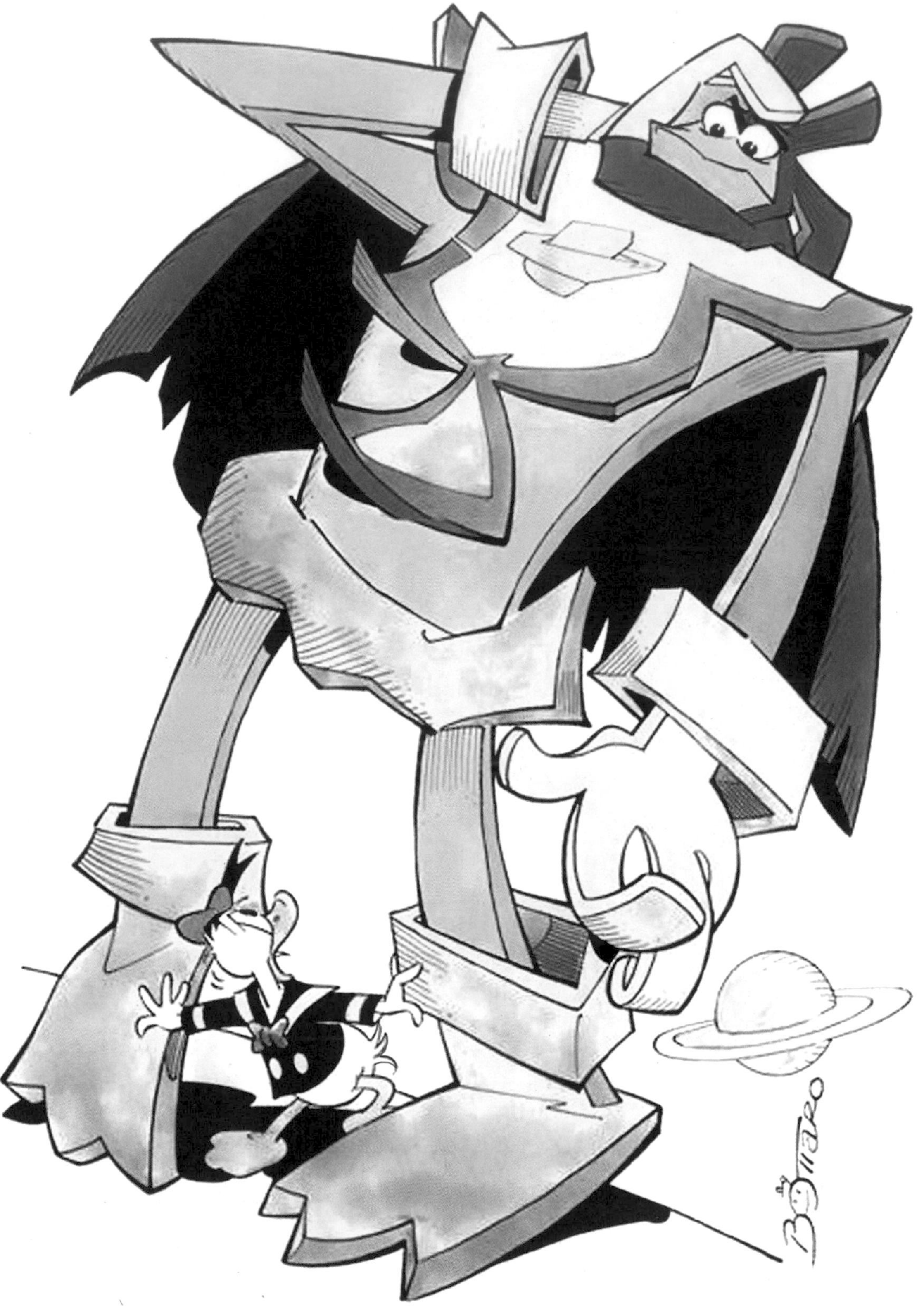

Donald meets his Saturnian match in this publicity drawing by Luciano Bottaro. Image courtesy Disney Publishing Worldwide.

Walt Disney

Donald Duck & Uncle $crooge in The Return of Rebo

CHAPTER 1

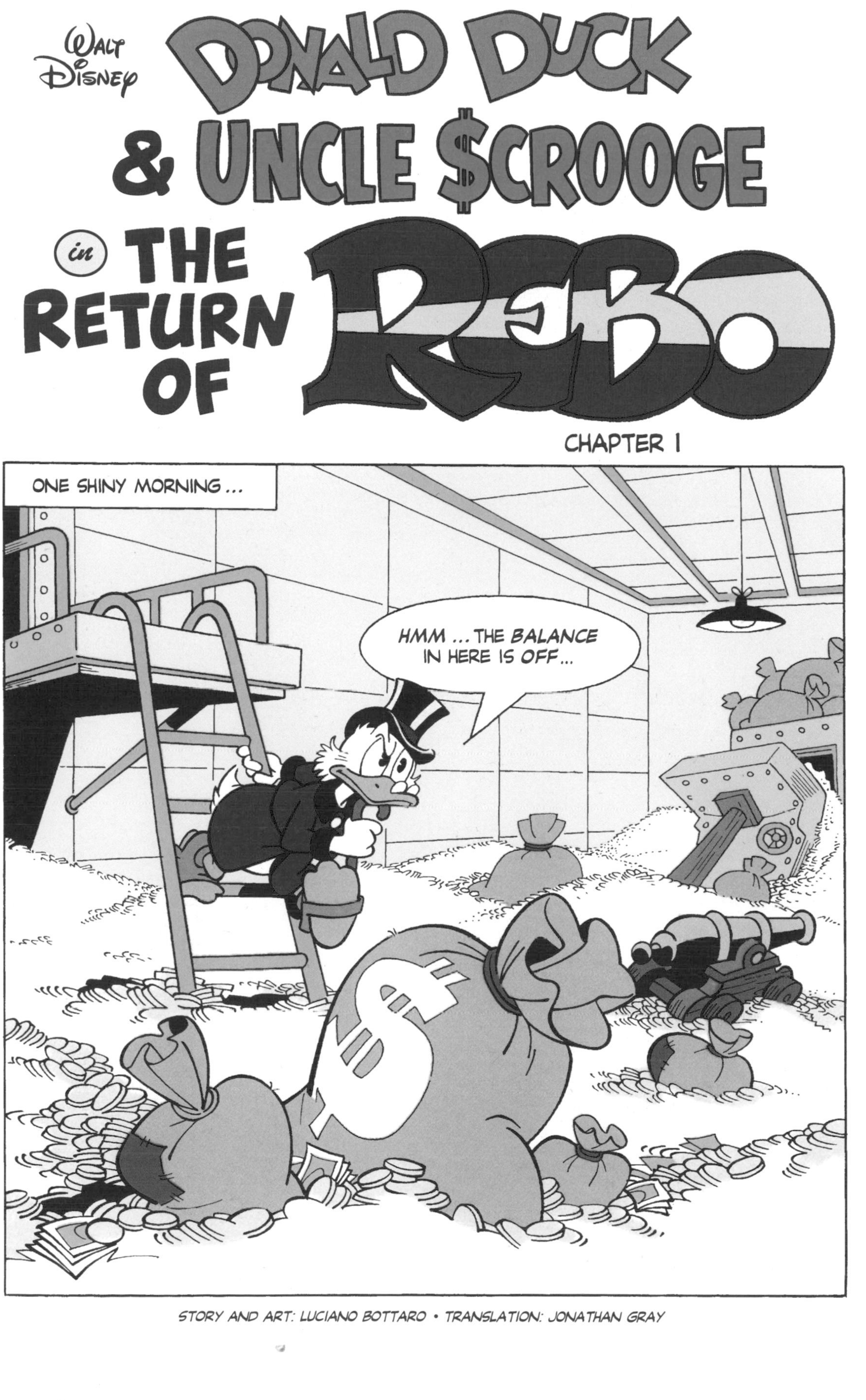
ONE SHINY MORNING...
HMM ... THE BALANCE IN HERE IS OFF...

STORY AND ART: LUCIANO BOTTARO • TRANSLATION: JONATHAN GRAY

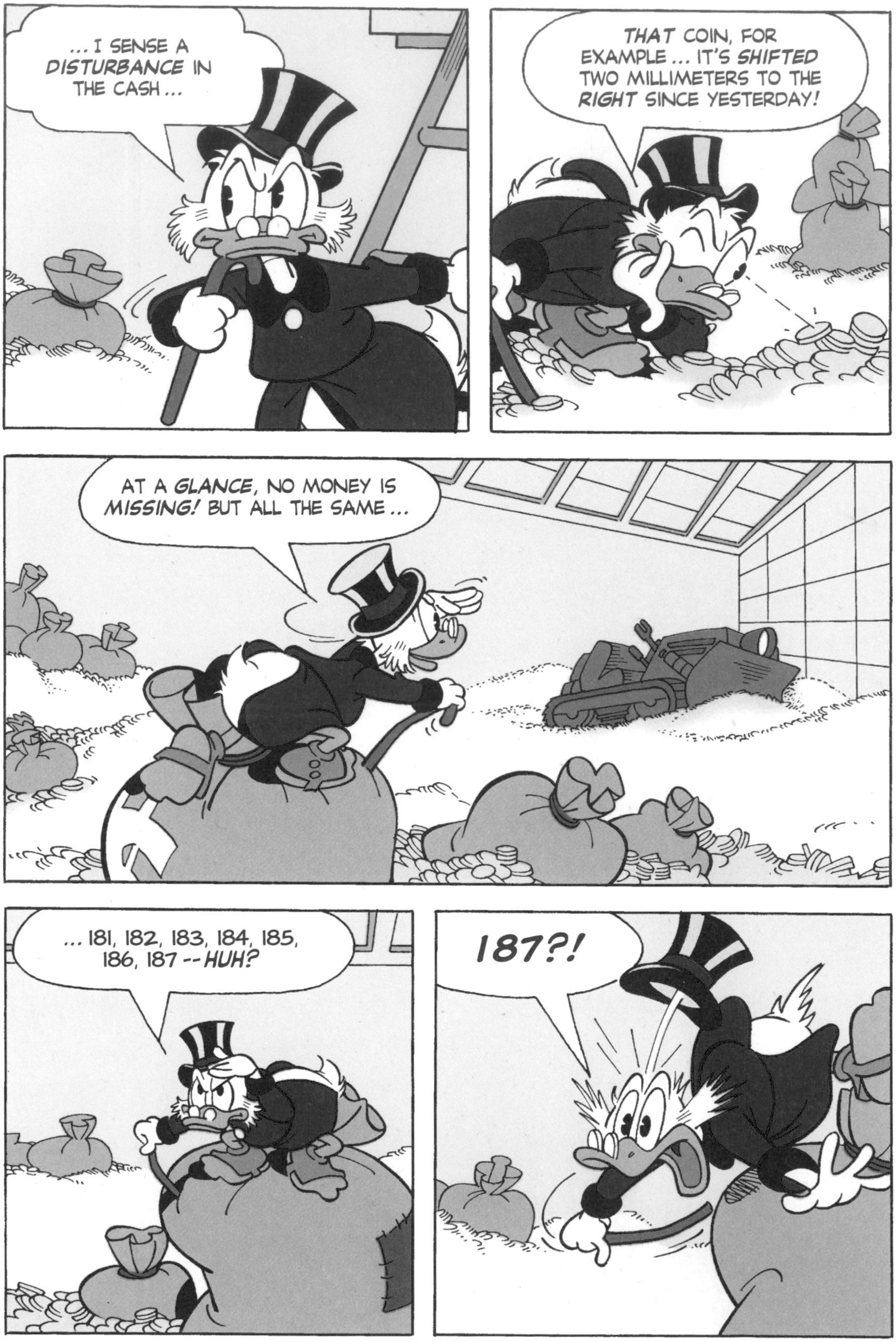
... I SENSE A DISTURBANCE IN THE CASH ...
THAT COIN, FOR EXAMPLE ... IT'S SHIFTED TWO MILLIMETERS TO THE RIGHT SINCE YESTERDAY!
AT A GLANCE, NO MONEY IS MISSING! BUT ALL THE SAME ...
... 181, 182, 183, 184, 185, 186, 187 -- HUH?
187?!

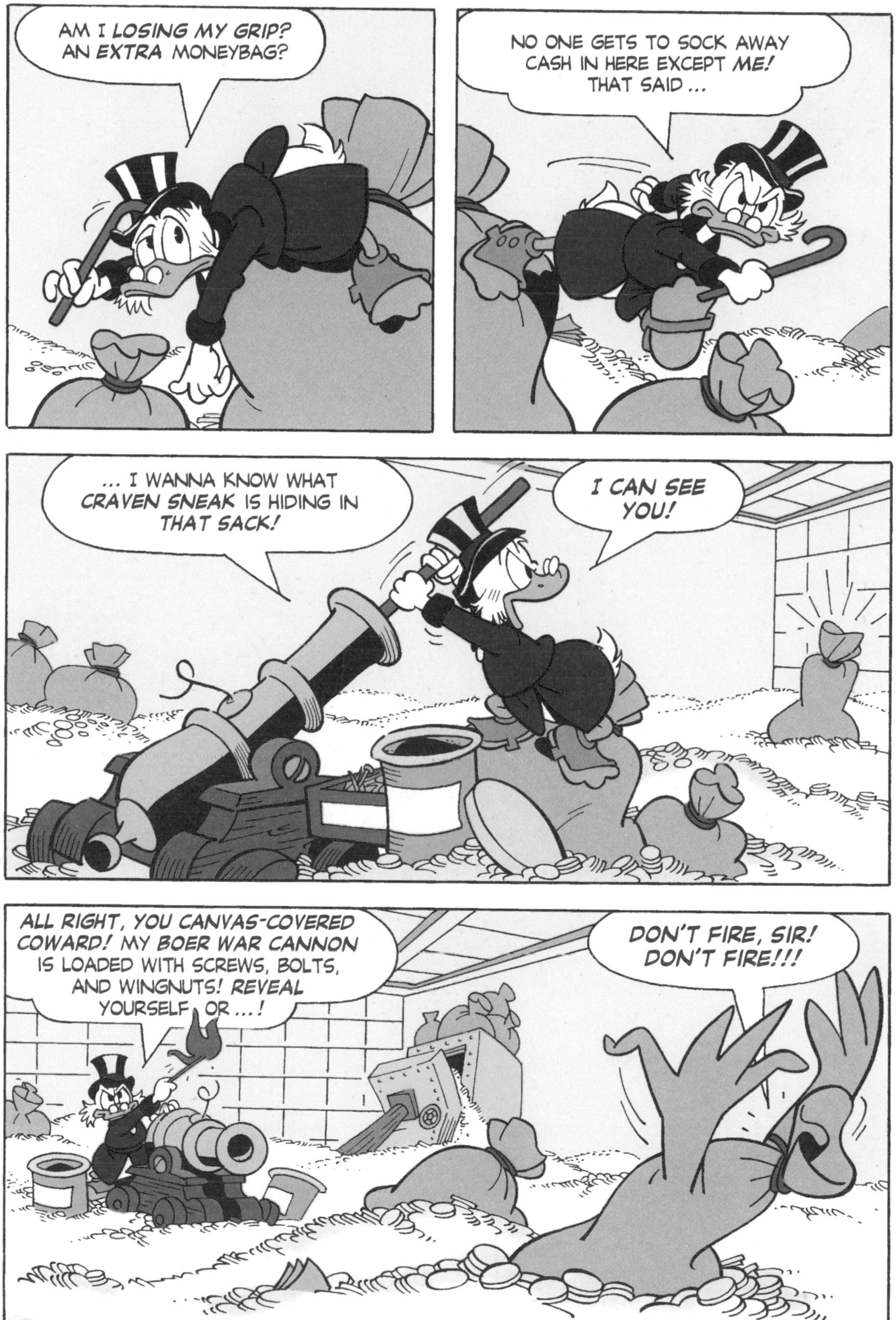
AM I LOSING MY GRIP? AN EXTRA MONEYBAG?
NO ONE GETS TO SOCK AWAY CASH IN HERE EXCEPT ME! THAT SAID ...
... I WANNA KNOW WHAT CRAVEN SNEAK IS HIDING IN THAT SACK!
I CAN SEE YOU!
ALL RIGHT, YOU CANVAS-COVERED COWARD! MY BOER WAR CANNON IS LOADED WITH SCREWS, BOLTS, AND WINGNUTS! REVEAL YOURSELF, OR ...!
DON'T FIRE, SIR! DON'T FIRE!!!

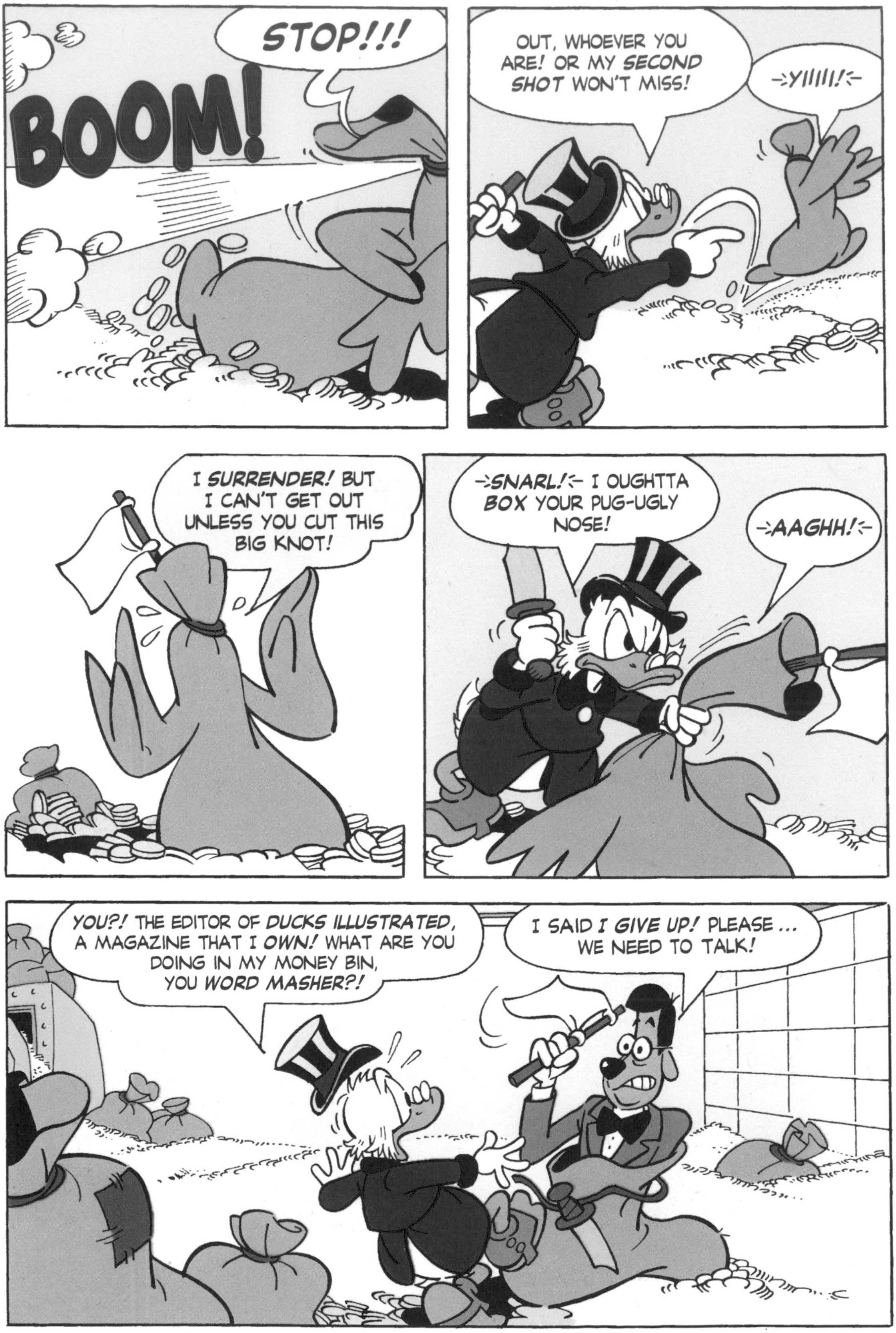
BOOM!
STOP!!!
OUT, WHOEVER YOU ARE! OR MY SECOND SHOT WON'T MISS!
-YIIIII!-
I SURRENDER! BUT I CAN'T GET OUT UNLESS YOU CUT THIS BIG KNOT!
-SNARL!- I OUGHTTA BOX YOUR PUG-UGLY NOSE!
-AAGHH!-
YOU?! THE EDITOR OF DUCKS ILLUSTRATED, A MAGAZINE THAT I OWN! WHAT ARE YOU DOING IN MY MONEY BIN, YOU WORD MASHER?!
I SAID I GIVE UP! PLEASE ... WE NEED TO TALK!

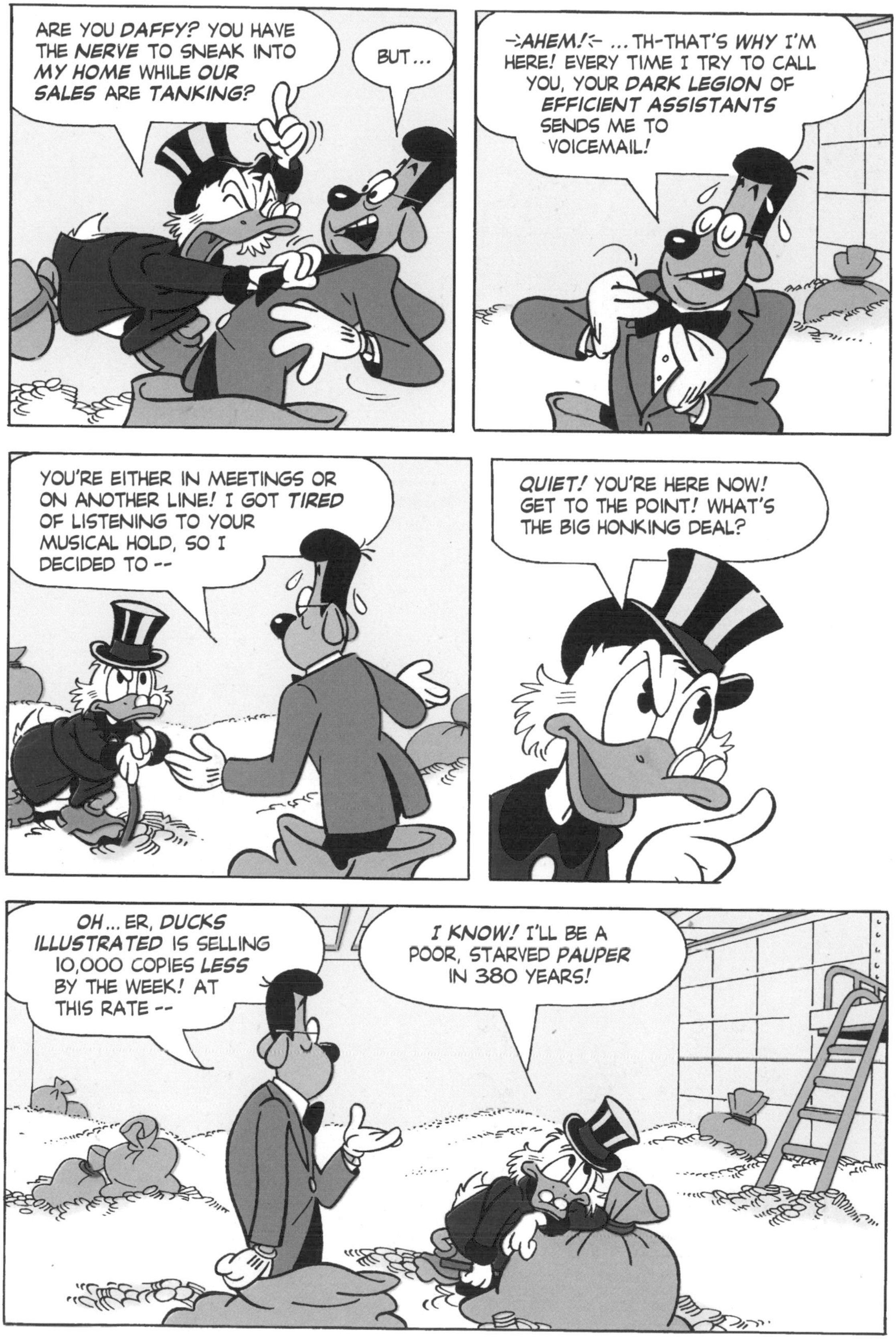
ARE YOU DAFFY? YOU HAVE THE NERVE TO SNEAK INTO MY HOME WHILE OUR SALES ARE TANKING?
BUT...
-AHEM!- ...TH-THAT'S WHY I'M HERE! EVERY TIME I TRY TO CALL YOU, YOUR DARK LEGION OF EFFICIENT ASSISTANTS SENDS ME TO VOICEMAIL!
YOU'RE EITHER IN MEETINGS OR ON ANOTHER LINE! I GOT TIRED OF LISTENING TO YOUR MUSICAL HOLD, SO I DECIDED TO --
QUIET! YOU'RE HERE NOW! GET TO THE POINT! WHAT'S THE BIG HONKING DEAL?
OH... ER, DUCKS ILLUSTRATED IS SELLING 10,000 COPIES LESS BY THE WEEK! AT THIS RATE --
I KNOW! I'LL BE A POOR, STARVED PAUPER IN 380 YEARS!

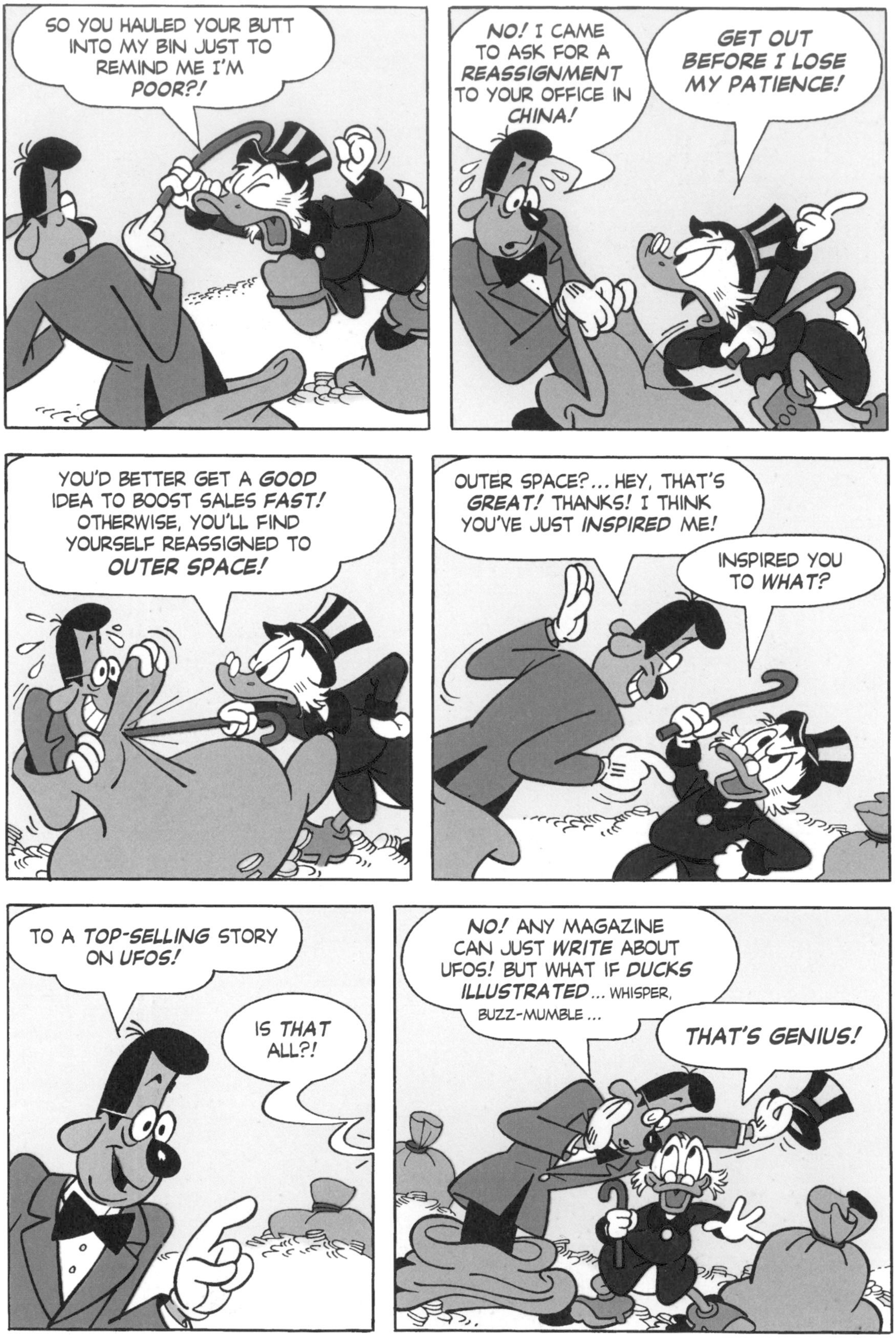
SO YOU HAULED YOUR BUTT INTO MY BIN JUST TO REMIND ME I'M POOR?!
NO! I CAME TO ASK FOR A REASSIGNMENT TO YOUR OFFICE IN CHINA!
GET OUT BEFORE I LOSE MY PATIENCE!
YOU'D BETTER GET A GOOD IDEA TO BOOST SALES FAST! OTHERWISE, YOU'LL FIND YOURSELF REASSIGNED TO OUTER SPACE!
OUTER SPACE?... HEY, THAT'S GREAT! THANKS! I THINK YOU'VE JUST INSPIRED ME!
INSPIRED YOU TO WHAT?
TO A TOP-SELLING STORY ON UFOS!
IS THAT ALL?!
NO! ANY MAGAZINE CAN JUST WRITE ABOUT UFOS! BUT WHAT IF DUCKS ILLUSTRATED... WHISPER, BUZZ-MUMBLE...
THAT'S GENIUS!

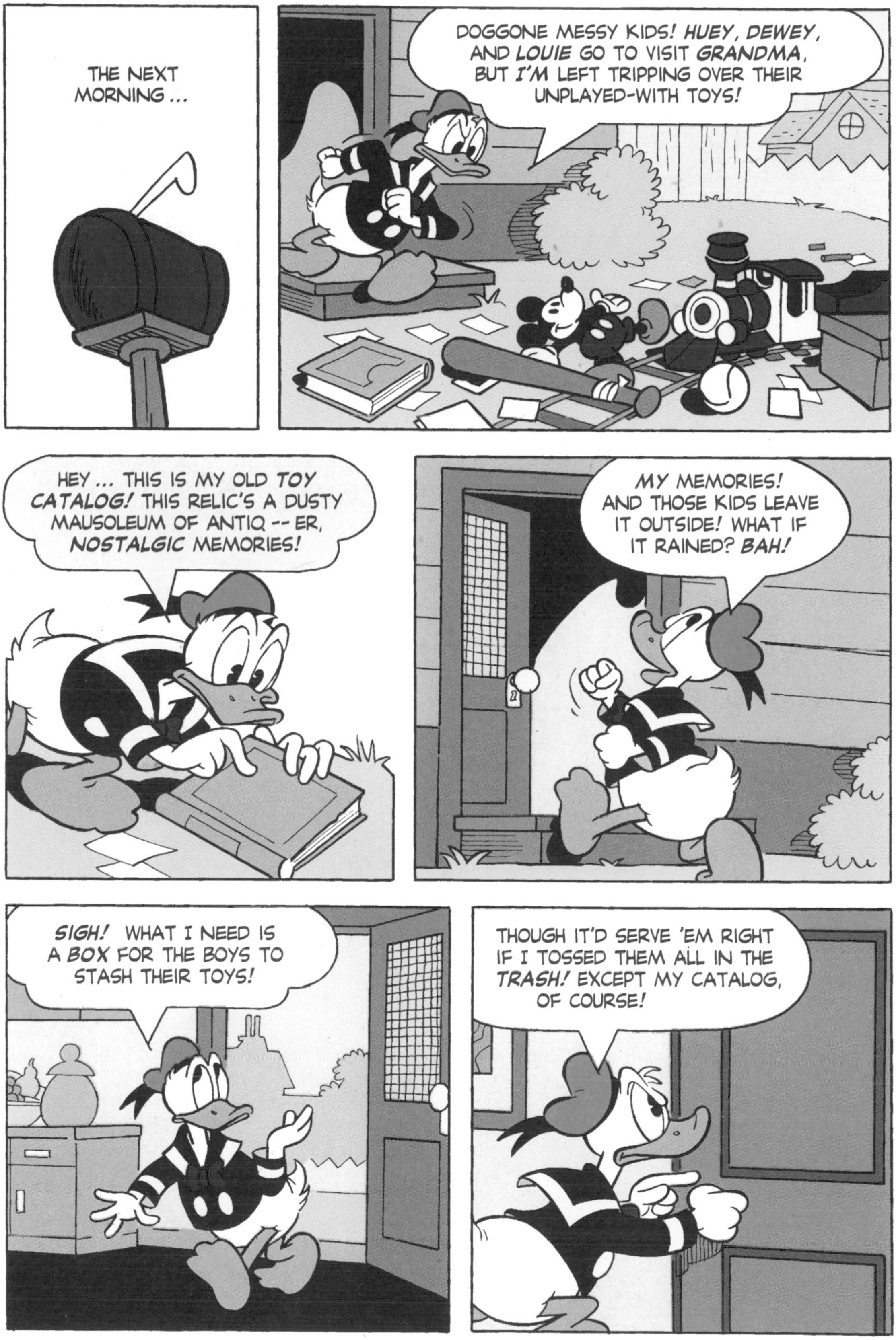
THE NEXT MORNING ...
DOGGONE MESSY KIDS! HUEY, DEWEY, AND LOUIE GO TO VISIT GRANDMA, BUT I'M LEFT TRIPPING OVER THEIR UNPLAYED-WITH TOYS!
HEY ... THIS IS MY OLD TOY CATALOG! THIS RELIC'S A DUSTY MAUSOLEUM OF ANTIQ -- ER, NOSTALGIC MEMORIES!
MY MEMORIES! AND THOSE KIDS LEAVE IT OUTSIDE! WHAT IF IT RAINED? BAH!
SIGH! WHAT I NEED IS A BOX FOR THE BOYS TO STASH THEIR TOYS!
THOUGH IT'D SERVE 'EM RIGHT IF I TOSSED THEM ALL IN THE TRASH! EXCEPT MY CATALOG, OF COURSE!

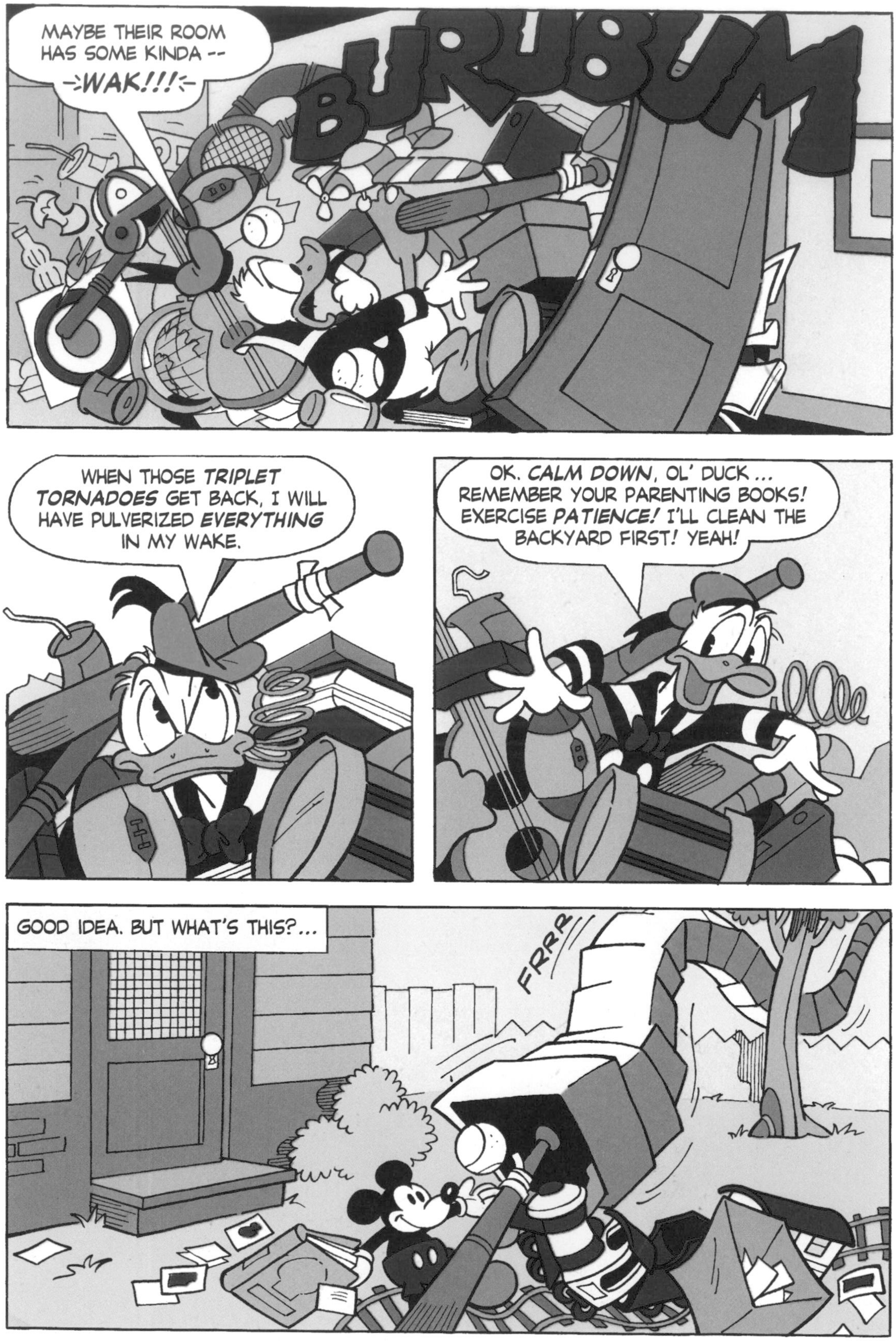
MAYBE THEIR ROOM HAS SOME KINDA -- -WAK!!!-
BURUBUM
WHEN THOSE *TRIPLET TORNADOES* GET BACK, I WILL HAVE PULVERIZED *EVERYTHING* IN MY WAKE.
OK. *CALM DOWN*, OL' DUCK ... REMEMBER YOUR PARENTING BOOKS! EXERCISE *PATIENCE!* I'LL CLEAN THE BACKYARD FIRST! YEAH!
GOOD IDEA. BUT WHAT'S THIS?...
FRRR

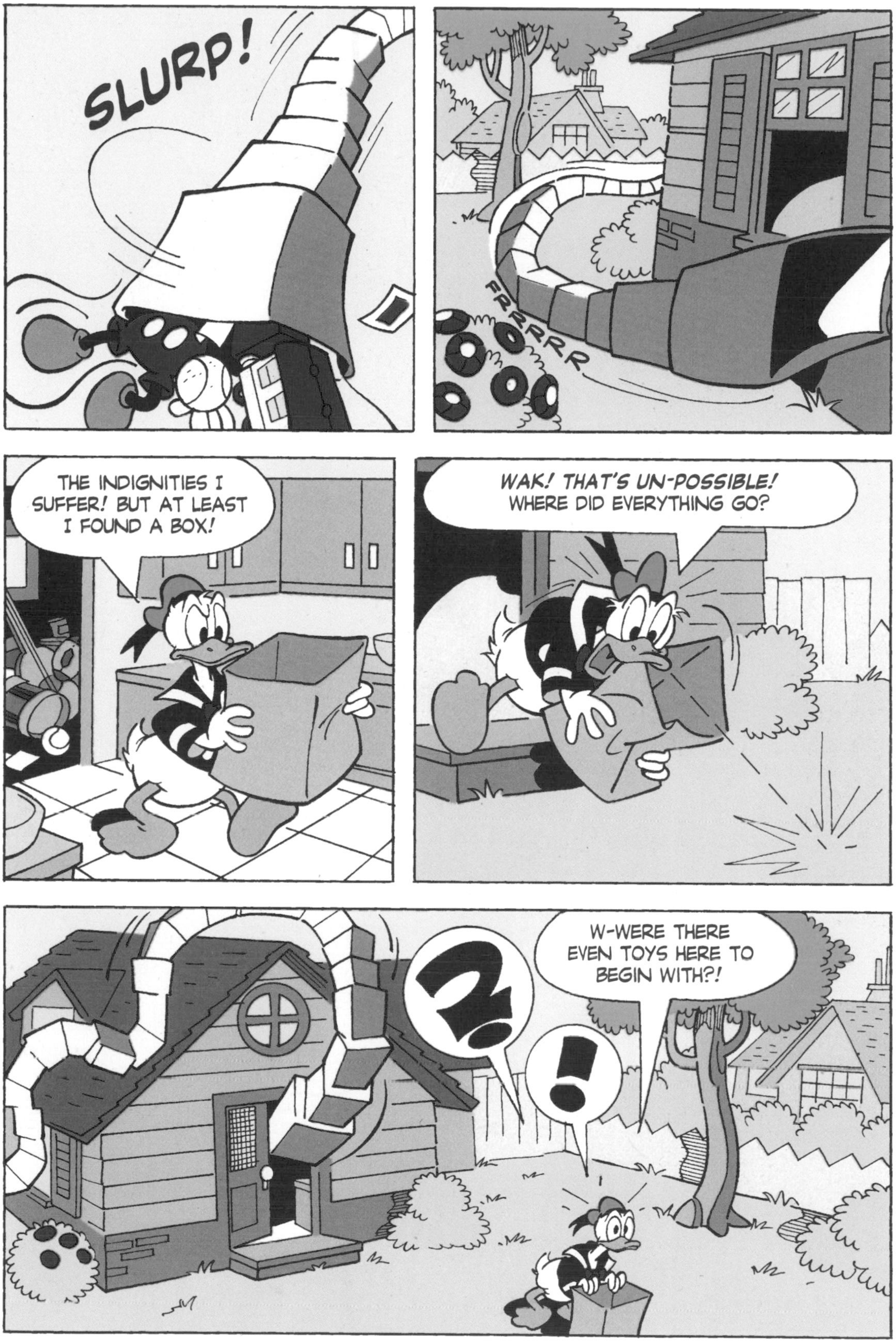
SLURP!
FRRRRRR
THE INDIGNITIES I SUFFER! BUT AT LEAST I FOUND A BOX!
WAK! THAT'S UN-POSSIBLE! WHERE DID EVERYTHING GO?
?
!
W-WERE THERE EVEN TOYS HERE TO BEGIN WITH?!

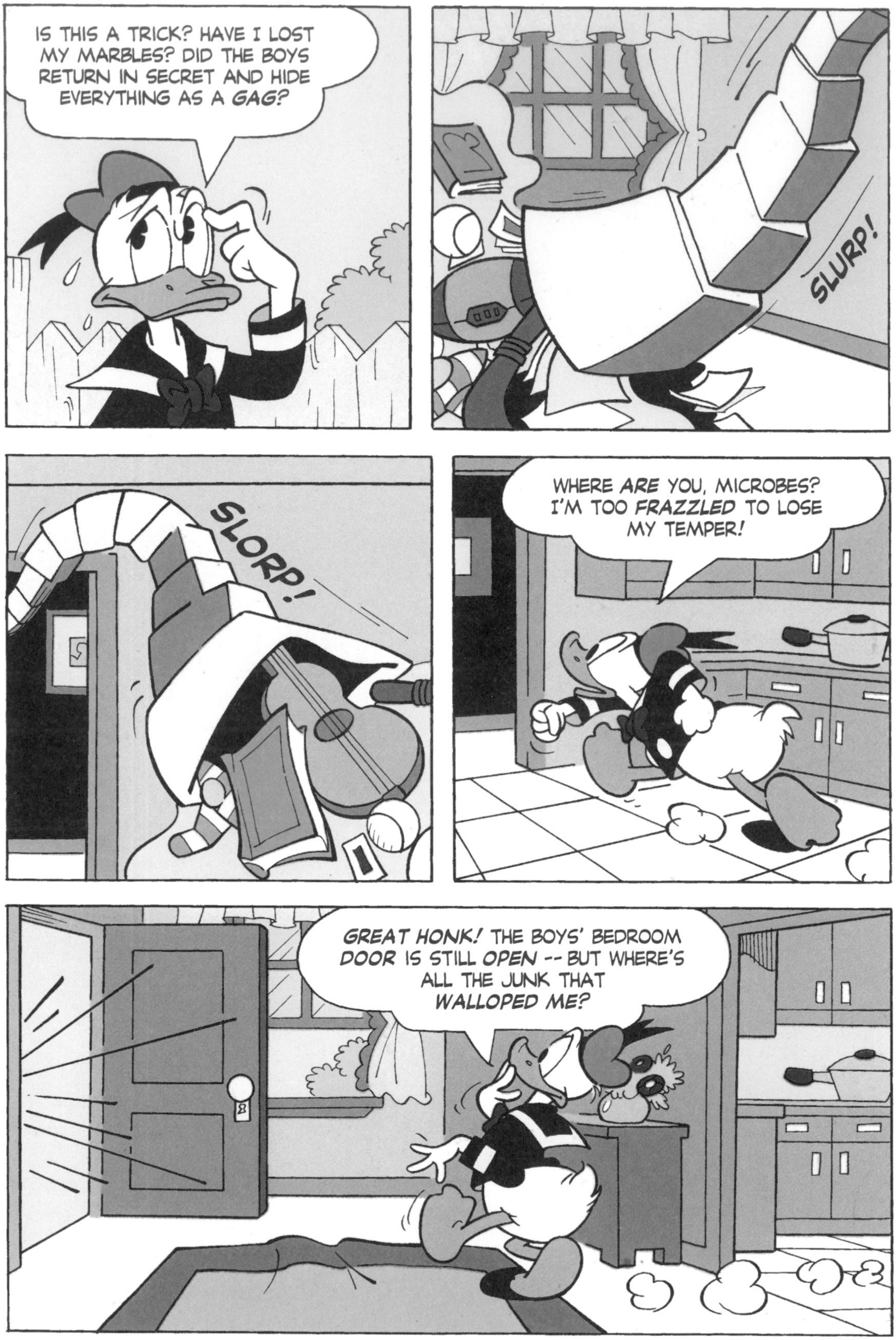
IS THIS A TRICK? HAVE I LOST MY MARBLES? DID THE BOYS RETURN IN SECRET AND HIDE EVERYTHING AS A *GAG?*
SLURP!
SLORP!
WHERE *ARE* YOU, MICROBES? I'M TOO *FRAZZLED* TO LOSE MY TEMPER!
GREAT HONK! THE BOYS' BEDROOM *DOOR* IS STILL *OPEN* -- BUT WHERE'S ALL THE JUNK THAT *WALLOPED ME?*

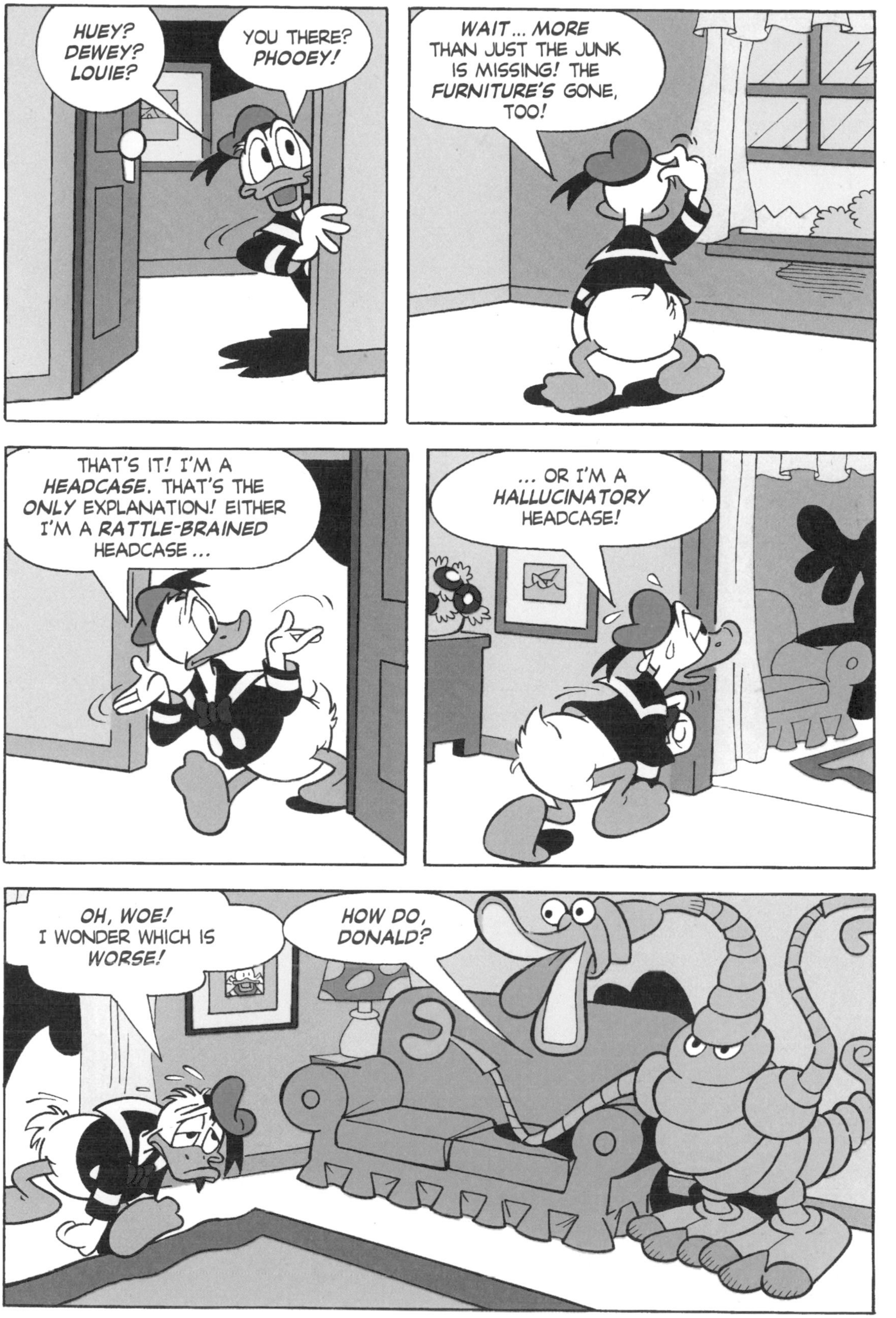
HUEY? DEWEY? LOUIE?
YOU THERE? PHOOEY!
WAIT ... MORE THAN JUST THE JUNK IS MISSING! THE FURNITURE'S GONE, TOO!
THAT'S IT! I'M A HEADCASE. THAT'S THE ONLY EXPLANATION! EITHER I'M A RATTLE-BRAINED HEADCASE ...
... OR I'M A HALLUCINATORY HEADCASE!
OH, WOE! I WONDER WHICH IS WORSE!
HOW DO, DONALD?

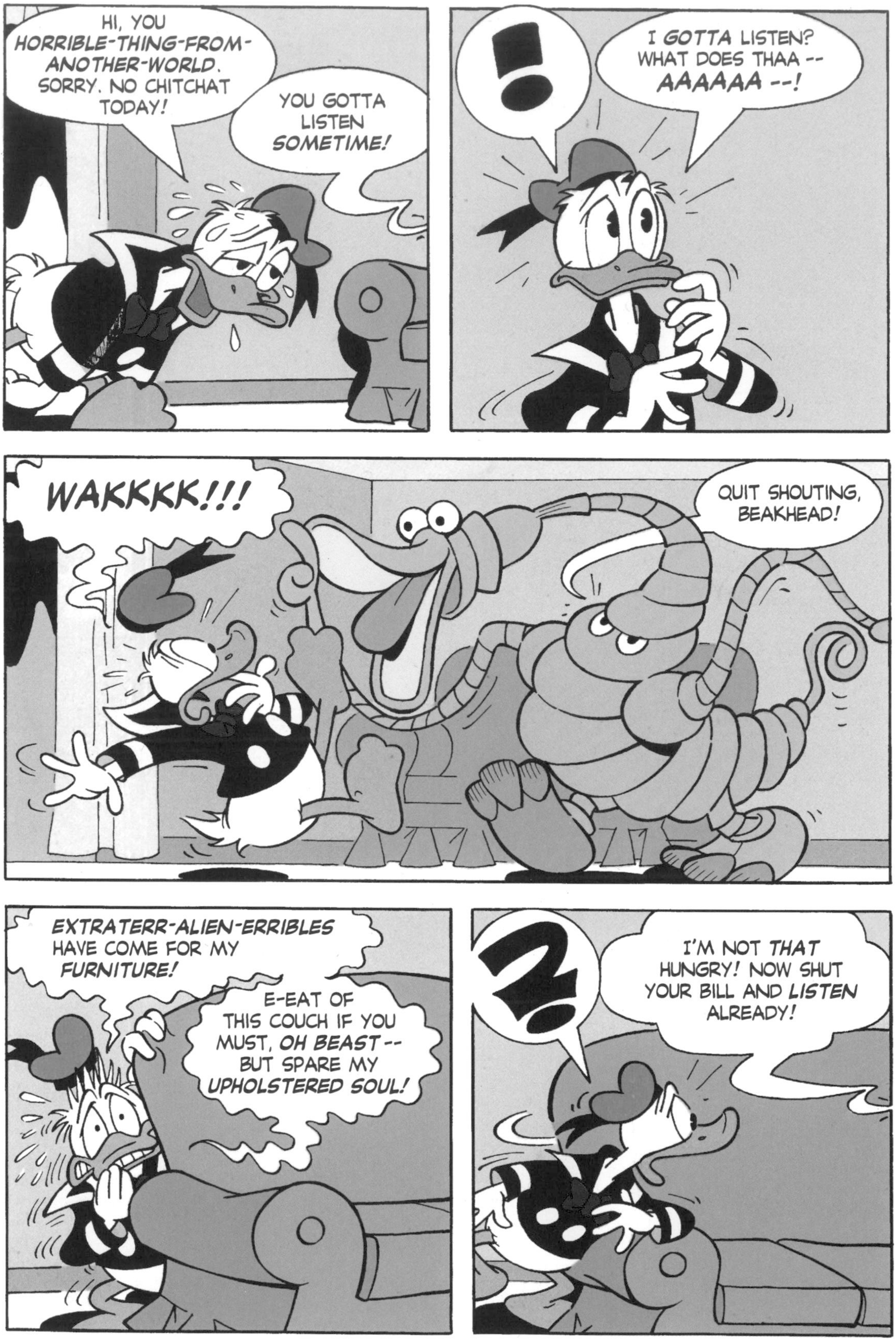

HI, YOU HORRIBLE-THING-FROM-ANOTHER-WORLD. SORRY. NO CHITCHAT TODAY!
YOU GOTTA LISTEN SOMETIME!
!
I GOTTA LISTEN? WHAT DOES THAA -- AAAAAA --!
WAKKKK!!!
QUIT SHOUTING, BEAKHEAD!
EXTRATERR-ALIEN-ERRIBLES HAVE COME FOR MY FURNITURE!
E-EAT OF THIS COUCH IF YOU MUST, OH BEAST -- BUT SPARE MY UPHOLSTERED SOUL!
?
I'M NOT THAT HUNGRY! NOW SHUT YOUR BILL AND LISTEN ALREADY!

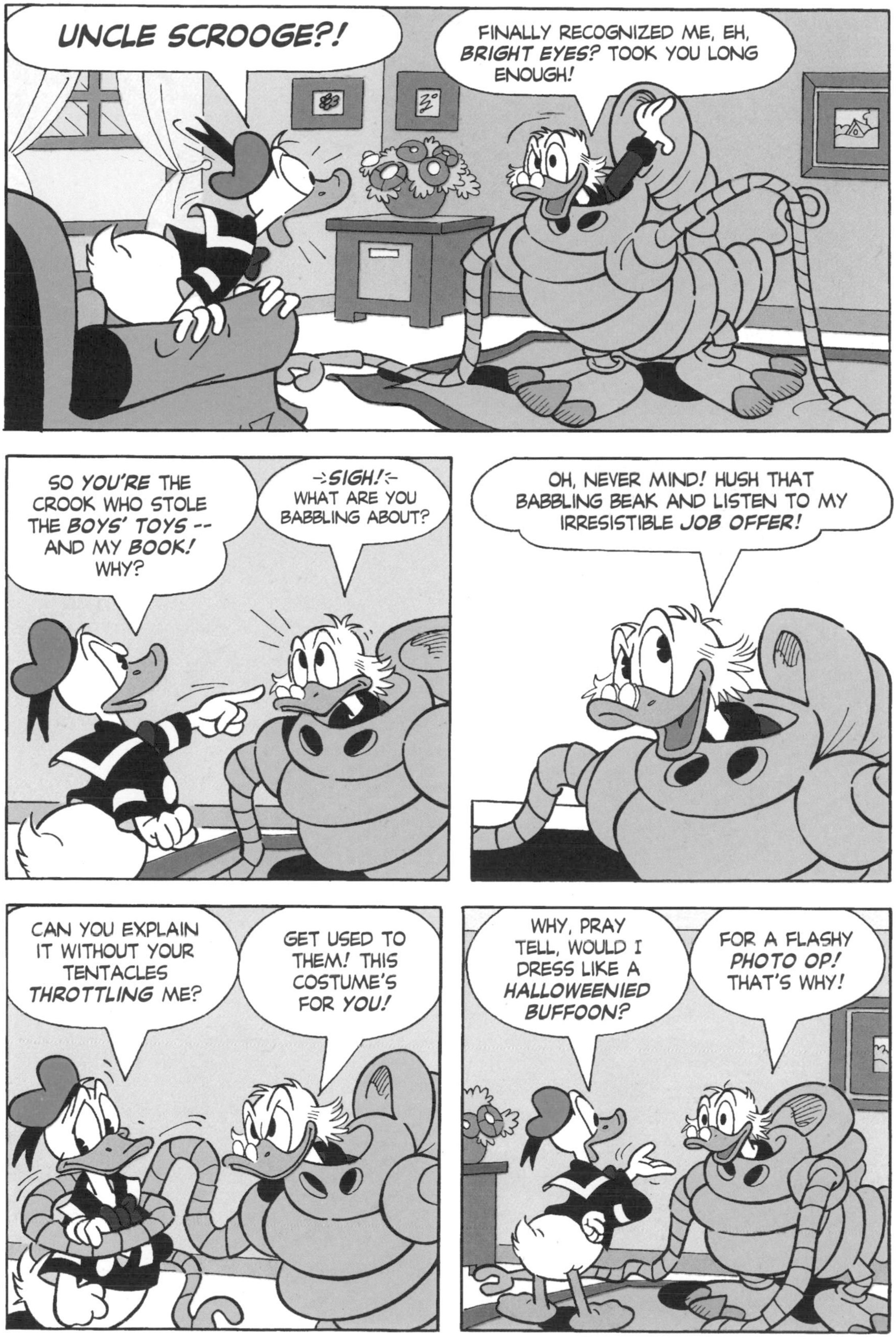
UNCLE SCROOGE?!
FINALLY RECOGNIZED ME, EH, BRIGHT EYES? TOOK YOU LONG ENOUGH!
SO YOU'RE THE CROOK WHO STOLE THE BOYS' TOYS -- AND MY BOOK! WHY?
-SIGH!- WHAT ARE YOU BABBLING ABOUT?
OH, NEVER MIND! HUSH THAT BABBLING BEAK AND LISTEN TO MY IRRESISTIBLE JOB OFFER!
CAN YOU EXPLAIN IT WITHOUT YOUR TENTACLES THROTTLING ME?
GET USED TO THEM! THIS COSTUME'S FOR YOU!
WHY, PRAY TELL, WOULD I DRESS LIKE A HALLOWEENIED BUFFOON?
FOR A FLASHY PHOTO OP! THAT'S WHY!

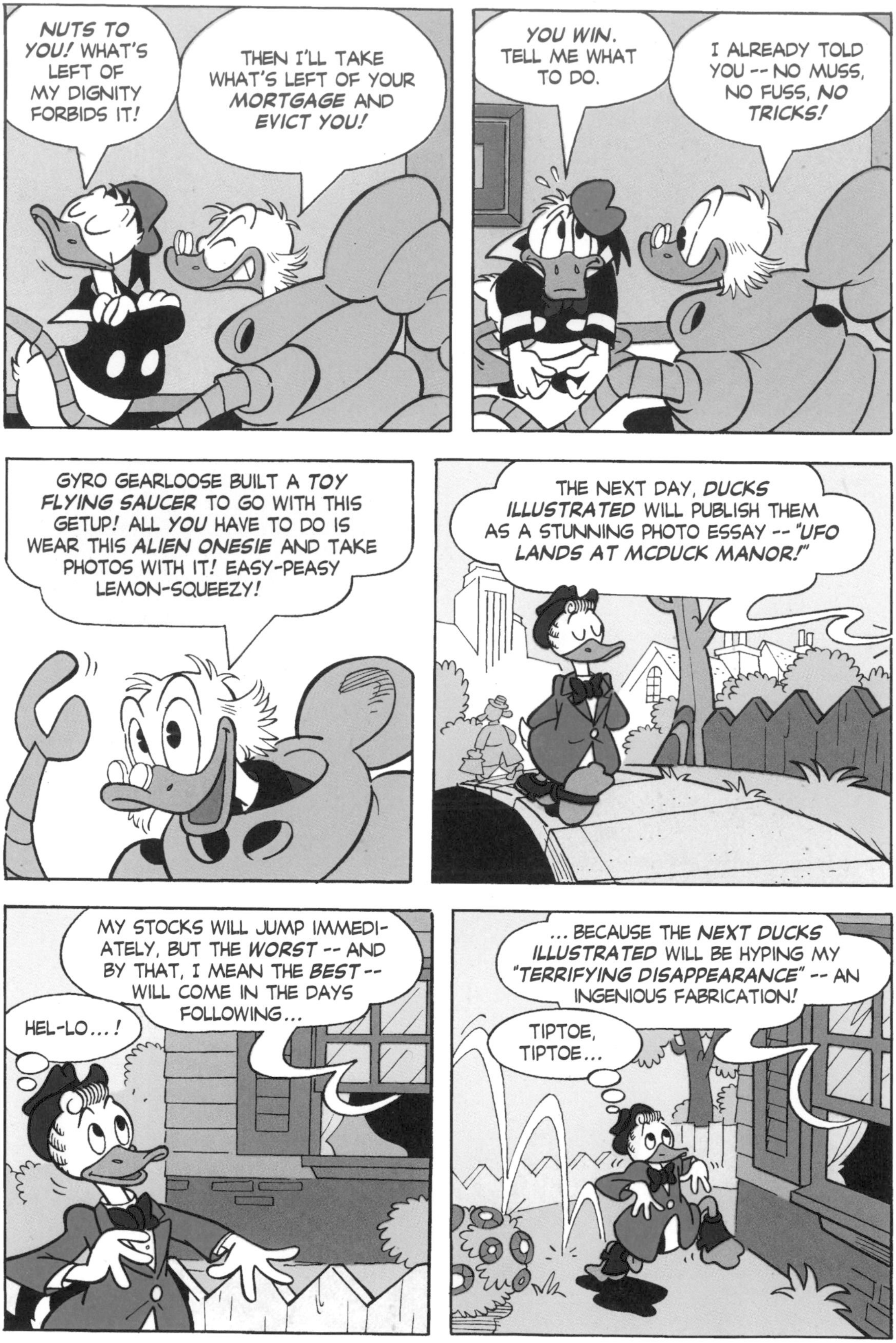
NUTS TO YOU! WHAT'S LEFT OF MY DIGNITY FORBIDS IT!
THEN I'LL TAKE WHAT'S LEFT OF YOUR MORTGAGE AND EVICT YOU!
YOU WIN. TELL ME WHAT TO DO.
I ALREADY TOLD YOU -- NO MUSS, NO FUSS, NO TRICKS!
GYRO GEARLOOSE BUILT A TOY FLYING SAUCER TO GO WITH THIS GETUP! ALL YOU HAVE TO DO IS WEAR THIS ALIEN ONESIE AND TAKE PHOTOS WITH IT! EASY-PEASY LEMON-SQUEEZY!
THE NEXT DAY, DUCKS ILLUSTRATED WILL PUBLISH THEM AS A STUNNING PHOTO ESSAY -- "UFO LANDS AT MCDUCK MANOR!"
MY STOCKS WILL JUMP IMMEDI-ATELY, BUT THE WORST -- AND BY THAT, I MEAN THE BEST -- WILL COME IN THE DAYS FOLLOWING...
HEL-LO...!
...BECAUSE THE NEXT DUCKS ILLUSTRATED WILL BE HYPING MY "TERRIFYING DISAPPEARANCE" -- AN INGENIOUS FABRICATION!
TIPTOE, TIPTOE...

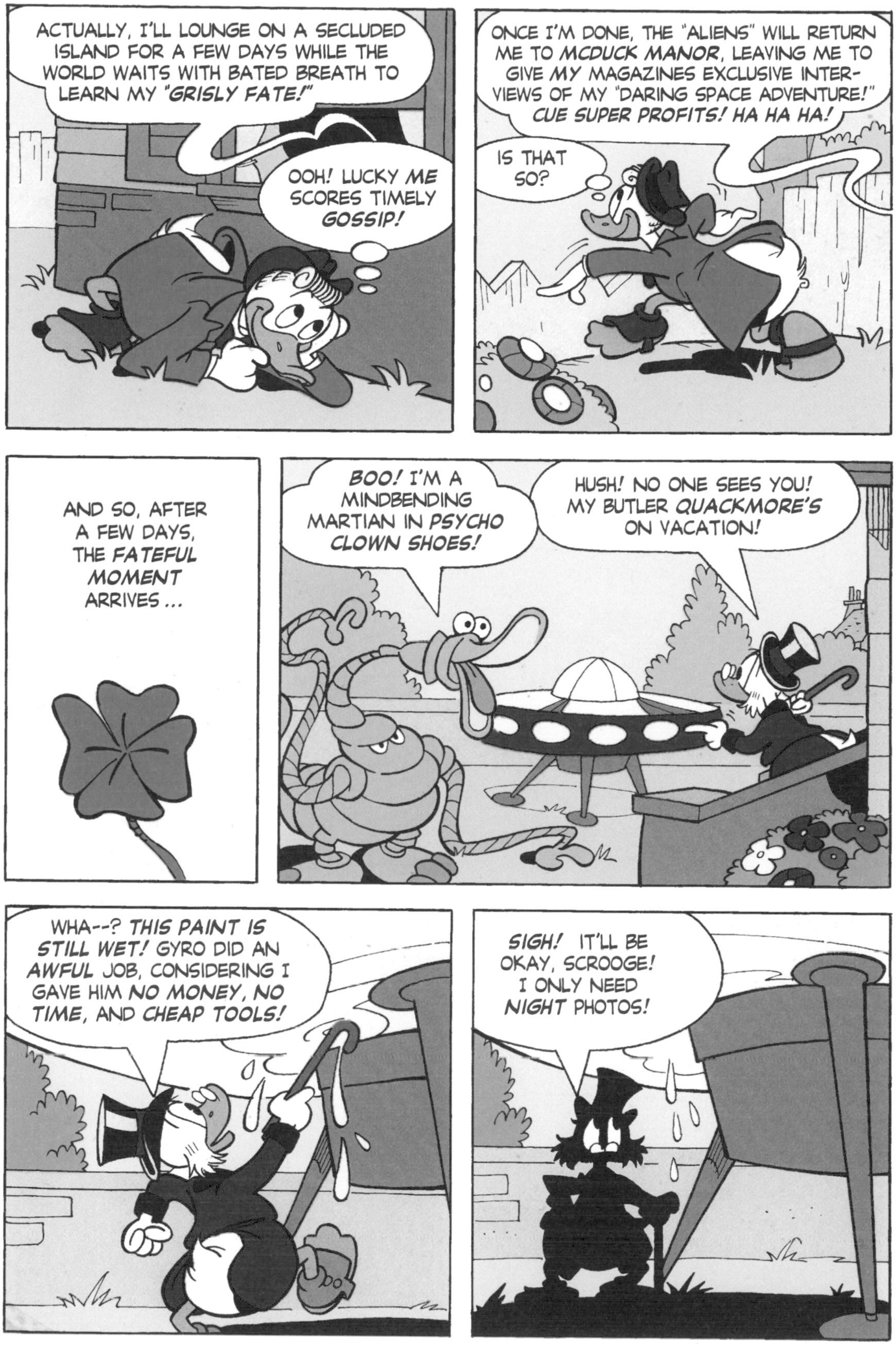
ACTUALLY, I'LL LOUNGE ON A SECLUDED ISLAND FOR A FEW DAYS WHILE THE WORLD WAITS WITH BATED BREATH TO LEARN MY "GRISLY FATE!"
OOH! LUCKY ME SCORES TIMELY GOSSIP!
ONCE I'M DONE, THE "ALIENS" WILL RETURN ME TO MCDUCK MANOR, LEAVING ME TO GIVE MY MAGAZINES EXCLUSIVE INTERVIEWS OF MY "DARING SPACE ADVENTURE!" CUE SUPER PROFITS! HA HA HA!
IS THAT SO?
AND SO, AFTER A FEW DAYS, THE FATEFUL MOMENT ARRIVES ...
BOO! I'M A MINDBENDING MARTIAN IN PSYCHO CLOWN SHOES!
HUSH! NO ONE SEES YOU! MY BUTLER QUACKMORE'S ON VACATION!
WHA--? THIS PAINT IS STILL WET! GYRO DID AN AWFUL JOB, CONSIDERING I GAVE HIM NO MONEY, NO TIME, AND CHEAP TOOLS!
SIGH! IT'LL BE OKAY, SCROOGE! I ONLY NEED NIGHT PHOTOS!

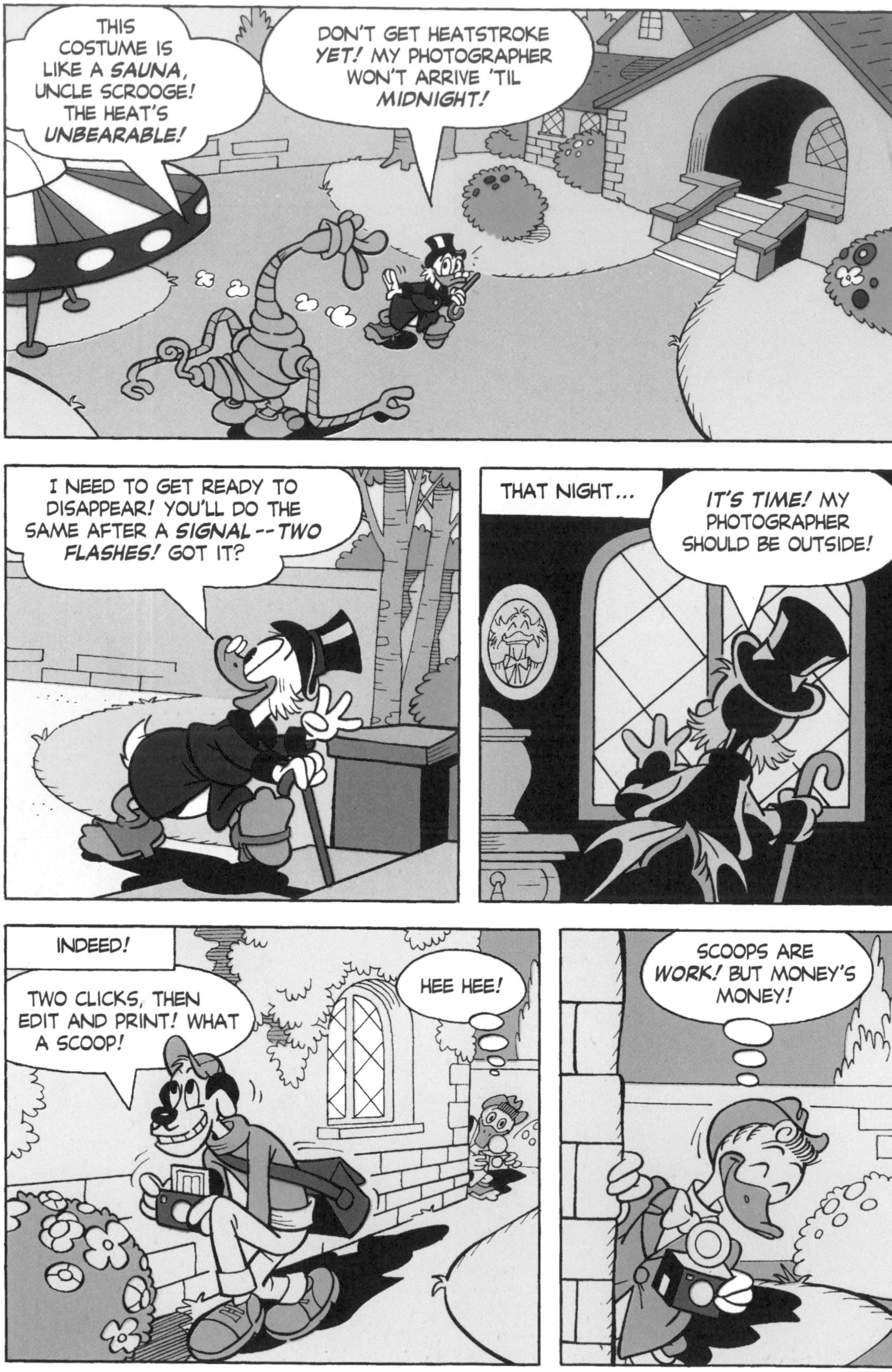

THIS COSTUME IS LIKE A *SAUNA*, UNCLE SCROOGE! THE HEAT'S *UNBEARABLE!*
DON'T GET HEATSTROKE *YET!* MY PHOTOGRAPHER WON'T ARRIVE 'TIL *MIDNIGHT!*
I NEED TO GET READY TO DISAPPEAR! YOU'LL DO THE SAME AFTER A *SIGNAL--TWO FLASHES!* GOT IT?
THAT NIGHT...
IT'S TIME! MY PHOTOGRAPHER SHOULD BE OUTSIDE!
INDEED!
TWO CLICKS, THEN EDIT AND PRINT! WHAT A SCOOP!
HEE HEE!
SCOOPS ARE *WORK!* BUT MONEY'S MONEY!

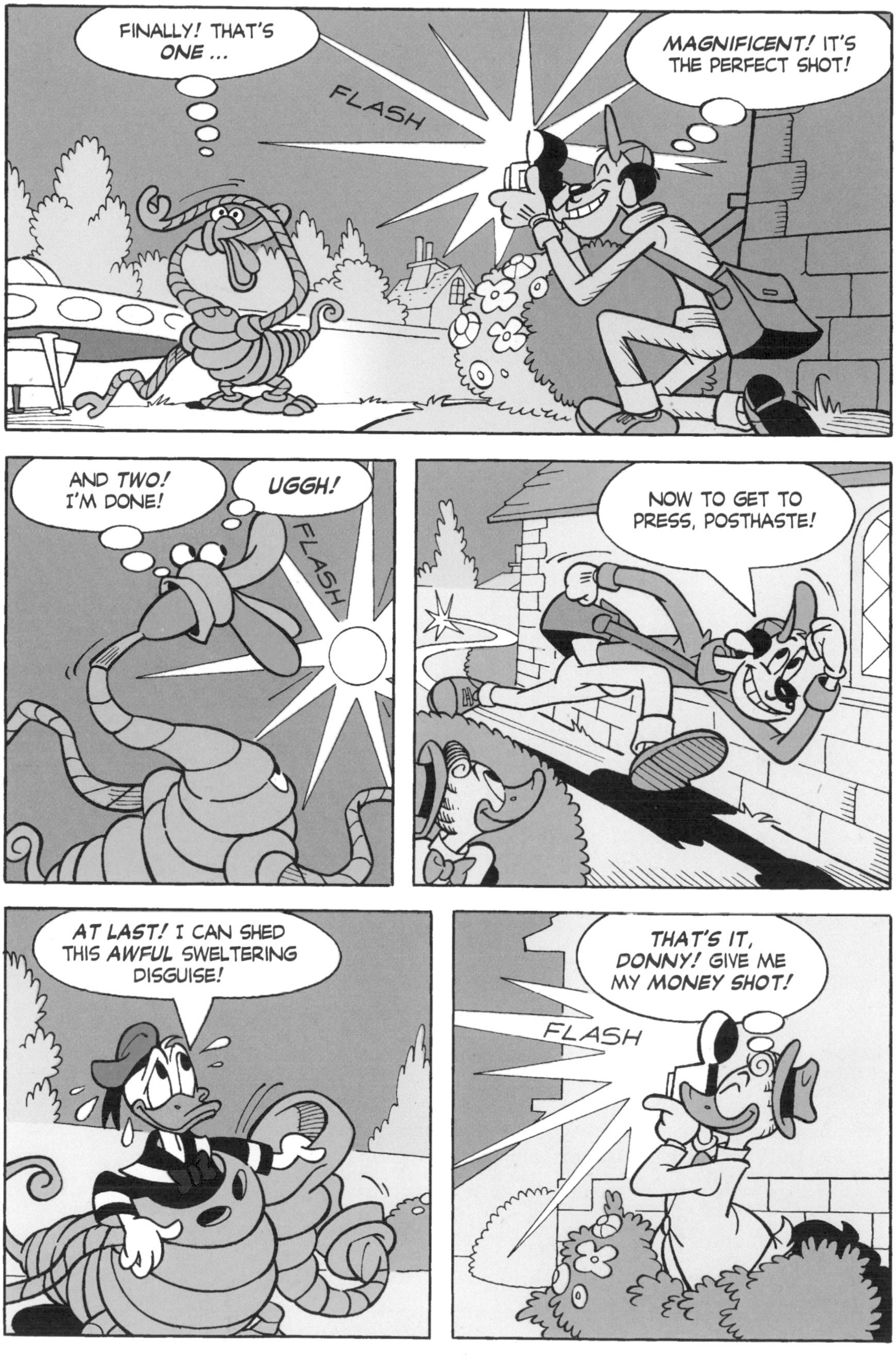
FINALLY! THAT'S ONE ...
FLASH
MAGNIFICENT! IT'S THE PERFECT SHOT!
AND TWO! I'M DONE!
UGGH!
FLASH
NOW TO GET TO PRESS, POSTHASTE!
AT LAST! I CAN SHED THIS AWFUL SWELTERING DISGUISE!
THAT'S IT, DONNY! GIVE ME MY MONEY SHOT!
FLASH

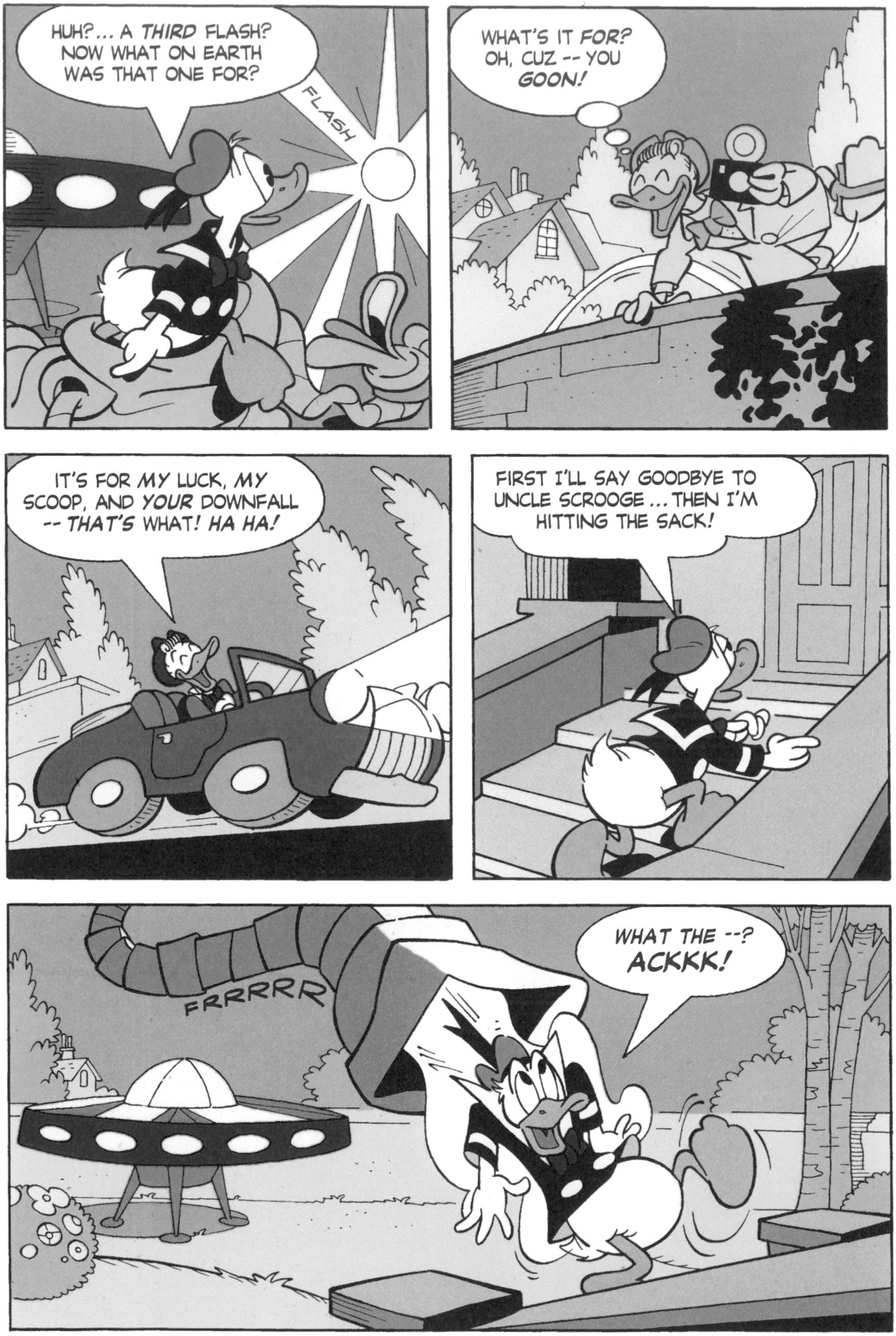
HUH?... A THIRD FLASH? NOW WHAT ON EARTH WAS THAT ONE FOR?
FLASH
WHAT'S IT FOR? OH, CUZ -- YOU GOON!
IT'S FOR MY LUCK, MY SCOOP, AND YOUR DOWNFALL -- THAT'S WHAT! HA HA!
FIRST I'LL SAY GOODBYE TO UNCLE SCROOGE ... THEN I'M HITTING THE SACK!
FRRRRR
WHAT THE --? ACKKK!

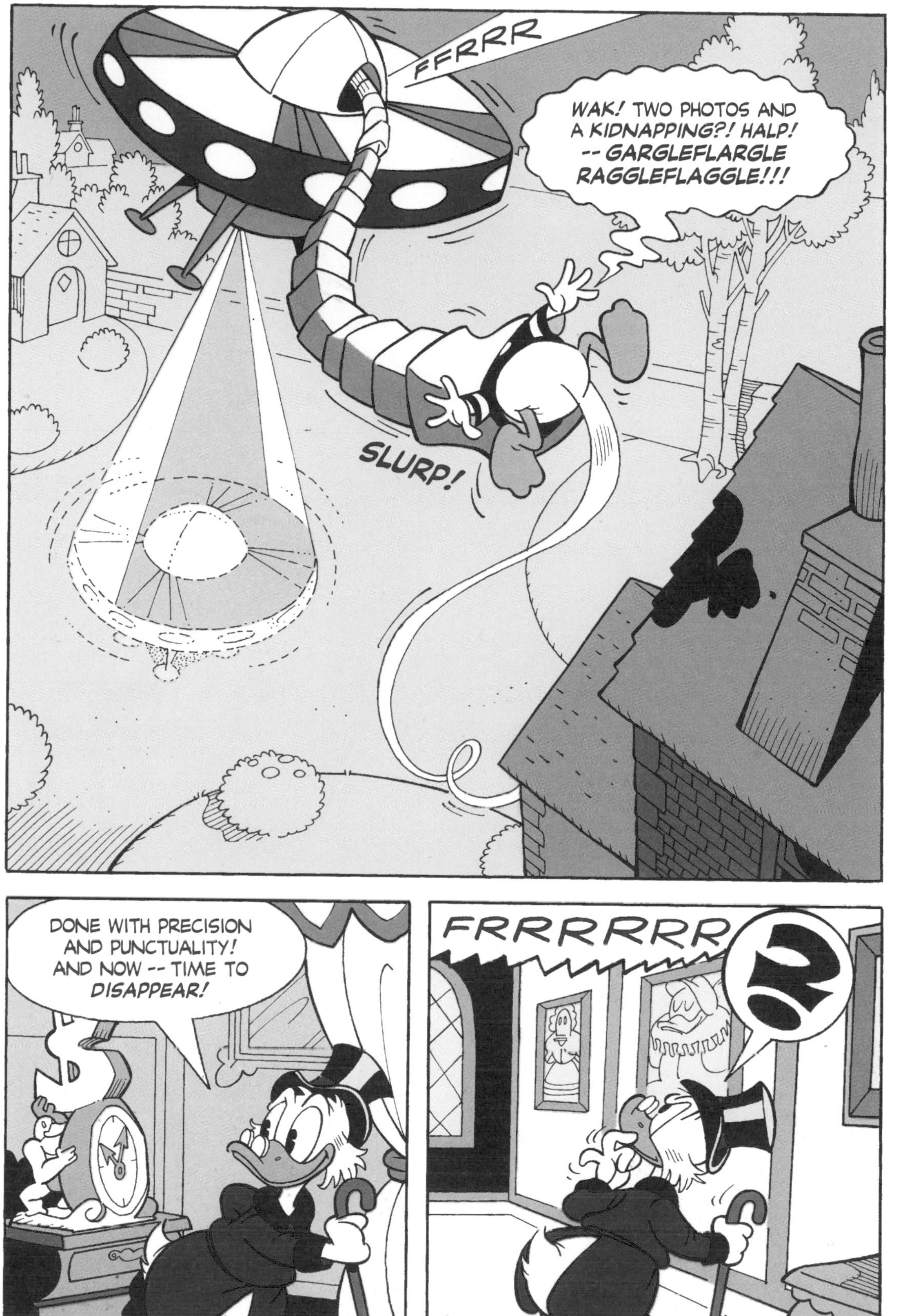
FFRRR
WAK! TWO PHOTOS AND A KIDNAPPING?! HALP! -- GARGLEFLARGLE RAGGLEFLAGGLE!!!
SLURP!
DONE WITH PRECISION AND PUNCTUALITY! AND NOW -- TIME TO DISAPPEAR!
FRRRRRRR
?

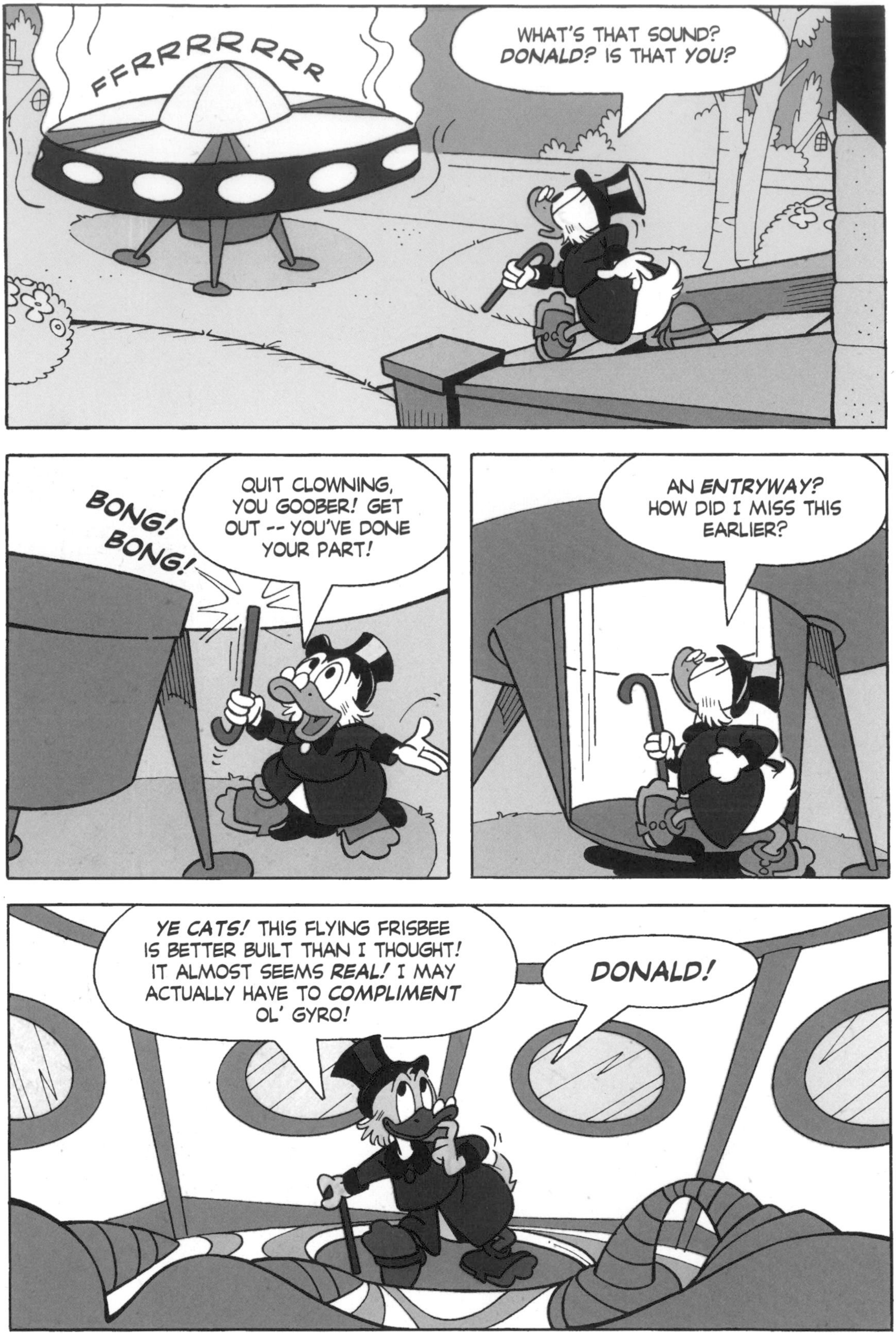
FFRRRRRRRR
WHAT'S THAT SOUND? DONALD? IS THAT YOU?
BONG! BONG!
QUIT CLOWNING, YOU GOOBER! GET OUT -- YOU'VE DONE YOUR PART!
AN ENTRYWAY? HOW DID I MISS THIS EARLIER?
YE CATS! THIS FLYING FRISBEE IS BETTER BUILT THAN I THOUGHT! IT ALMOST SEEMS REAL! I MAY ACTUALLY HAVE TO COMPLIMENT OL' GYRO!
DONALD!

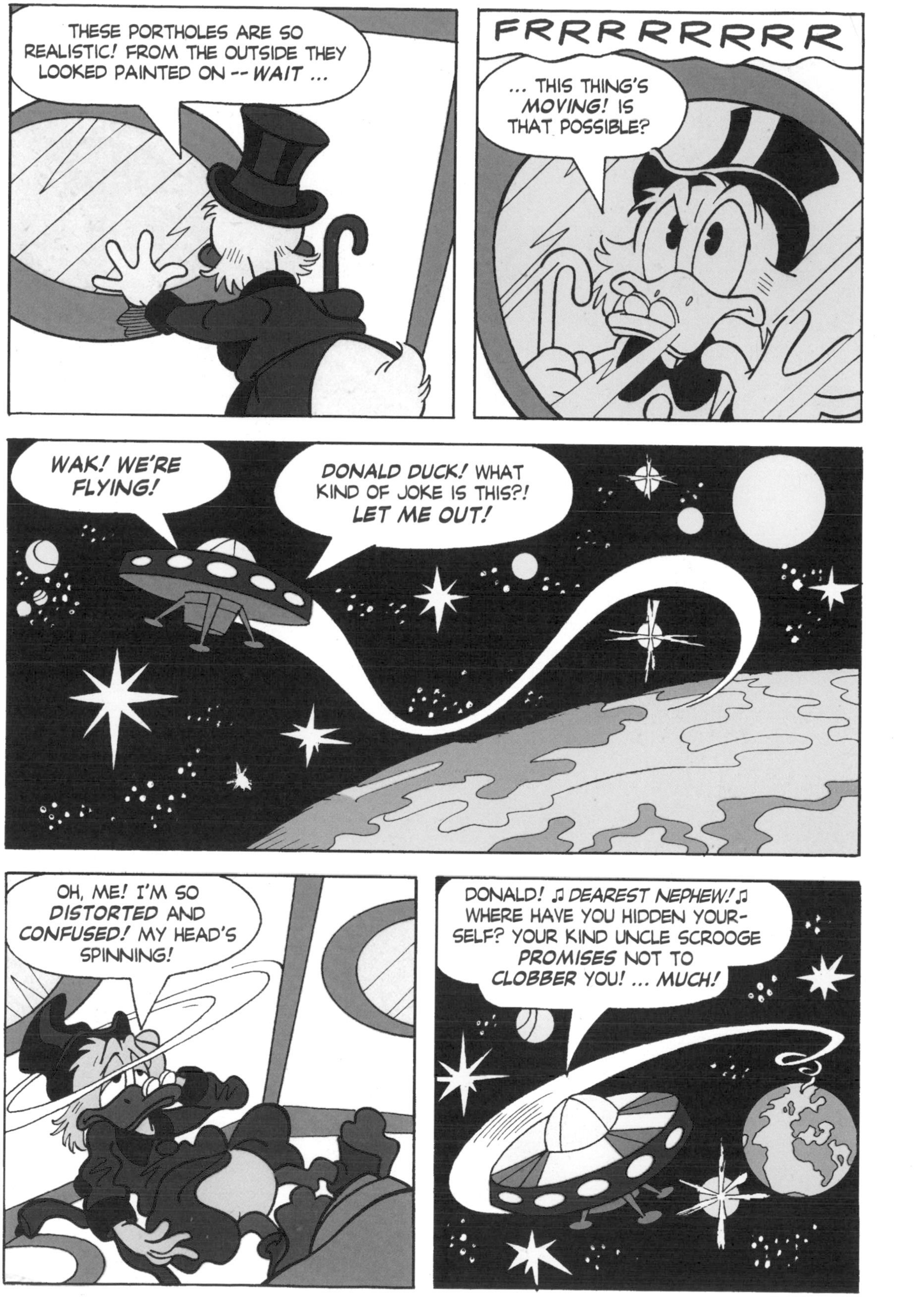
THESE PORTHOLES ARE SO REALISTIC! FROM THE OUTSIDE THEY LOOKED PAINTED ON -- WAIT ...
FRRRRRRRR
... THIS THING'S MOVING! IS THAT POSSIBLE?
WAK! WE'RE FLYING!
DONALD DUCK! WHAT KIND OF JOKE IS THIS?! LET ME OUT!
OH, ME! I'M SO DISTORTED AND CONFUSED! MY HEAD'S SPINNING!
DONALD! ♫ DEAREST NEPHEW! ♫ WHERE HAVE YOU HIDDEN YOURSELF? YOUR KIND UNCLE SCROOGE PROMISES NOT TO CLOBBER YOU! ... MUCH!

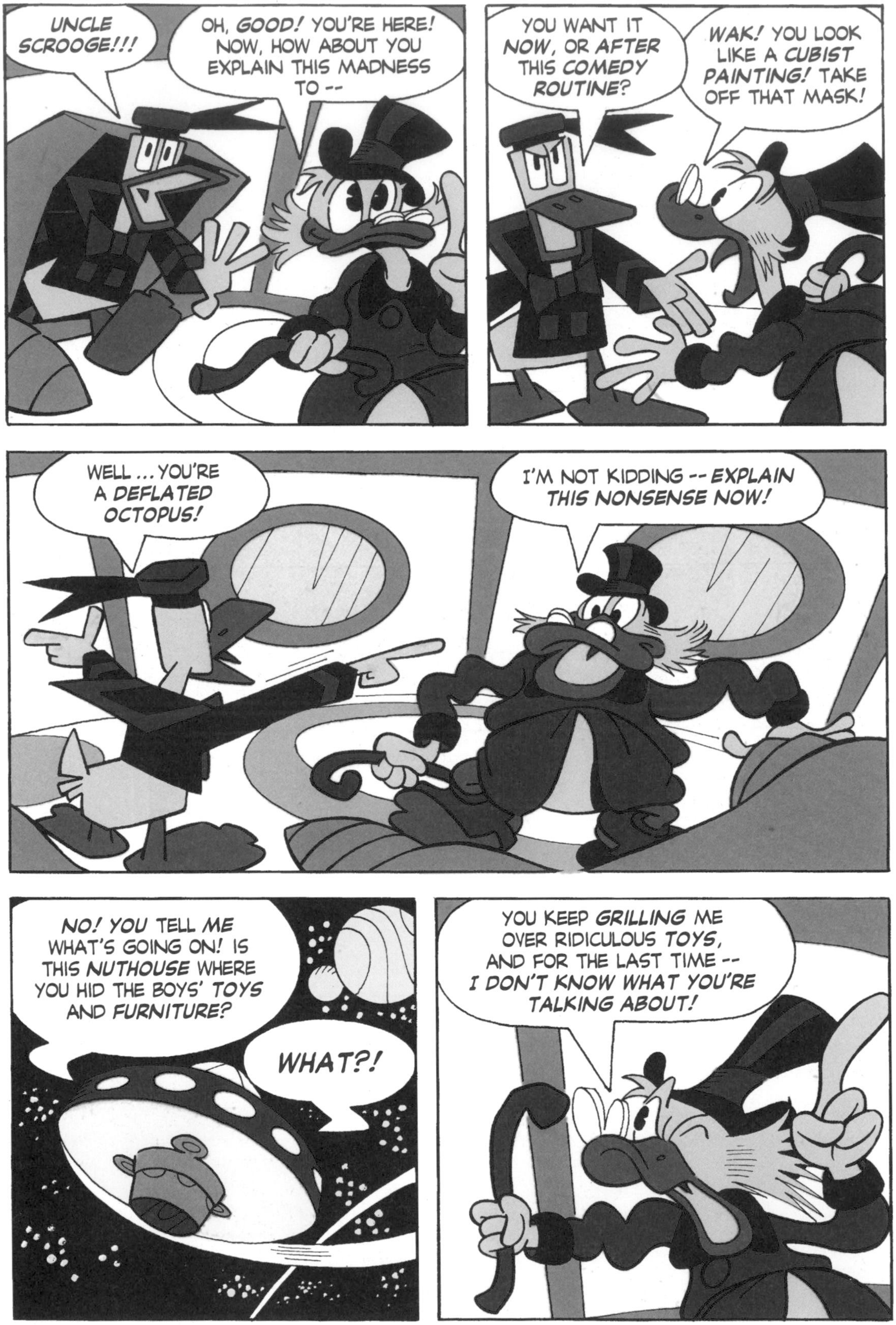
UNCLE SCROOGE!!!
OH, GOOD! YOU'RE HERE! NOW, HOW ABOUT YOU EXPLAIN THIS MADNESS TO --
YOU WANT IT NOW, OR AFTER THIS COMEDY ROUTINE?
WAK! YOU LOOK LIKE A CUBIST PAINTING! TAKE OFF THAT MASK!
WELL ... YOU'RE A DEFLATED OCTOPUS!
I'M NOT KIDDING -- EXPLAIN THIS NONSENSE NOW!
NO! YOU TELL ME WHAT'S GOING ON! IS THIS NUTHOUSE WHERE YOU HID THE BOYS' TOYS AND FURNITURE?
WHAT?!
YOU KEEP GRILLING ME OVER RIDICULOUS TOYS, AND FOR THE LAST TIME -- I DON'T KNOW WHAT YOU'RE TALKING ABOUT!

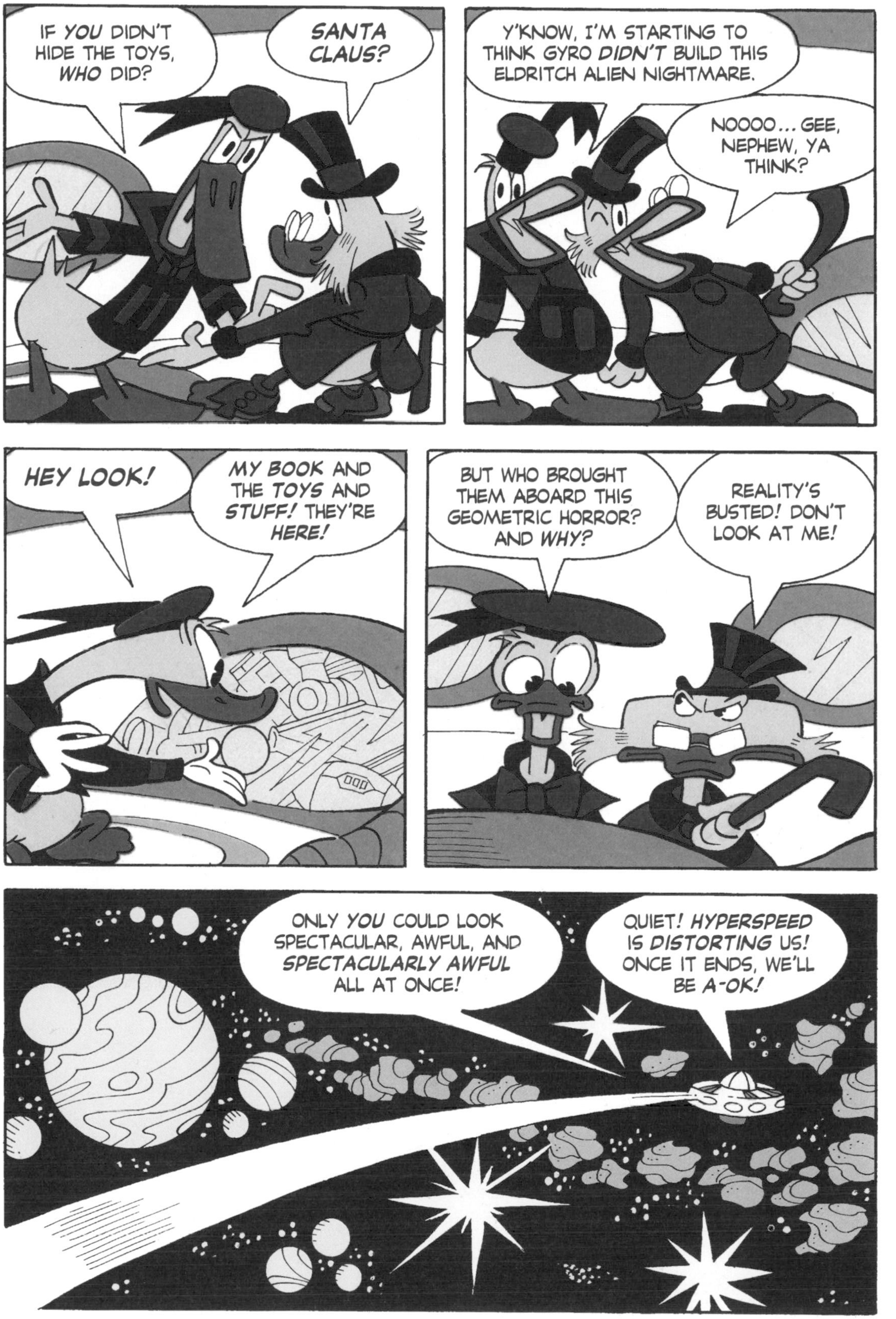
IF YOU DIDN'T HIDE THE TOYS, WHO DID?
SANTA CLAUS?
Y'KNOW, I'M STARTING TO THINK GYRO DIDN'T BUILD THIS ELDRITCH ALIEN NIGHTMARE.
NOOOO... GEE, NEPHEW, YA THINK?
HEY LOOK!
MY BOOK AND THE TOYS AND STUFF! THEY'RE HERE!
BUT WHO BROUGHT THEM ABOARD THIS GEOMETRIC HORROR? AND WHY?
REALITY'S BUSTED! DON'T LOOK AT ME!
ONLY YOU COULD LOOK SPECTACULAR, AWFUL, AND SPECTACULARLY AWFUL ALL AT ONCE!
QUIET! HYPERSPEED IS DISTORTING US! ONCE IT ENDS, WE'LL BE A-OK!

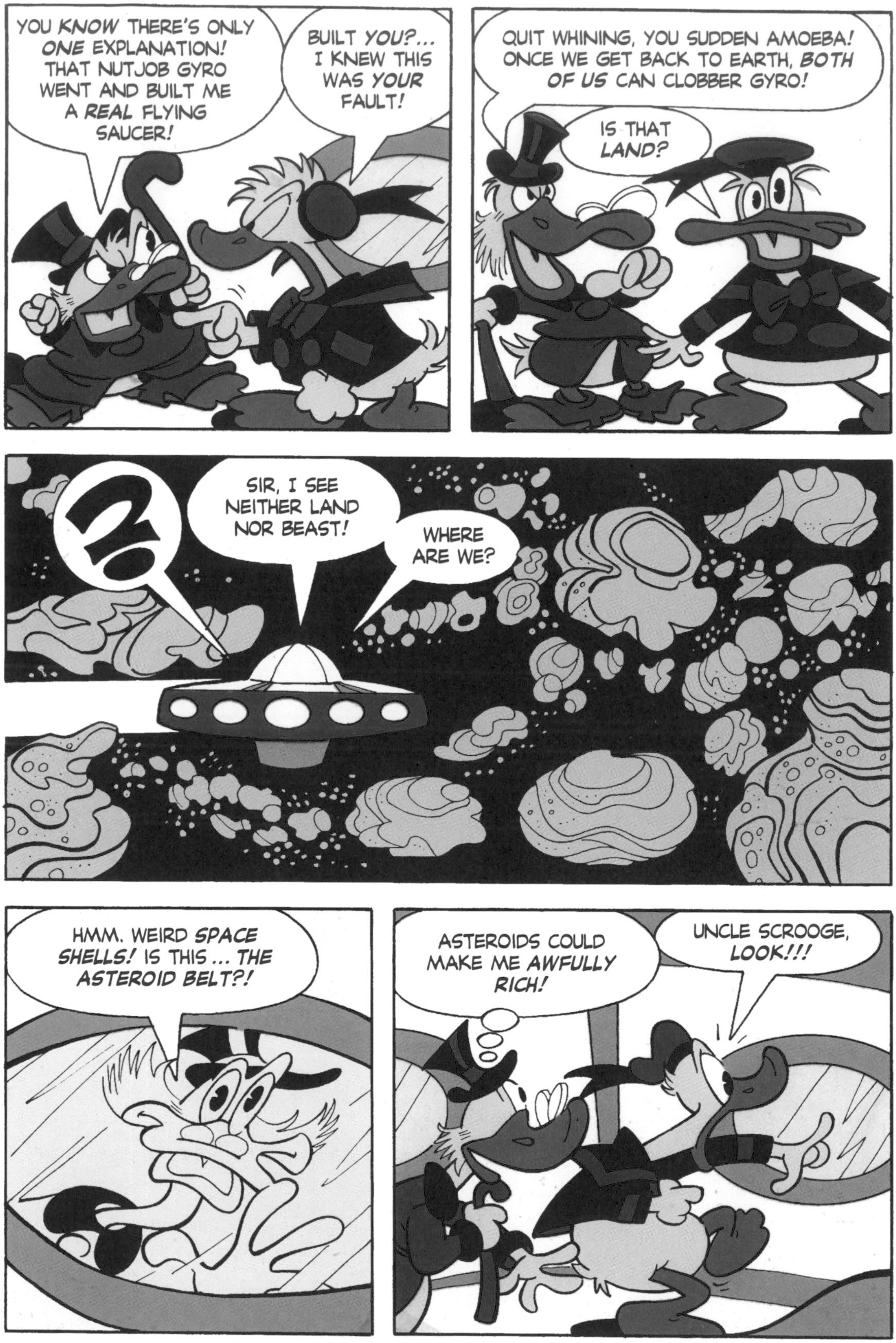
YOU KNOW THERE'S ONLY ONE EXPLANATION! THAT NUTJOB GYRO WENT AND BUILT ME A REAL FLYING SAUCER!
BUILT YOU?... I KNEW THIS WAS YOUR FAULT!
QUIT WHINING, YOU SUDDEN AMOEBA! ONCE WE GET BACK TO EARTH, BOTH OF US CAN CLOBBER GYRO!
IS THAT LAND?
?
SIR, I SEE NEITHER LAND NOR BEAST!
WHERE ARE WE?
HMM. WEIRD SPACE SHELLS! IS THIS ... THE ASTEROID BELT?!
ASTEROIDS COULD MAKE ME AWFULLY RICH!
UNCLE SCROOGE, LOOK!!!

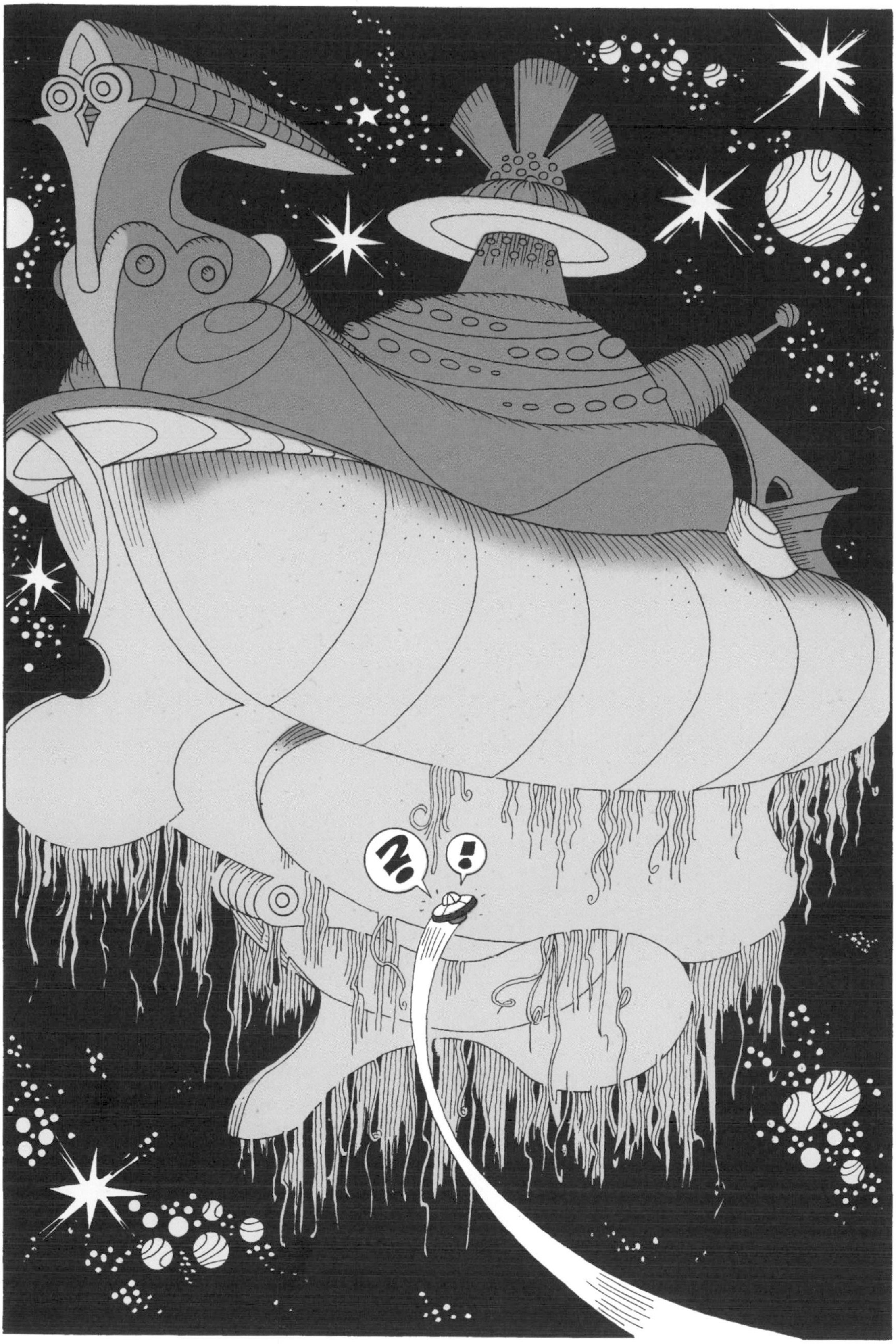
?
!

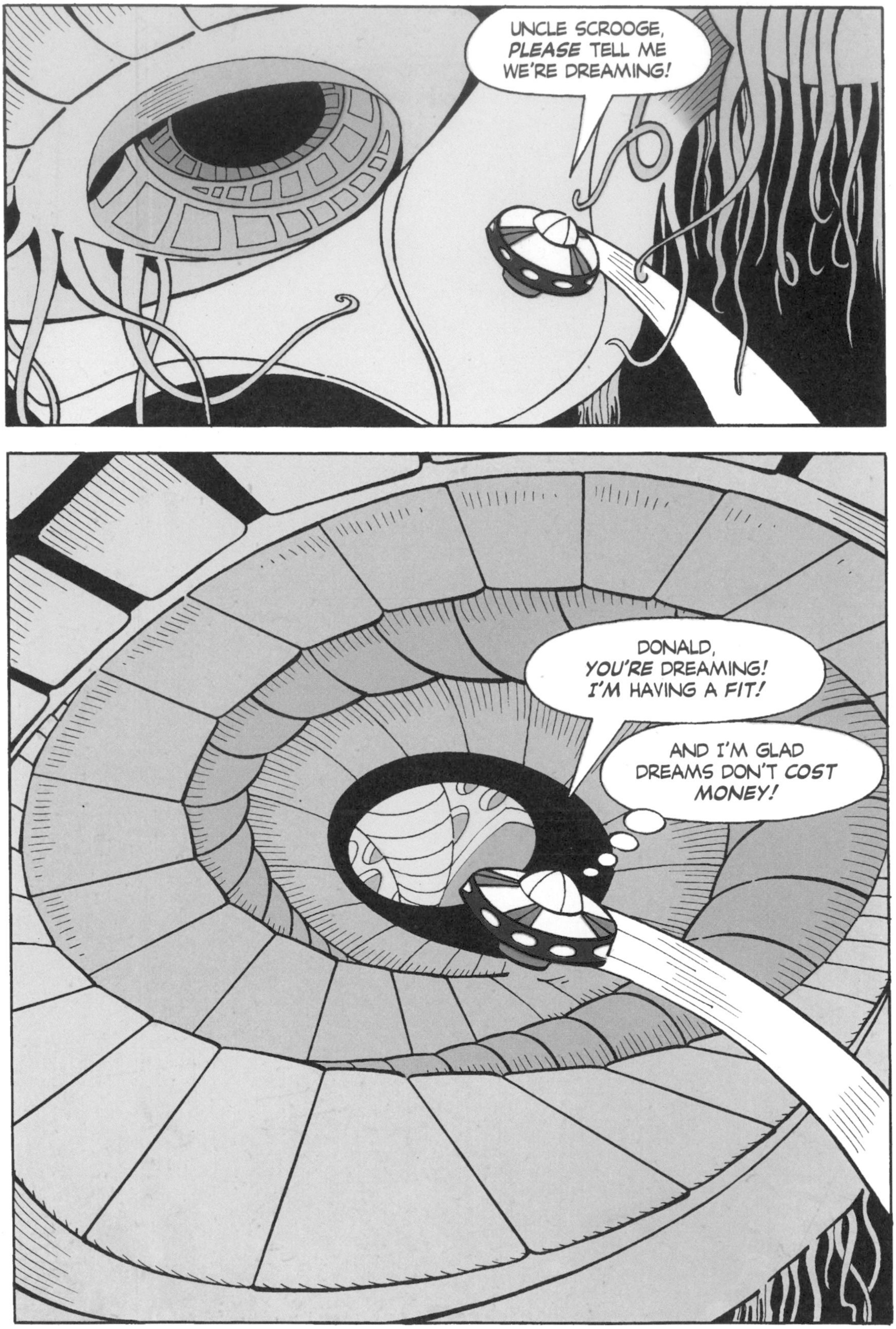
UNCLE SCROOGE, PLEASE TELL ME WE'RE DREAMING!
DONALD, YOU'RE DREAMING! I'M HAVING A FIT!
AND I'M GLAD DREAMS DON'T COST MONEY!

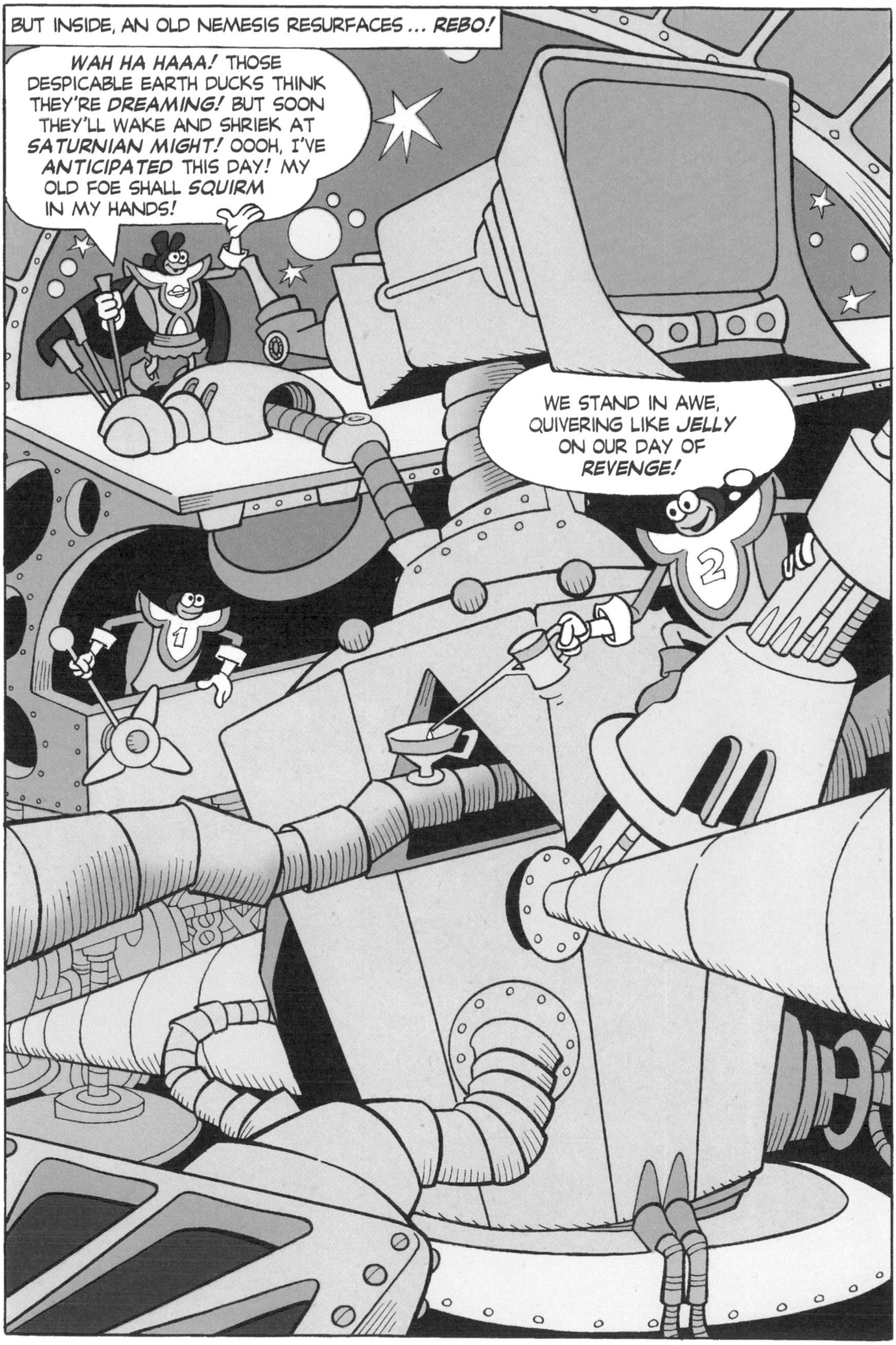

BUT INSIDE, AN OLD NEMESIS RESURFACES ... REBO!
WAH HA HAAA! THOSE DESPICABLE EARTH DUCKS THINK THEY'RE DREAMING! BUT SOON THEY'LL WAKE AND SHRIEK AT SATURNIAN MIGHT! OOOH, I'VE ANTICIPATED THIS DAY! MY OLD FOE SHALL SQUIRM IN MY HANDS!
WE STAND IN AWE, QUIVERING LIKE JELLY ON OUR DAY OF REVENGE!

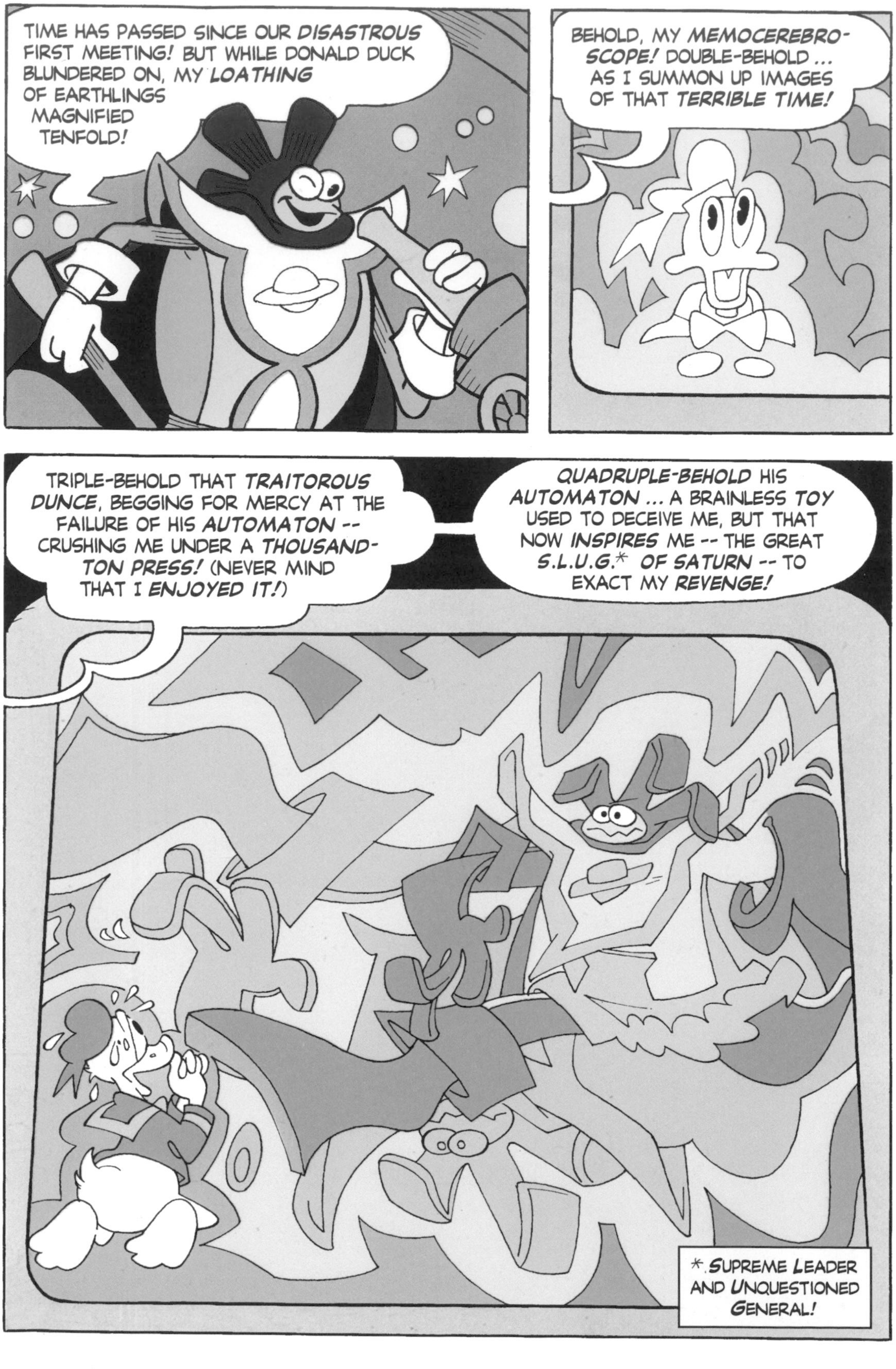

TIME HAS PASSED SINCE OUR DISASTROUS FIRST MEETING! BUT WHILE DONALD DUCK BLUNDERED ON, MY LOATHING OF EARTHLINGS MAGNIFIED TENFOLD!
BEHOLD, MY MEMOCEREBRO-SCOPE! DOUBLE-BEHOLD ... AS I SUMMON UP IMAGES OF THAT TERRIBLE TIME!
TRIPLE-BEHOLD THAT TRAITOROUS DUNCE, BEGGING FOR MERCY AT THE FAILURE OF HIS AUTOMATON -- CRUSHING ME UNDER A THOUSAND-TON PRESS! (NEVER MIND THAT I ENJOYED IT!)
QUADRUPLE-BEHOLD HIS AUTOMATON ... A BRAINLESS TOY USED TO DECEIVE ME, BUT THAT NOW INSPIRES ME -- THE GREAT S.L.U.G.* OF SATURN -- TO EXACT MY REVENGE!
*. SUPREME LEADER AND UNQUESTIONED GENERAL!

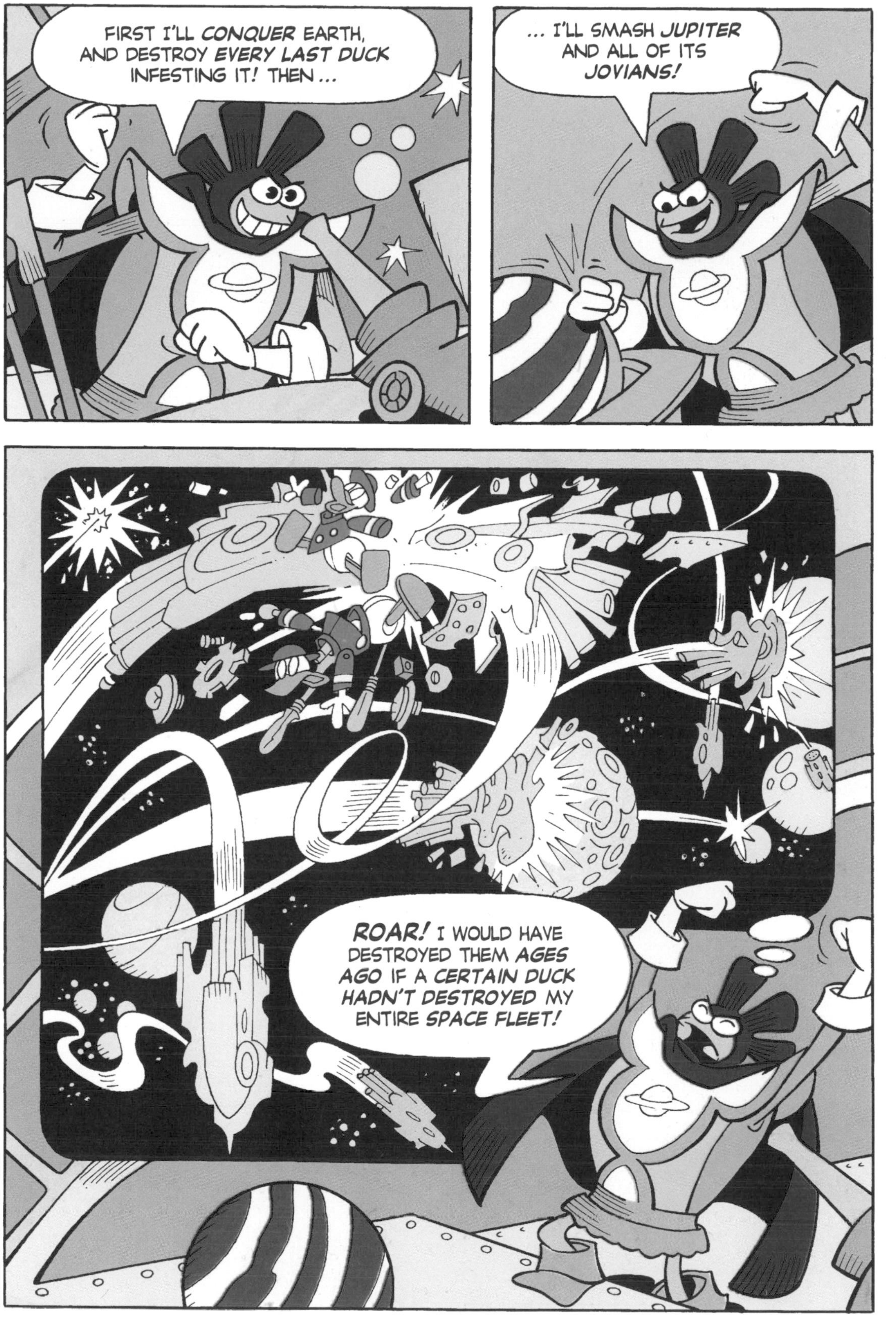
FIRST I'LL CONQUER EARTH, AND DESTROY EVERY LAST DUCK INFESTING IT! THEN ...
... I'LL SMASH JUPITER AND ALL OF ITS JOVIANS!
ROAR! I WOULD HAVE DESTROYED THEM AGES AGO IF A CERTAIN DUCK HADN'T DESTROYED MY ENTIRE SPACE FLEET!

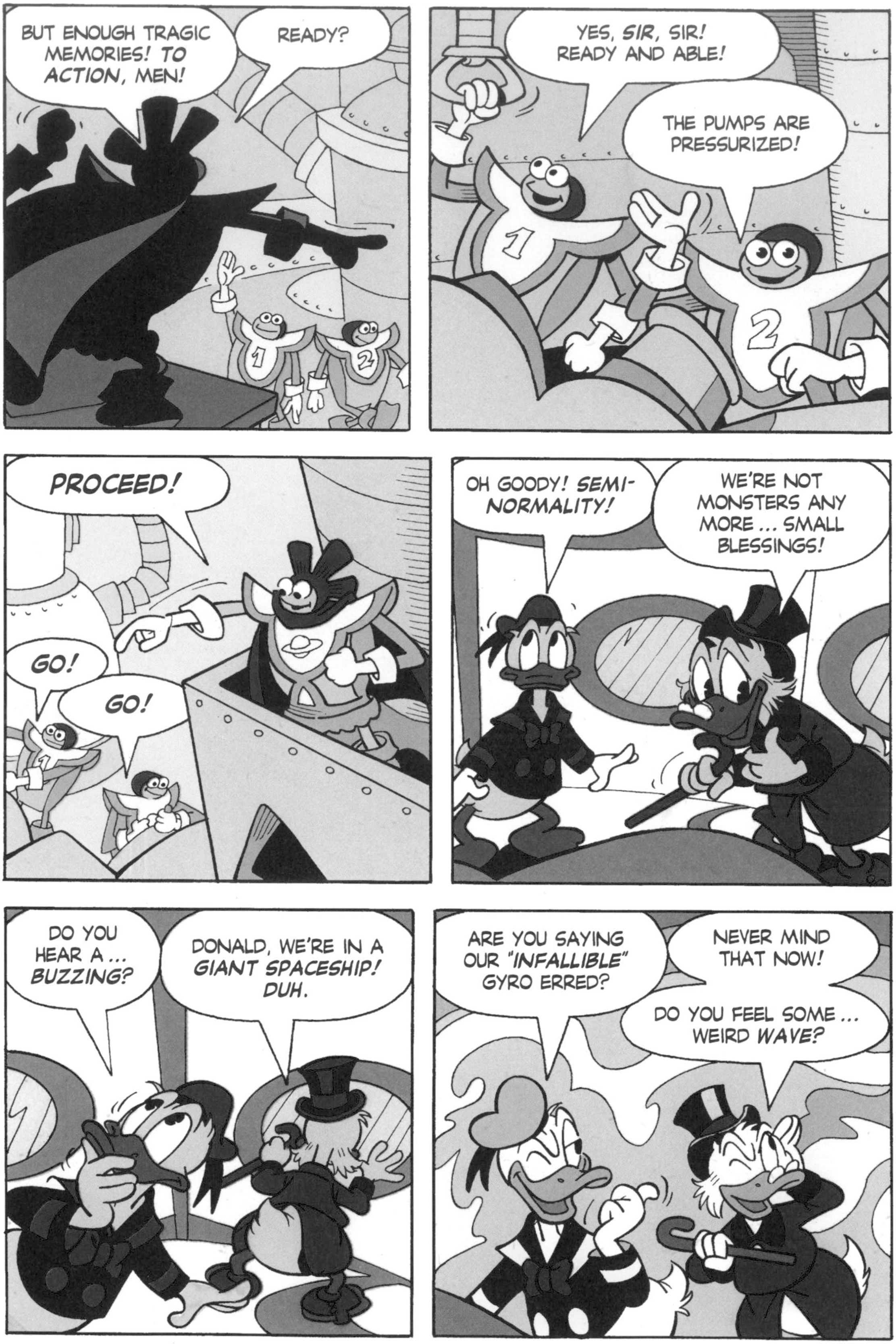
BUT ENOUGH TRAGIC MEMORIES! TO ACTION, MEN!
READY?
YES, SIR, SIR! READY AND ABLE!
THE PUMPS ARE PRESSURIZED!
PROCEED!
GO!
GO!
OH GOODY! SEMI-NORMALITY!
WE'RE NOT MONSTERS ANY MORE ... SMALL BLESSINGS!
DO YOU HEAR A ... BUZZING?
DONALD, WE'RE IN A GIANT SPACESHIP! DUH.
ARE YOU SAYING OUR "INFALLIBLE" GYRO ERRED?
NEVER MIND THAT NOW!
DO YOU FEEL SOME ... WEIRD WAVE?

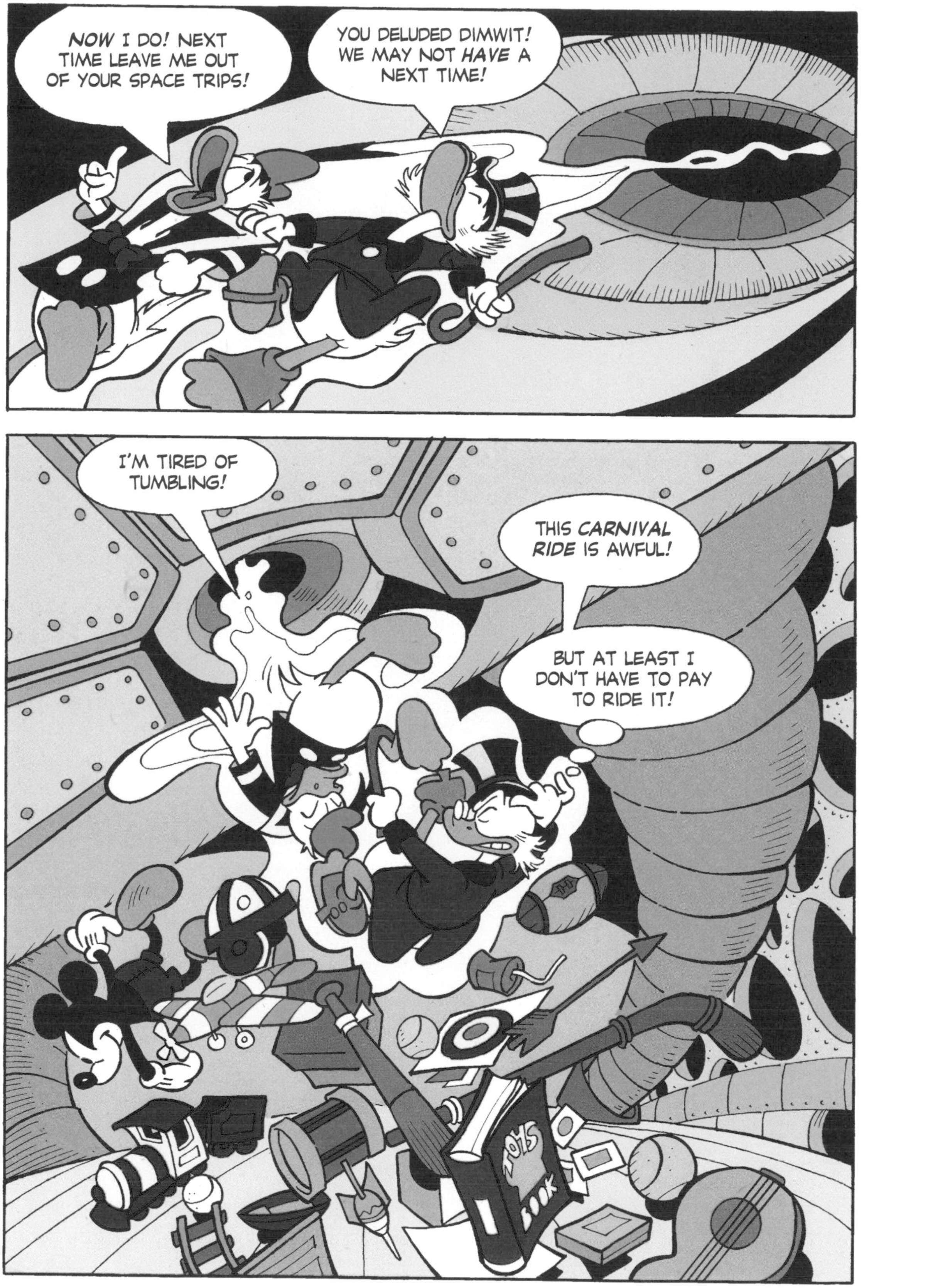
NOW I DO! NEXT TIME LEAVE ME OUT OF YOUR SPACE TRIPS!
YOU DELUDED DIMWIT! WE MAY NOT HAVE A NEXT TIME!
I'M TIRED OF TUMBLING!
THIS CARNIVAL RIDE IS AWFUL!
BUT AT LEAST I DON'T HAVE TO PAY TO RIDE IT!
TOYS BOOK

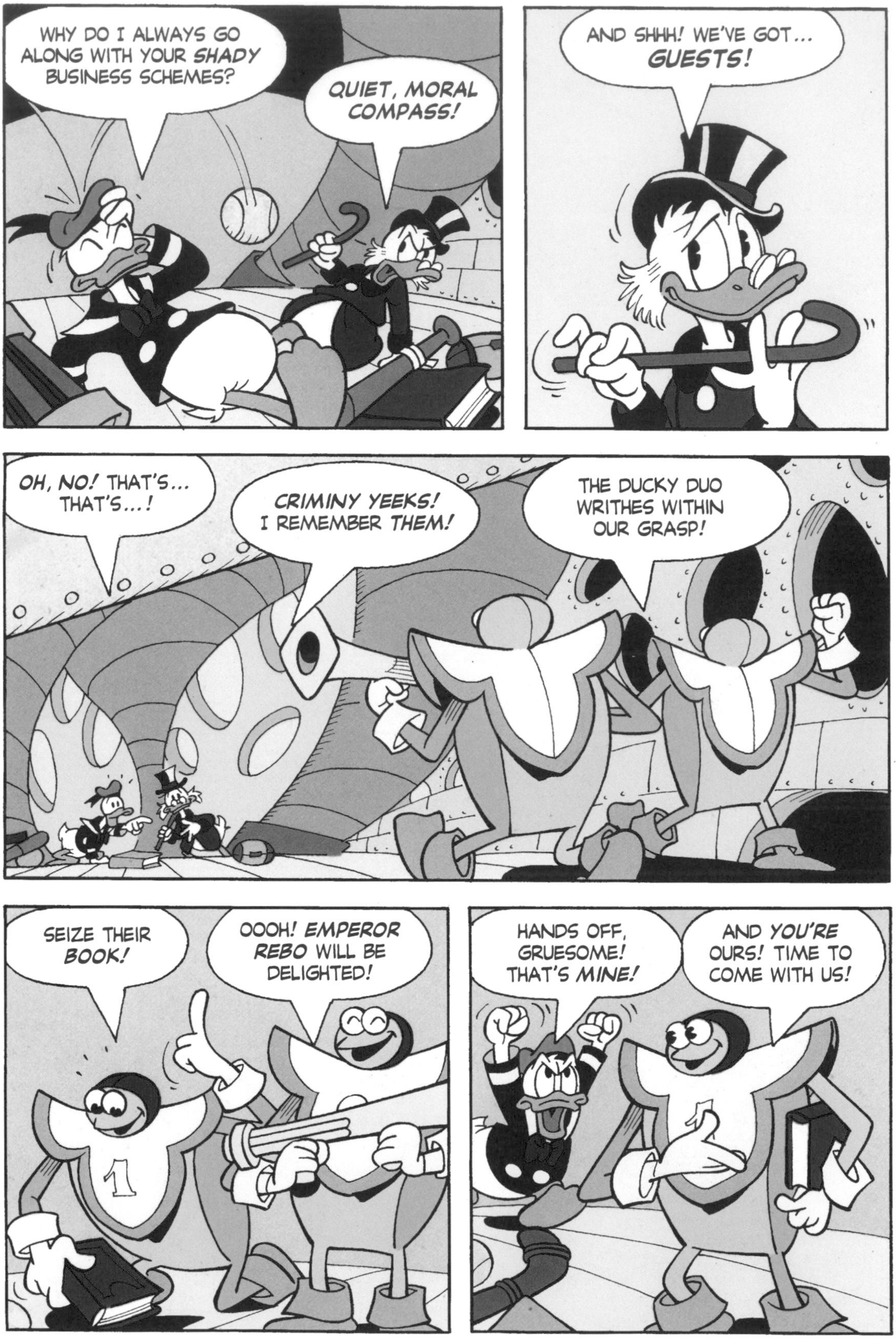
WHY DO I ALWAYS GO ALONG WITH YOUR SHADY BUSINESS SCHEMES?
QUIET, MORAL COMPASS!
AND SHHH! WE'VE GOT... GUESTS!
OH, NO! THAT'S... THAT'S...!
CRIMINY YEEKS! I REMEMBER THEM!
THE DUCKY DUO WRITHES WITHIN OUR GRASP!
SEIZE THEIR BOOK!
OOOH! EMPEROR REBO WILL BE DELIGHTED!
HANDS OFF, GRUESOME! THAT'S MINE!
AND YOU'RE OURS! TIME TO COME WITH US!

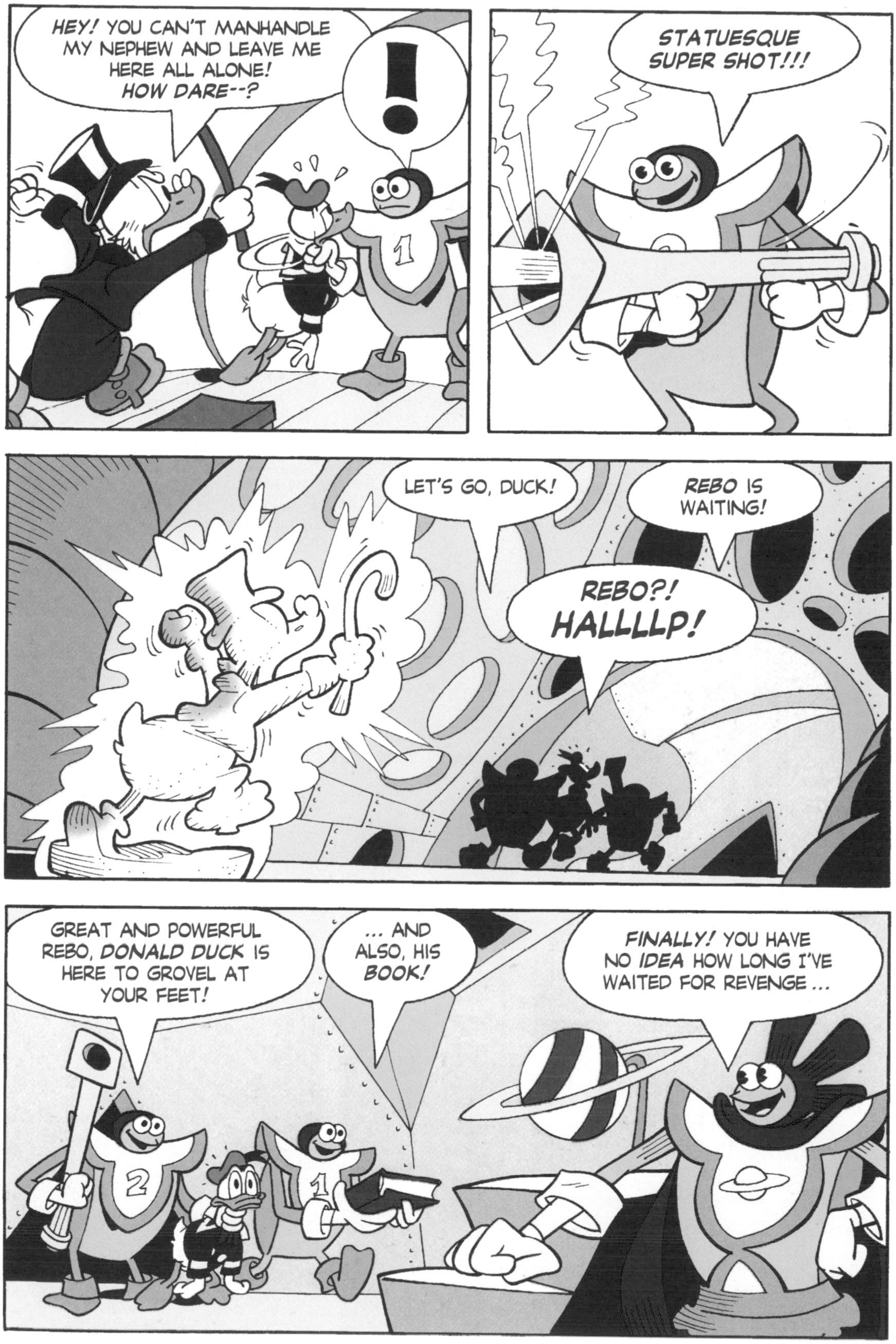

HEY! YOU CAN'T MANHANDLE MY NEPHEW AND LEAVE ME HERE ALL ALONE! HOW DARE--?
!
STATUESQUE SUPER SHOT!!!
LET'S GO, DUCK!
REBO IS WAITING!
REBO?! HALLLLP!
GREAT AND POWERFUL REBO, DONALD DUCK IS HERE TO GROVEL AT YOUR FEET!
... AND ALSO, HIS BOOK!
FINALLY! YOU HAVE NO IDEA HOW LONG I'VE WAITED FOR REVENGE ...

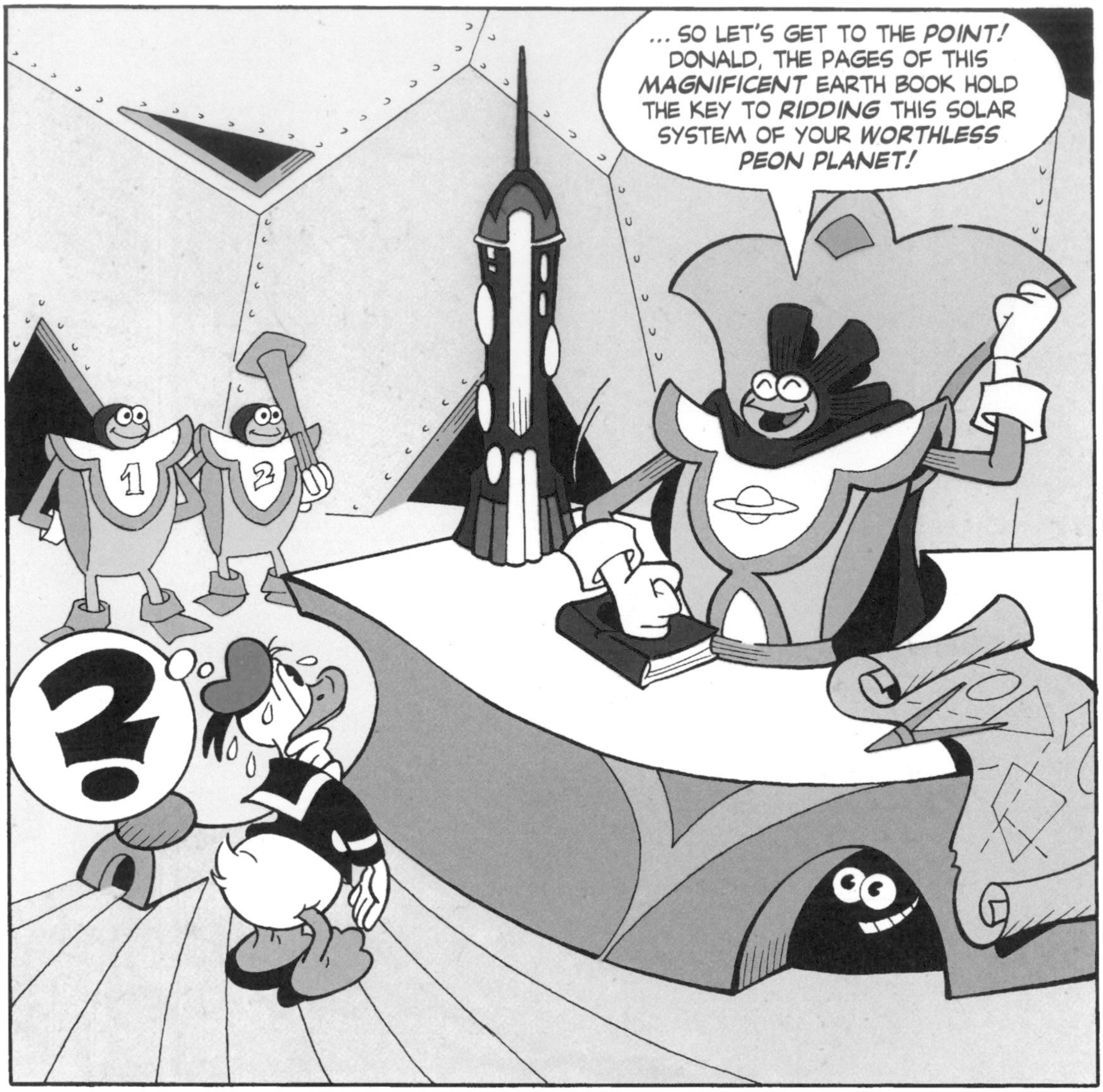
... SO LET'S GET TO THE POINT! DONALD, THE PAGES OF THIS MAGNIFICENT EARTH BOOK HOLD THE KEY TO RIDDING THIS SOLAR SYSTEM OF YOUR WORTHLESS PEON PLANET!
?

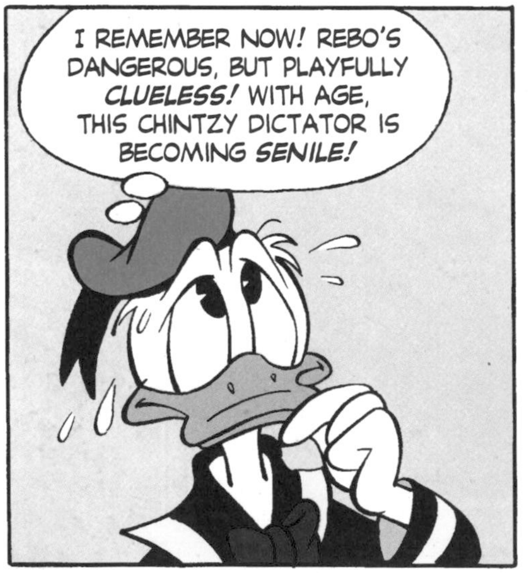
I REMEMBER NOW! REBO'S DANGEROUS, BUT PLAYFULLY CLUELESS! WITH AGE, THIS CHINTZY DICTATOR IS BECOMING SENILE!

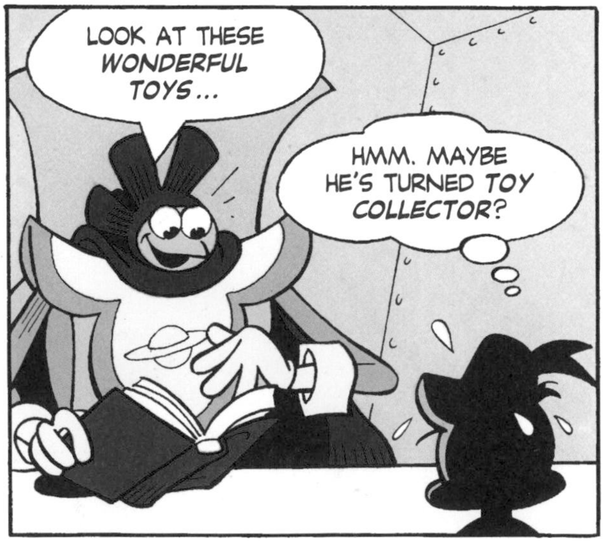
LOOK AT THESE WONDERFUL TOYS...
HMM. MAYBE HE'S TURNED TOY COLLECTOR?

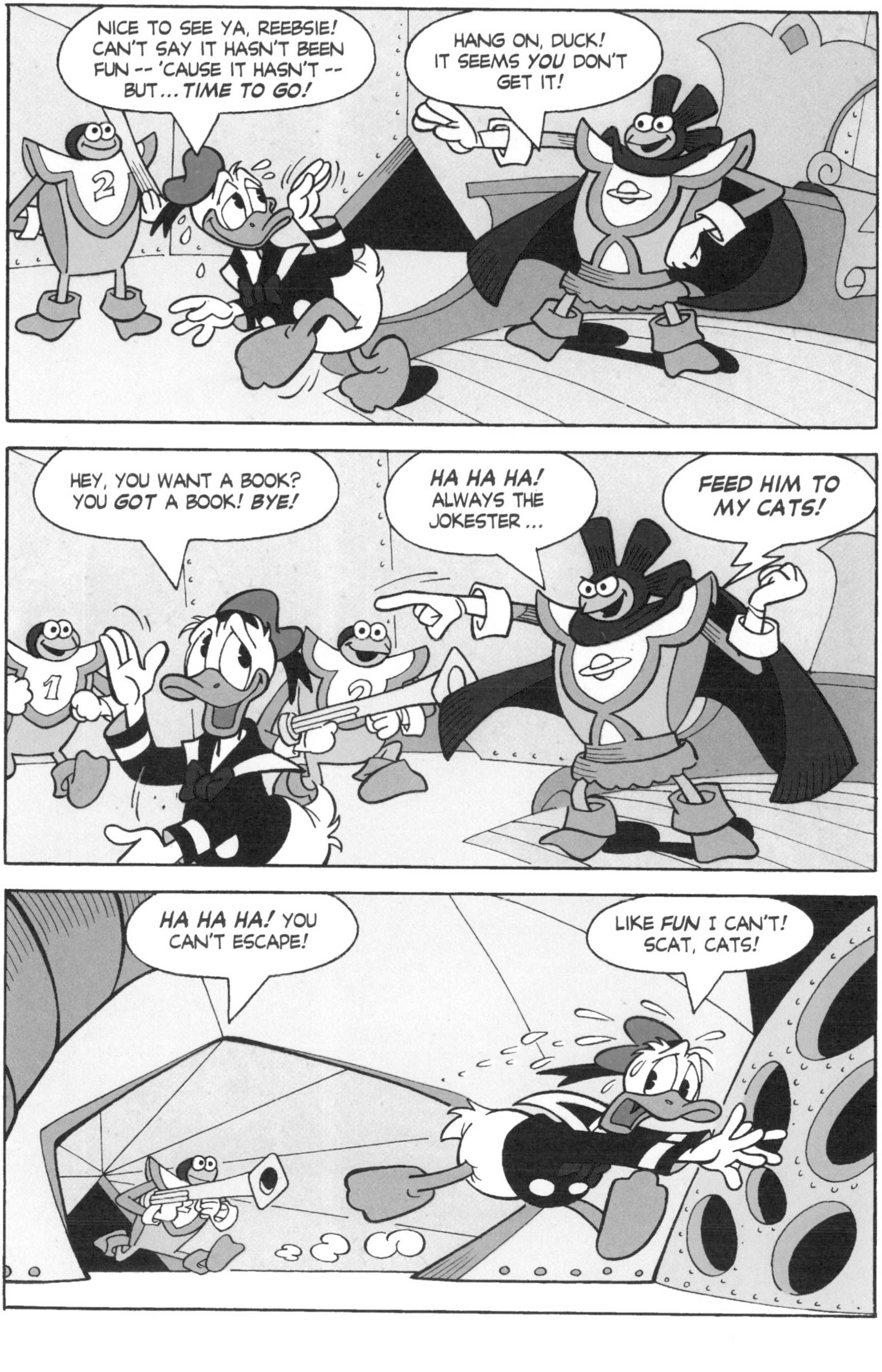
NICE TO SEE YA, REEBSIE! CAN'T SAY IT HASN'T BEEN FUN -- 'CAUSE IT HASN'T -- BUT... TIME TO GO!
HANG ON, DUCK! IT SEEMS YOU DON'T GET IT!
HEY, YOU WANT A BOOK? YOU GOT A BOOK! BYE!
HA HA HA! ALWAYS THE JOKESTER...
FEED HIM TO MY CATS!
HA HA HA! YOU CAN'T ESCAPE!
LIKE FUN I CAN'T! SCAT, CATS!

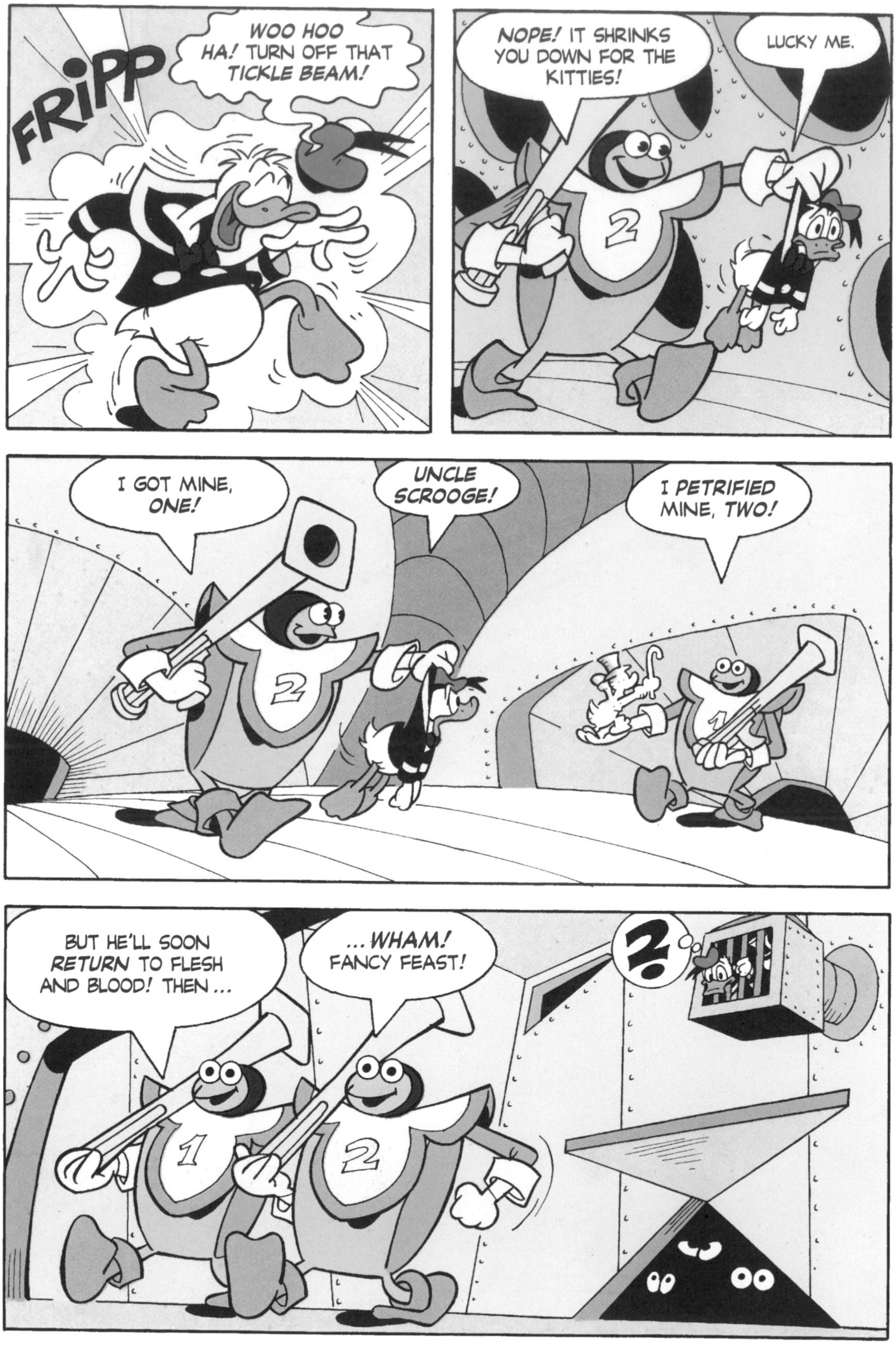
FRIPP
WOO HOO HA! TURN OFF THAT TICKLE BEAM!
NOPE! IT SHRINKS YOU DOWN FOR THE KITTIES!
LUCKY ME.
I GOT MINE, ONE!
UNCLE SCROOGE!
I PETRIFIED MINE, TWO!
BUT HE'LL SOON RETURN TO FLESH AND BLOOD! THEN ...
...WHAM! FANCY FEAST!

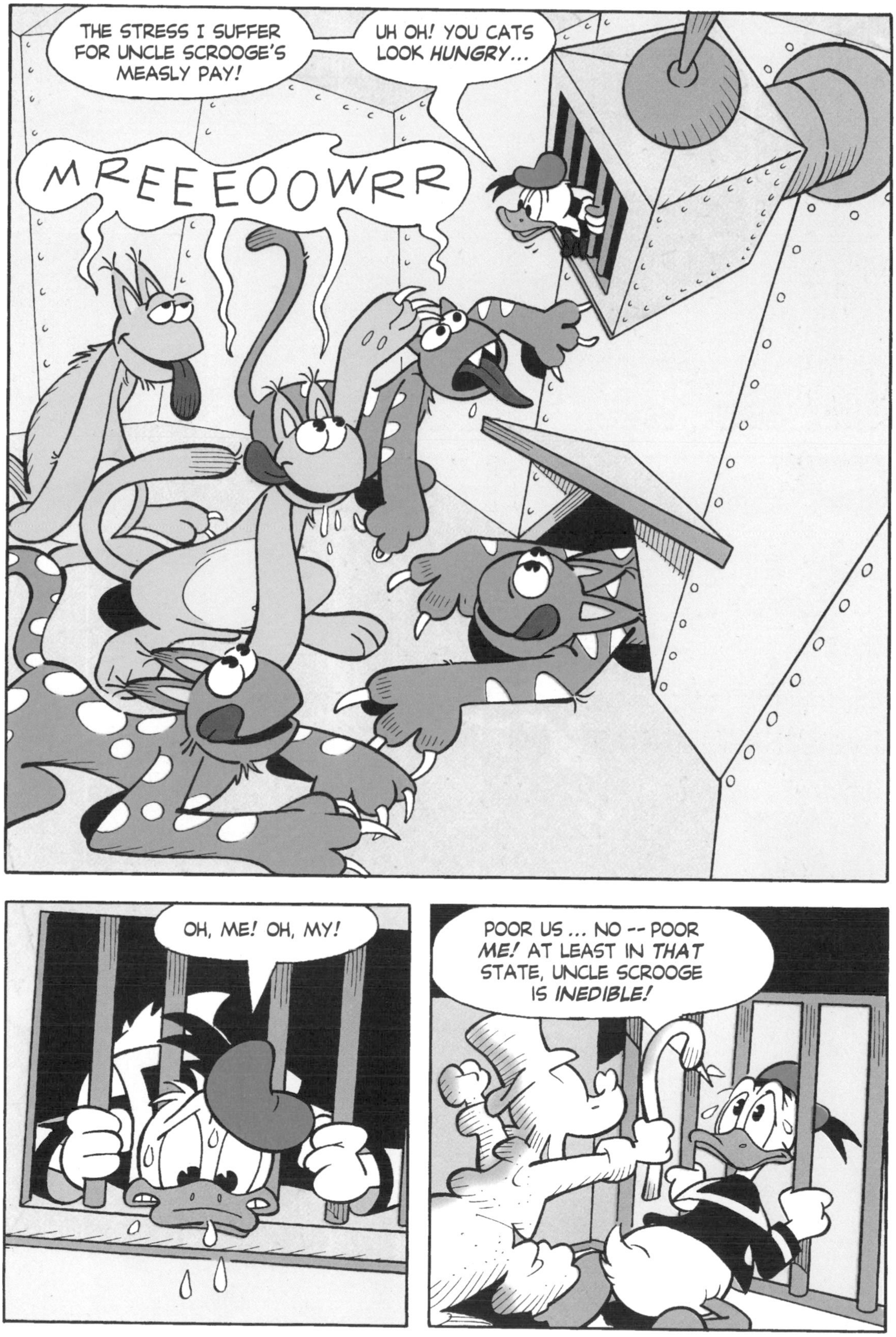
THE STRESS I SUFFER FOR UNCLE SCROOGE'S MEASLY PAY!
UH OH! YOU CATS LOOK HUNGRY...
MREEEOOWRR
OH, ME! OH, MY!
POOR US ... NO -- POOR ME! AT LEAST IN THAT STATE, UNCLE SCROOGE IS INEDIBLE!

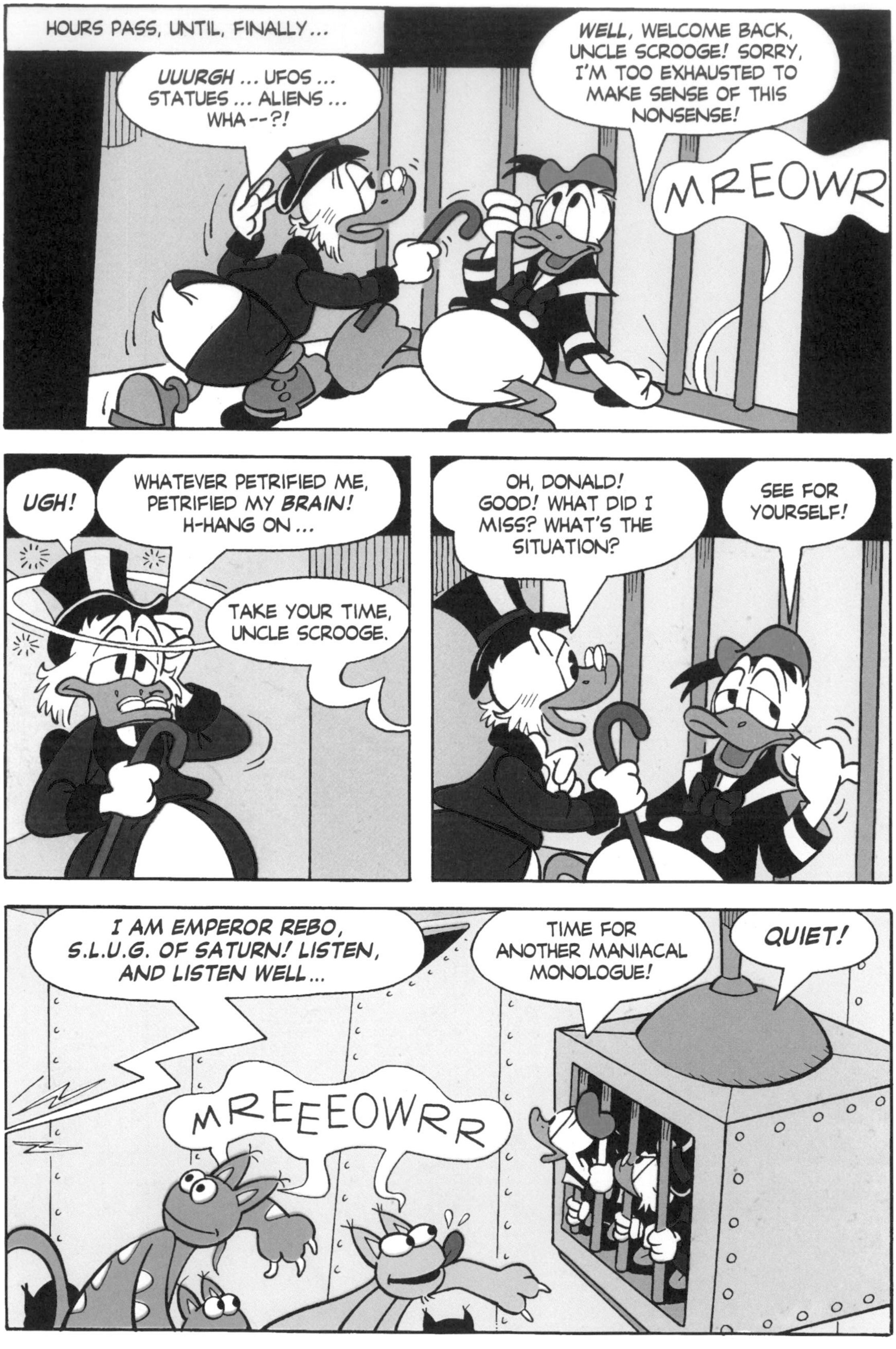

HOURS PASS, UNTIL, FINALLY...
UUURGH ... UFOS ... STATUES ... ALIENS ... WHA--?!
WELL, WELCOME BACK, UNCLE SCROOGE! SORRY, I'M TOO EXHAUSTED TO MAKE SENSE OF THIS NONSENSE!
MREOWR
UGH!
WHATEVER PETRIFIED ME, PETRIFIED MY BRAIN! H-HANG ON ...
TAKE YOUR TIME, UNCLE SCROOGE.
OH, DONALD! GOOD! WHAT DID I MISS? WHAT'S THE SITUATION?
SEE FOR YOURSELF!
I AM EMPEROR REBO, S.L.U.G. OF SATURN! LISTEN, AND LISTEN WELL...
TIME FOR ANOTHER MANIACAL MONOLOGUE!
QUIET!
MREEEEOWRR

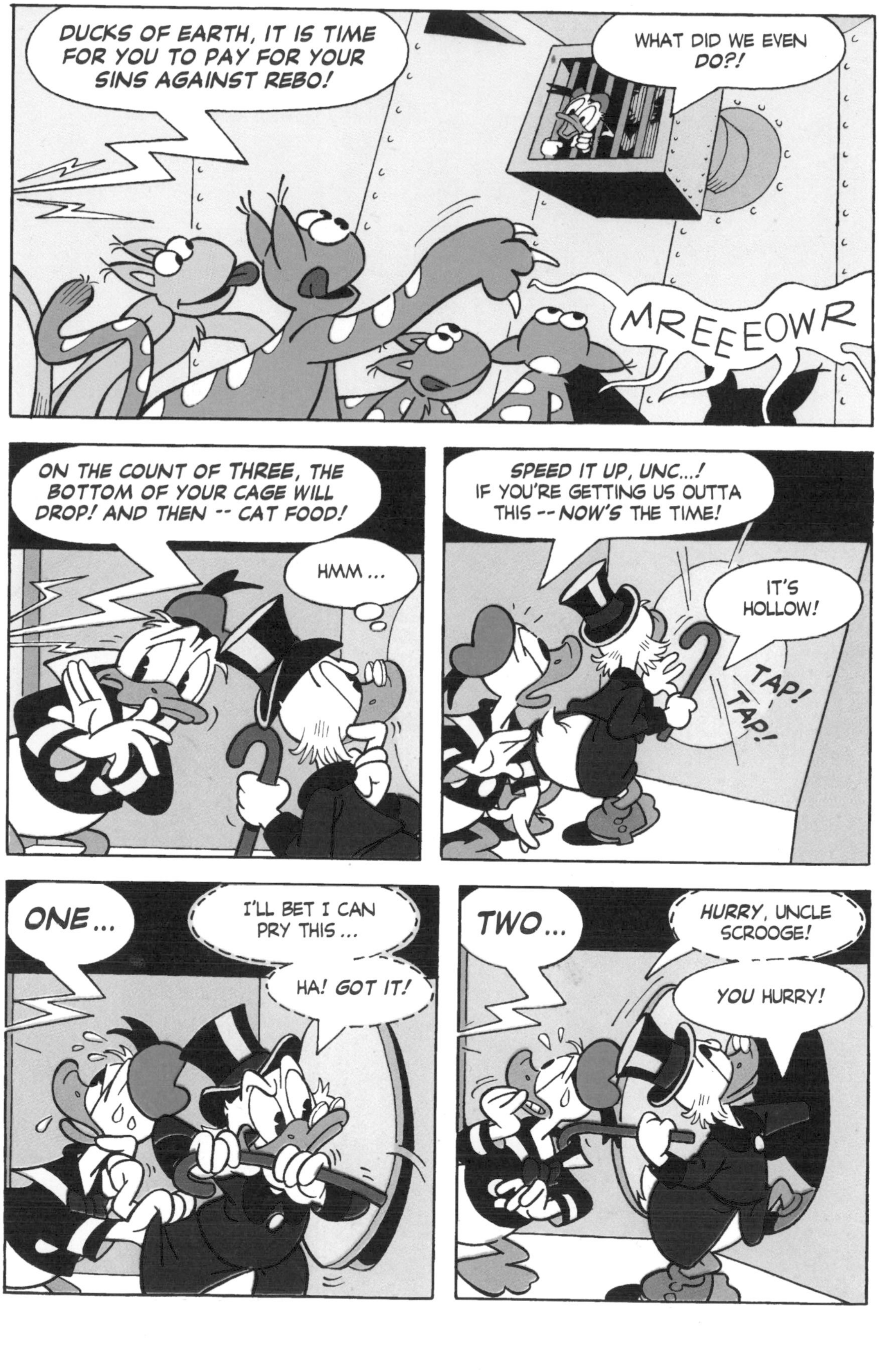
DUCKS OF EARTH, IT IS TIME FOR YOU TO PAY FOR YOUR SINS AGAINST REBO!
WHAT DID WE EVEN DO?!
MREEEEOWR
ON THE COUNT OF THREE, THE BOTTOM OF YOUR CAGE WILL DROP! AND THEN -- CAT FOOD!
HMM ...
SPEED IT UP, UNC...! IF YOU'RE GETTING US OUTTA THIS -- NOW'S THE TIME!
IT'S HOLLOW!
TAP! TAP!
ONE...
I'LL BET I CAN PRY THIS ...
HA! GOT IT!
TWO...
HURRY, UNCLE SCROOGE!
YOU HURRY!

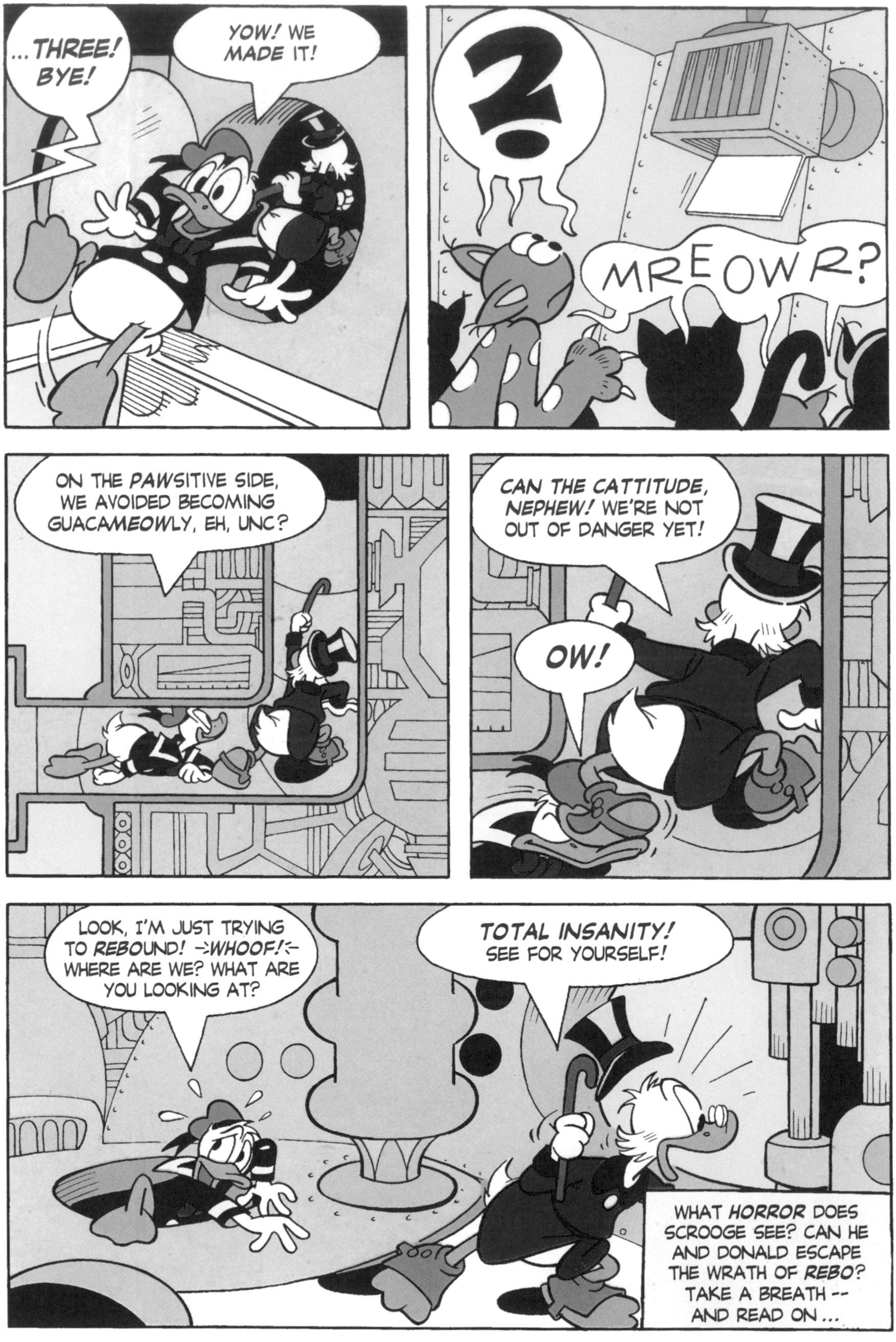
...THREE! BYE!
YOW! WE MADE IT!
2
MREOWR?
ON THE PAWSITIVE SIDE, WE AVOIDED BECOMING GUACAMEOWLY, EH, UNC?
CAN THE CATTITUDE, NEPHEW! WE'RE NOT OUT OF DANGER YET!
OW!
LOOK, I'M JUST TRYING TO REBOUND! ⇛WHOOF!⇚ WHERE ARE WE? WHAT ARE YOU LOOKING AT?
TOTAL INSANITY! SEE FOR YOURSELF!
WHAT HORROR DOES SCROOGE SEE? CAN HE AND DONALD ESCAPE THE WRATH OF REBO? TAKE A BREATH -- AND READ ON...

Walt Disney Donald Duck & Uncle $crooge in The Return of Rebo

CHAPTER 2

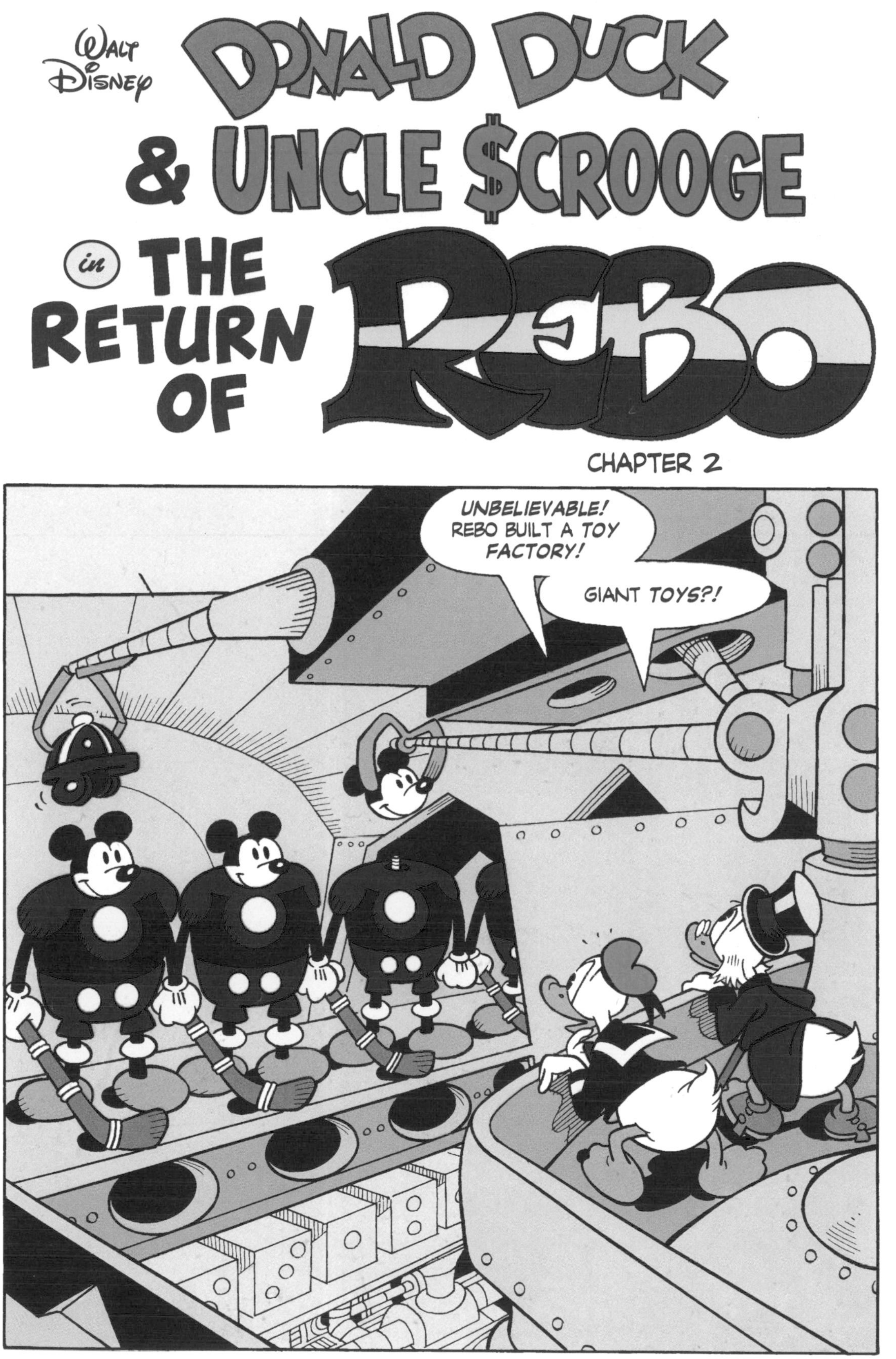
UNBELIEVABLE! REBO BUILT A TOY FACTORY!
GIANT TOYS?!

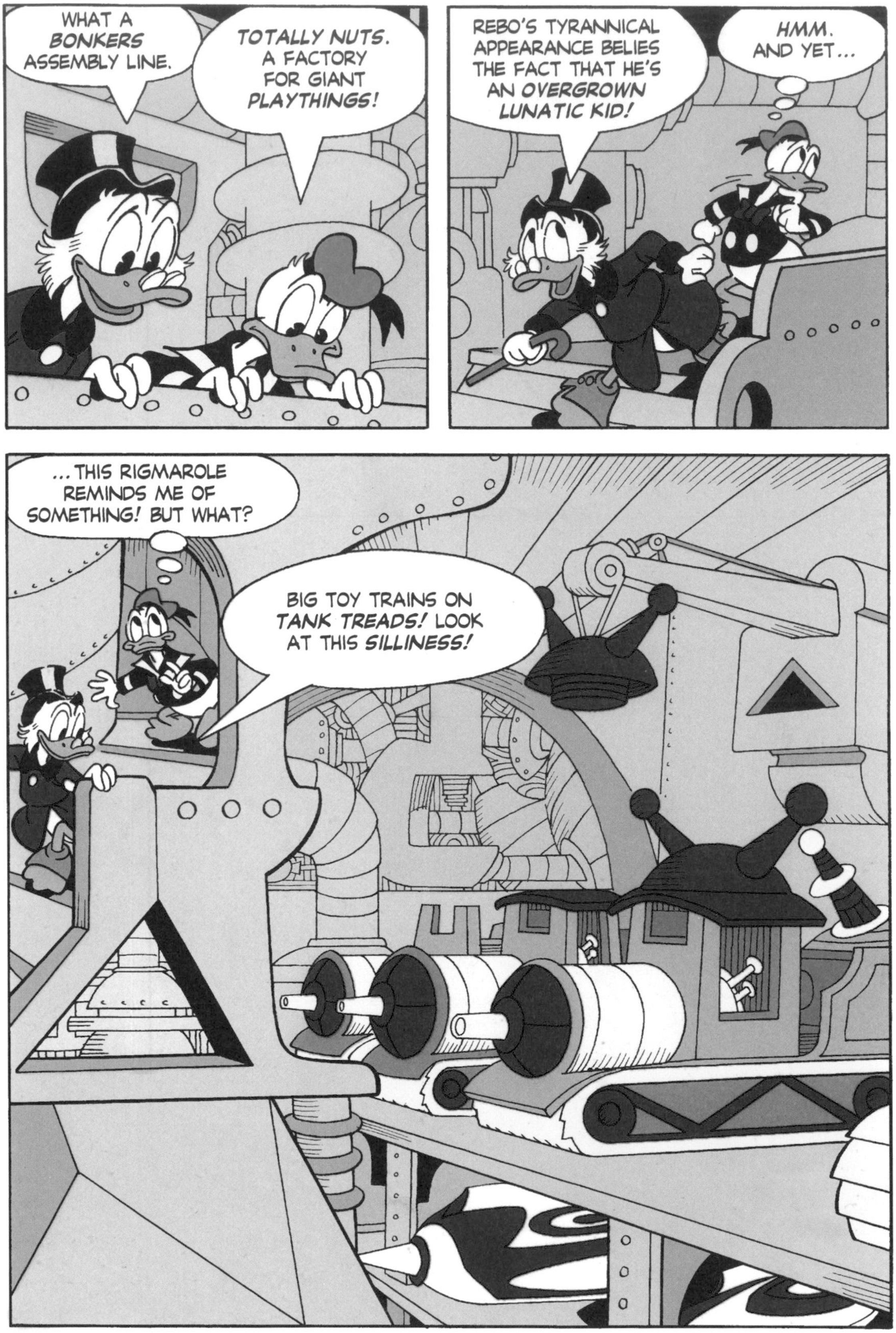
WHAT A BONKERS ASSEMBLY LINE.
TOTALLY NUTS. A FACTORY FOR GIANT PLAYTHINGS!
REBO'S TYRANNICAL APPEARANCE BELIES THE FACT THAT HE'S AN OVERGROWN LUNATIC KID!
HMM. AND YET...
...THIS RIGMAROLE REMINDS ME OF SOMETHING! BUT WHAT?
BIG TOY TRAINS ON TANK TREADS! LOOK AT THIS SILLINESS!

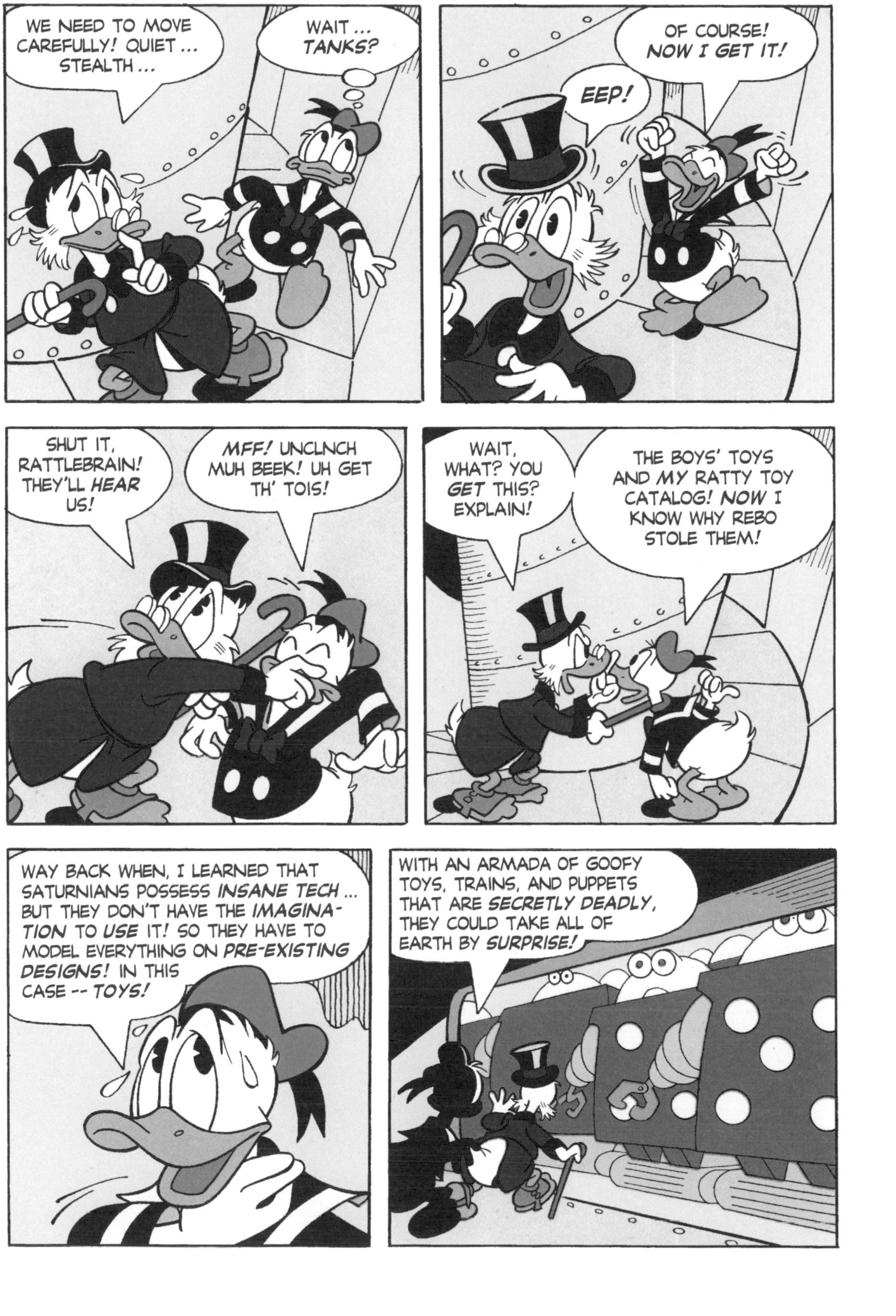
WE NEED TO MOVE CAREFULLY! QUIET ... STEALTH ...
WAIT ... TANKS?
EEP!
OF COURSE! NOW I GET IT!
SHUT IT, RATTLEBRAIN! THEY'LL HEAR US!
MFF! UNCLNCH MUH BEEK! UH GET TH' TOIS!
WAIT, WHAT? YOU GET THIS? EXPLAIN!
THE BOYS' TOYS AND MY RATTY TOY CATALOG! NOW I KNOW WHY REBO STOLE THEM!
WAY BACK WHEN, I LEARNED THAT SATURNIANS POSSESS INSANE TECH ... BUT THEY DON'T HAVE THE IMAGINATION TO USE IT! SO THEY HAVE TO MODEL EVERYTHING ON PRE-EXISTING DESIGNS! IN THIS CASE -- TOYS!
WITH AN ARMADA OF GOOFY TOYS, TRAINS, AND PUPPETS THAT ARE SECRETLY DEADLY, THEY COULD TAKE ALL OF EARTH BY SURPRISE!

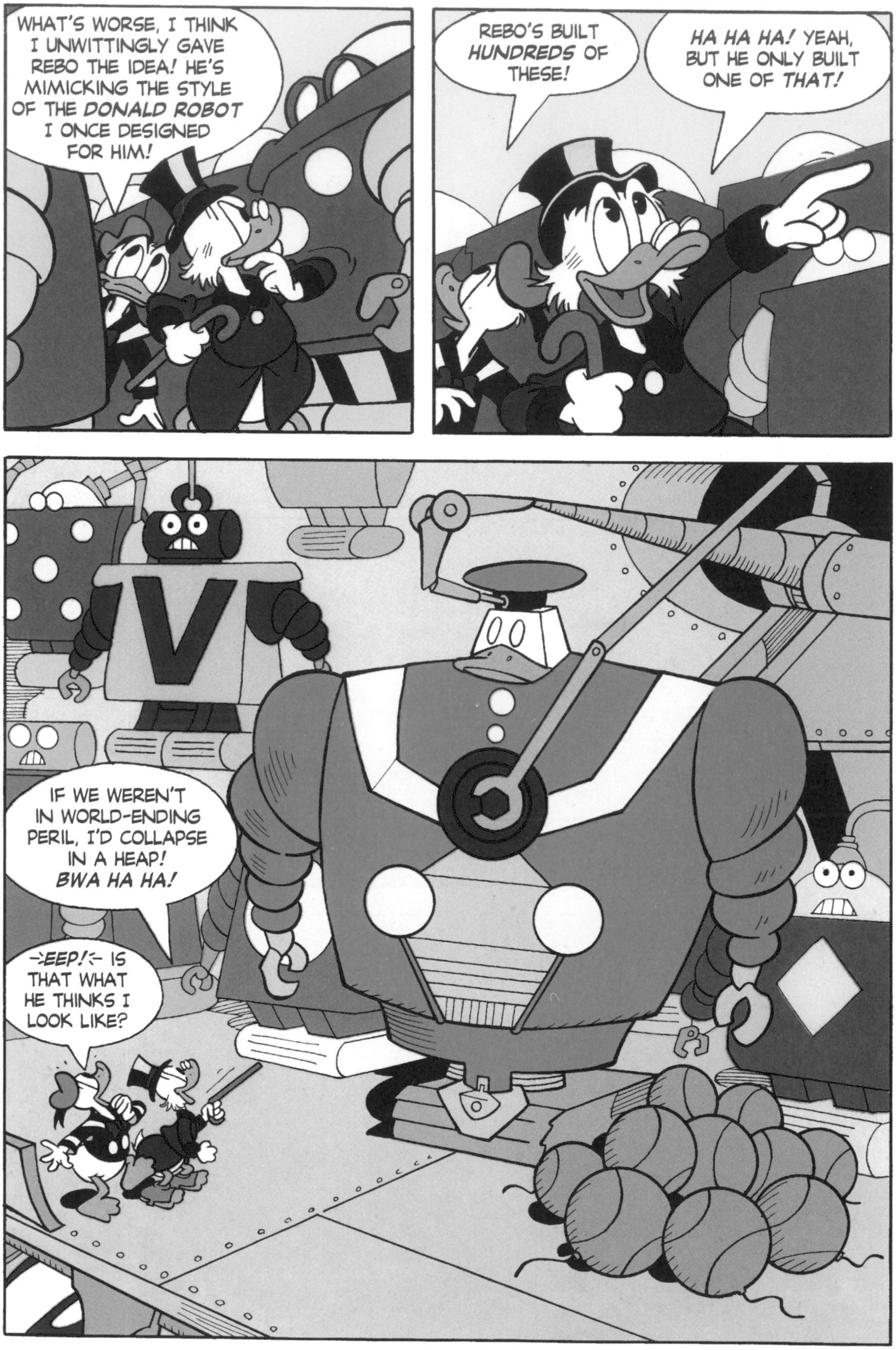
WHAT'S WORSE, I THINK I UNWITTINGLY GAVE REBO THE IDEA! HE'S MIMICKING THE STYLE OF THE DONALD ROBOT I ONCE DESIGNED FOR HIM!
REBO'S BUILT HUNDREDS OF THESE!
HA HA HA! YEAH, BUT HE ONLY BUILT ONE OF THAT!
V
IF WE WEREN'T IN WORLD-ENDING PERIL, I'D COLLAPSE IN A HEAP! BWA HA HA!
EEP! IS THAT WHAT HE THINKS I LOOK LIKE?

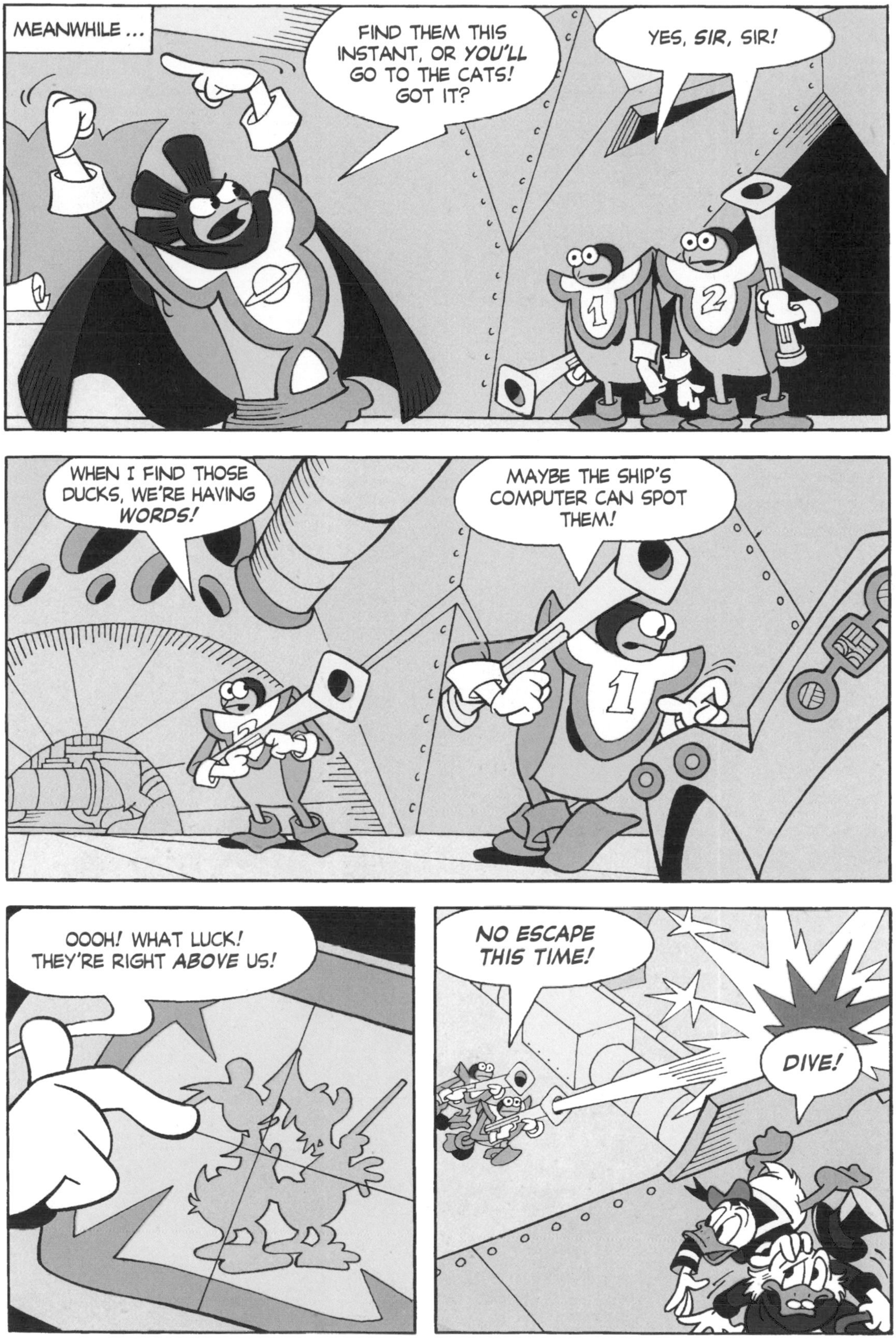
MEANWHILE ...
FIND THEM THIS INSTANT, OR YOU'LL GO TO THE CATS! GOT IT?
YES, SIR, SIR!
WHEN I FIND THOSE DUCKS, WE'RE HAVING WORDS!
MAYBE THE SHIP'S COMPUTER CAN SPOT THEM!
OOOH! WHAT LUCK! THEY'RE RIGHT ABOVE US!
NO ESCAPE THIS TIME!
DIVE!

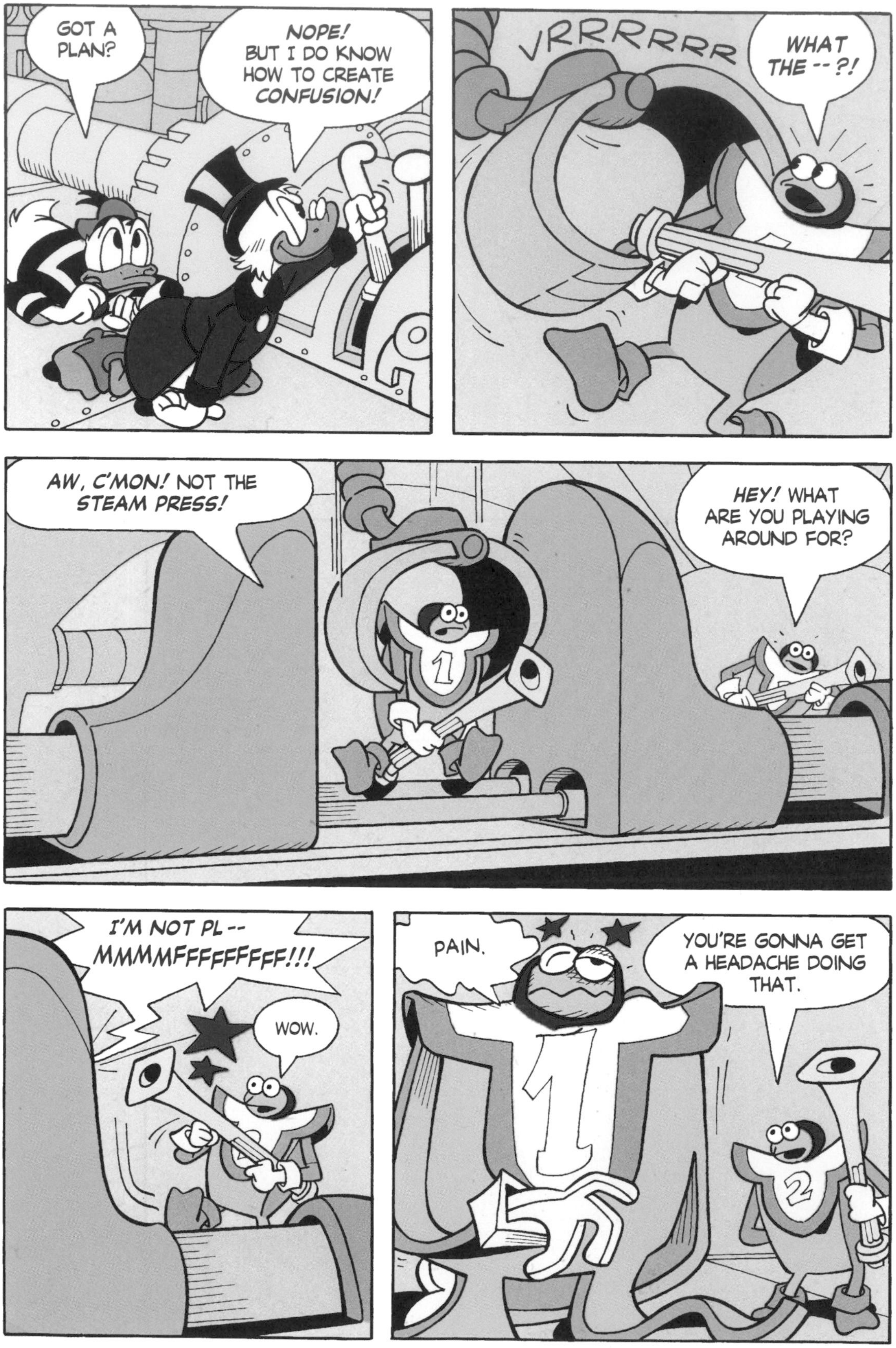
GOT A PLAN?
NOPE! BUT I DO KNOW HOW TO CREATE CONFUSION!
VRRRRRRR
WHAT THE --?!
AW, C'MON! NOT THE STEAM PRESS!
HEY! WHAT ARE YOU PLAYING AROUND FOR?
I'M NOT PL-- MMMMFFFFFFFFF!!!
WOW.
PAIN.
YOU'RE GONNA GET A HEADACHE DOING THAT.

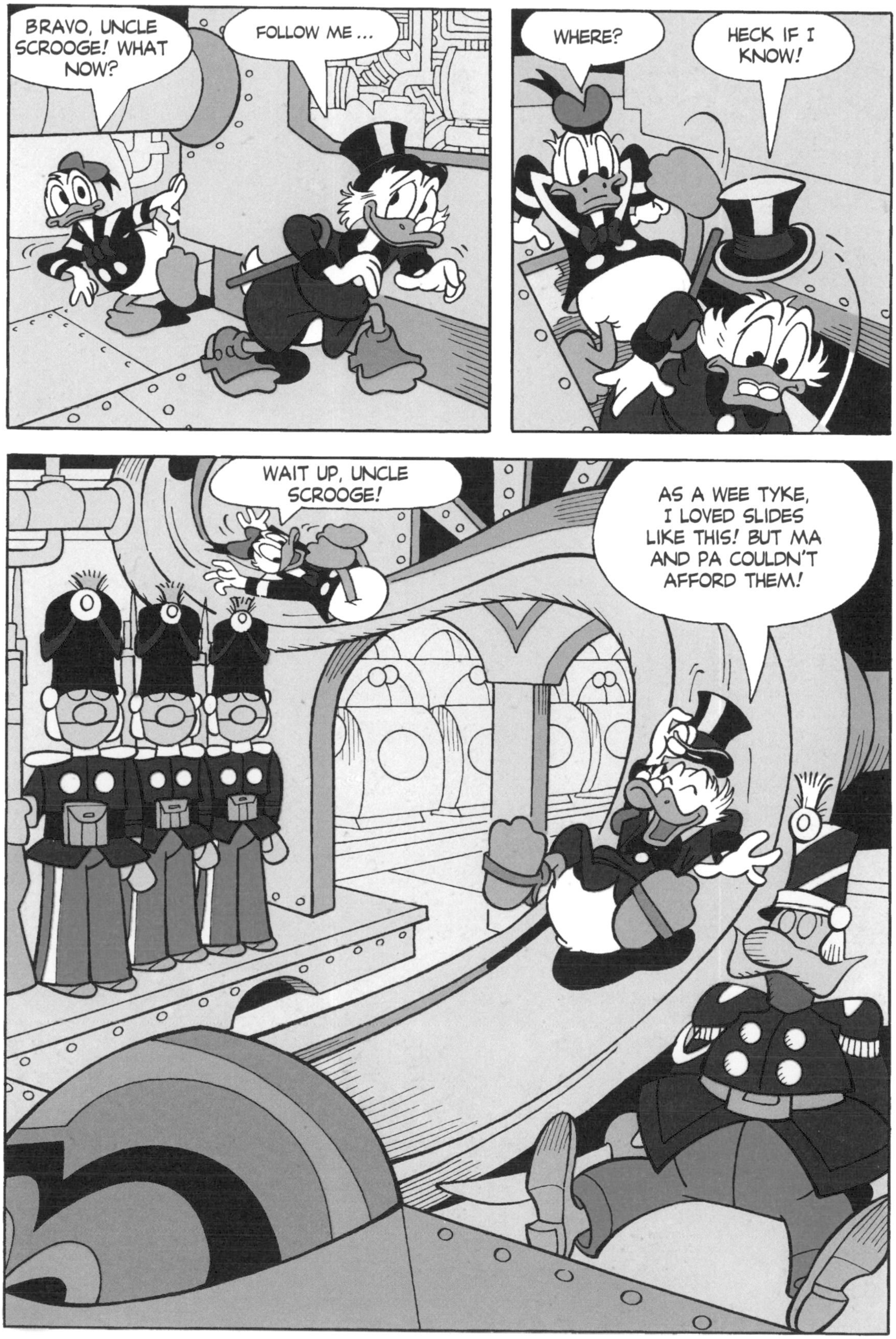
BRAVO, UNCLE SCROOGE! WHAT NOW?
FOLLOW ME ...
WHERE?
HECK IF I KNOW!
WAIT UP, UNCLE SCROOGE!
AS A WEE TYKE, I LOVED SLIDES LIKE THIS! BUT MA AND PA COULDN'T AFFORD THEM!

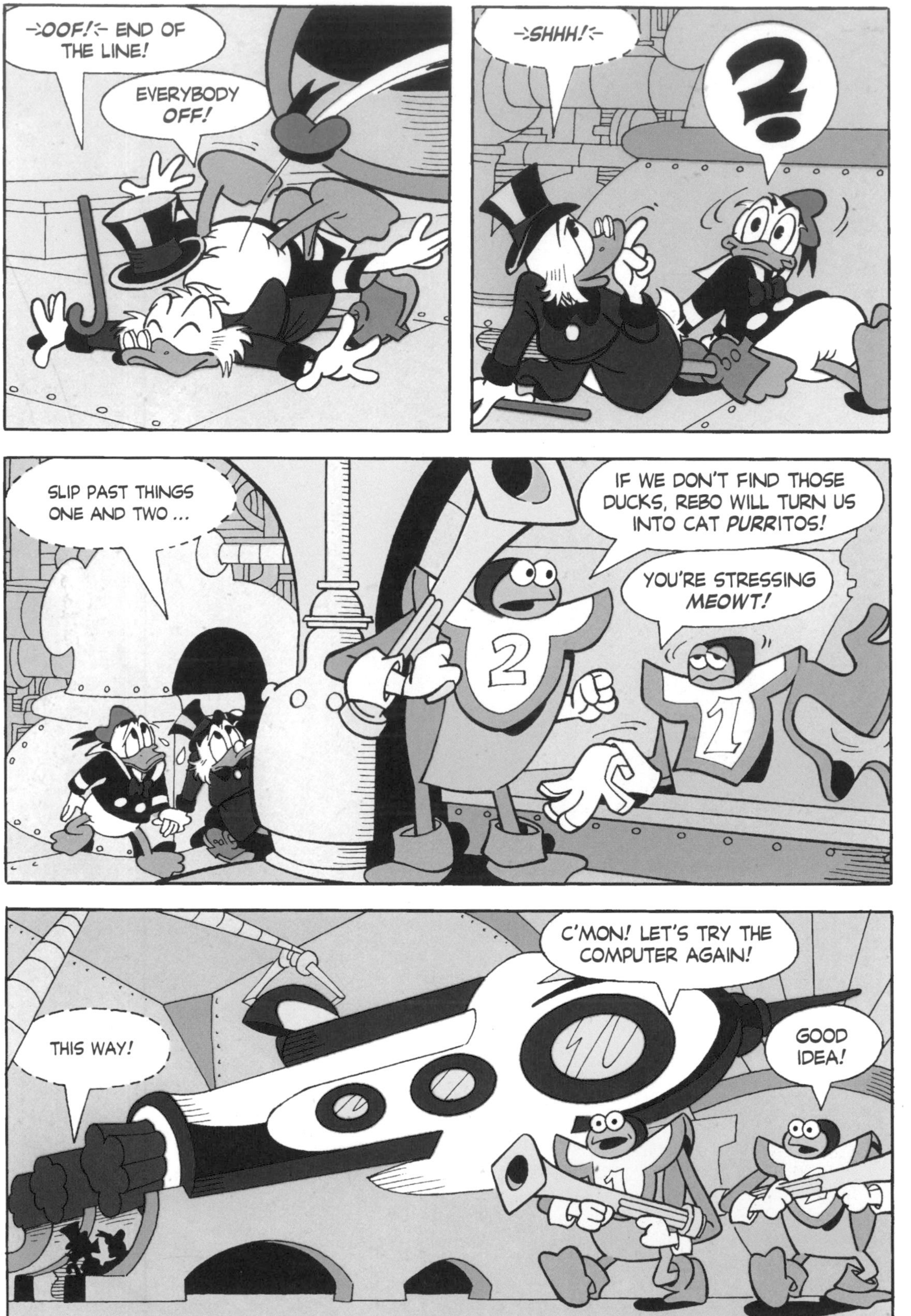

-OOF!- END OF THE LINE!
EVERYBODY OFF!
-SHHH!-
?
SLIP PAST THINGS ONE AND TWO ...
IF WE DON'T FIND THOSE DUCKS, REBO WILL TURN US INTO CAT PURRITOS!
YOU'RE STRESSING MEOWT!
C'MON! LET'S TRY THE COMPUTER AGAIN!
THIS WAY!
GOOD IDEA!

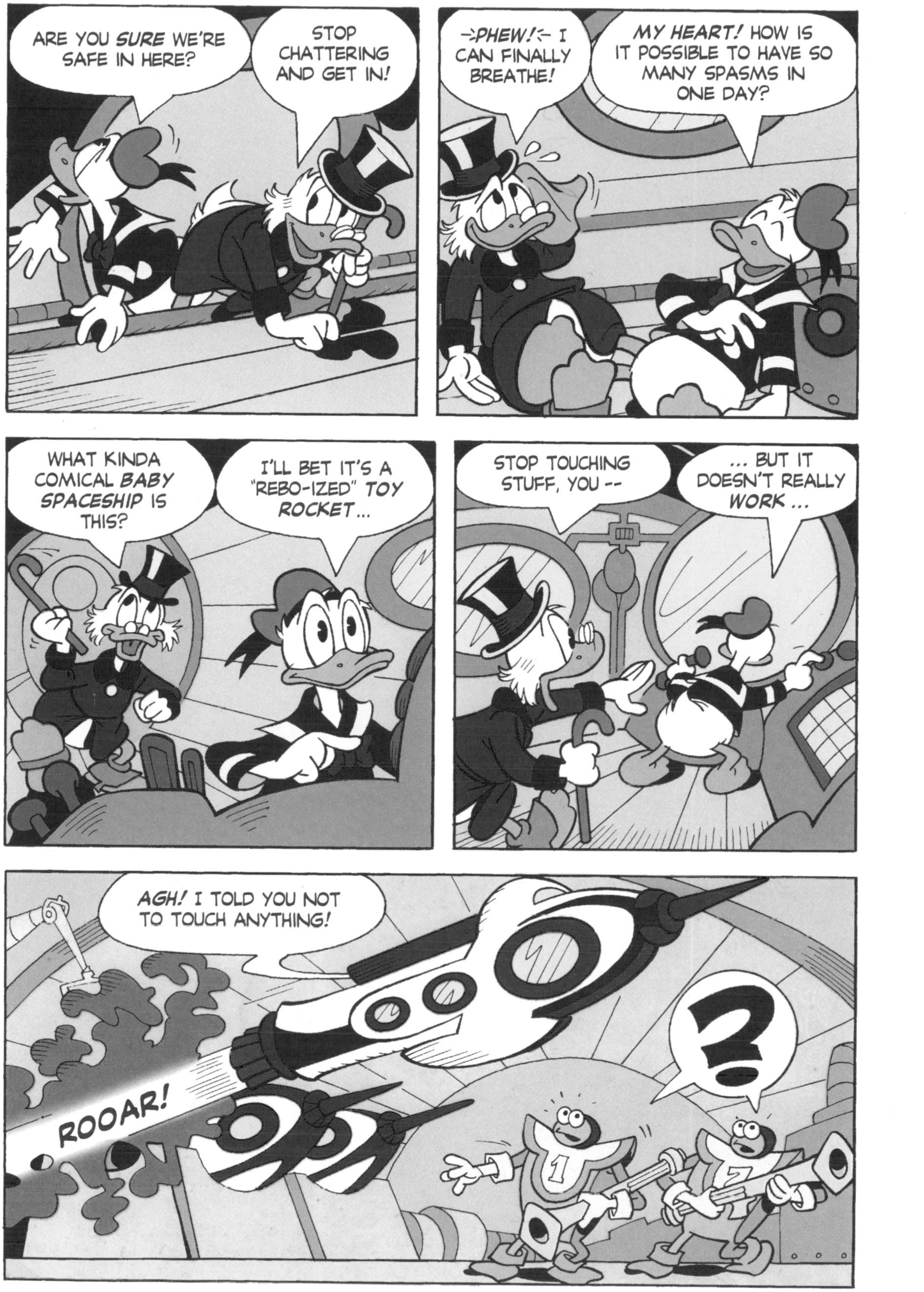
ARE YOU SURE WE'RE SAFE IN HERE?
STOP CHATTERING AND GET IN!
PHEW! I CAN FINALLY BREATHE!
MY HEART! HOW IS IT POSSIBLE TO HAVE SO MANY SPASMS IN ONE DAY?
WHAT KINDA COMICAL BABY SPACESHIP IS THIS?
I'LL BET IT'S A "REBO-IZED" TOY ROCKET...
STOP TOUCHING STUFF, YOU --
... BUT IT DOESN'T REALLY WORK ...
AGH! I TOLD YOU NOT TO TOUCH ANYTHING!
ROOAR!
?

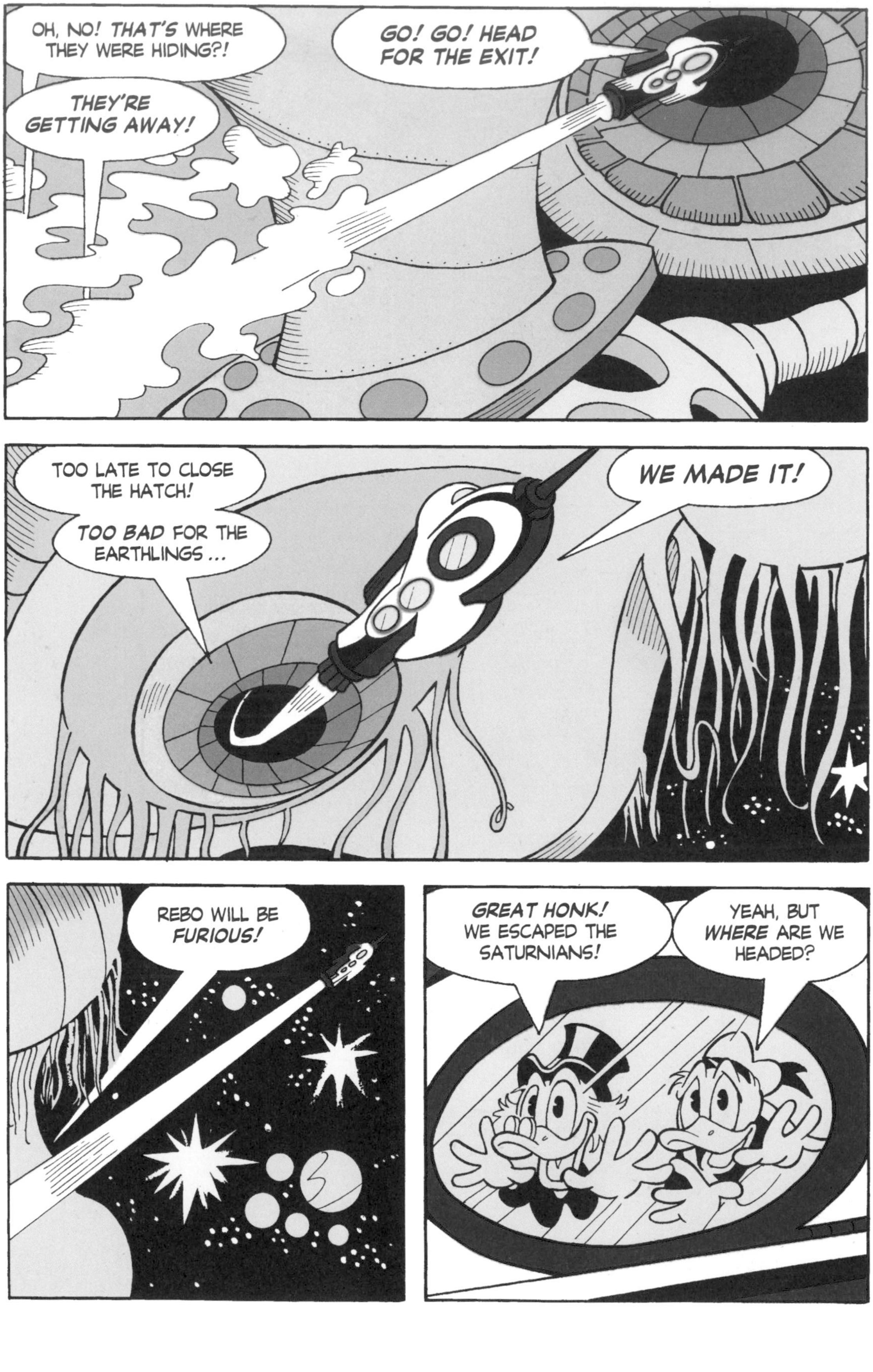
OH, NO! THAT'S WHERE THEY WERE HIDING?!
THEY'RE GETTING AWAY!
GO! GO! HEAD FOR THE EXIT!
TOO LATE TO CLOSE THE HATCH!
TOO BAD FOR THE EARTHLINGS ...
WE MADE IT!
REBO WILL BE FURIOUS!
GREAT HONK! WE ESCAPED THE SATURNIANS!
YEAH, BUT WHERE ARE WE HEADED?

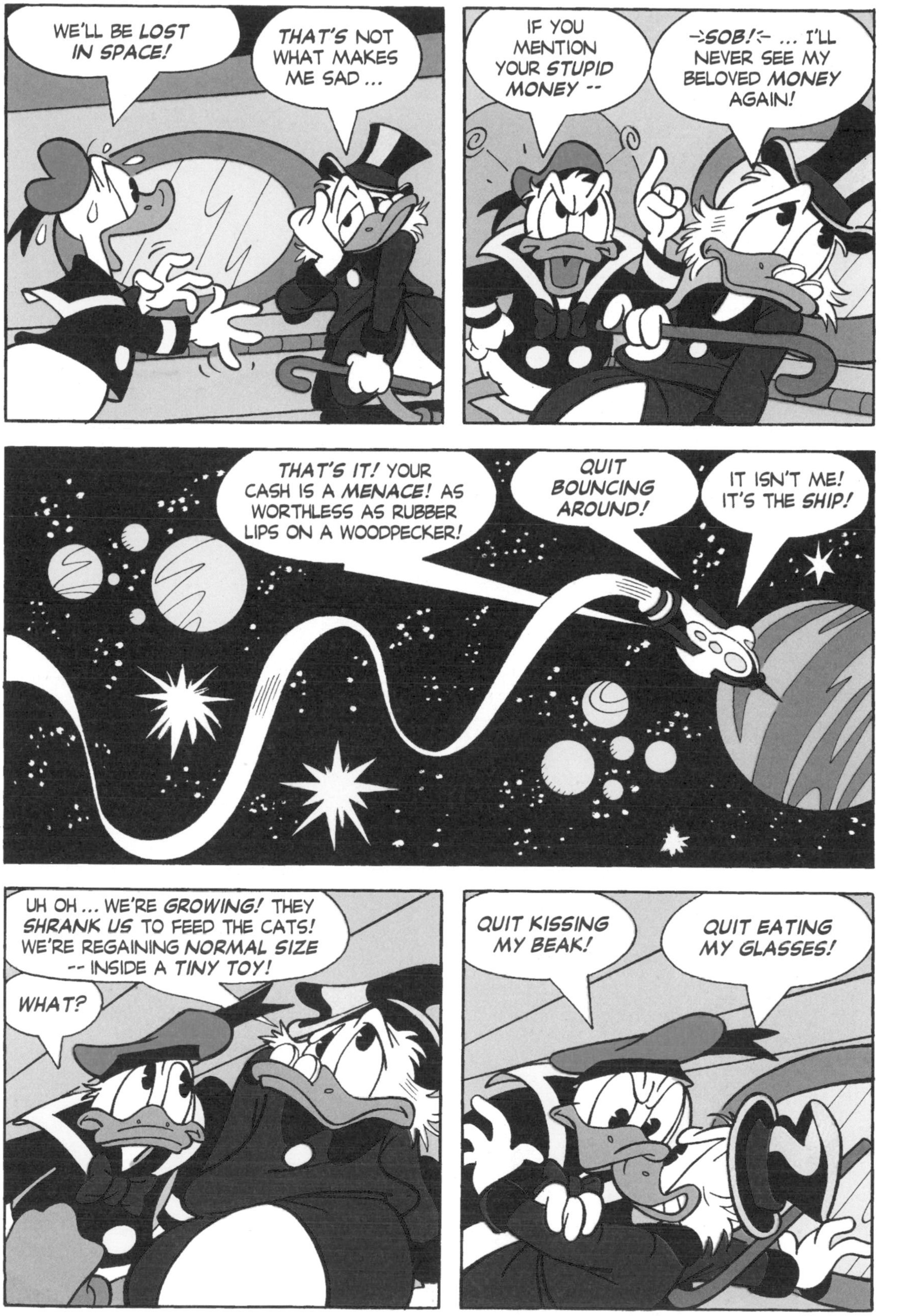
WE'LL BE LOST IN SPACE!
THAT'S NOT WHAT MAKES ME SAD ...
IF YOU MENTION YOUR STUPID MONEY --
-SOB!- ... I'LL NEVER SEE MY BELOVED MONEY AGAIN!
THAT'S IT! YOUR CASH IS A MENACE! AS WORTHLESS AS RUBBER LIPS ON A WOODPECKER!
QUIT BOUNCING AROUND!
IT ISN'T ME! IT'S THE SHIP!
UH OH ... WE'RE GROWING! THEY SHRANK US TO FEED THE CATS! WE'RE REGAINING NORMAL SIZE -- INSIDE A TINY TOY!
WHAT?
QUIT KISSING MY BEAK!
QUIT EATING MY GLASSES!

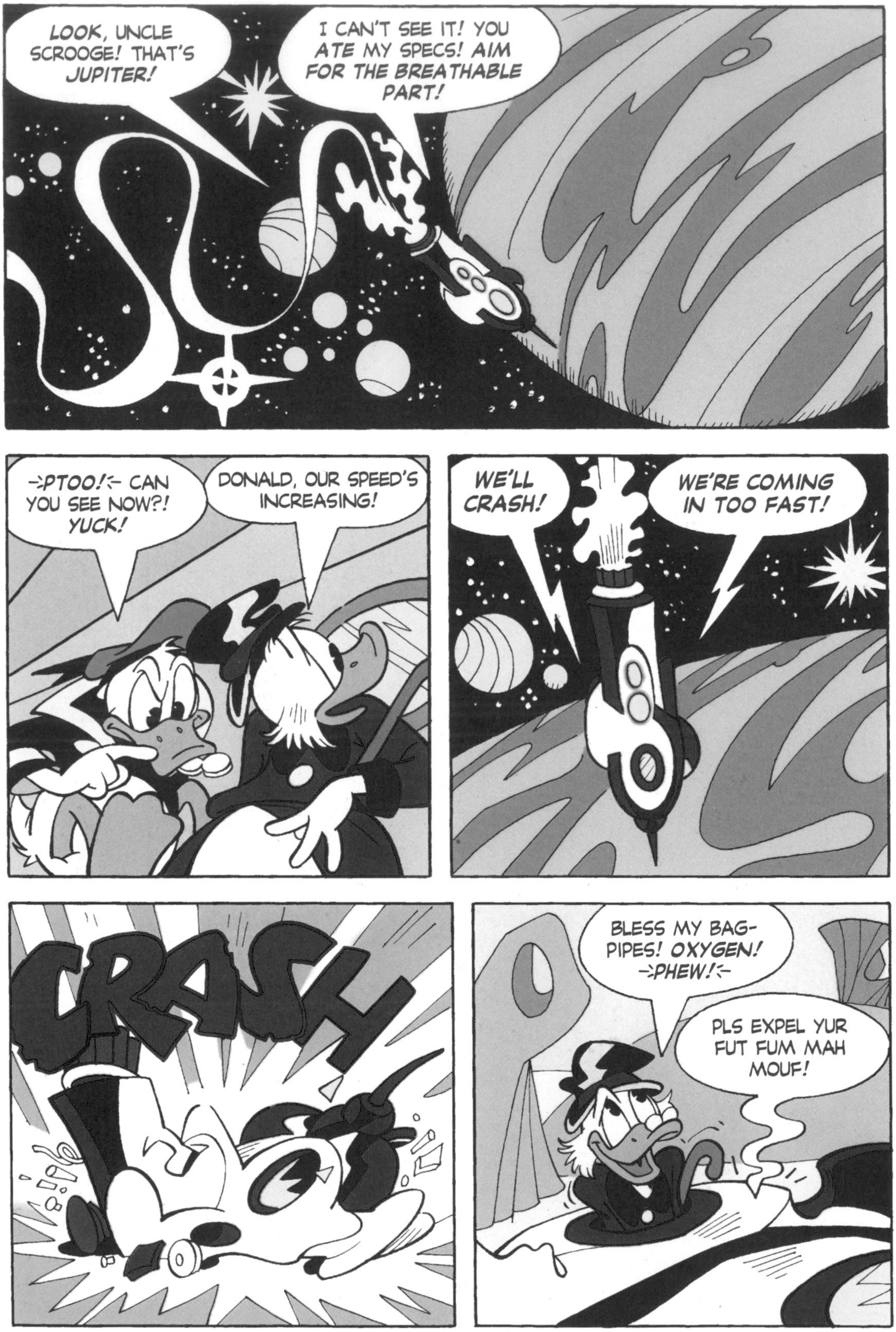
LOOK, UNCLE SCROOGE! THAT'S JUPITER!
I CAN'T SEE IT! YOU ATE MY SPECS! AIM FOR THE BREATHABLE PART!
–PTOO!– CAN YOU SEE NOW?! YUCK!
DONALD, OUR SPEED'S INCREASING!
WE'LL CRASH!
WE'RE COMING IN TOO FAST!
CRASH
BLESS MY BAG-PIPES! OXYGEN! –PHEW!–
PLS EXPEL YUR FUT FUM MAH MOUF!

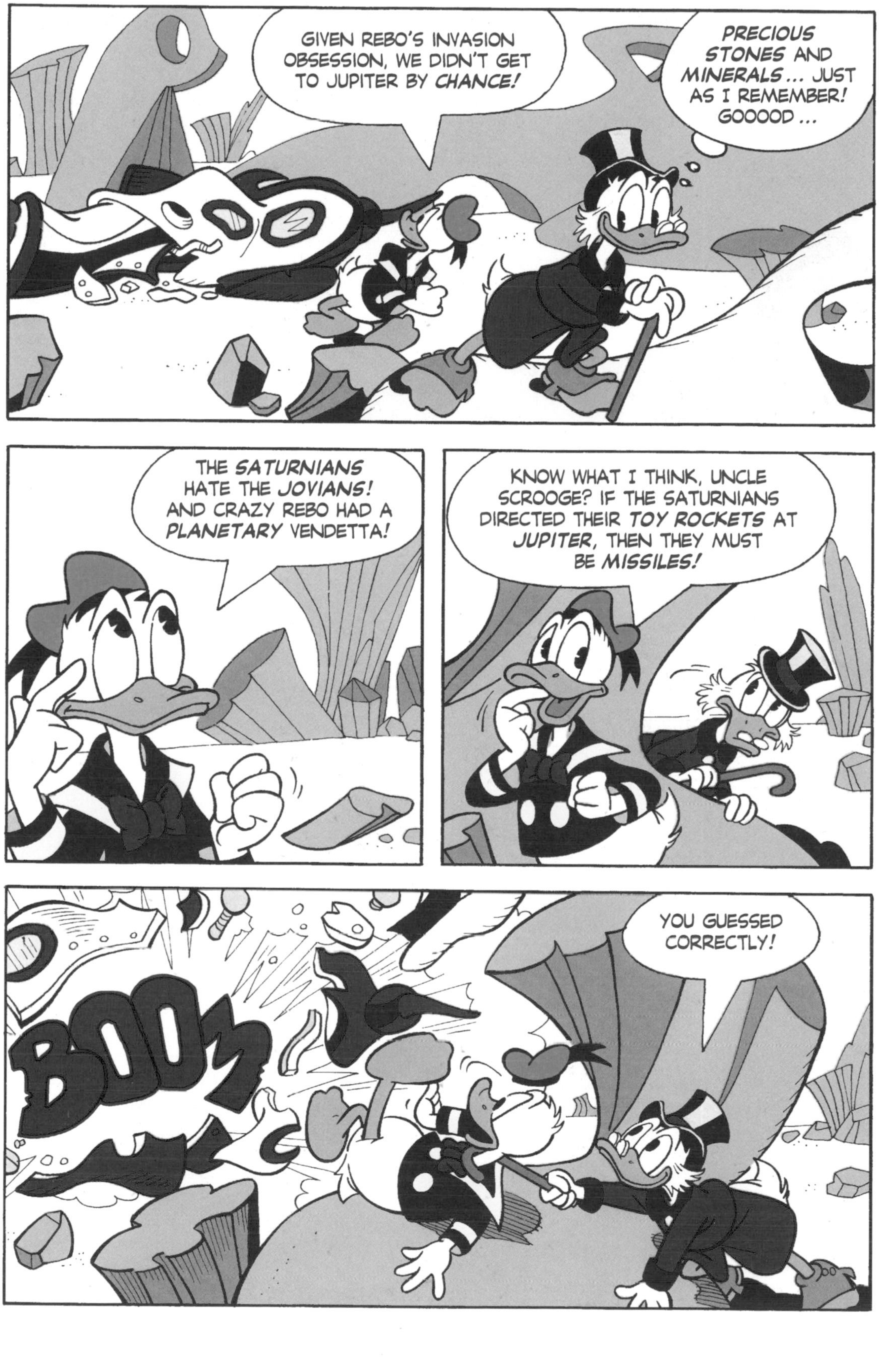
GIVEN REBO'S INVASION OBSESSION, WE DIDN'T GET TO JUPITER BY CHANCE!
PRECIOUS STONES AND MINERALS... JUST AS I REMEMBER! GOOOOD...
THE SATURNIANS HATE THE JOVIANS! AND CRAZY REBO HAD A PLANETARY VENDETTA!
KNOW WHAT I THINK, UNCLE SCROOGE? IF THE SATURNIANS DIRECTED THEIR TOY ROCKETS AT JUPITER, THEN THEY MUST BE MISSILES!
BOOM
YOU GUESSED CORRECTLY!

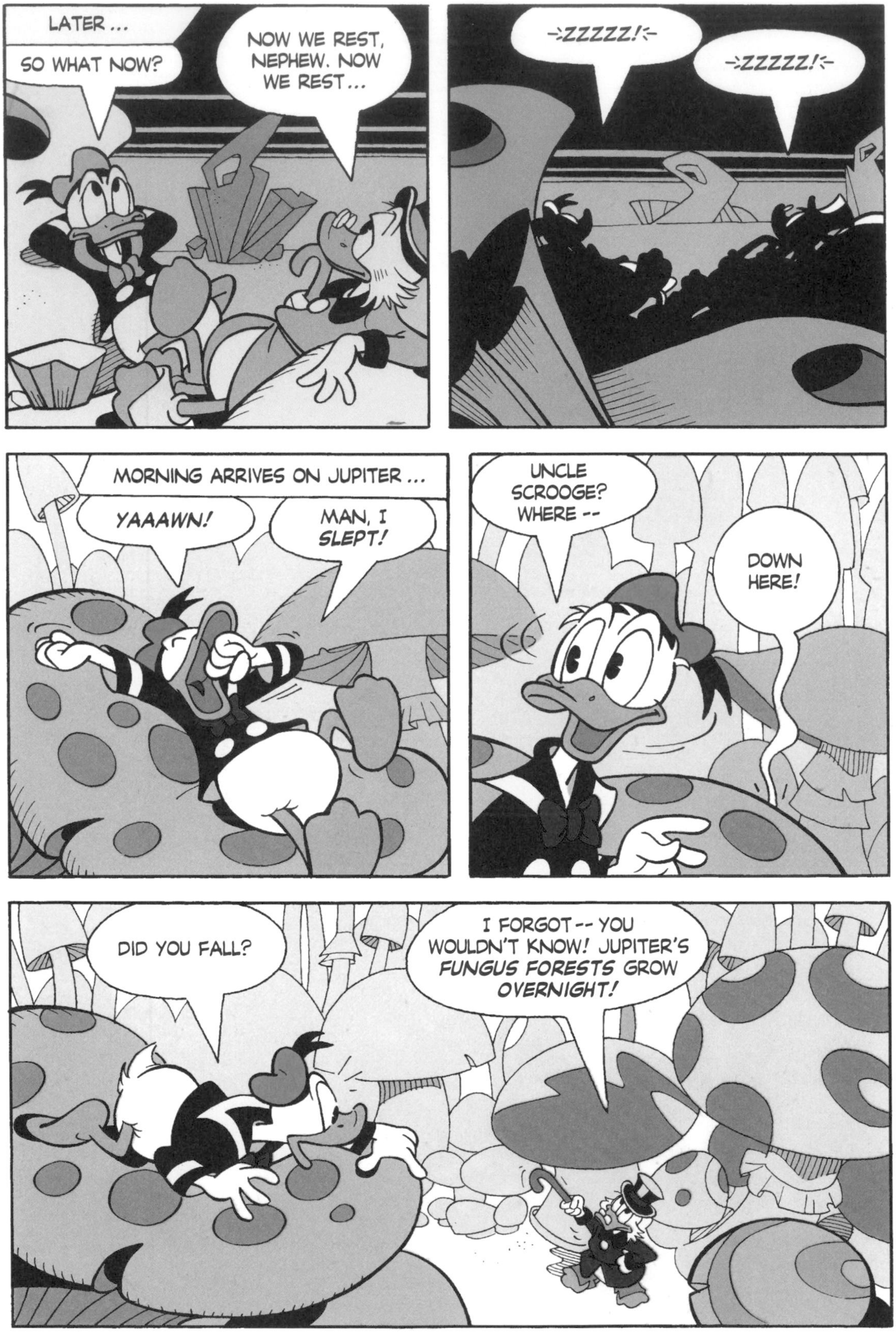
LATER ...
SO WHAT NOW?
NOW WE REST, NEPHEW. NOW WE REST...
-ZZZZZ!-
-ZZZZZ!-
MORNING ARRIVES ON JUPITER ...
YAAAWN!
MAN, I SLEPT!
UNCLE SCROOGE? WHERE --
DOWN HERE!
DID YOU FALL?
I FORGOT -- YOU WOULDN'T KNOW! JUPITER'S FUNGUS FORESTS GROW OVERNIGHT!

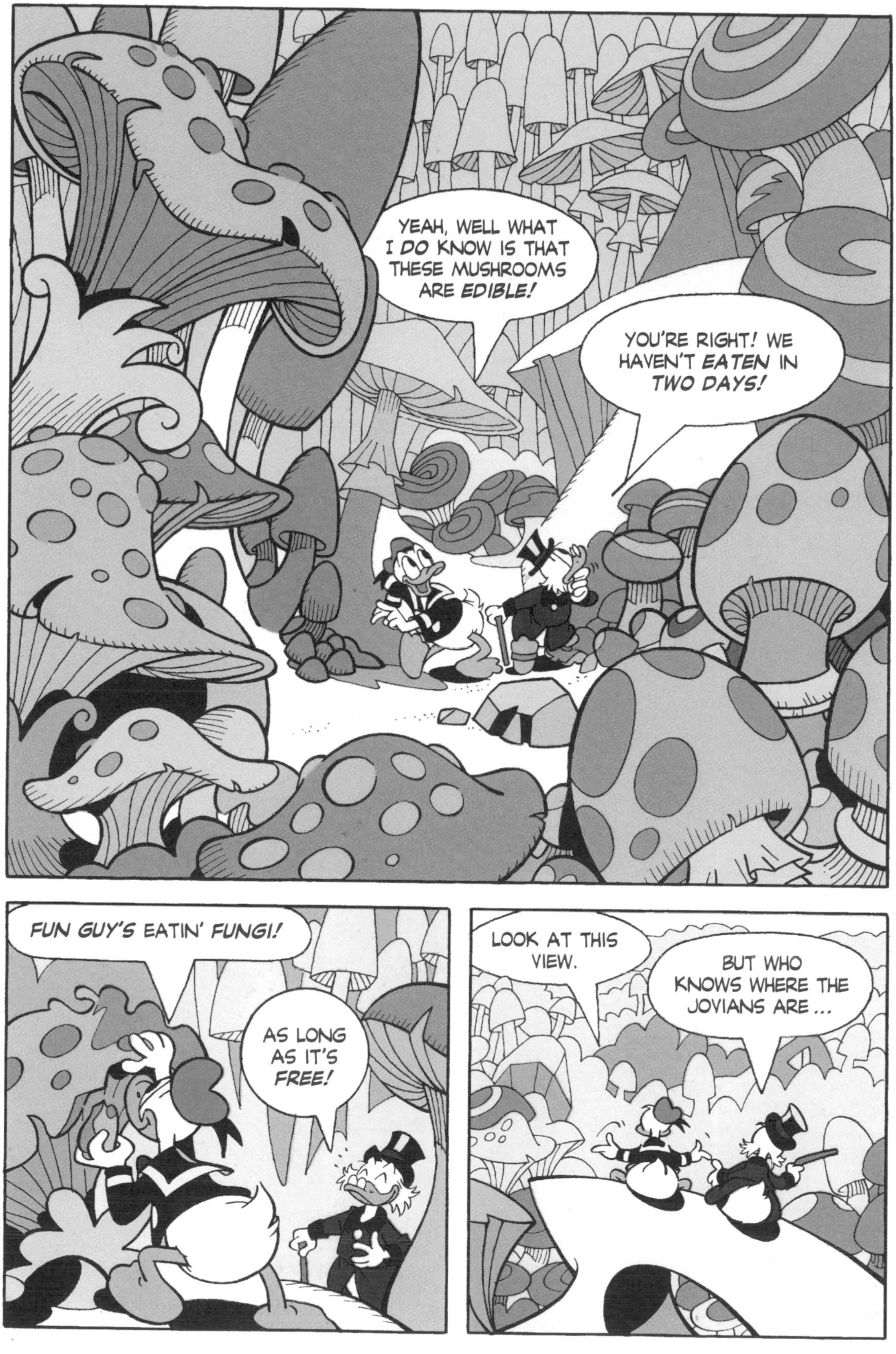
YEAH, WELL WHAT I DO KNOW IS THAT THESE MUSHROOMS ARE EDIBLE!
YOU'RE RIGHT! WE HAVEN'T EATEN IN TWO DAYS!
FUN GUY'S EATIN' FUNGI!
AS LONG AS IT'S FREE!
LOOK AT THIS VIEW.
BUT WHO KNOWS WHERE THE JOVIANS ARE ...

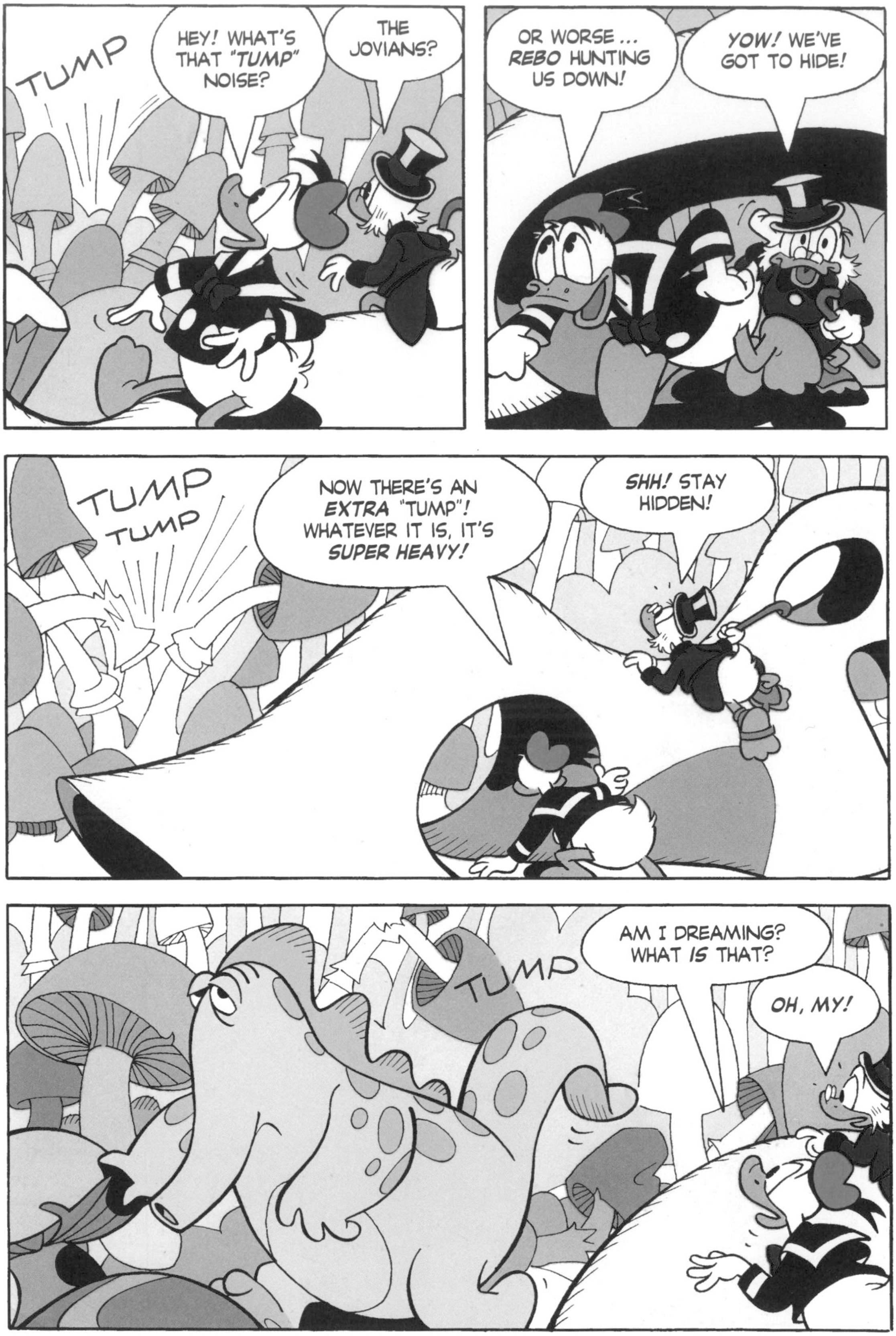
TUMP
HEY! WHAT'S THAT "TUMP" NOISE?
THE JOVIANS?
OR WORSE ... REBO HUNTING US DOWN!
YOW! WE'VE GOT TO HIDE!
TUMP TUMP
NOW THERE'S AN EXTRA "TUMP"! WHATEVER IT IS, IT'S SUPER HEAVY!
SHH! STAY HIDDEN!
TUMP
AM I DREAMING? WHAT IS THAT?
OH, MY!

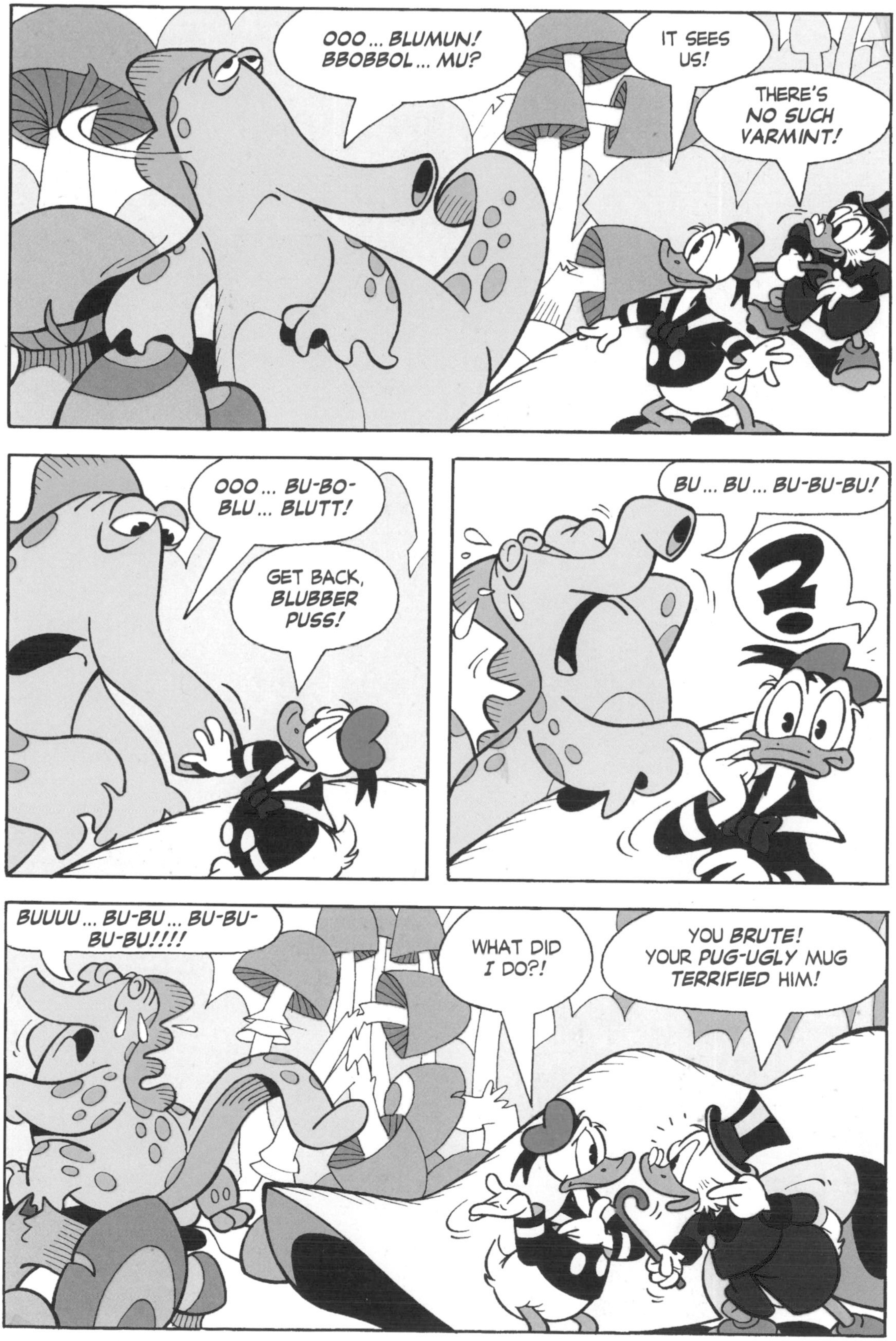
OOO ... BLUMUN! BBOBBOL ... MU?
IT SEES US!
THERE'S NO SUCH VARMINT!
OOO ... BU-BO-BLU ... BLUTT!
GET BACK, BLUBBER PUSS!
BU ... BU ... BU-BU-BU!
?
BUUUU ... BU-BU ... BU-BU-BU-BU!!!!
WHAT DID I DO?!
YOU BRUTE! YOUR PUG-UGLY MUG TERRIFIED HIM!

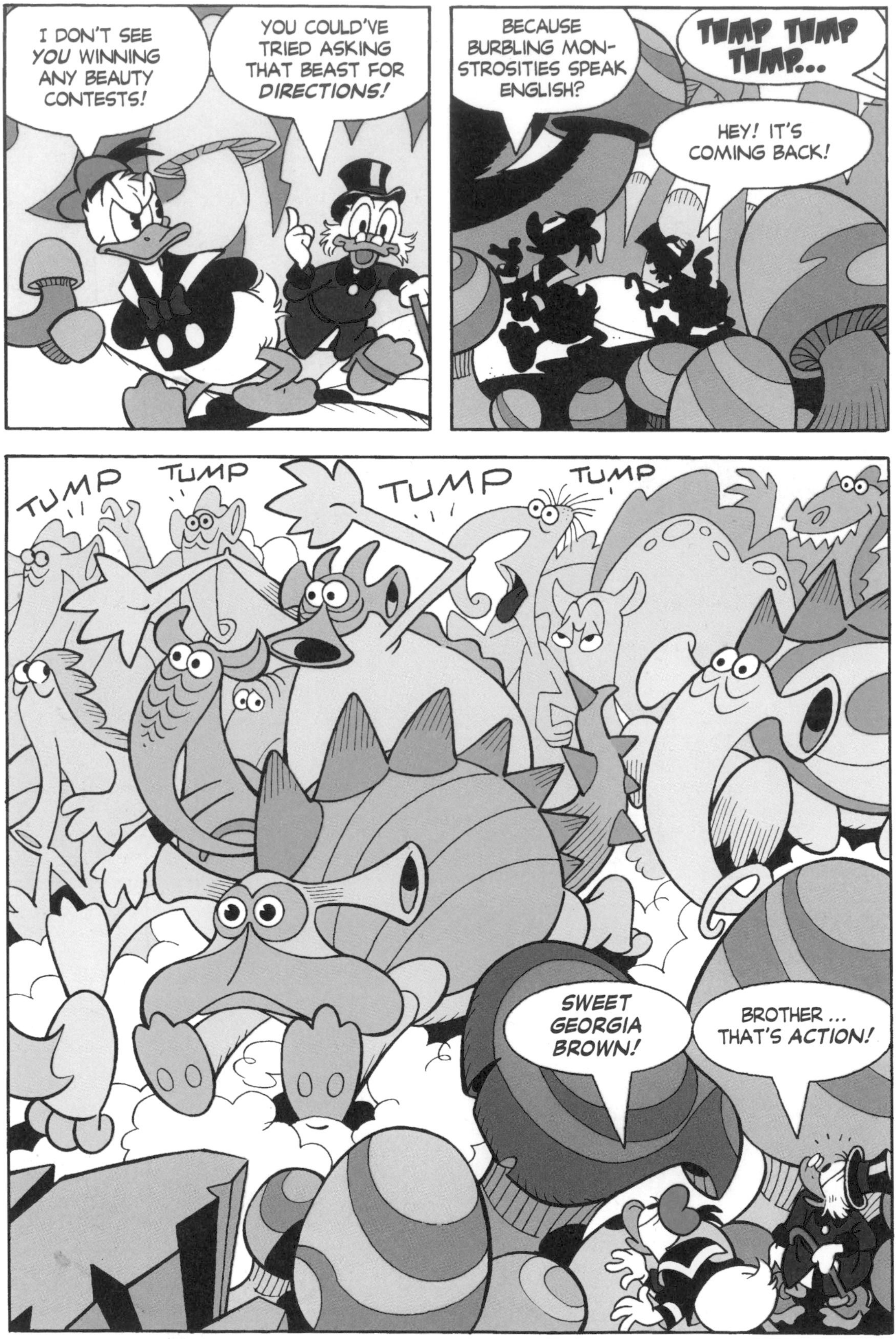
I DON'T SEE *YOU* WINNING ANY BEAUTY CONTESTS!
YOU COULD'VE TRIED ASKING THAT BEAST FOR *DIRECTIONS!*
BECAUSE BURBLING MON-STROSITIES SPEAK ENGLISH?
TUMP TUMP TUMP...
HEY! IT'S COMING BACK!
TUMP
TUMP
TUMP
TUMP
SWEET GEORGIA BROWN!
BROTHER ... THAT'S *ACTION!*

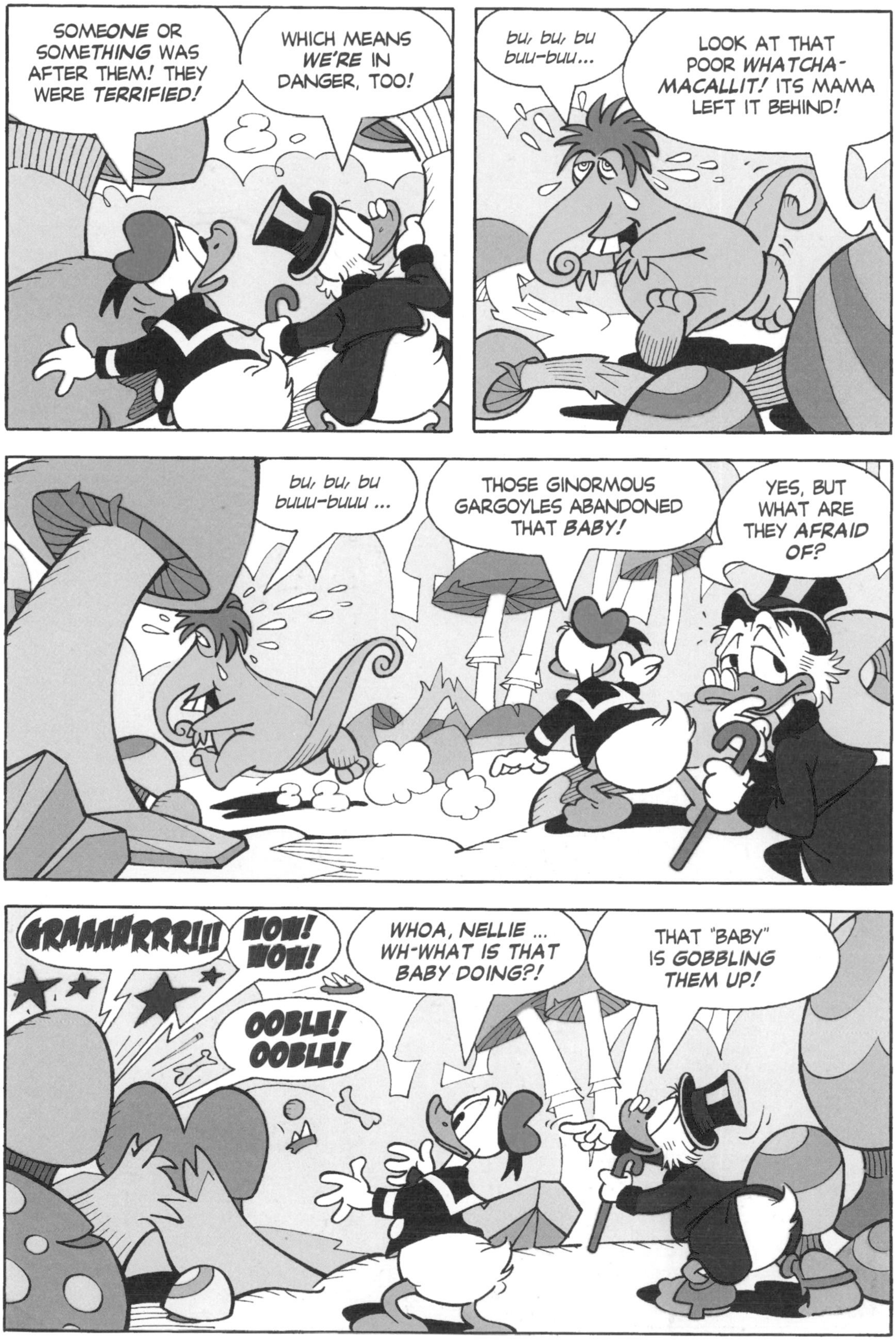
SOMEONE OR SOMETHING WAS AFTER THEM! THEY WERE TERRIFIED!
WHICH MEANS WE'RE IN DANGER, TOO!
bu, bu, bu buu-buu...
LOOK AT THAT POOR WHATCHA-MACALLIT! ITS MAMA LEFT IT BEHIND!
bu, bu, bu buuu-buuu ...
THOSE GINORMOUS GARGOYLES ABANDONED THAT BABY!
YES, BUT WHAT ARE THEY AFRAID OF?
GRAAAHRRR!!!
WOW! WOW!
OOBLE! OOBLE!
WHOA, NELLIE ... WH-WHAT IS THAT BABY DOING?!
THAT "BABY" IS GOBBLING THEM UP!

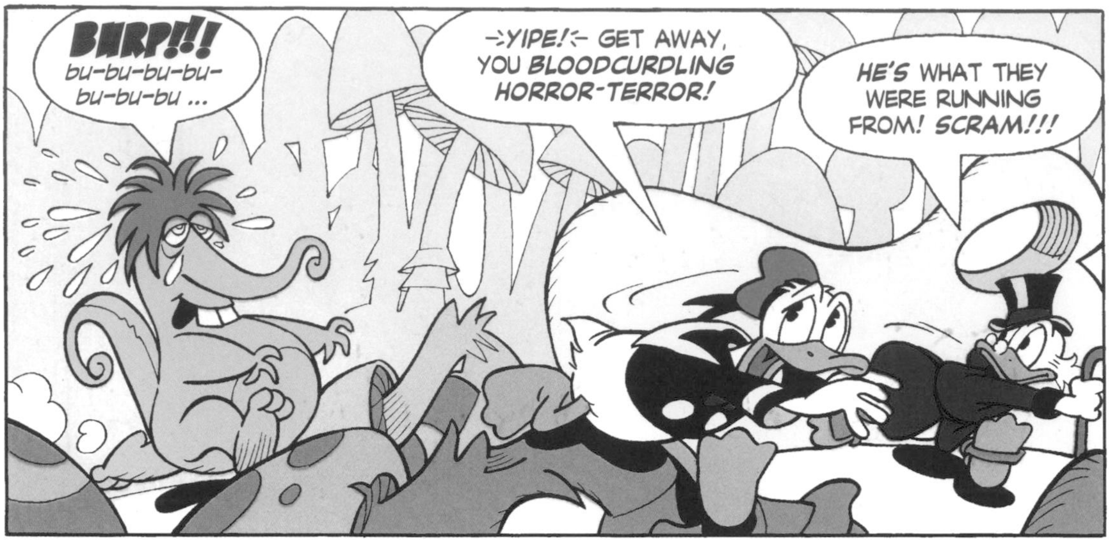
BURP!!!
bu-bu-bu-bu-bu-bu-bu ...
→YIPE!← GET AWAY, YOU BLOODCURDLING HORROR-TERROR!
HE'S WHAT THEY WERE RUNNING FROM! SCRAM!!!

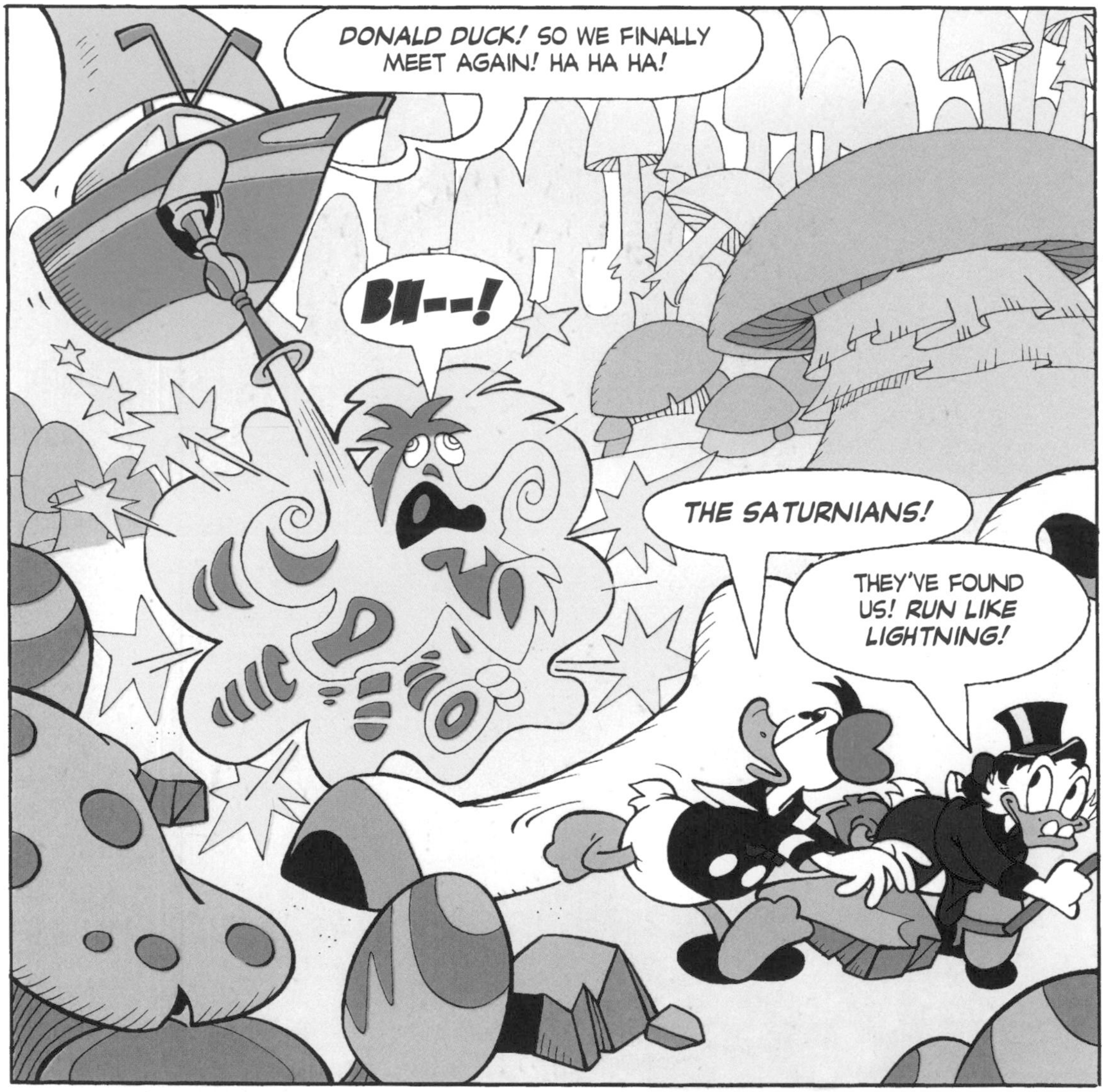
DONALD DUCK! SO WE FINALLY MEET AGAIN! HA HA HA!
BU--!
THE SATURNIANS!
THEY'VE FOUND US! RUN LIKE LIGHTNING!

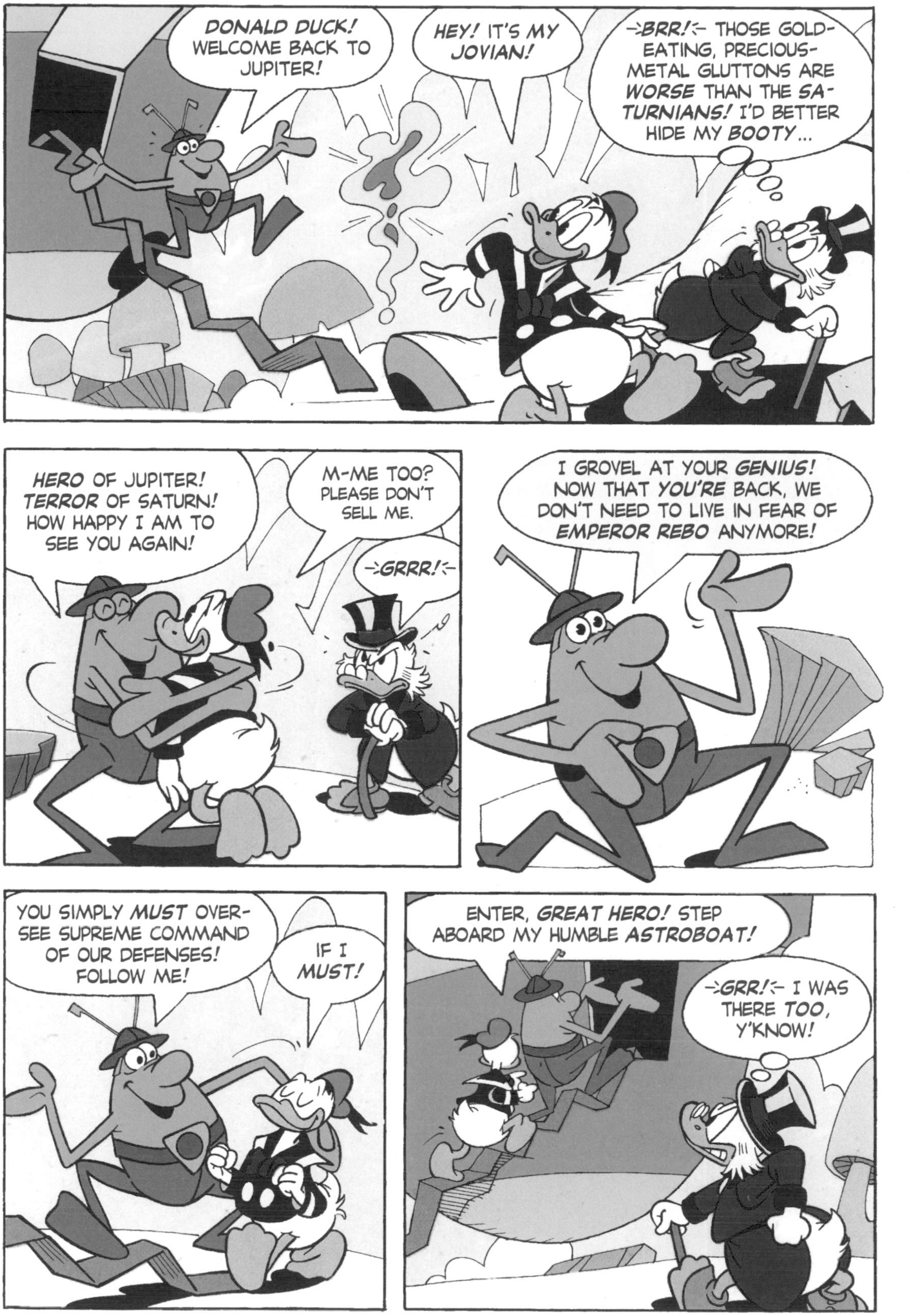
DONALD DUCK! WELCOME BACK TO JUPITER!
HEY! IT'S MY JOVIAN!
BRR! THOSE GOLD-EATING, PRECIOUS-METAL GLUTTONS ARE WORSE THAN THE SATURNIANS! I'D BETTER HIDE MY BOOTY...
HERO OF JUPITER! TERROR OF SATURN! HOW HAPPY I AM TO SEE YOU AGAIN!
M-ME TOO? PLEASE DON'T SELL ME.
GRRR!
I GROVEL AT YOUR GENIUS! NOW THAT YOU'RE BACK, WE DON'T NEED TO LIVE IN FEAR OF EMPEROR REBO ANYMORE!
YOU SIMPLY MUST OVERSEE SUPREME COMMAND OF OUR DEFENSES! FOLLOW ME!
IF I MUST!
ENTER, GREAT HERO! STEP ABOARD MY HUMBLE ASTROBOAT!
GRR! I WAS THERE TOO, Y'KNOW!

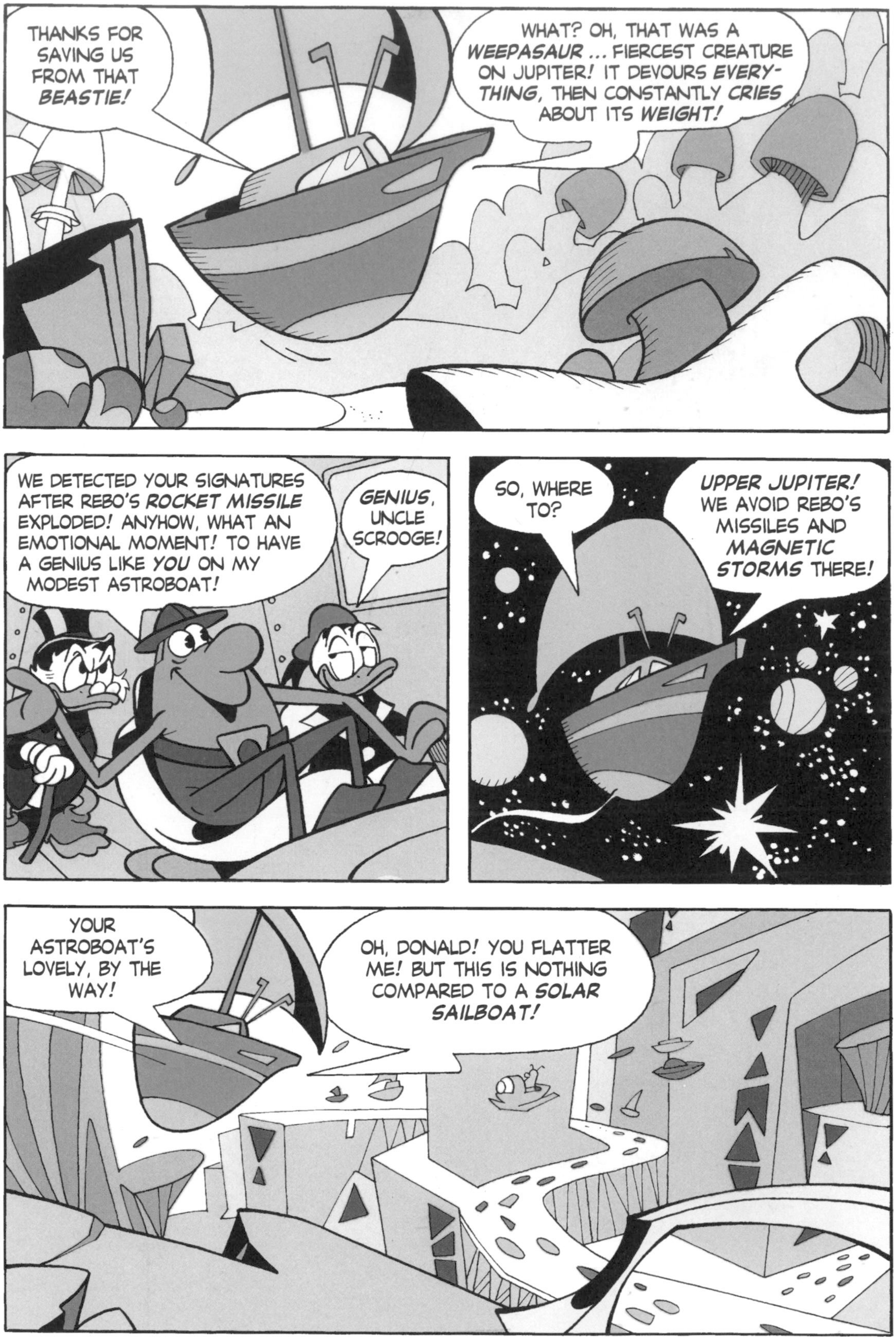
THANKS FOR SAVING US FROM THAT BEASTIE!
WHAT? OH, THAT WAS A WEEPASAUR ... FIERCEST CREATURE ON JUPITER! IT DEVOURS EVERY-THING, THEN CONSTANTLY CRIES ABOUT ITS WEIGHT!
WE DETECTED YOUR SIGNATURES AFTER REBO'S ROCKET MISSILE EXPLODED! ANYHOW, WHAT AN EMOTIONAL MOMENT! TO HAVE A GENIUS LIKE YOU ON MY MODEST ASTROBOAT!
GENIUS, UNCLE SCROOGE!
SO, WHERE TO?
UPPER JUPITER! WE AVOID REBO'S MISSILES AND MAGNETIC STORMS THERE!
YOUR ASTROBOAT'S LOVELY, BY THE WAY!
OH, DONALD! YOU FLATTER ME! BUT THIS IS NOTHING COMPARED TO A SOLAR SAILBOAT!

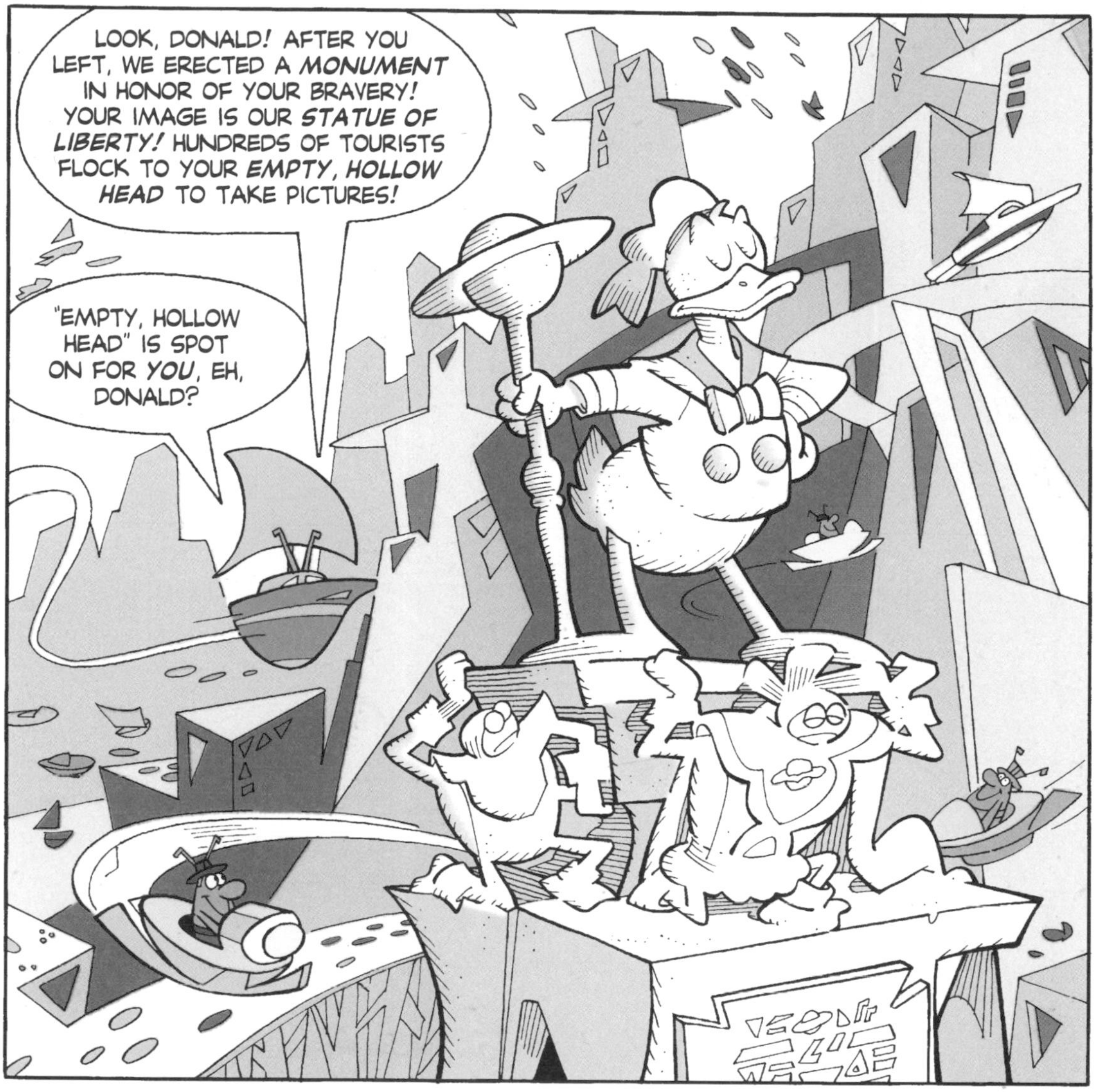
LOOK, DONALD! AFTER YOU LEFT, WE ERECTED A MONUMENT IN HONOR OF YOUR BRAVERY! YOUR IMAGE IS OUR STATUE OF LIBERTY! HUNDREDS OF TOURISTS FLOCK TO YOUR EMPTY, HOLLOW HEAD TO TAKE PICTURES!
"EMPTY, HOLLOW HEAD" IS SPOT ON FOR YOU, EH, DONALD?

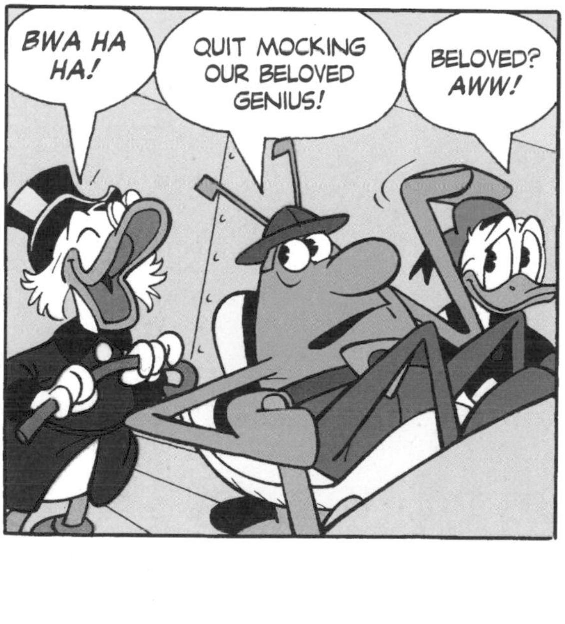
BWA HA HA!
QUIT MOCKING OUR BELOVED GENIUS!
BELOVED? AWW!

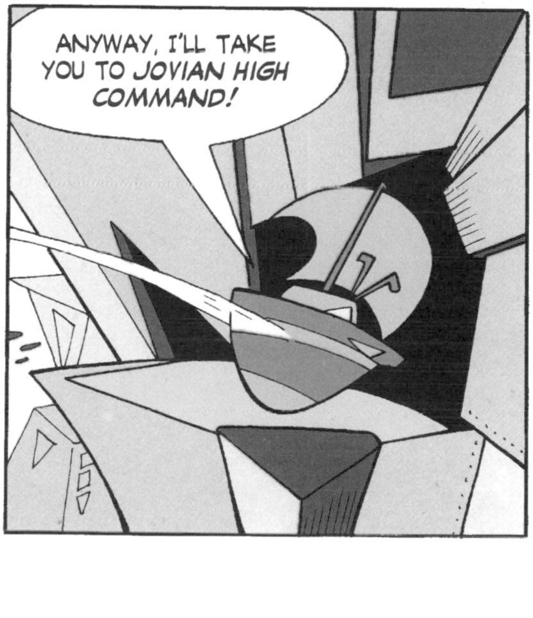
ANYWAY, I'LL TAKE YOU TO JOVIAN HIGH COMMAND!

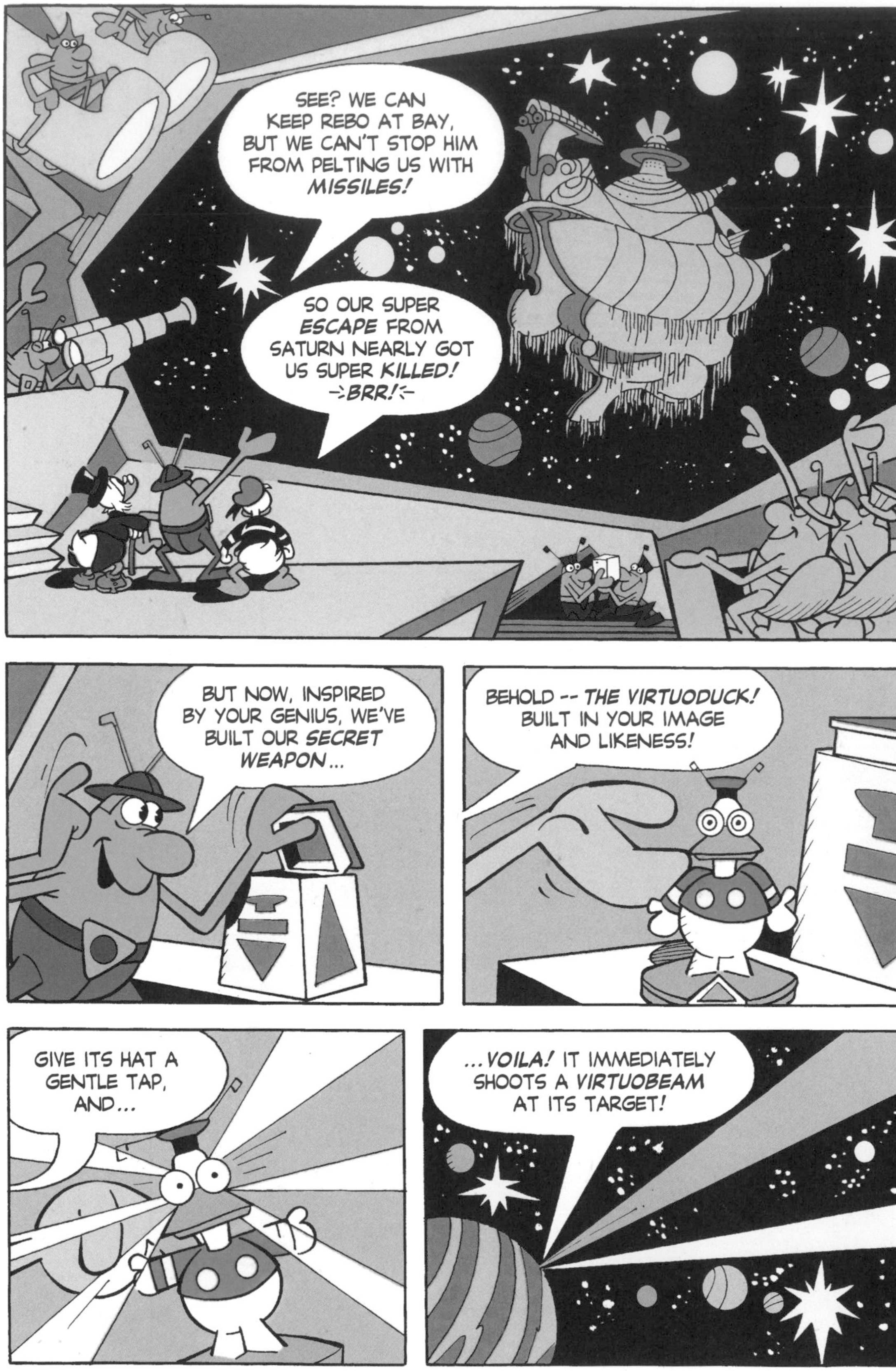
SEE? WE CAN KEEP REBO AT BAY, BUT WE CAN'T STOP HIM FROM PELTING US WITH MISSILES!
SO OUR SUPER ESCAPE FROM SATURN NEARLY GOT US SUPER KILLED! -BRR!-
BUT NOW, INSPIRED BY YOUR GENIUS, WE'VE BUILT OUR SECRET WEAPON...
BEHOLD -- THE VIRTUODUCK! BUILT IN YOUR IMAGE AND LIKENESS!
GIVE ITS HAT A GENTLE TAP, AND...
...VOILA! IT IMMEDIATELY SHOOTS A VIRTUOBEAM AT ITS TARGET!

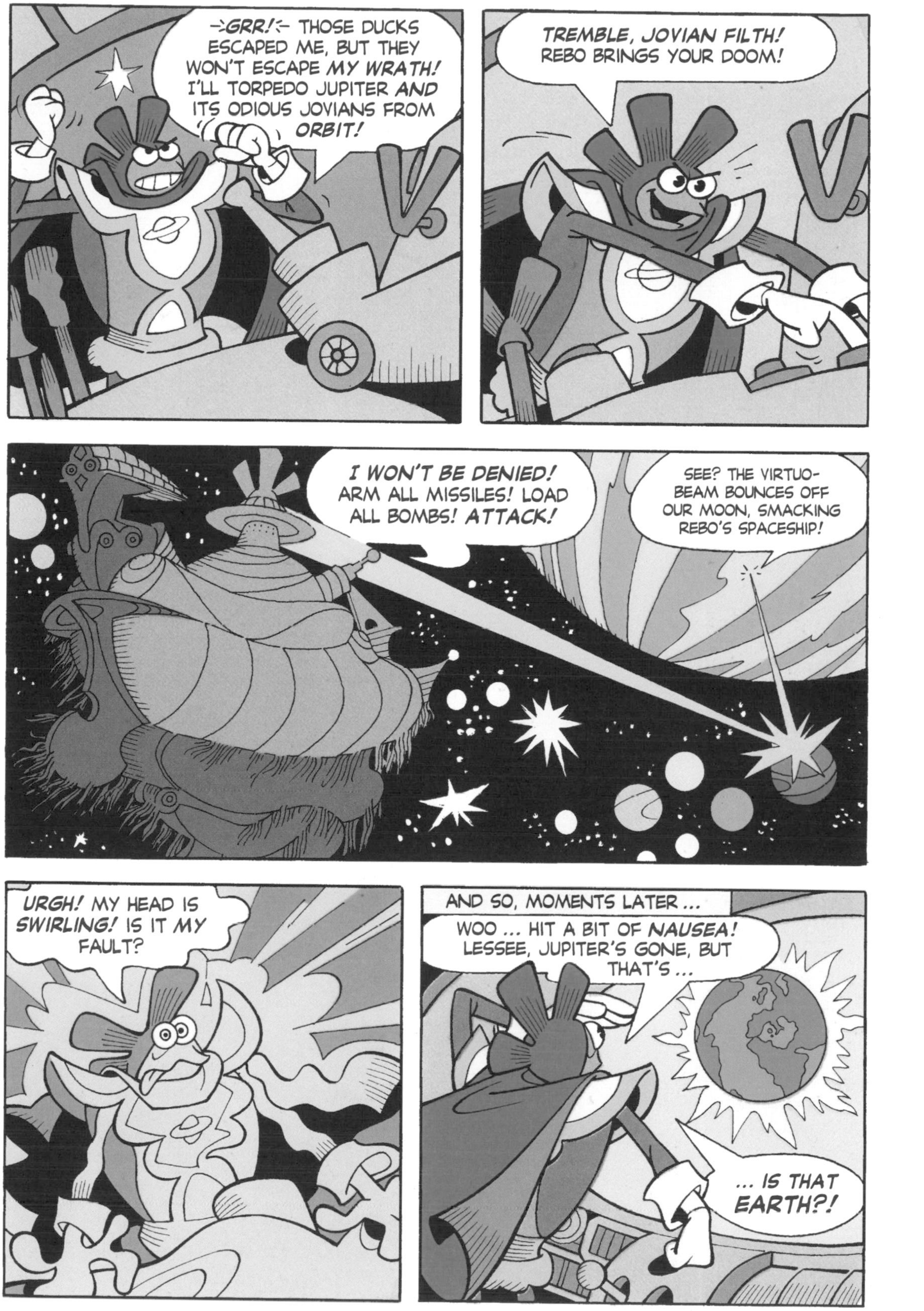

-GRR!- THOSE DUCKS ESCAPED ME, BUT THEY WON'T ESCAPE MY WRATH! I'LL TORPEDO JUPITER AND ITS ODIOUS JOVIANS FROM ORBIT!
TREMBLE, JOVIAN FILTH! REBO BRINGS YOUR DOOM!
I WON'T BE DENIED! ARM ALL MISSILES! LOAD ALL BOMBS! ATTACK!
SEE? THE VIRTUO-BEAM BOUNCES OFF OUR MOON, SMACKING REBO'S SPACESHIP!
URGH! MY HEAD IS SWIRLING! IS IT MY FAULT?
AND SO, MOMENTS LATER ...
WOO ... HIT A BIT OF NAUSEA! LESSEE, JUPITER'S GONE, BUT THAT'S ...
... IS THAT EARTH?!

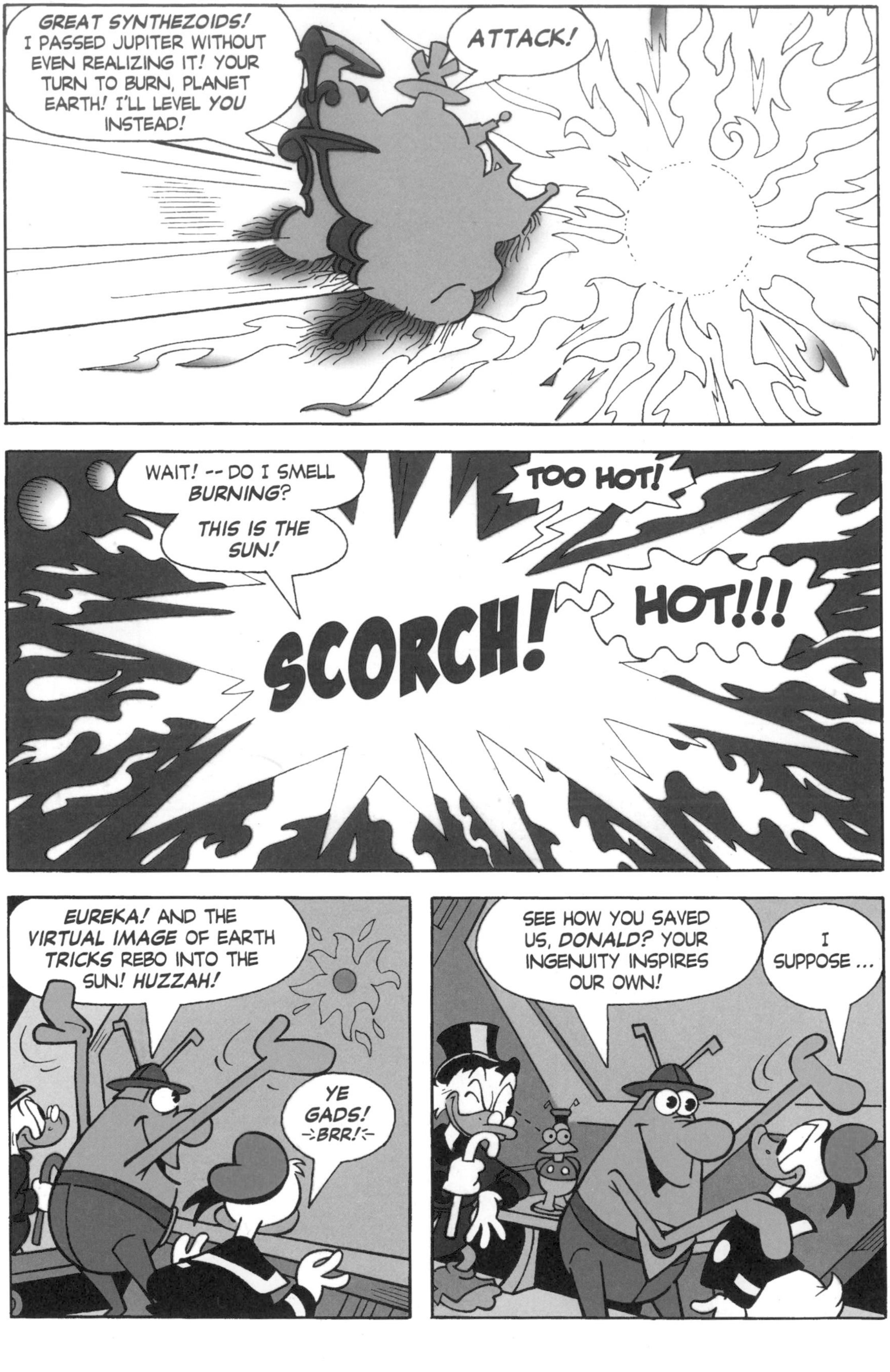
GREAT SYNTHEZOIDS! I PASSED JUPITER WITHOUT EVEN REALIZING IT! YOUR TURN TO BURN, PLANET EARTH! I'LL LEVEL YOU INSTEAD!
ATTACK!
WAIT! -- DO I SMELL BURNING?
THIS IS THE SUN!
TOO HOT!
SCORCH!
HOT!!!
EUREKA! AND THE VIRTUAL IMAGE OF EARTH TRICKS REBO INTO THE SUN! HUZZAH!
YE GADS! -BRR!-
SEE HOW YOU SAVED US, DONALD? YOUR INGENUITY INSPIRES OUR OWN!
I SUPPOSE ...

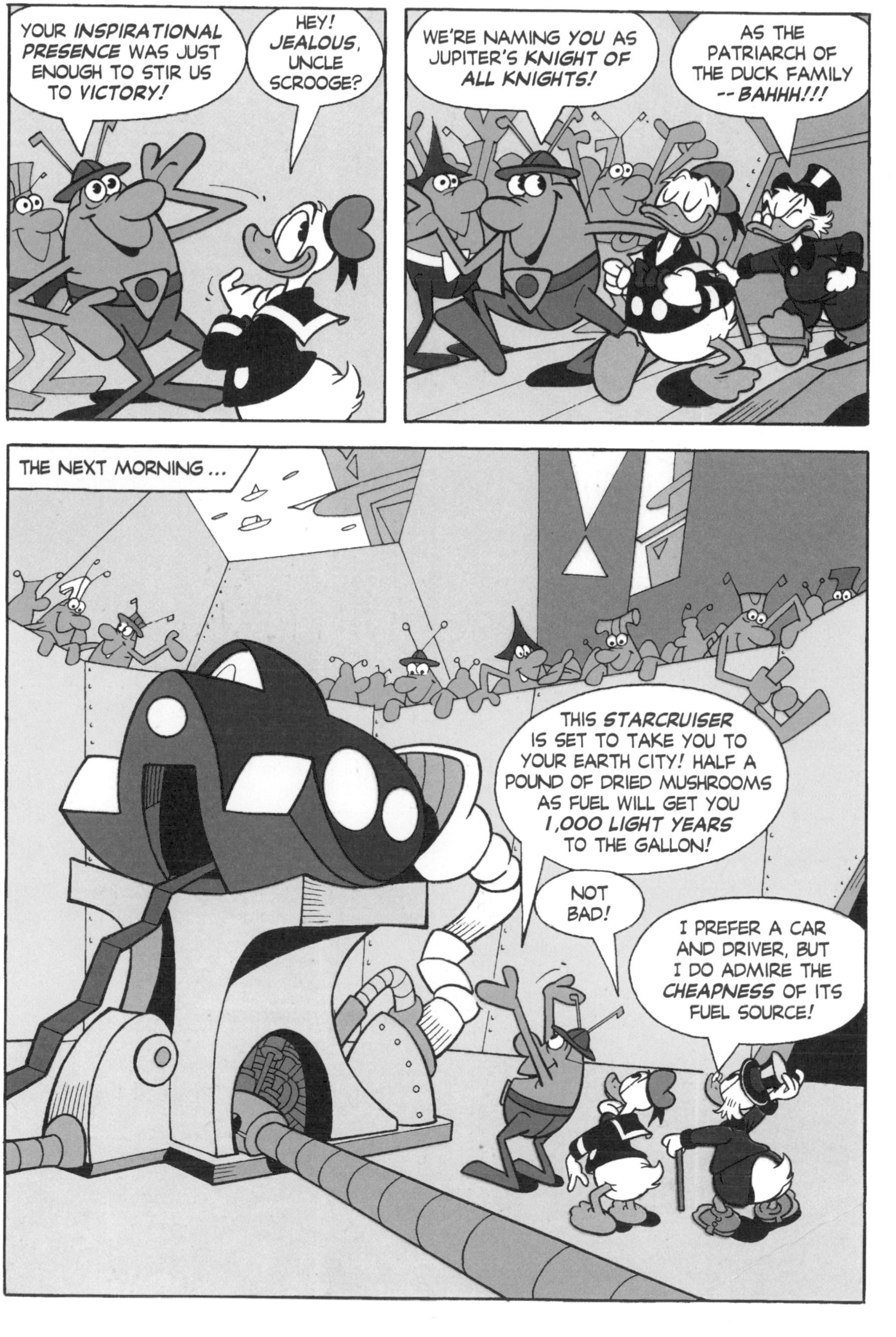
YOUR INSPIRATIONAL PRESENCE WAS JUST ENOUGH TO STIR US TO VICTORY!
HEY! JEALOUS, UNCLE SCROOGE?
WE'RE NAMING YOU AS JUPITER'S KNIGHT OF ALL KNIGHTS!
AS THE PATRIARCH OF THE DUCK FAMILY --BAHHH!!!
THE NEXT MORNING ...
THIS STARCRUISER IS SET TO TAKE YOU TO YOUR EARTH CITY! HALF A POUND OF DRIED MUSHROOMS AS FUEL WILL GET YOU 1,000 LIGHT YEARS TO THE GALLON!
NOT BAD!
I PREFER A CAR AND DRIVER, BUT I DO ADMIRE THE CHEAPNESS OF ITS FUEL SOURCE!

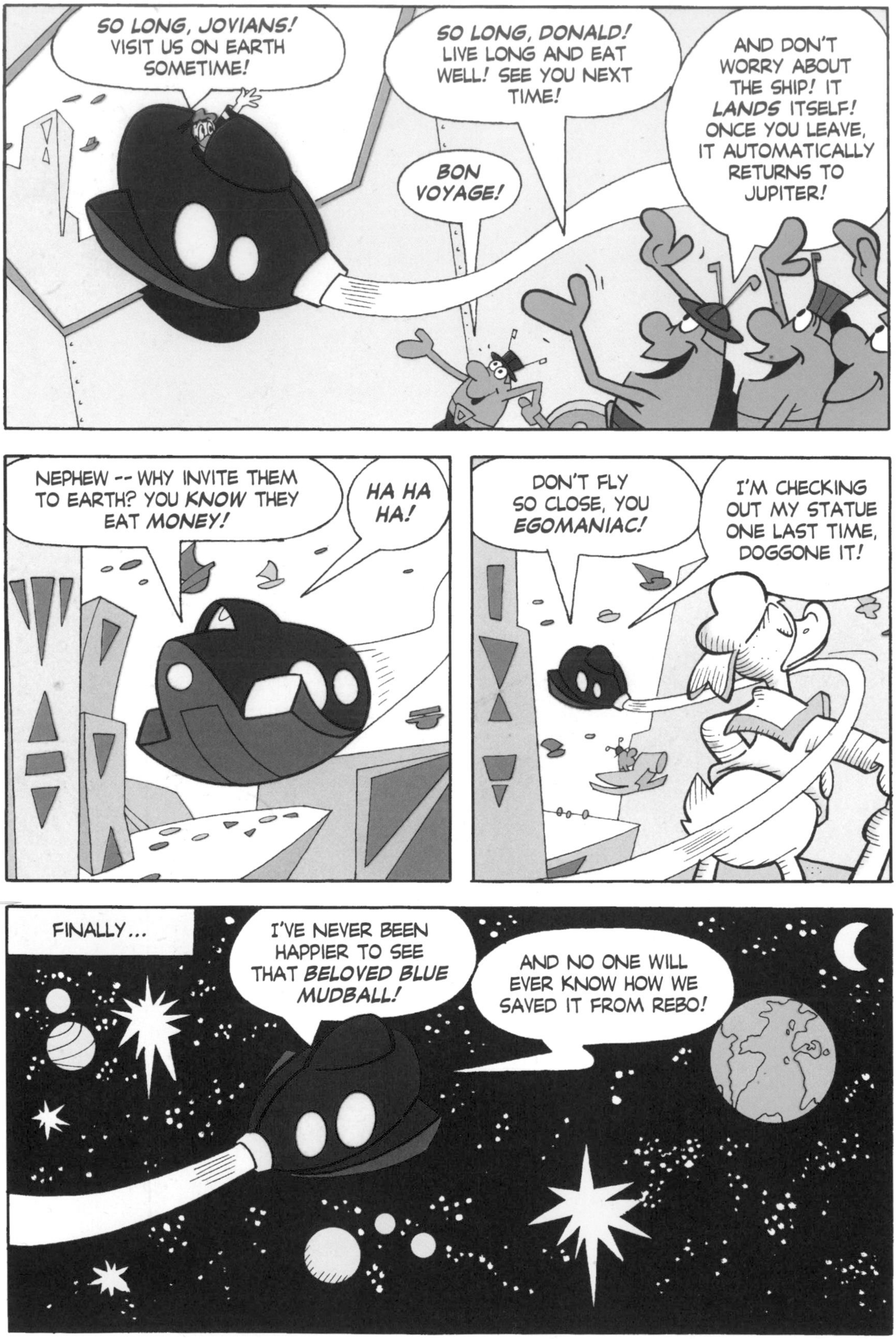
SO LONG, JOVIANS! VISIT US ON EARTH SOMETIME!
SO LONG, DONALD! LIVE LONG AND EAT WELL! SEE YOU NEXT TIME!
BON VOYAGE!
AND DON'T WORRY ABOUT THE SHIP! IT LANDS ITSELF! ONCE YOU LEAVE, IT AUTOMATICALLY RETURNS TO JUPITER!
NEPHEW -- WHY INVITE THEM TO EARTH? YOU KNOW THEY EAT MONEY!
HA HA HA!
DON'T FLY SO CLOSE, YOU EGOMANIAC!
I'M CHECKING OUT MY STATUE ONE LAST TIME, DOGGONE IT!
FINALLY...
I'VE NEVER BEEN HAPPIER TO SEE THAT BELOVED BLUE MUDBALL!
AND NO ONE WILL EVER KNOW HOW WE SAVED IT FROM REBO!

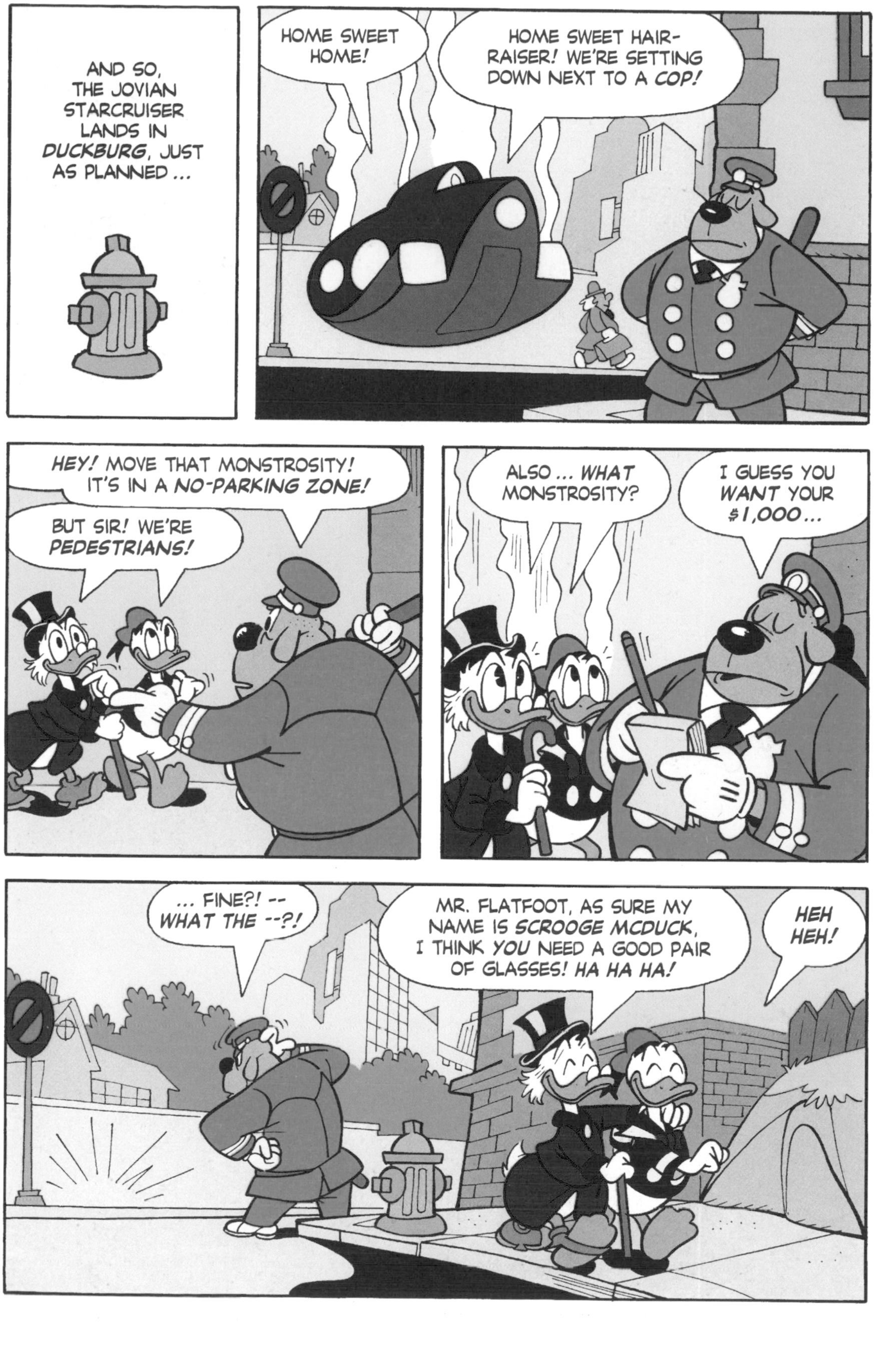
AND SO, THE JOVIAN STARCRUISER LANDS IN DUCKBURG, JUST AS PLANNED ...
HOME SWEET HOME!
HOME SWEET HAIR-RAISER! WE'RE SETTING DOWN NEXT TO A COP!
HEY! MOVE THAT MONSTROSITY! IT'S IN A NO-PARKING ZONE!
BUT SIR! WE'RE PEDESTRIANS!
ALSO ... WHAT MONSTROSITY?
I GUESS YOU WANT YOUR $1,000 ...
... FINE?! -- WHAT THE --?!
MR. FLATFOOT, AS SURE MY NAME IS SCROOGE MCDUCK, I THINK YOU NEED A GOOD PAIR OF GLASSES! HA HA HA!
HEH HEH!

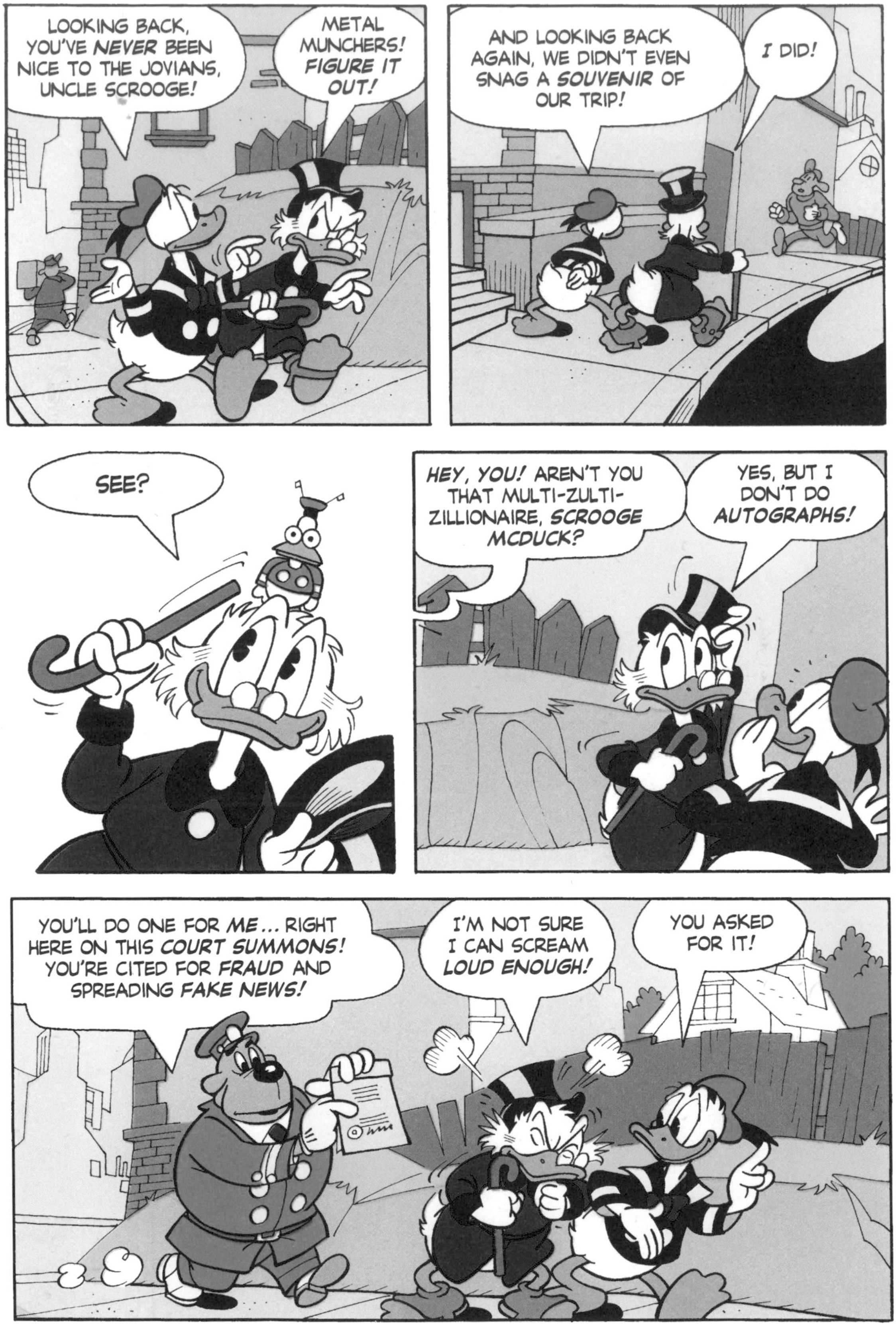
LOOKING BACK, YOU'VE NEVER BEEN NICE TO THE JOVIANS, UNCLE SCROOGE!
METAL MUNCHERS! FIGURE IT OUT!
AND LOOKING BACK AGAIN, WE DIDN'T EVEN SNAG A SOUVENIR OF OUR TRIP!
I DID!
SEE?
HEY, YOU! AREN'T YOU THAT MULTI-ZULTI-ZILLIONAIRE, SCROOGE MCDUCK?
YES, BUT I DON'T DO AUTOGRAPHS!
YOU'LL DO ONE FOR ME... RIGHT HERE ON THIS COURT SUMMONS! YOU'RE CITED FOR FRAUD AND SPREADING FAKE NEWS!
I'M NOT SURE I CAN SCREAM LOUD ENOUGH!
YOU ASKED FOR IT!

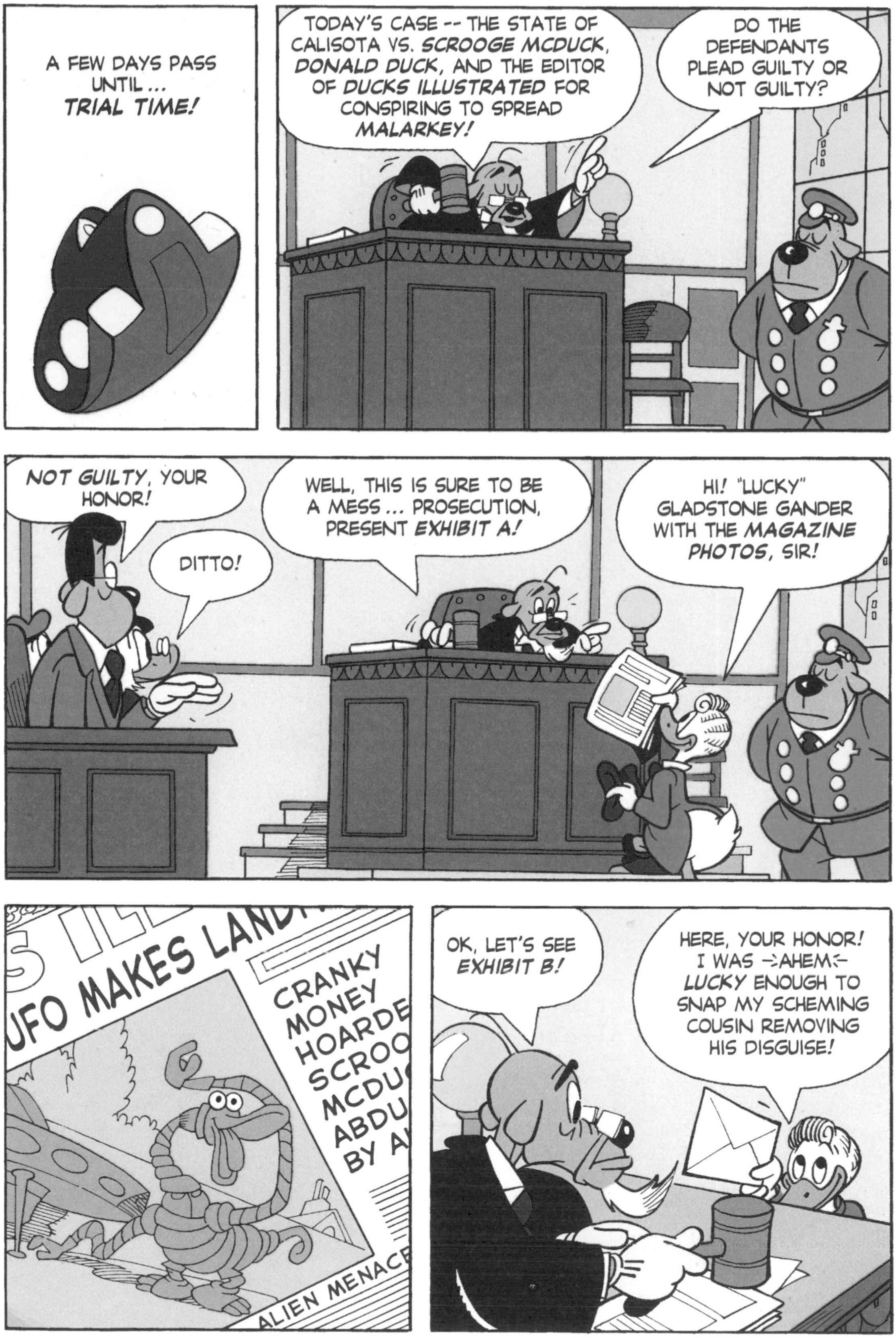
A FEW DAYS PASS UNTIL... TRIAL TIME!
TODAY'S CASE -- THE STATE OF CALISOTA VS. SCROOGE MCDUCK, DONALD DUCK, AND THE EDITOR OF DUCKS ILLUSTRATED FOR CONSPIRING TO SPREAD MALARKEY!
DO THE DEFENDANTS PLEAD GUILTY OR NOT GUILTY?
NOT GUILTY, YOUR HONOR!
DITTO!
WELL, THIS IS SURE TO BE A MESS... PROSECUTION, PRESENT EXHIBIT A!
HI! "LUCKY" GLADSTONE GANDER WITH THE MAGAZINE PHOTOS, SIR!
UFO MAKES LAND
CRANKY MONEY HOARDE SCROO MCDU ABDU BY A
ALIEN MENAC
OK, LET'S SEE EXHIBIT B!
HERE, YOUR HONOR! I WAS -AHEM- LUCKY ENOUGH TO SNAP MY SCHEMING COUSIN REMOVING HIS DISGUISE!

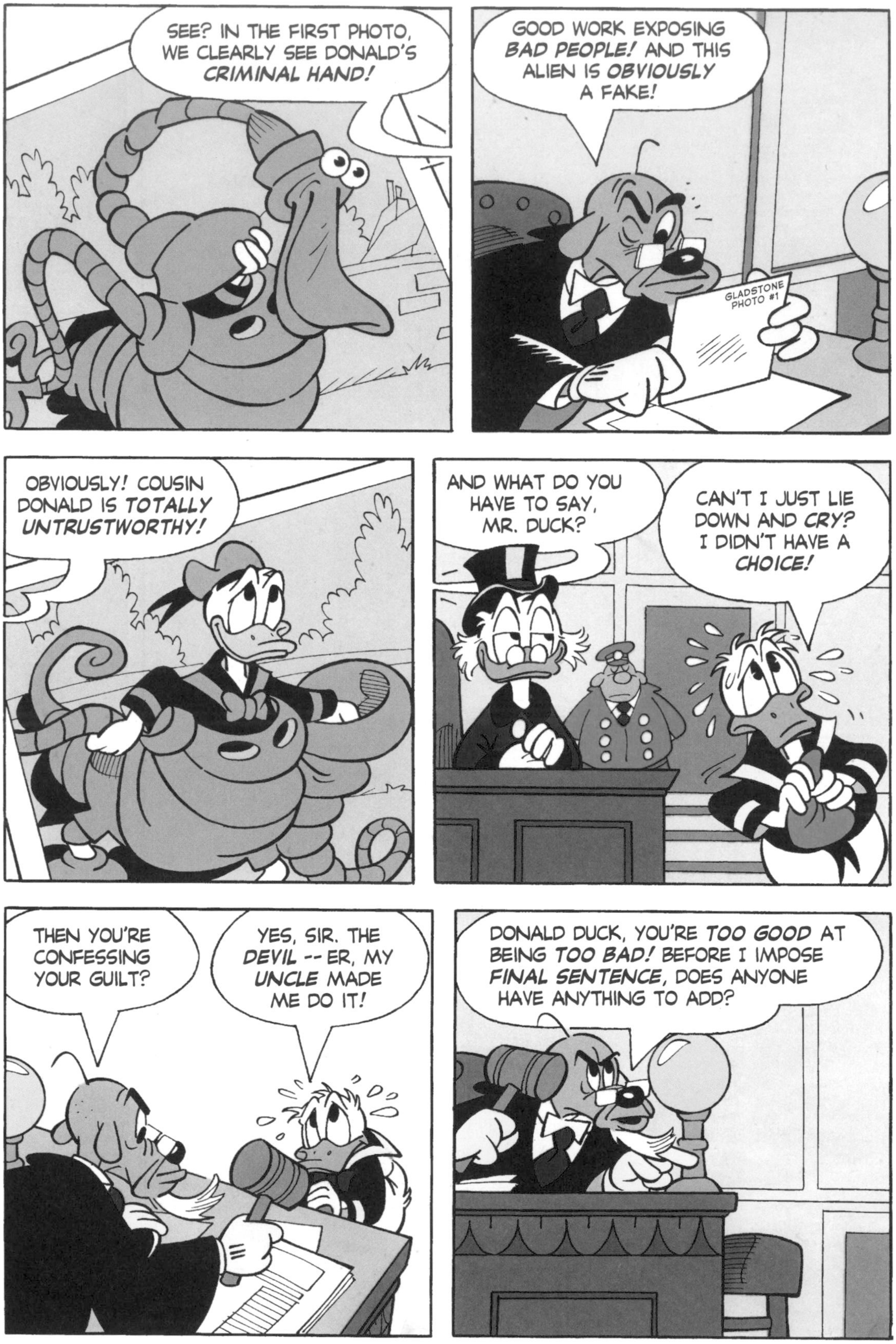
SEE? IN THE FIRST PHOTO, WE CLEARLY SEE DONALD'S CRIMINAL HAND!
GOOD WORK EXPOSING BAD PEOPLE! AND THIS ALIEN IS OBVIOUSLY A FAKE!
GLADSTONE PHOTO #1
OBVIOUSLY! COUSIN DONALD IS TOTALLY UNTRUSTWORTHY!
AND WHAT DO YOU HAVE TO SAY, MR. DUCK?
CAN'T I JUST LIE DOWN AND CRY? I DIDN'T HAVE A CHOICE!
THEN YOU'RE CONFESSING YOUR GUILT?
YES, SIR. THE DEVIL -- ER, MY UNCLE MADE ME DO IT!
DONALD DUCK, YOU'RE TOO GOOD AT BEING TOO BAD! BEFORE I IMPOSE FINAL SENTENCE, DOES ANYONE HAVE ANYTHING TO ADD?

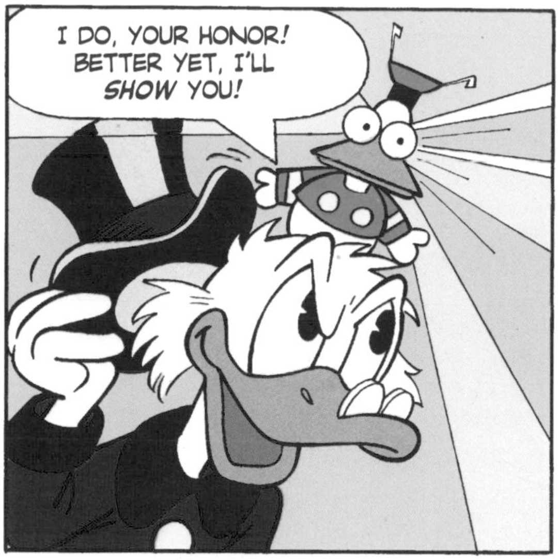
I DO, YOUR HONOR! BETTER YET, I'LL SHOW YOU!

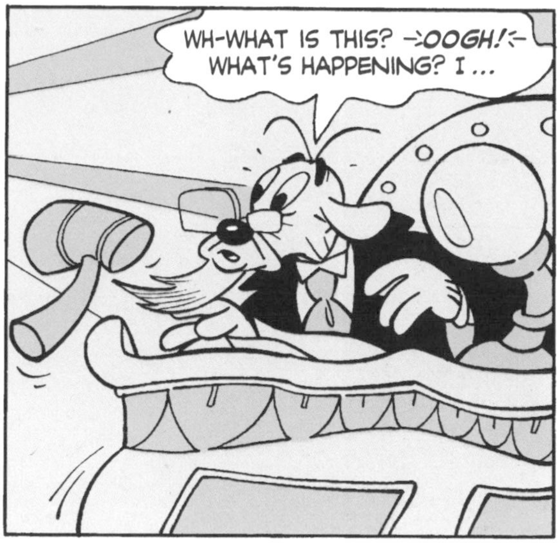
WH-WHAT IS THIS? -OOGH!- WHAT'S HAPPENING? I ...

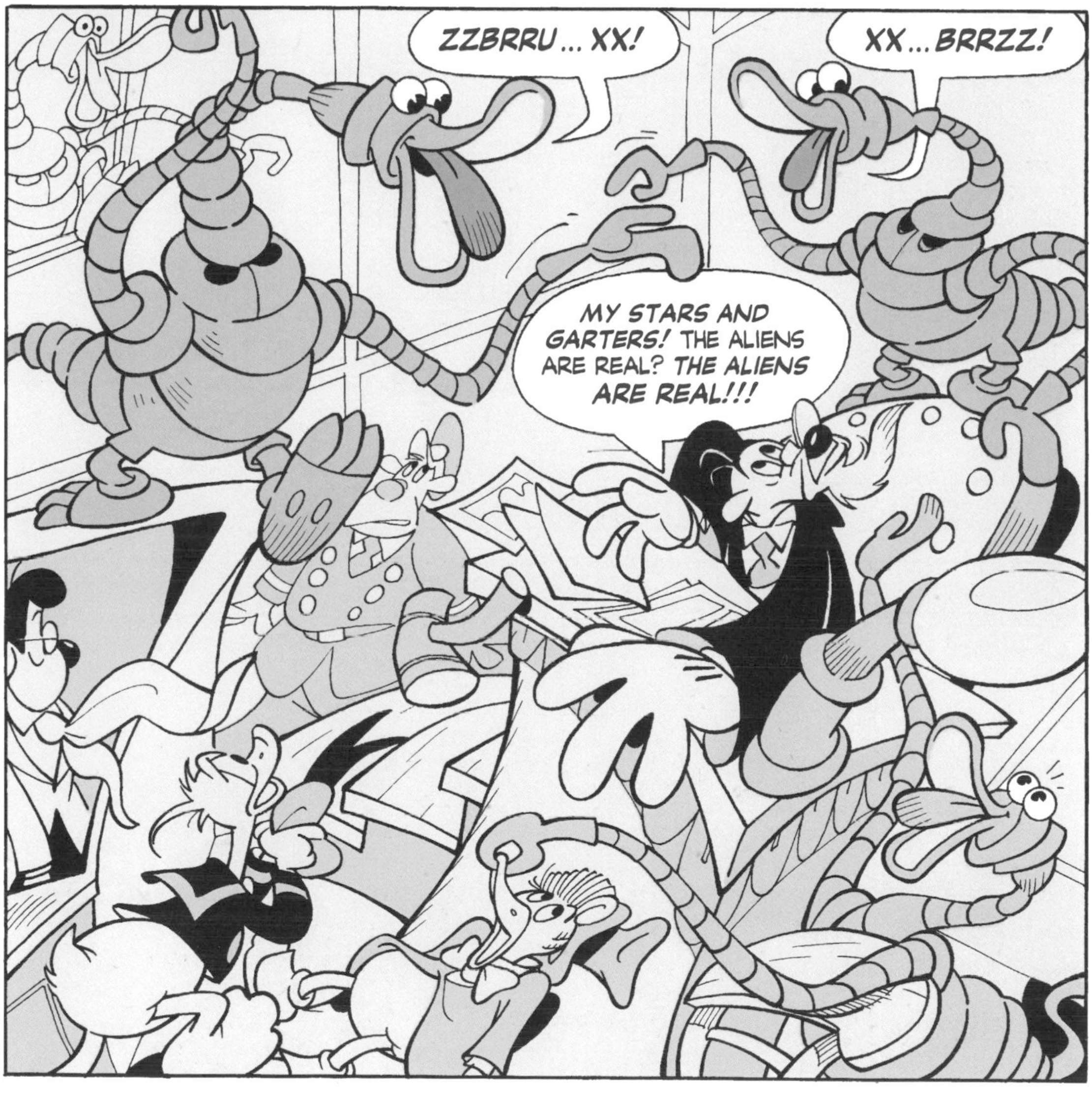
ZZBRRU ... XX!
XX ... BRRZZ!
MY STARS AND GARTERS! THE ALIENS ARE REAL? THE ALIENS ARE REAL!!!

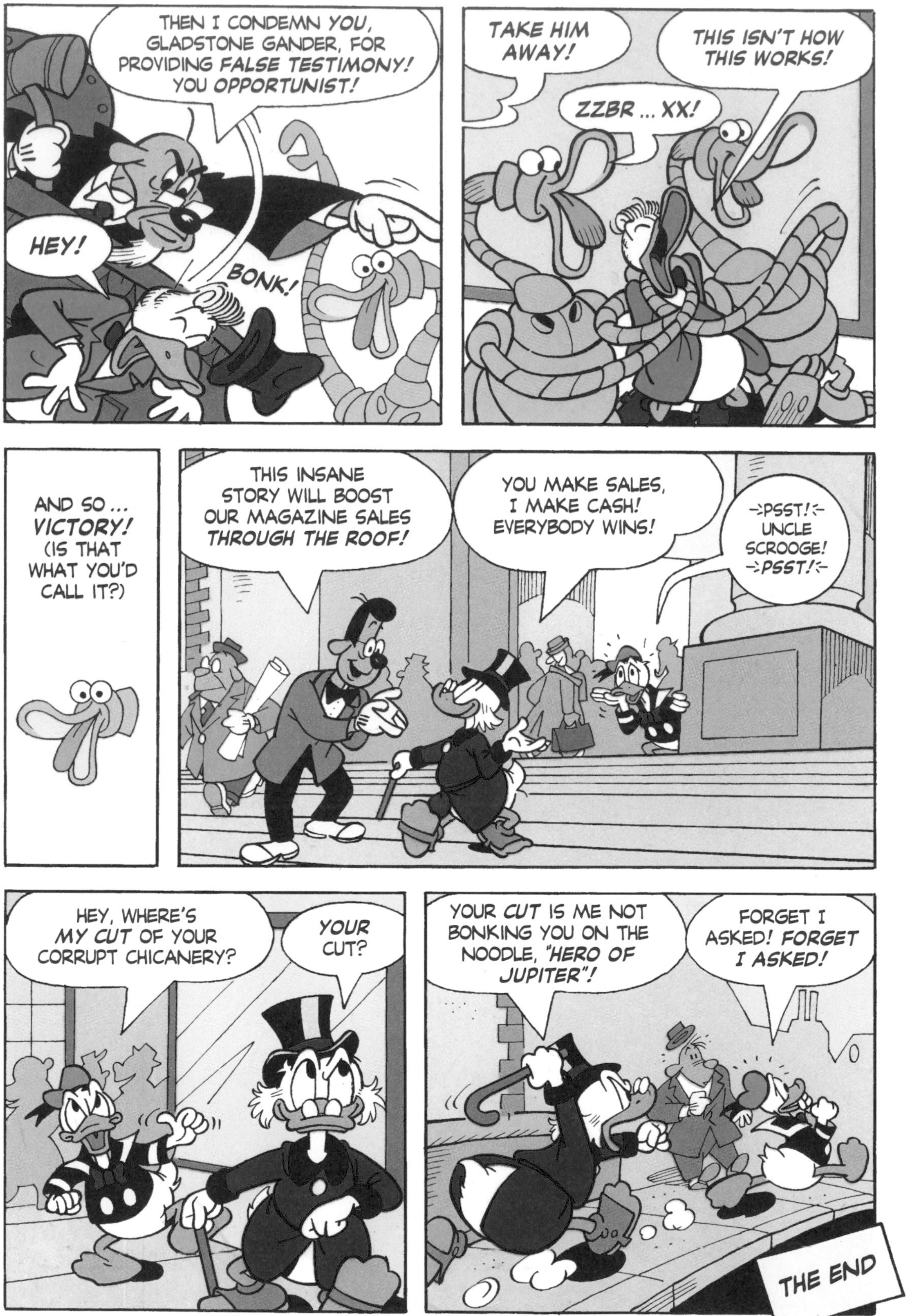
THEN I CONDEMN YOU, GLADSTONE GANDER, FOR PROVIDING FALSE TESTIMONY! YOU OPPORTUNIST!
HEY!
BONK!
TAKE HIM AWAY!
THIS ISN'T HOW THIS WORKS!
ZZBR ... XX!
AND SO ... VICTORY! (IS THAT WHAT YOU'D CALL IT?)
THIS INSANE STORY WILL BOOST OUR MAGAZINE SALES THROUGH THE ROOF!
YOU MAKE SALES, I MAKE CASH! EVERYBODY WINS!
PSST! UNCLE SCROOGE! PSST!
HEY, WHERE'S MY CUT OF YOUR CORRUPT CHICANERY?
YOUR CUT?
YOUR CUT IS ME NOT BONKING YOU ON THE NOODLE, "HERO OF JUPITER"!
FORGET I ASKED! FORGET I ASKED!
THE END

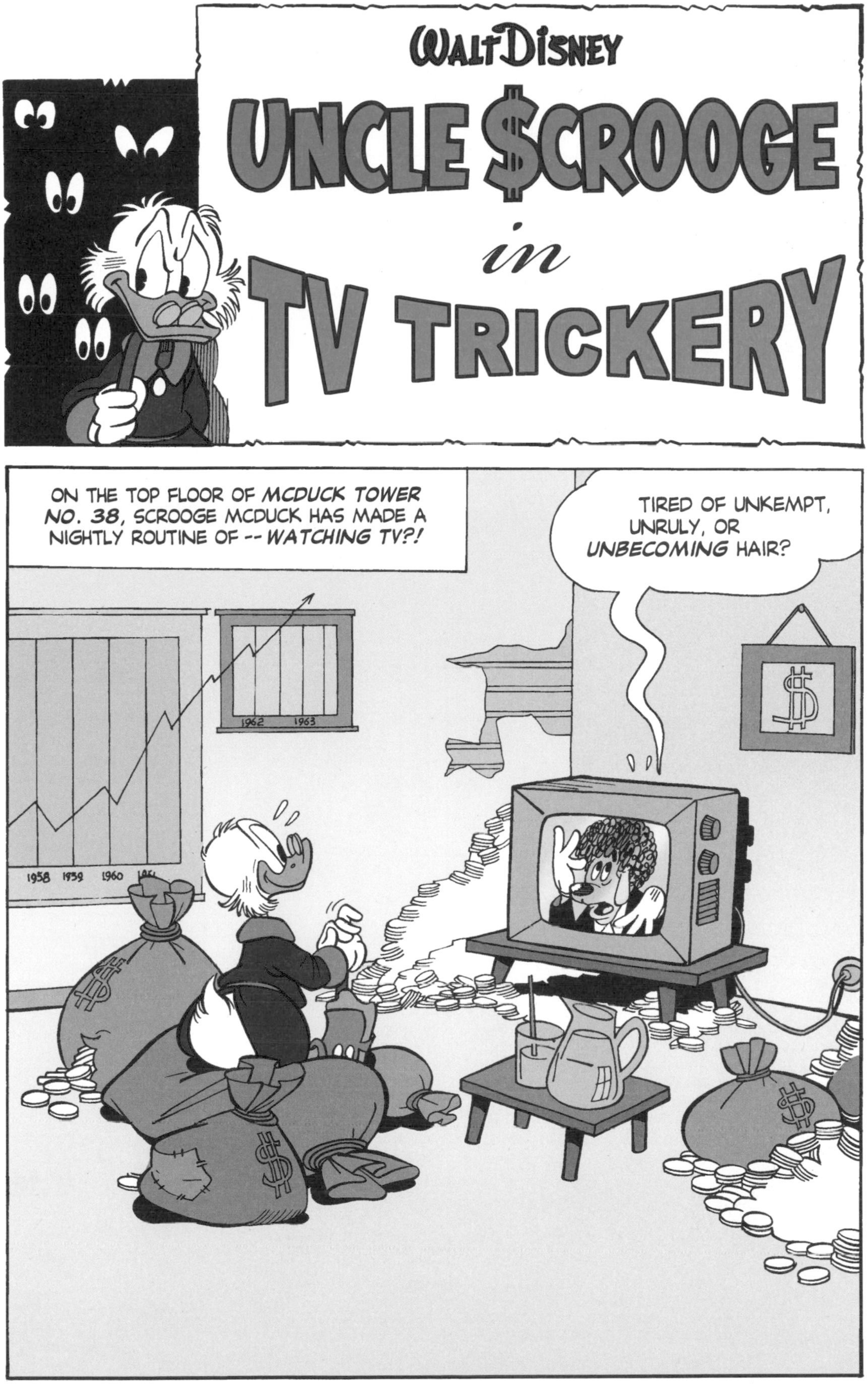
WALT DISNEY
UNCLE $CROOGE
in
TV TRICKERY
ON THE TOP FLOOR OF *MCDUCK TOWER NO. 38*, SCROOGE MCDUCK HAS MADE A NIGHTLY ROUTINE OF -- *WATCHING TV?!*
TIRED OF UNKEMPT, UNRULY, OR *UNBECOMING* HAIR?

STORY AND ART: LUCIANO BOTTARO • TRANSLATION: THAD KOMOROWSKI

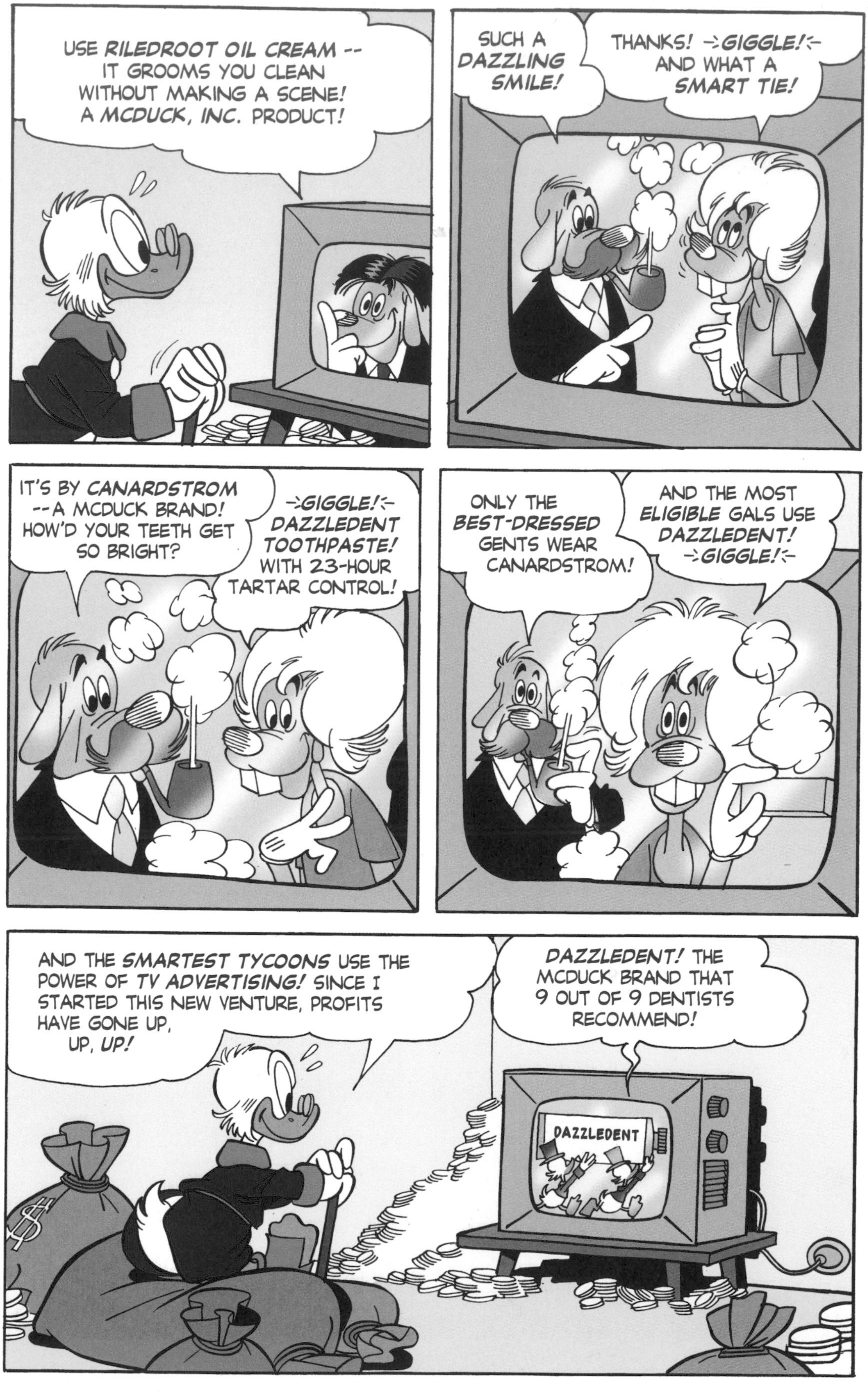
USE RILEDROOT OIL CREAM -- IT GROOMS YOU CLEAN WITHOUT MAKING A SCENE! A MCDUCK, INC. PRODUCT!
SUCH A DAZZLING SMILE!
THANKS! GIGGLE! AND WHAT A SMART TIE!
IT'S BY CANARDSTROM -- A MCDUCK BRAND! HOW'D YOUR TEETH GET SO BRIGHT?
GIGGLE! DAZZLEDENT TOOTHPASTE! WITH 23-HOUR TARTAR CONTROL!
ONLY THE BEST-DRESSED GENTS WEAR CANARDSTROM!
AND THE MOST ELIGIBLE GALS USE DAZZLEDENT! GIGGLE!
AND THE SMARTEST TYCOONS USE THE POWER OF TV ADVERTISING! SINCE I STARTED THIS NEW VENTURE, PROFITS HAVE GONE UP, UP, UP!
DAZZLEDENT! THE MCDUCK BRAND THAT 9 OUT OF 9 DENTISTS RECOMMEND!
DAZZLEDENT

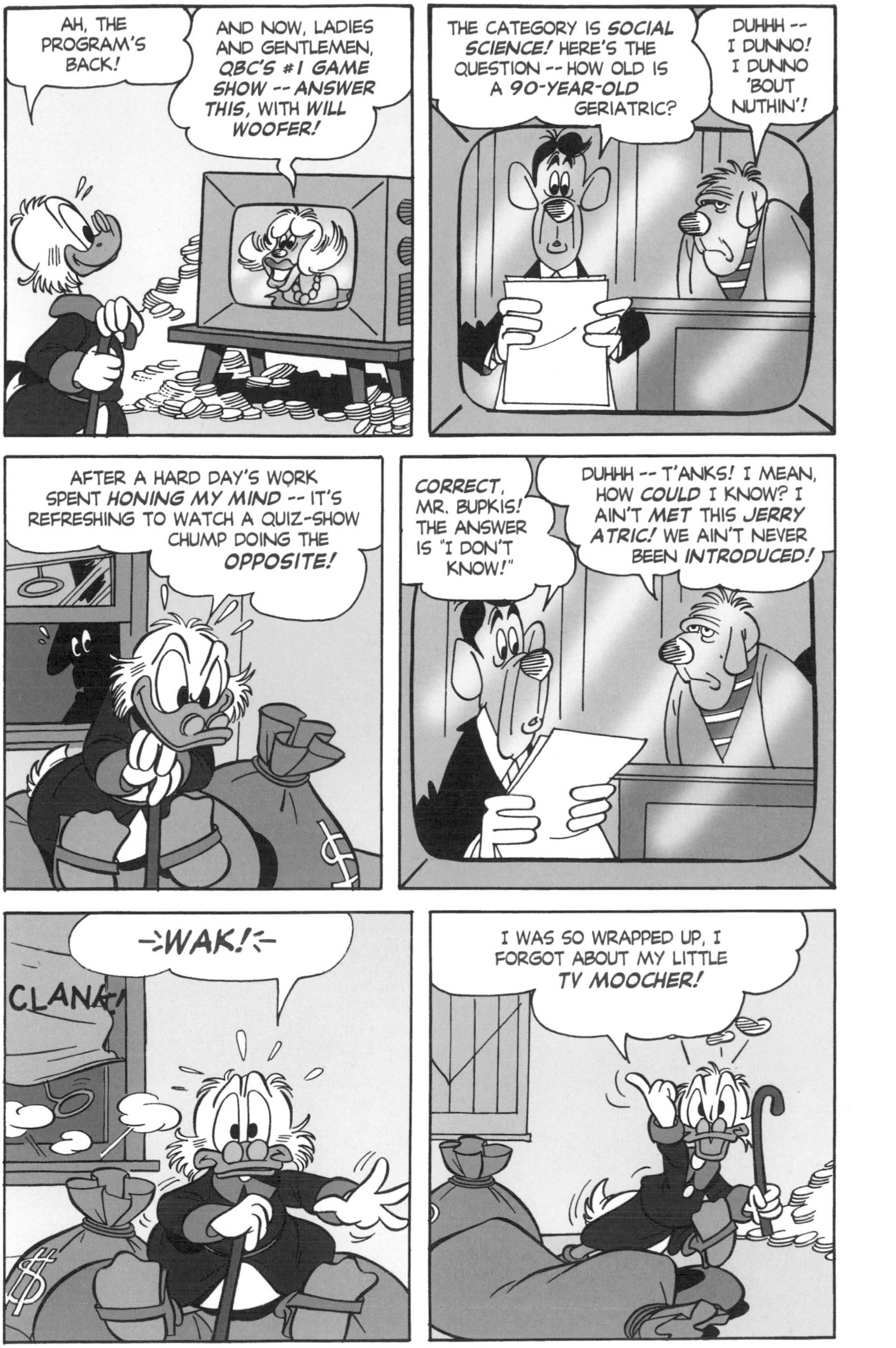
AH, THE PROGRAM'S BACK!
AND NOW, LADIES AND GENTLEMEN, QBC'S #1 GAME SHOW -- ANSWER THIS, WITH WILL WOOFER!
THE CATEGORY IS SOCIAL SCIENCE! HERE'S THE QUESTION -- HOW OLD IS A 90-YEAR-OLD GERIATRIC?
DUHHH -- I DUNNO! I DUNNO 'BOUT NUTHIN'!
AFTER A HARD DAY'S WORK SPENT HONING MY MIND -- IT'S REFRESHING TO WATCH A QUIZ-SHOW CHUMP DOING THE OPPOSITE!
CORRECT, MR. BUPKIS! THE ANSWER IS "I DON'T KNOW!"
DUHHH -- T'ANKS! I MEAN, HOW COULD I KNOW? I AIN'T MET THIS JERRY ATRIC! WE AIN'T NEVER BEEN INTRODUCED!
-WAK!-
CLANG
I WAS SO WRAPPED UP, I FORGOT ABOUT MY LITTLE TV MOOCHER!

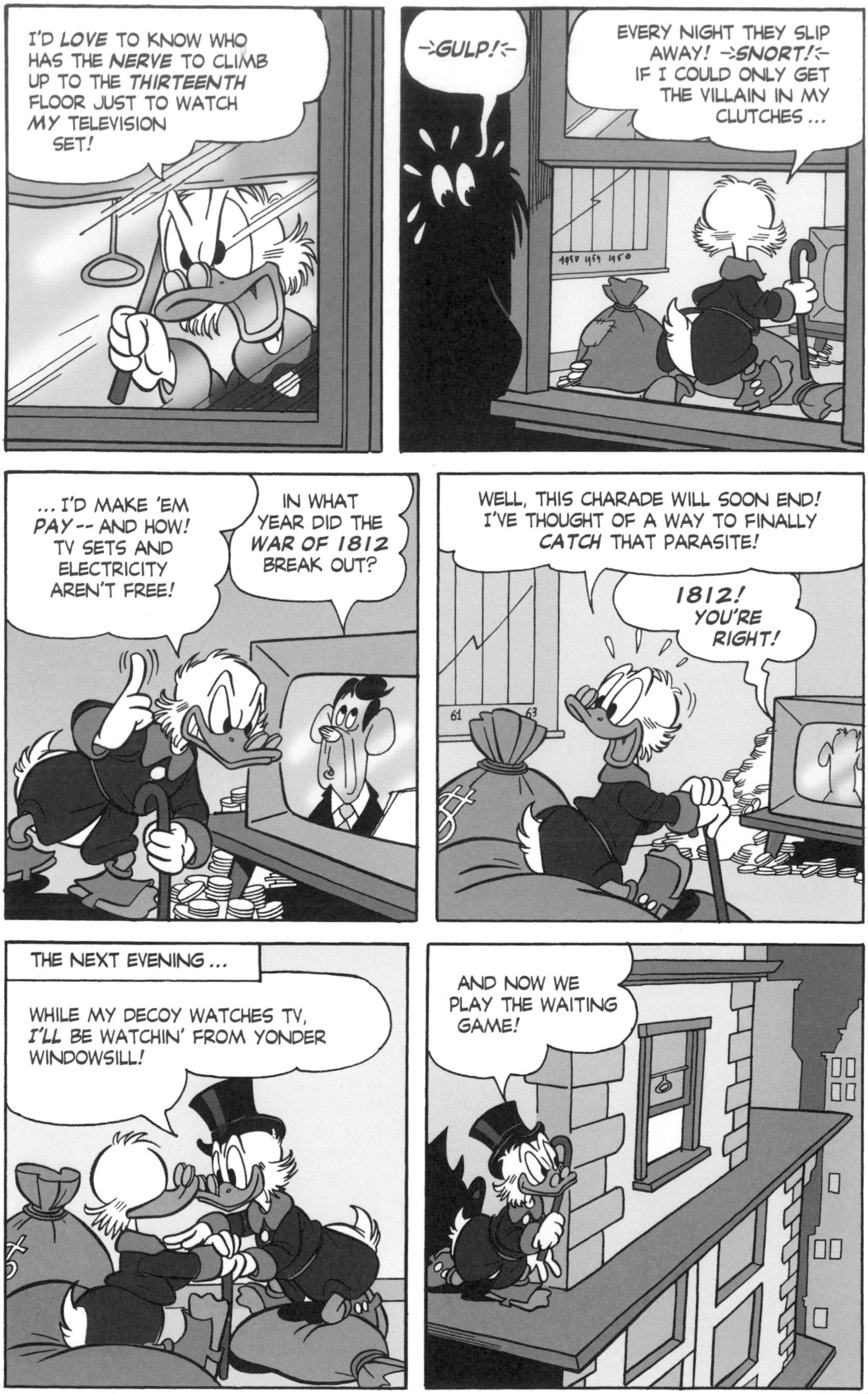
I'D LOVE TO KNOW WHO HAS THE NERVE TO CLIMB UP TO THE THIRTEENTH FLOOR JUST TO WATCH MY TELEVISION SET!
-GULP!-
EVERY NIGHT THEY SLIP AWAY! -SNORT!- IF I COULD ONLY GET THE VILLAIN IN MY CLUTCHES ...
... I'D MAKE 'EM PAY -- AND HOW! TV SETS AND ELECTRICITY AREN'T FREE!
IN WHAT YEAR DID THE WAR OF 1812 BREAK OUT?
WELL, THIS CHARADE WILL SOON END! I'VE THOUGHT OF A WAY TO FINALLY CATCH THAT PARASITE!
1812! YOU'RE RIGHT!
THE NEXT EVENING ...
WHILE MY DECOY WATCHES TV, I'LL BE WATCHIN' FROM YONDER WINDOWSILL!
AND NOW WE PLAY THE WAITING GAME!

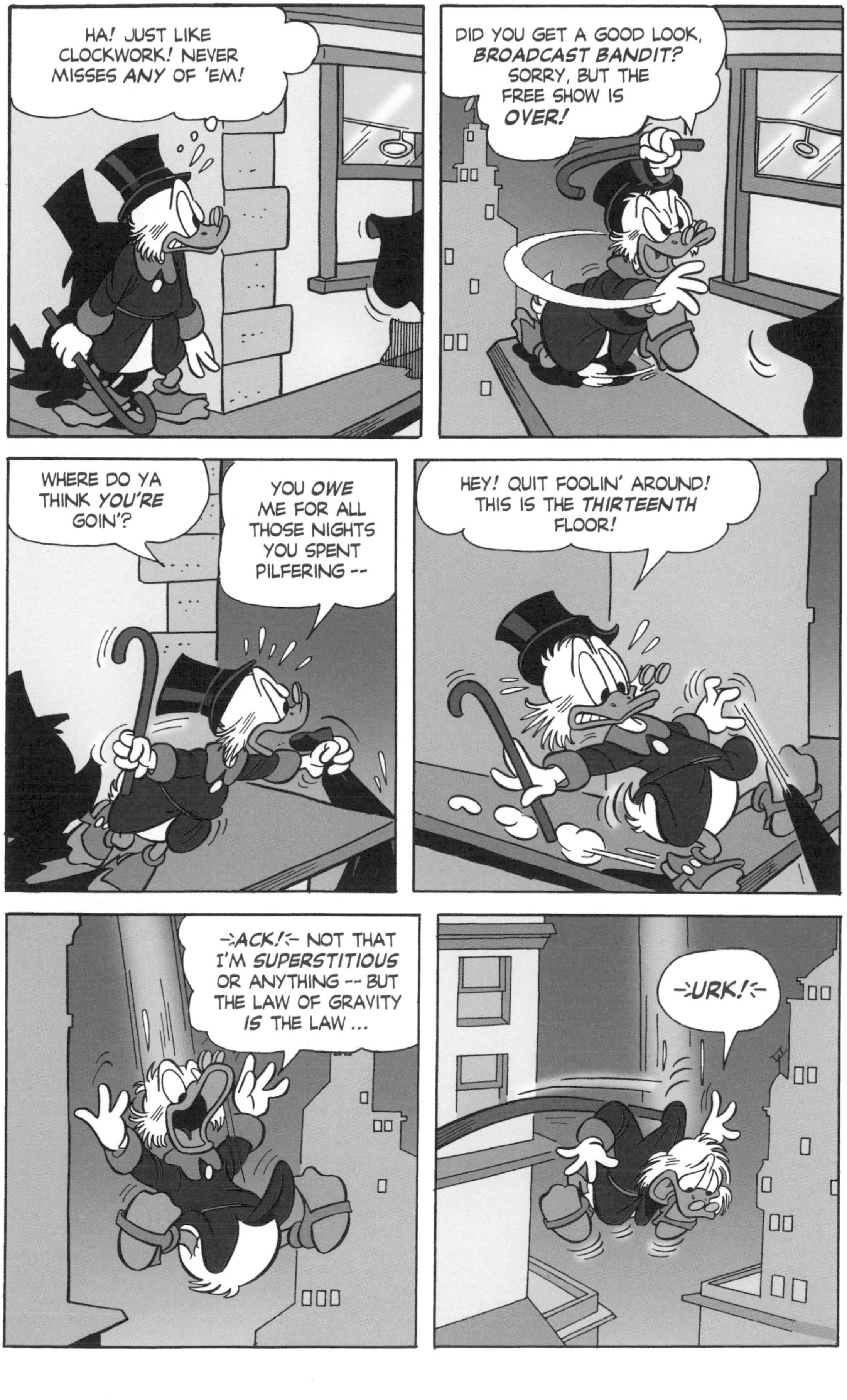

HA! JUST LIKE CLOCKWORK! NEVER MISSES ANY OF 'EM!
DID YOU GET A GOOD LOOK, BROADCAST BANDIT? SORRY, BUT THE FREE SHOW IS OVER!
WHERE DO YA THINK YOU'RE GOIN'?
YOU OWE ME FOR ALL THOSE NIGHTS YOU SPENT PILFERING --
HEY! QUIT FOOLIN' AROUND! THIS IS THE THIRTEENTH FLOOR!
-ACK!- NOT THAT I'M SUPERSTITIOUS OR ANYTHING -- BUT THE LAW OF GRAVITY IS THE LAW ...
-URK!-

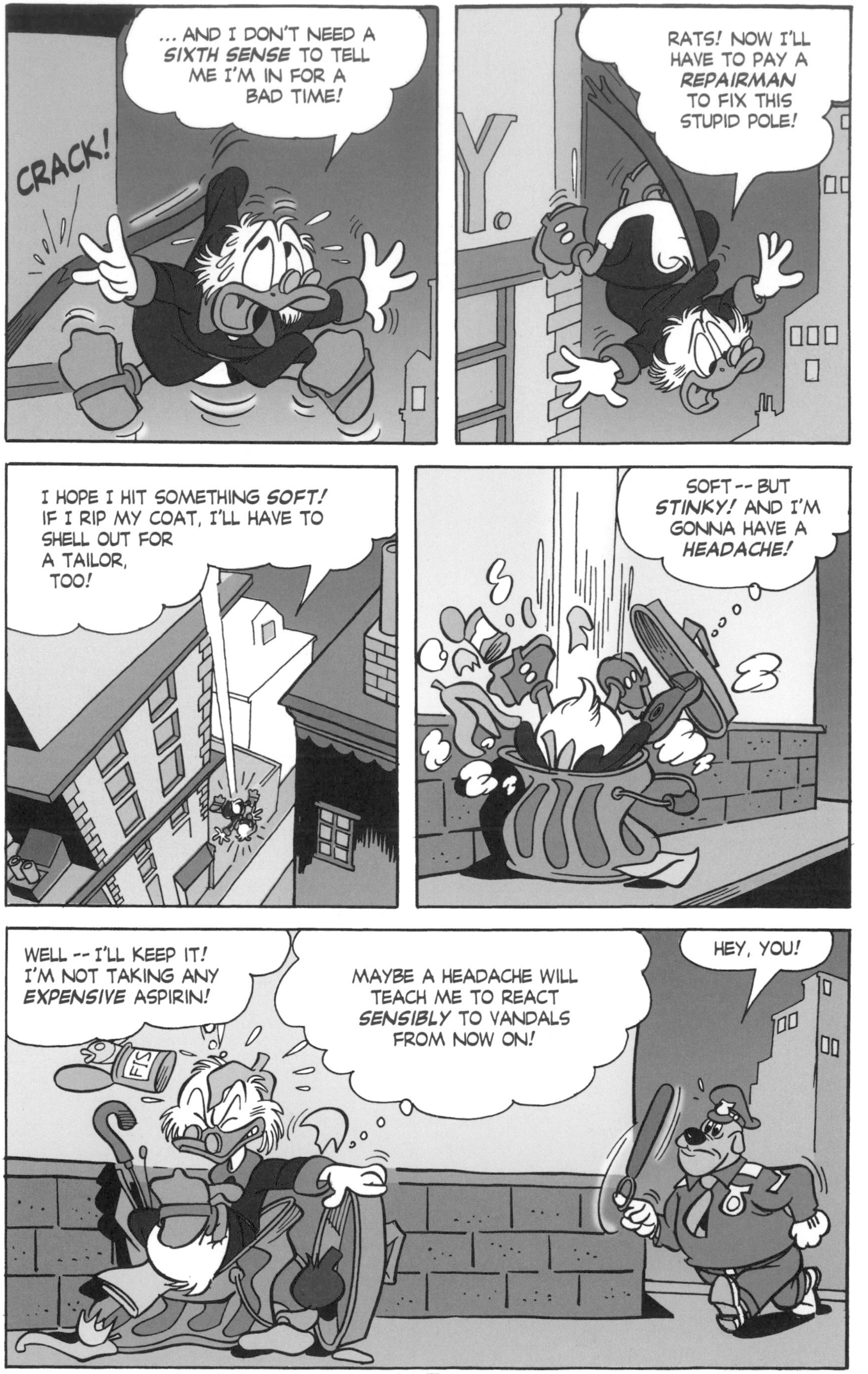
CRACK!
... AND I DON'T NEED A SIXTH SENSE TO TELL ME I'M IN FOR A BAD TIME!
RATS! NOW I'LL HAVE TO PAY A REPAIRMAN TO FIX THIS STUPID POLE!
I HOPE I HIT SOMETHING SOFT! IF I RIP MY COAT, I'LL HAVE TO SHELL OUT FOR A TAILOR, TOO!
SOFT -- BUT STINKY! AND I'M GONNA HAVE A HEADACHE!
WELL -- I'LL KEEP IT! I'M NOT TAKING ANY EXPENSIVE ASPIRIN!
MAYBE A HEADACHE WILL TEACH ME TO REACT SENSIBLY TO VANDALS FROM NOW ON!
HEY, YOU!

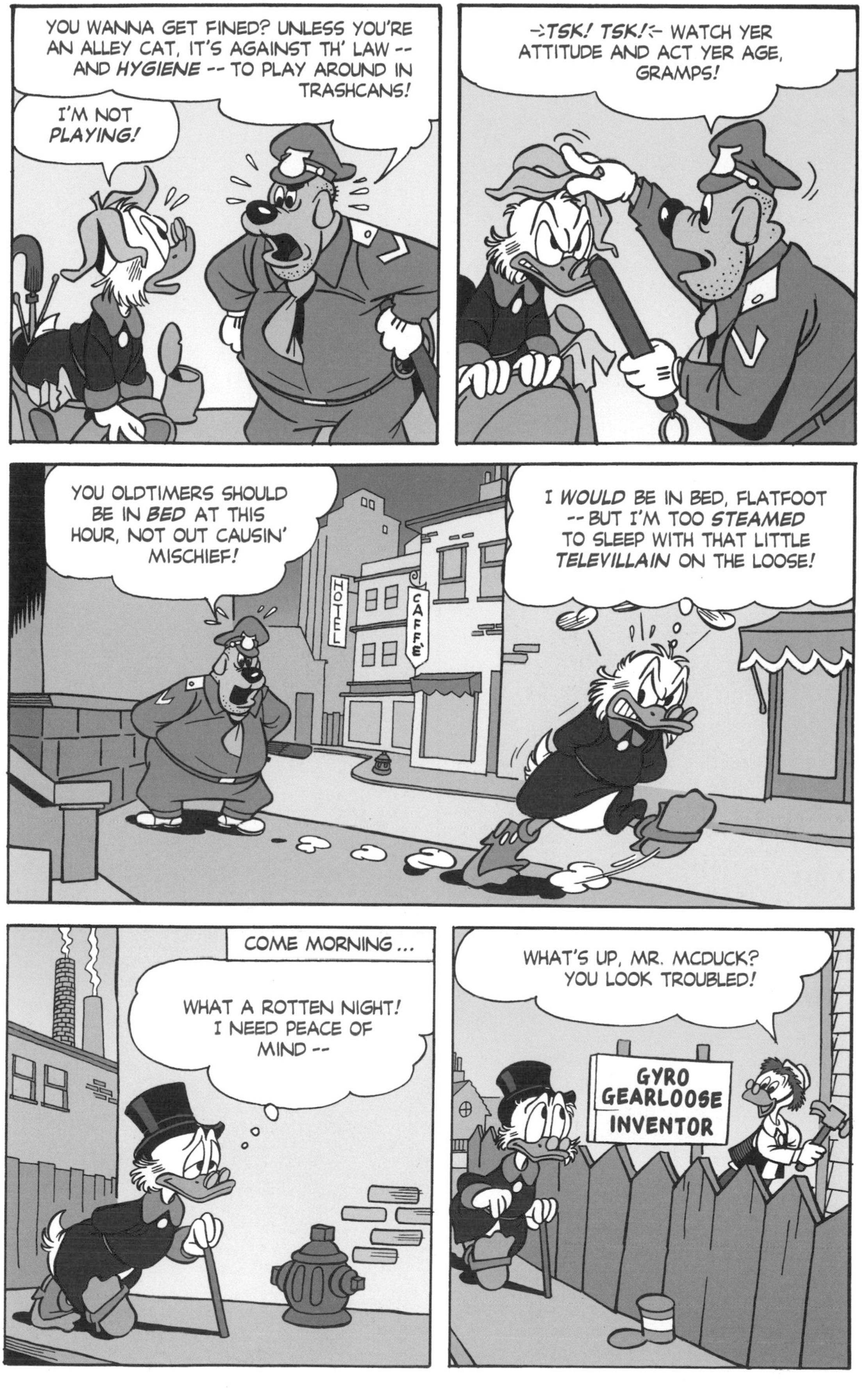
YOU WANNA GET FINED? UNLESS YOU'RE AN ALLEY CAT, IT'S AGAINST TH' LAW -- AND HYGIENE -- TO PLAY AROUND IN TRASHCANS!
I'M NOT PLAYING!
-TSK! TSK!- WATCH YER ATTITUDE AND ACT YER AGE, GRAMPS!
YOU OLDTIMERS SHOULD BE IN BED AT THIS HOUR, NOT OUT CAUSIN' MISCHIEF!
HOTEL
CAFFÈ
I WOULD BE IN BED, FLATFOOT -- BUT I'M TOO STEAMED TO SLEEP WITH THAT LITTLE TELEVILLAIN ON THE LOOSE!
COME MORNING ...
WHAT A ROTTEN NIGHT! I NEED PEACE OF MIND --
WHAT'S UP, MR. MCDUCK? YOU LOOK TROUBLED!
GYRO GEARLOOSE INVENTOR

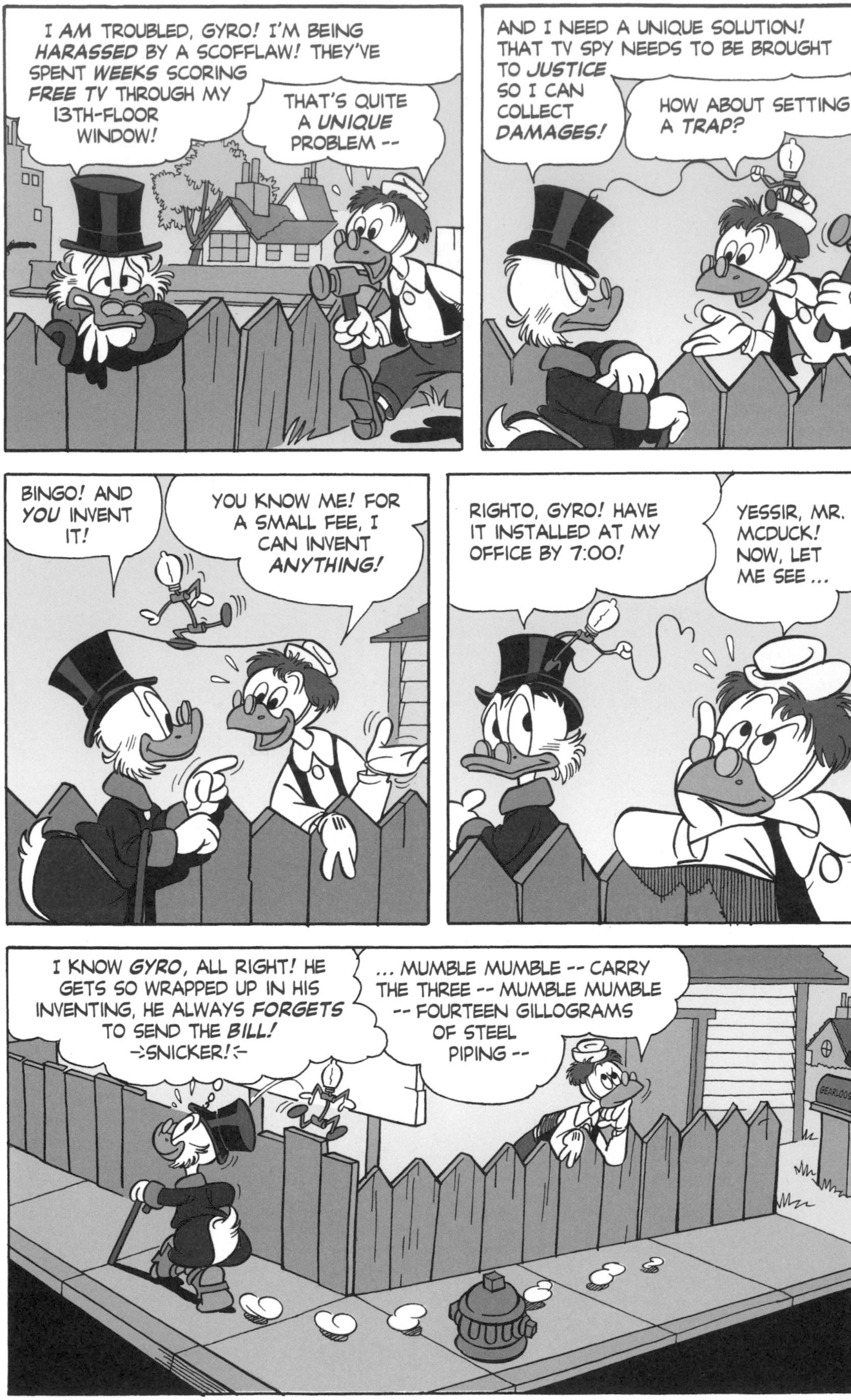

I AM TROUBLED, GYRO! I'M BEING HARASSED BY A SCOFFLAW! THEY'VE SPENT WEEKS SCORING FREE TV THROUGH MY 13TH-FLOOR WINDOW!
THAT'S QUITE A UNIQUE PROBLEM --
AND I NEED A UNIQUE SOLUTION! THAT TV SPY NEEDS TO BE BROUGHT TO JUSTICE SO I CAN COLLECT DAMAGES!
HOW ABOUT SETTING A TRAP?
BINGO! AND YOU INVENT IT!
YOU KNOW ME! FOR A SMALL FEE, I CAN INVENT ANYTHING!
RIGHTO, GYRO! HAVE IT INSTALLED AT MY OFFICE BY 7:00!
YESSIR, MR. MCDUCK! NOW, LET ME SEE ...
I KNOW GYRO, ALL RIGHT! HE GETS SO WRAPPED UP IN HIS INVENTING, HE ALWAYS FORGETS TO SEND THE BILL!
-SNICKER!-
... MUMBLE MUMBLE -- CARRY THE THREE -- MUMBLE MUMBLE -- FOURTEEN GILLOGRAMS OF STEEL PIPING --
GEARLOOSE

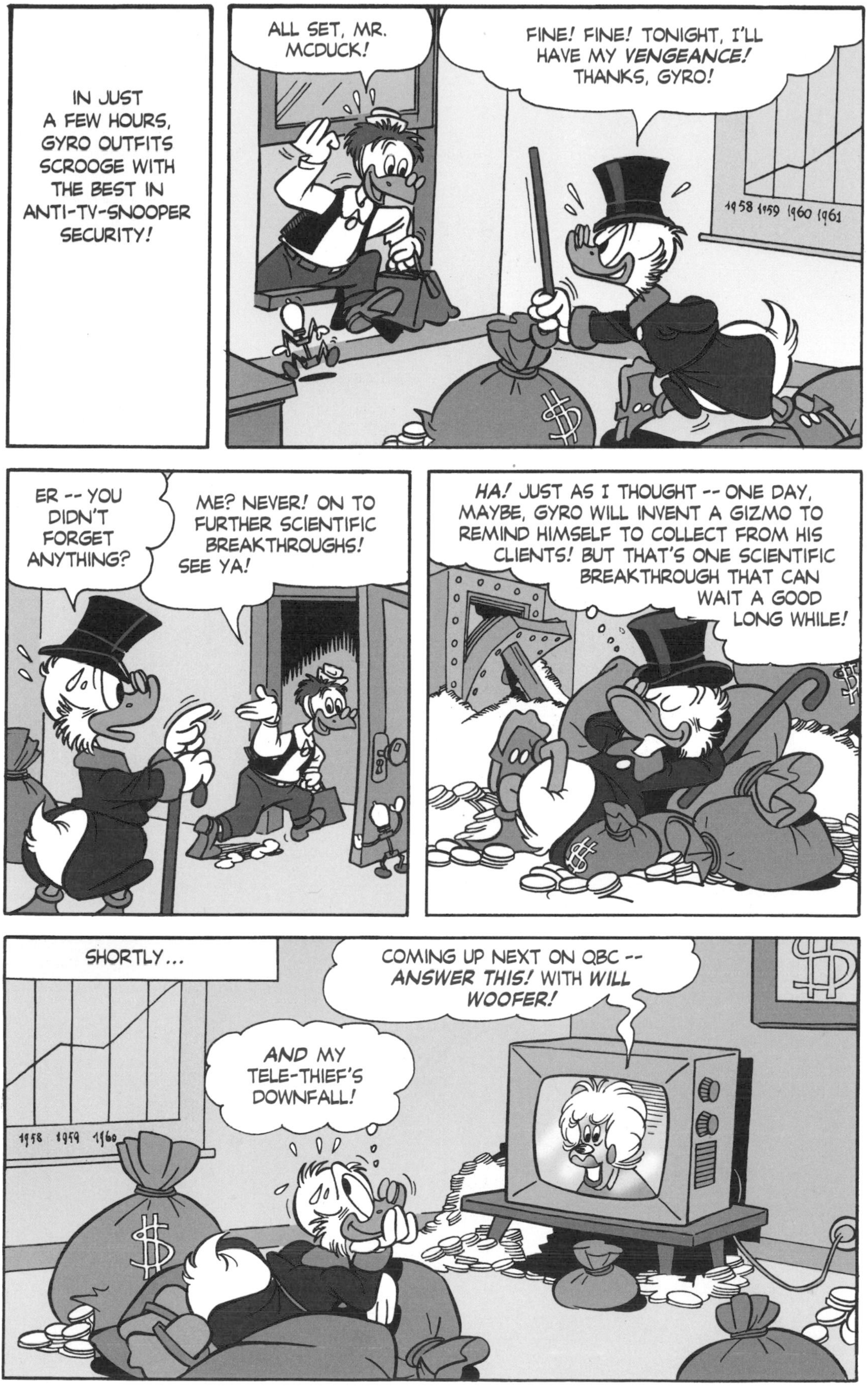
IN JUST A FEW HOURS, GYRO OUTFITS SCROOGE WITH THE BEST IN ANTI-TV-SNOOPER SECURITY!
ALL SET, MR. MCDUCK!
FINE! FINE! TONIGHT, I'LL HAVE MY VENGEANCE! THANKS, GYRO!
1958 1959 1960 1961
ER -- YOU DIDN'T FORGET ANYTHING?
ME? NEVER! ON TO FURTHER SCIENTIFIC BREAKTHROUGHS! SEE YA!
HA! JUST AS I THOUGHT -- ONE DAY, MAYBE, GYRO WILL INVENT A GIZMO TO REMIND HIMSELF TO COLLECT FROM HIS CLIENTS! BUT THAT'S ONE SCIENTIFIC BREAKTHROUGH THAT CAN WAIT A GOOD LONG WHILE!
SHORTLY...
COMING UP NEXT ON QBC -- ANSWER THIS! WITH WILL WOOFER!
AND MY TELE-THIEF'S DOWNFALL!
1958 1959 1960

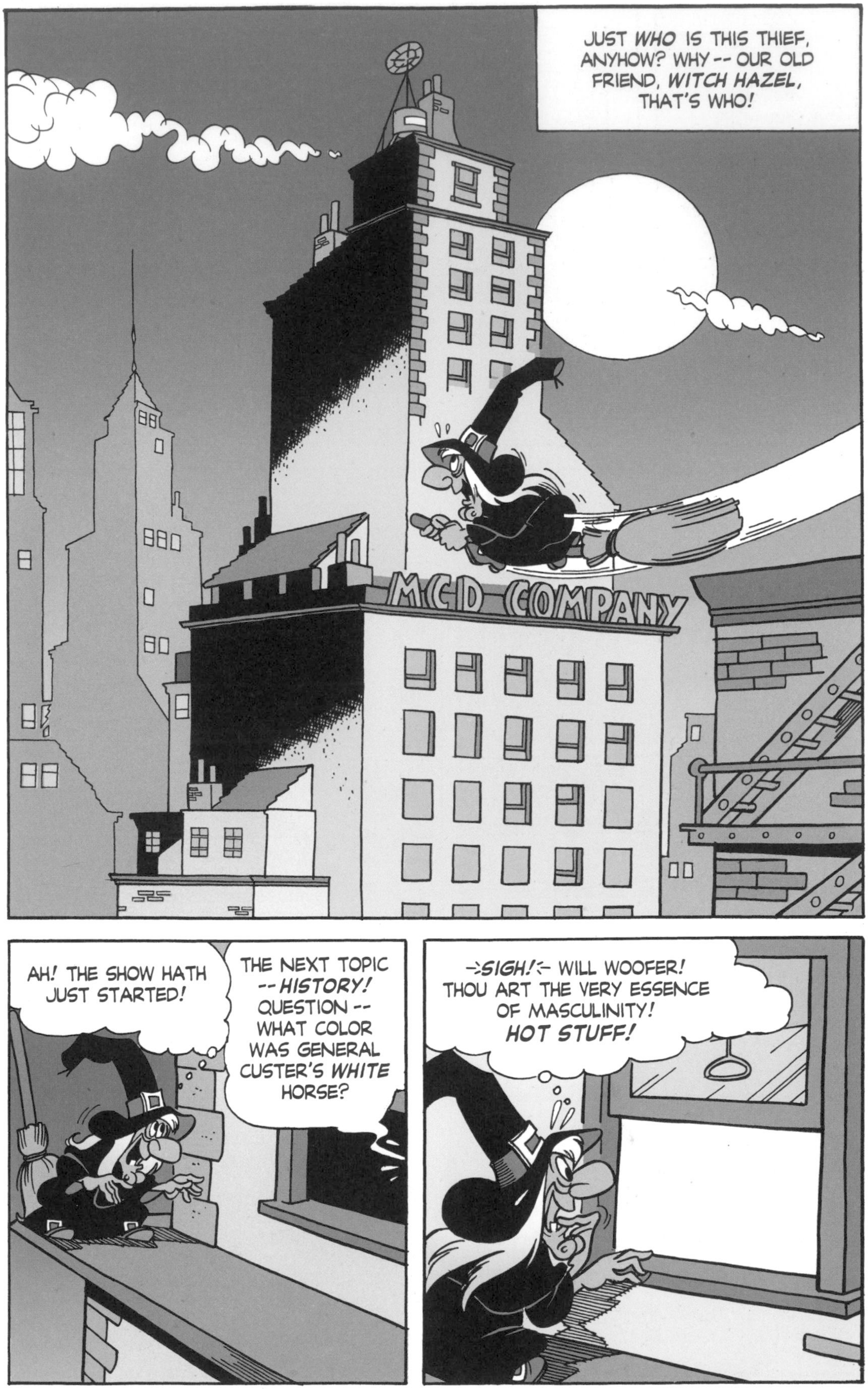
JUST WHO IS THIS THIEF, ANYHOW? WHY -- OUR OLD FRIEND, WITCH HAZEL, THAT'S WHO!
MCD COMPANY
AH! THE SHOW HATH JUST STARTED!
THE NEXT TOPIC -- HISTORY! QUESTION -- WHAT COLOR WAS GENERAL CUSTER'S WHITE HORSE?
-SIGH!- WILL WOOFER! THOU ART THE VERY ESSENCE OF MASCULINITY! HOT STUFF!

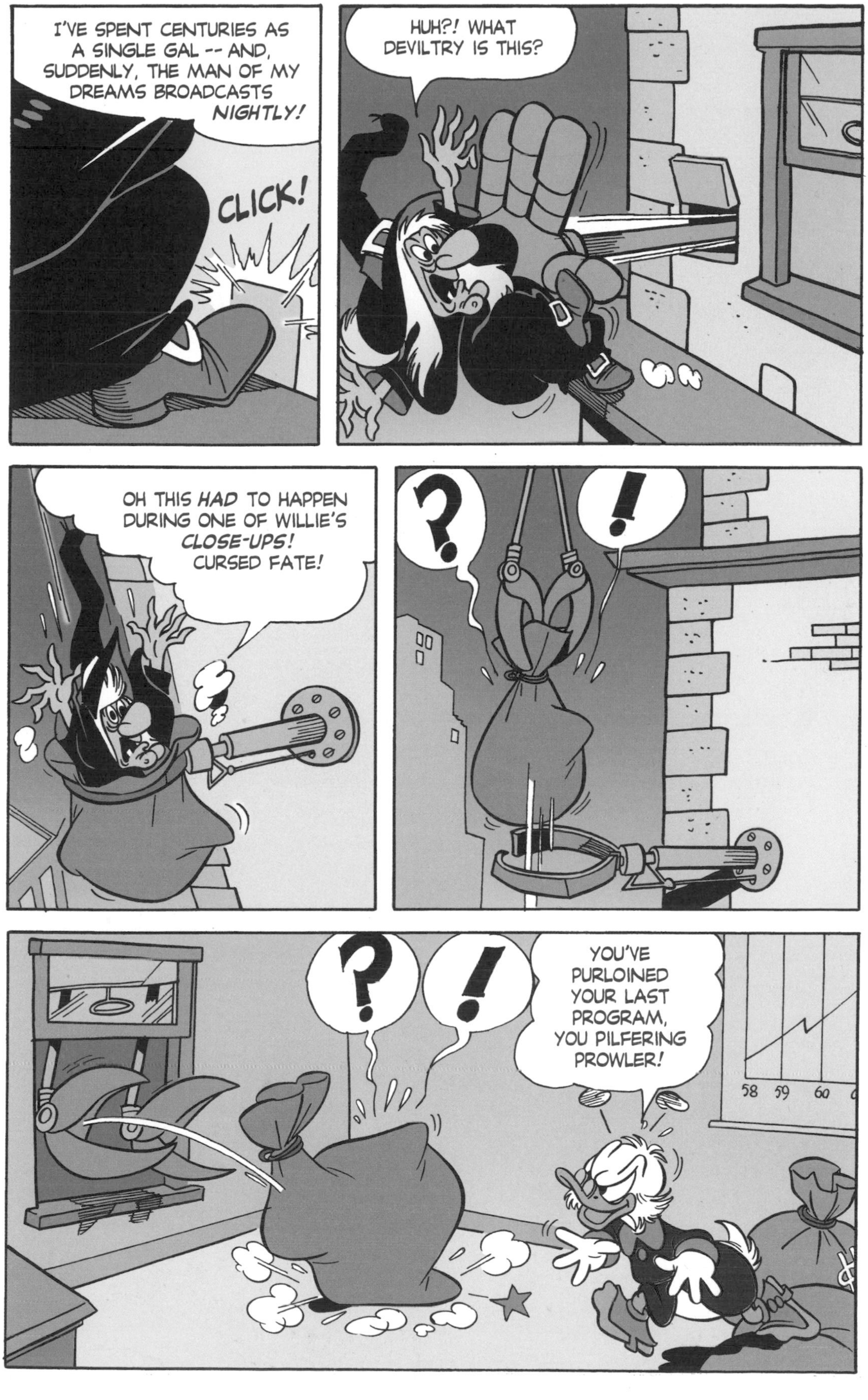
I'VE SPENT CENTURIES AS A SINGLE GAL -- AND, SUDDENLY, THE MAN OF MY DREAMS BROADCASTS *NIGHTLY!*
CLICK!
HUH?! WHAT DEVILTRY IS THIS?
OH THIS *HAD* TO HAPPEN DURING ONE OF WILLIE'S *CLOSE-UPS!* CURSED FATE!
?
!
?
!
YOU'VE PURLOINED YOUR LAST PROGRAM, YOU PILFERING PROWLER!
58 59 60

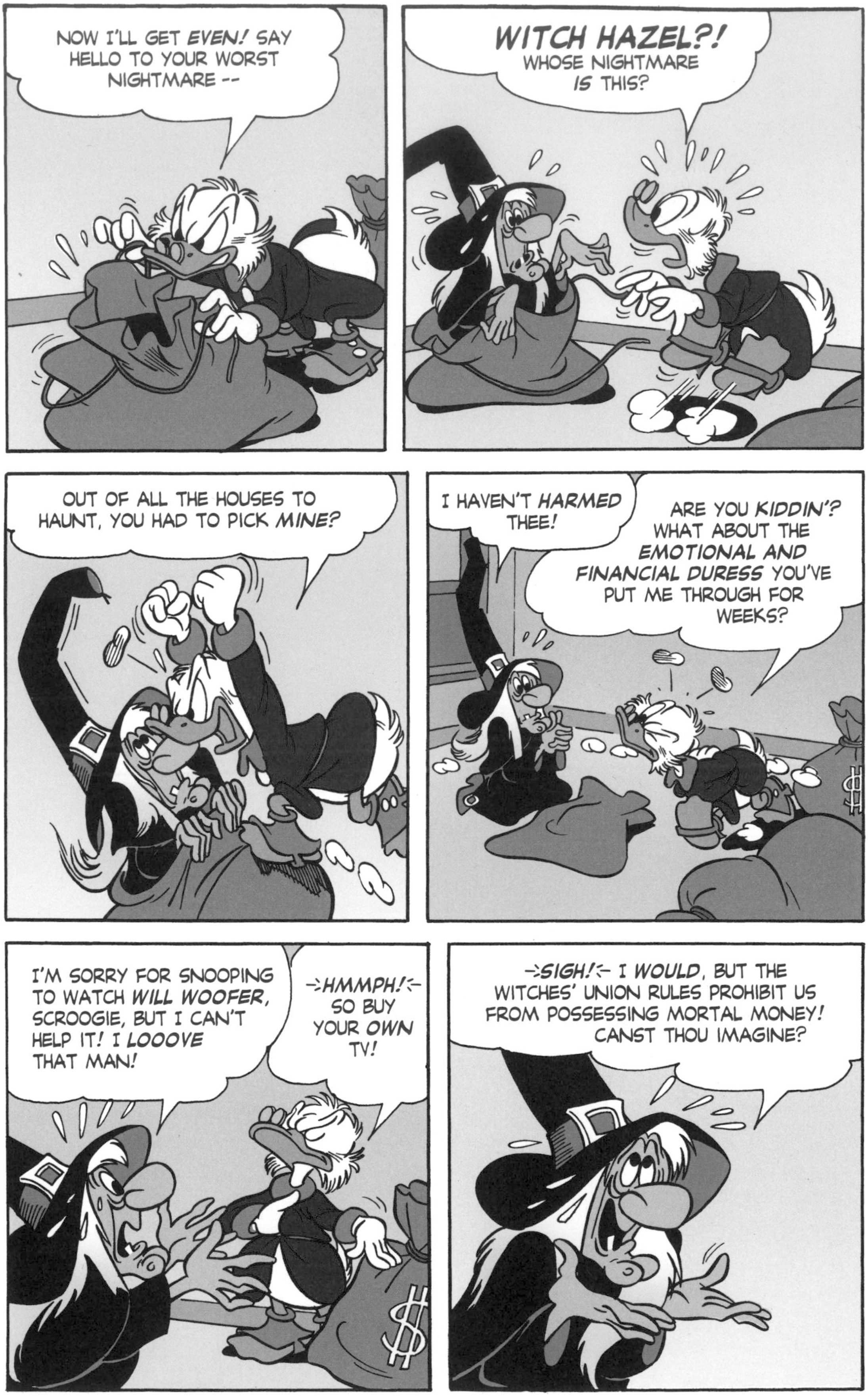
NOW I'LL GET EVEN! SAY HELLO TO YOUR WORST NIGHTMARE --
WITCH HAZEL?! WHOSE NIGHTMARE IS THIS?
OUT OF ALL THE HOUSES TO HAUNT, YOU HAD TO PICK MINE?
I HAVEN'T HARMED THEE!
ARE YOU KIDDIN'? WHAT ABOUT THE EMOTIONAL AND FINANCIAL DURESS YOU'VE PUT ME THROUGH FOR WEEKS?
I'M SORRY FOR SNOOPING TO WATCH WILL WOOFER, SCROOGIE, BUT I CAN'T HELP IT! I LOOOVE THAT MAN!
-HMMPH!- SO BUY YOUR OWN TV!
-SIGH!- I WOULD, BUT THE WITCHES' UNION RULES PROHIBIT US FROM POSSESSING MORTAL MONEY! CANST THOU IMAGINE?

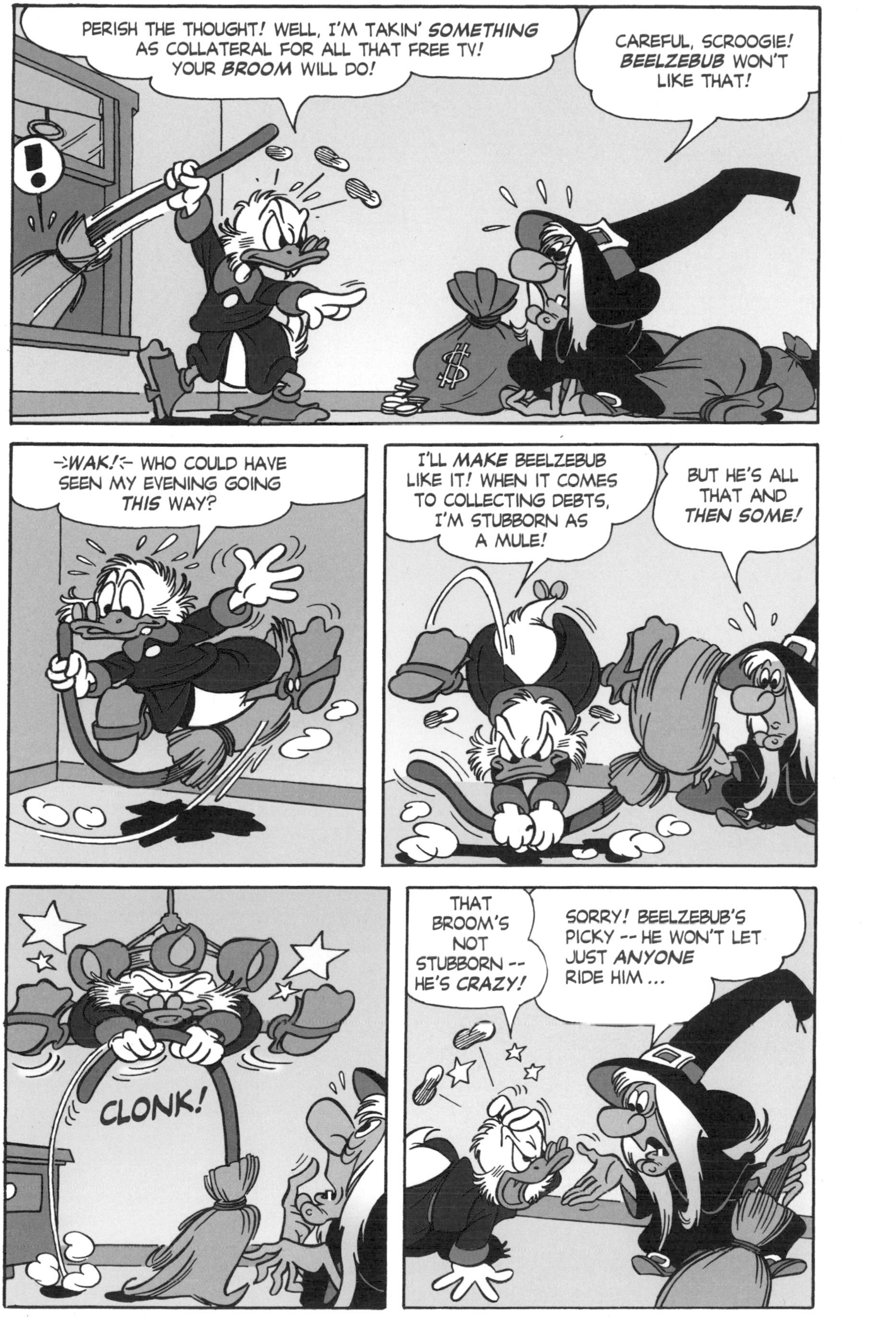
PERISH THE THOUGHT! WELL, I'M TAKIN' SOMETHING AS COLLATERAL FOR ALL THAT FREE TV! YOUR BROOM WILL DO!
CAREFUL, SCROOGIE! BEELZEBUB WON'T LIKE THAT!
!
-WAK!- WHO COULD HAVE SEEN MY EVENING GOING THIS WAY?
I'LL MAKE BEELZEBUB LIKE IT! WHEN IT COMES TO COLLECTING DEBTS, I'M STUBBORN AS A MULE!
BUT HE'S ALL THAT AND THEN SOME!
CLONK!
THAT BROOM'S NOT STUBBORN -- HE'S CRAZY!
SORRY! BEELZEBUB'S PICKY -- HE WON'T LET JUST ANYONE RIDE HIM ...

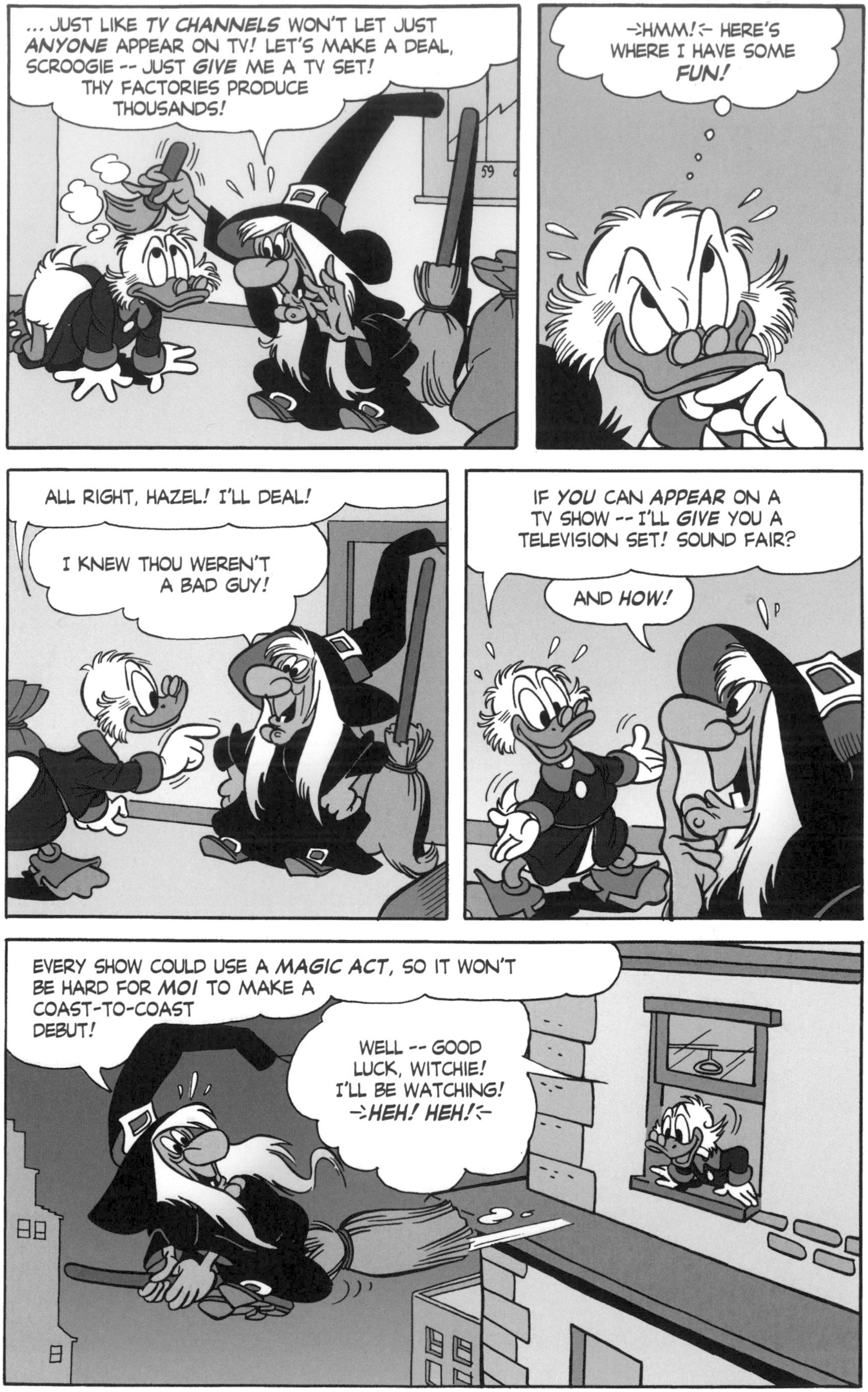

... JUST LIKE TV CHANNELS WON'T LET JUST ANYONE APPEAR ON TV! LET'S MAKE A DEAL, SCROOGIE -- JUST GIVE ME A TV SET! THY FACTORIES PRODUCE THOUSANDS!
59
-HMM!- HERE'S WHERE I HAVE SOME FUN!
ALL RIGHT, HAZEL! I'LL DEAL!
I KNEW THOU WEREN'T A BAD GUY!
IF YOU CAN APPEAR ON A TV SHOW -- I'LL GIVE YOU A TELEVISION SET! SOUND FAIR?
AND HOW!
EVERY SHOW COULD USE A MAGIC ACT, SO IT WON'T BE HARD FOR MOI TO MAKE A COAST-TO-COAST DEBUT!
WELL -- GOOD LUCK, WITCHIE! I'LL BE WATCHING! -HEH! HEH!-

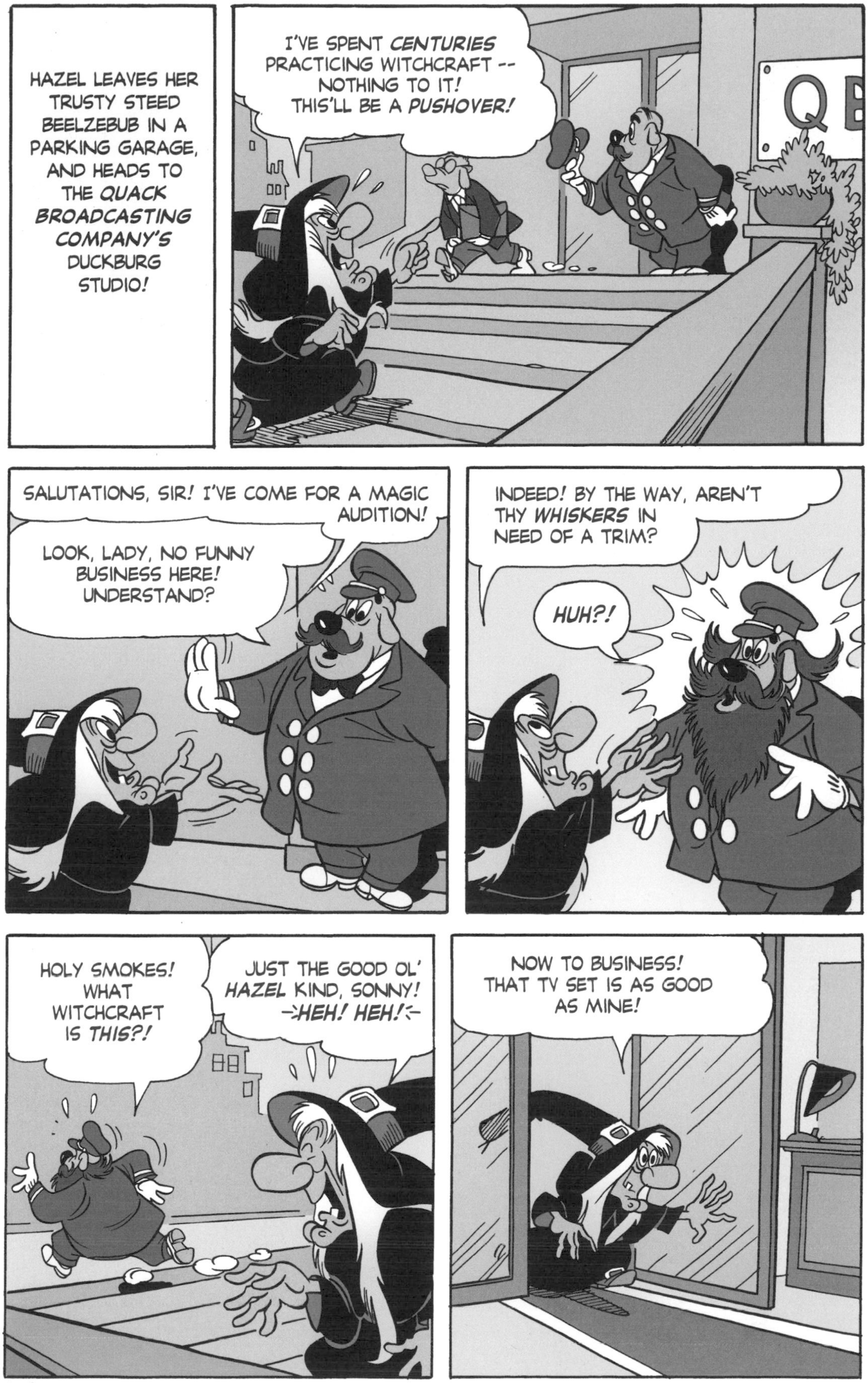
HAZEL LEAVES HER TRUSTY STEED BEELZEBUB IN A PARKING GARAGE, AND HEADS TO THE QUACK BROADCASTING COMPANY'S DUCKBURG STUDIO!
I'VE SPENT CENTURIES PRACTICING WITCHCRAFT -- NOTHING TO IT! THIS'LL BE A PUSHOVER!
QB
SALUTATIONS, SIR! I'VE COME FOR A MAGIC AUDITION!
LOOK, LADY, NO FUNNY BUSINESS HERE! UNDERSTAND?
INDEED! BY THE WAY, AREN'T THY WHISKERS IN NEED OF A TRIM?
HUH?!
HOLY SMOKES! WHAT WITCHCRAFT IS THIS?!
JUST THE GOOD OL' HAZEL KIND, SONNY! HEH! HEH!
NOW TO BUSINESS! THAT TV SET IS AS GOOD AS MINE!

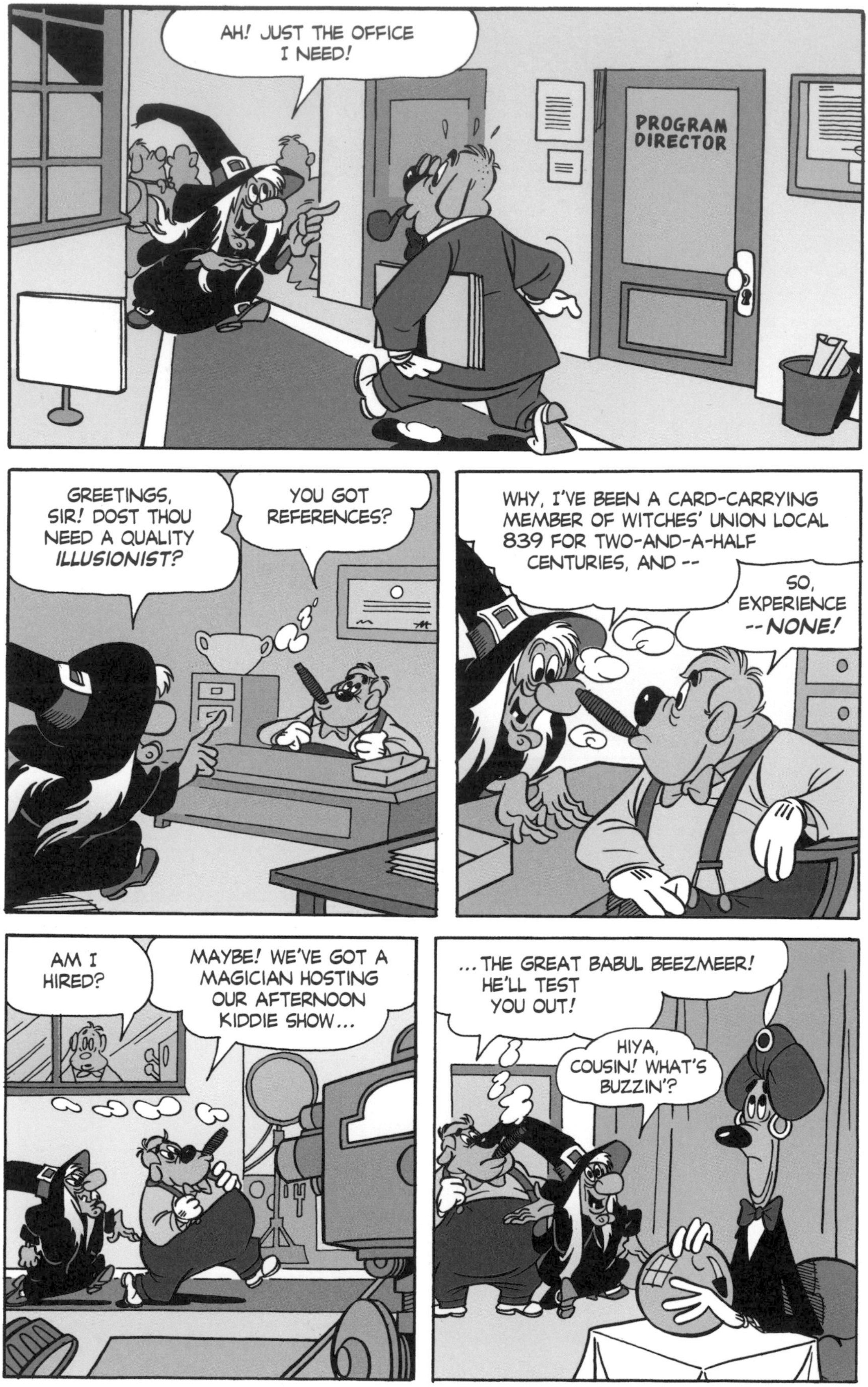
AH! JUST THE OFFICE I NEED!
PROGRAM DIRECTOR
GREETINGS, SIR! DOST THOU NEED A QUALITY *ILLUSIONIST?*
YOU GOT REFERENCES?
WHY, I'VE BEEN A CARD-CARRYING MEMBER OF WITCHES' UNION LOCAL 839 FOR TWO-AND-A-HALF CENTURIES, AND --
SO, EXPERIENCE -- *NONE!*
AM I HIRED?
MAYBE! WE'VE GOT A MAGICIAN HOSTING OUR AFTERNOON KIDDIE SHOW...
...THE GREAT BABUL BEEZMEER! HE'LL TEST YOU OUT!
HIYA, COUSIN! WHAT'S BUZZIN'?

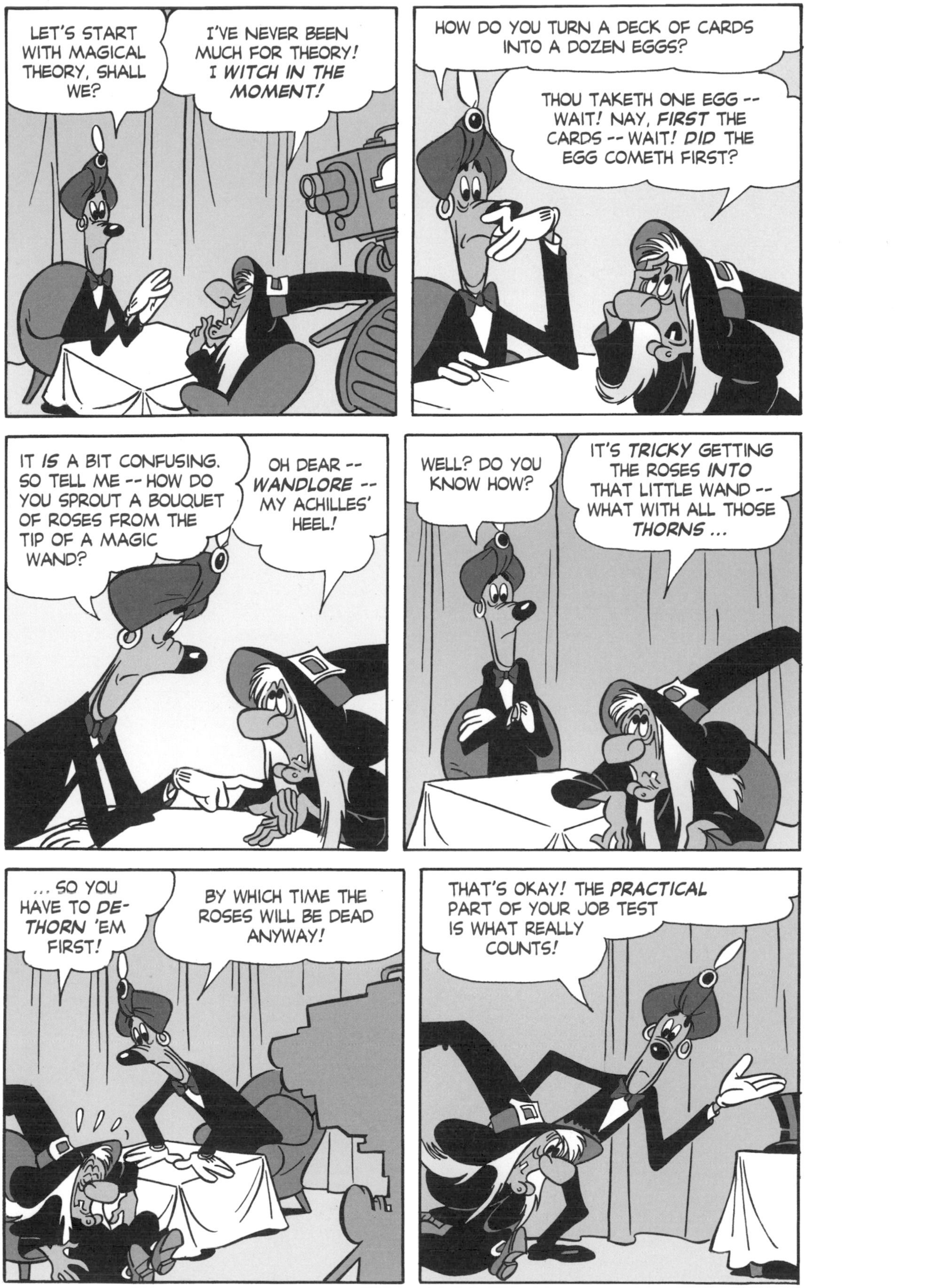

LET'S START WITH MAGICAL THEORY, SHALL WE?
I'VE NEVER BEEN MUCH FOR THEORY! I WITCH IN THE MOMENT!
HOW DO YOU TURN A DECK OF CARDS INTO A DOZEN EGGS?
THOU TAKETH ONE EGG -- WAIT! NAY, FIRST THE CARDS -- WAIT! DID THE EGG COMETH FIRST?
IT IS A BIT CONFUSING. SO TELL ME -- HOW DO YOU SPROUT A BOUQUET OF ROSES FROM THE TIP OF A MAGIC WAND?
OH DEAR -- WANDLORE -- MY ACHILLES' HEEL!
WELL? DO YOU KNOW HOW?
IT'S TRICKY GETTING THE ROSES INTO THAT LITTLE WAND -- WHAT WITH ALL THOSE THORNS ...
... SO YOU HAVE TO DE-THORN 'EM FIRST!
BY WHICH TIME THE ROSES WILL BE DEAD ANYWAY!
THAT'S OKAY! THE PRACTICAL PART OF YOUR JOB TEST IS WHAT REALLY COUNTS!

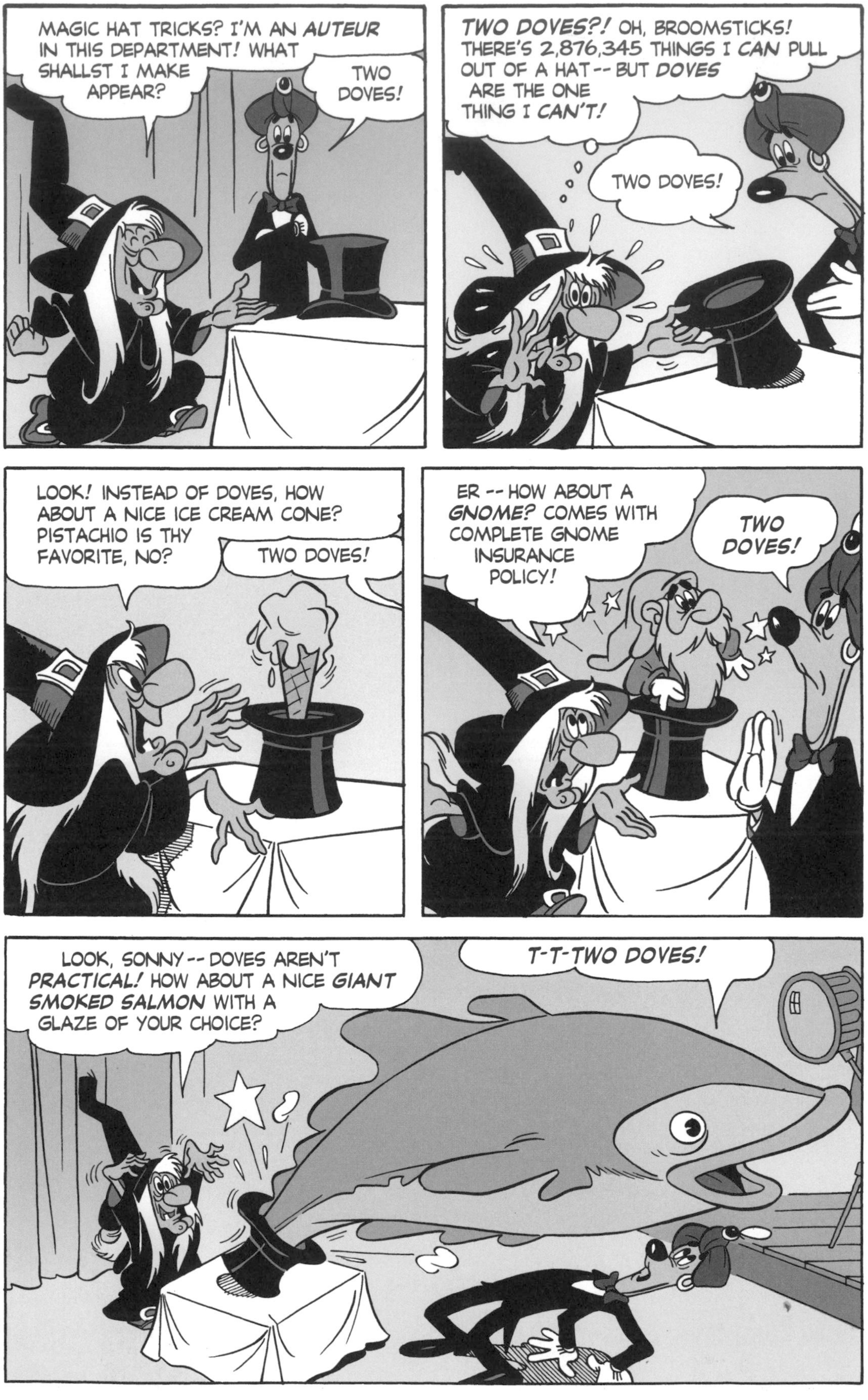
MAGIC HAT TRICKS? I'M AN AUTEUR IN THIS DEPARTMENT! WHAT SHALLST I MAKE APPEAR?
TWO DOVES!
TWO DOVES?! OH, BROOMSTICKS! THERE'S 2,876,345 THINGS I CAN PULL OUT OF A HAT -- BUT DOVES ARE THE ONE THING I CAN'T!
TWO DOVES!
LOOK! INSTEAD OF DOVES, HOW ABOUT A NICE ICE CREAM CONE? PISTACHIO IS THY FAVORITE, NO?
TWO DOVES!
ER -- HOW ABOUT A GNOME? COMES WITH COMPLETE GNOME INSURANCE POLICY!
TWO DOVES!
LOOK, SONNY -- DOVES AREN'T PRACTICAL! HOW ABOUT A NICE GIANT SMOKED SALMON WITH A GLAZE OF YOUR CHOICE?
T-T-TWO DOVES!

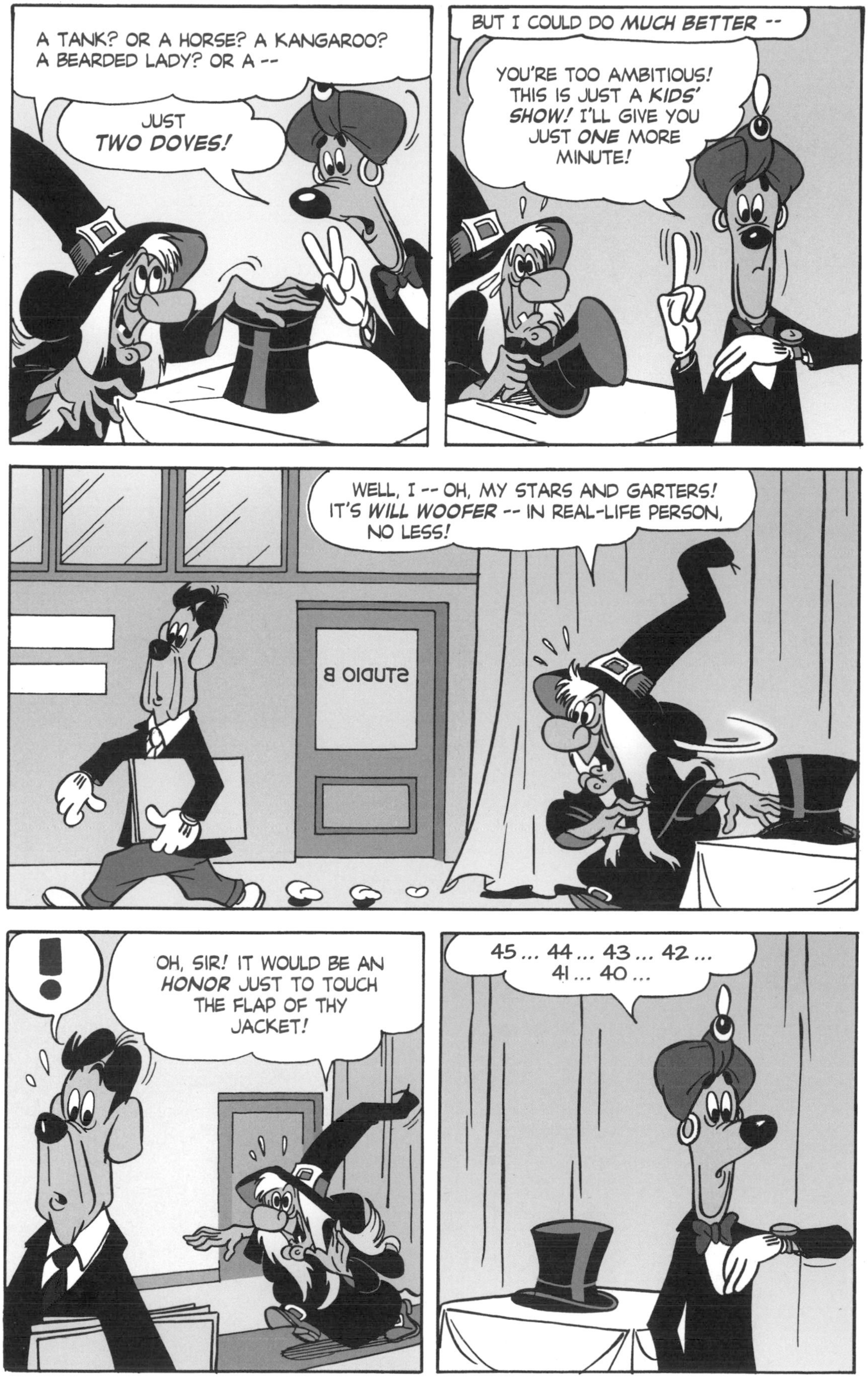
A TANK? OR A HORSE? A KANGAROO? A BEARDED LADY? OR A --
JUST TWO DOVES!
BUT I COULD DO MUCH BETTER --
YOU'RE TOO AMBITIOUS! THIS IS JUST A KIDS' SHOW! I'LL GIVE YOU JUST ONE MORE MINUTE!
WELL, I -- OH, MY STARS AND GARTERS! IT'S WILL WOOFER -- IN REAL-LIFE PERSON, NO LESS!
STUDIO B
!
OH, SIR! IT WOULD BE AN HONOR JUST TO TOUCH THE FLAP OF THY JACKET!
45 ... 44 ... 43 ... 42 ... 41 ... 40 ...

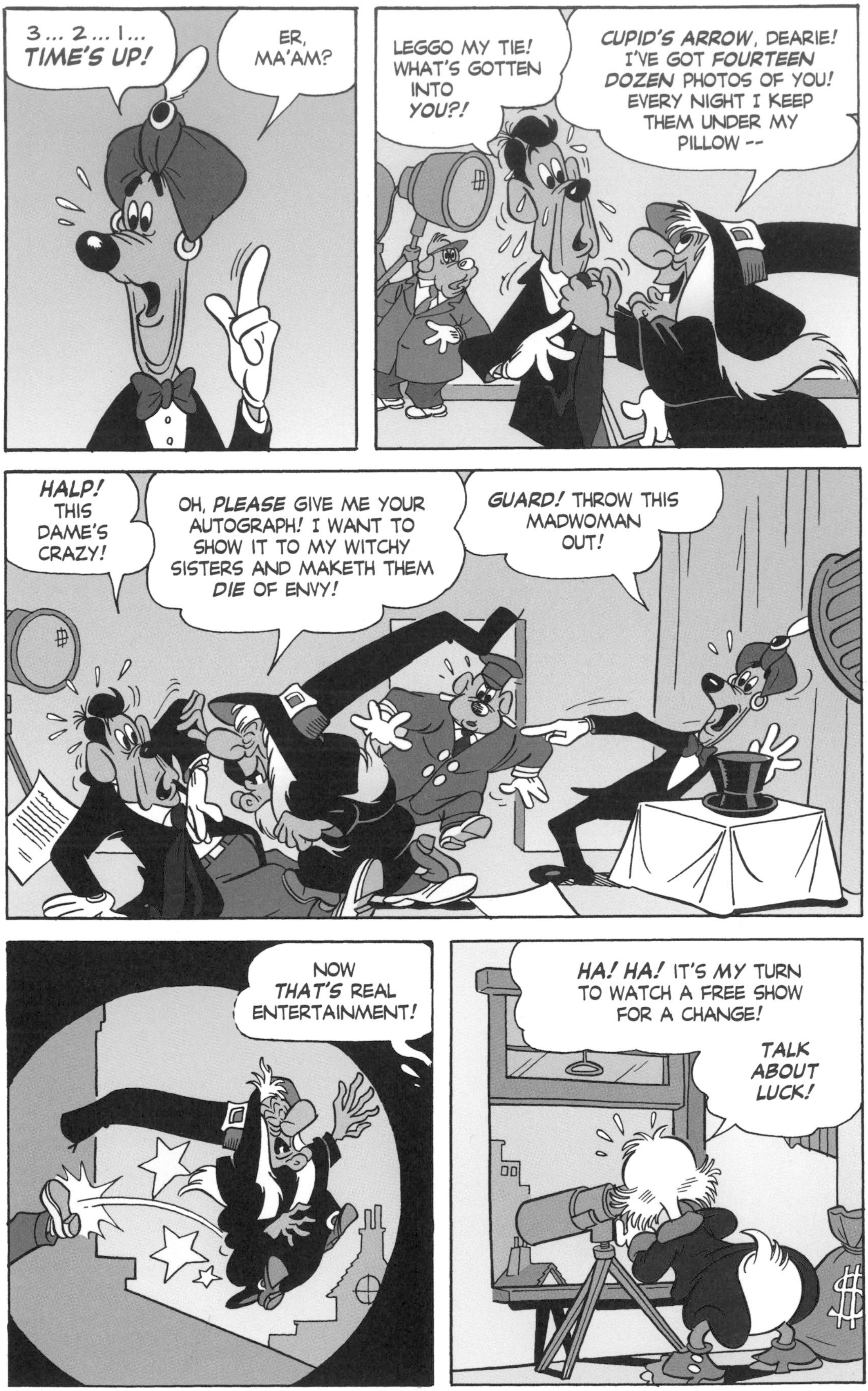
3... 2... 1... TIME'S UP!
ER, MA'AM?
LEGGO MY TIE! WHAT'S GOTTEN INTO YOU?!
CUPID'S ARROW, DEARIE! I'VE GOT FOURTEEN DOZEN PHOTOS OF YOU! EVERY NIGHT I KEEP THEM UNDER MY PILLOW --
HALP! THIS DAME'S CRAZY!
OH, PLEASE GIVE ME YOUR AUTOGRAPH! I WANT TO SHOW IT TO MY WITCHY SISTERS AND MAKETH THEM DIE OF ENVY!
GUARD! THROW THIS MADWOMAN OUT!
NOW THAT'S REAL ENTERTAINMENT!
HA! HA! IT'S MY TURN TO WATCH A FREE SHOW FOR A CHANGE!
TALK ABOUT LUCK!

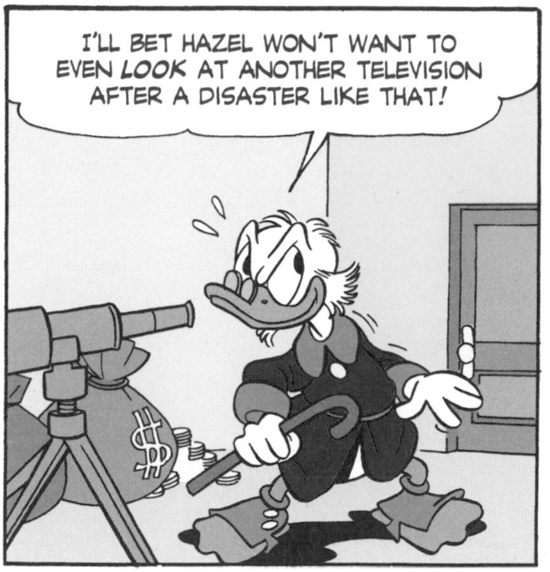
I'LL BET HAZEL WON'T WANT TO EVEN *LOOK* AT ANOTHER TELEVISION AFTER A DISASTER LIKE THAT!

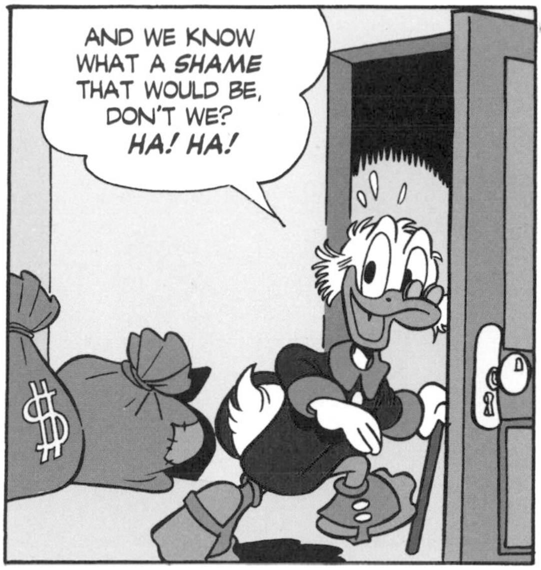
AND WE KNOW WHAT A *SHAME* THAT WOULD BE, DON'T WE? *HA! HA!*

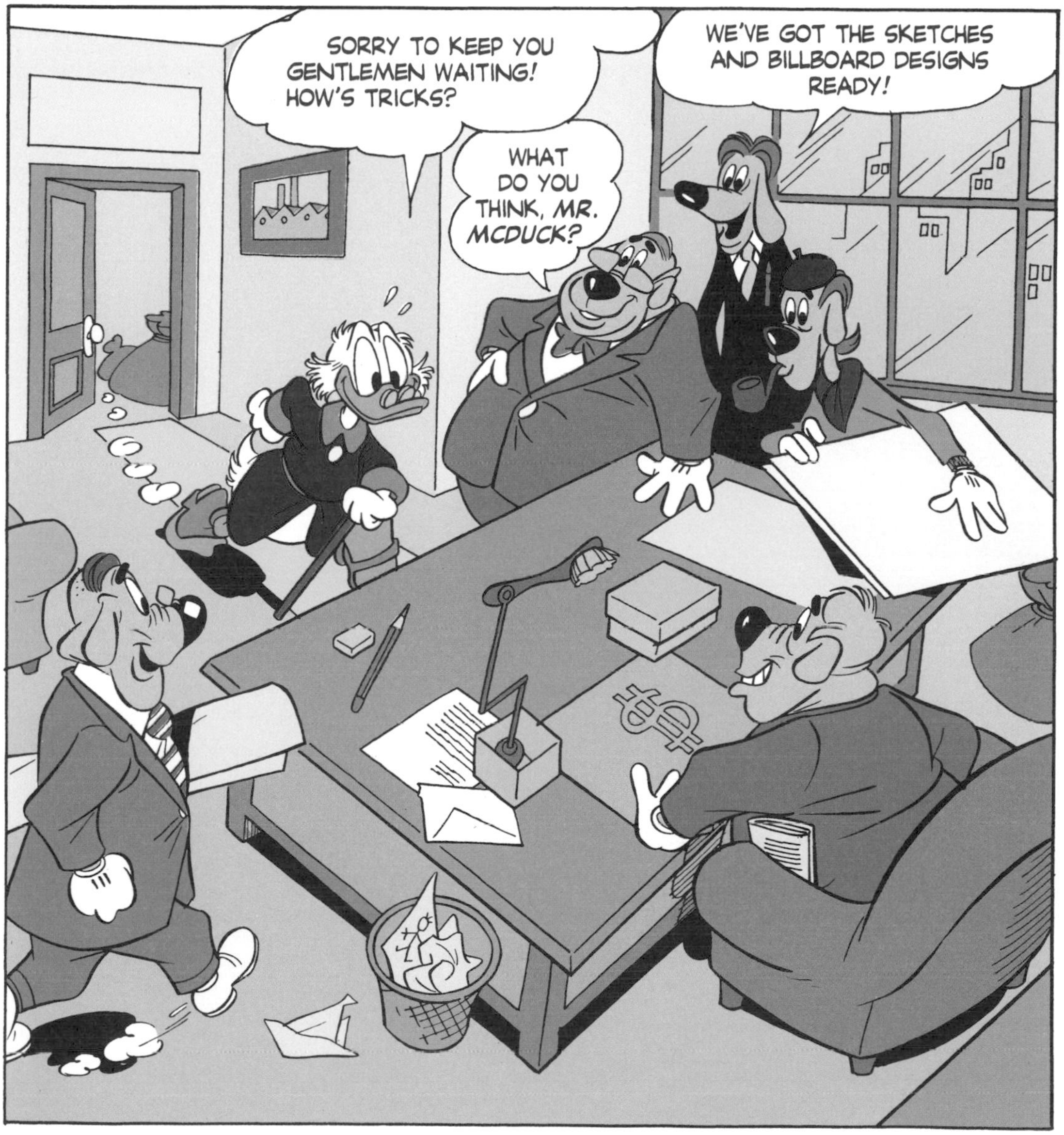
SORRY TO KEEP YOU GENTLEMEN WAITING! HOW'S TRICKS?
WE'VE GOT THE SKETCHES AND BILLBOARD DESIGNS READY!
WHAT DO YOU THINK, *MR. MCDUCK?*

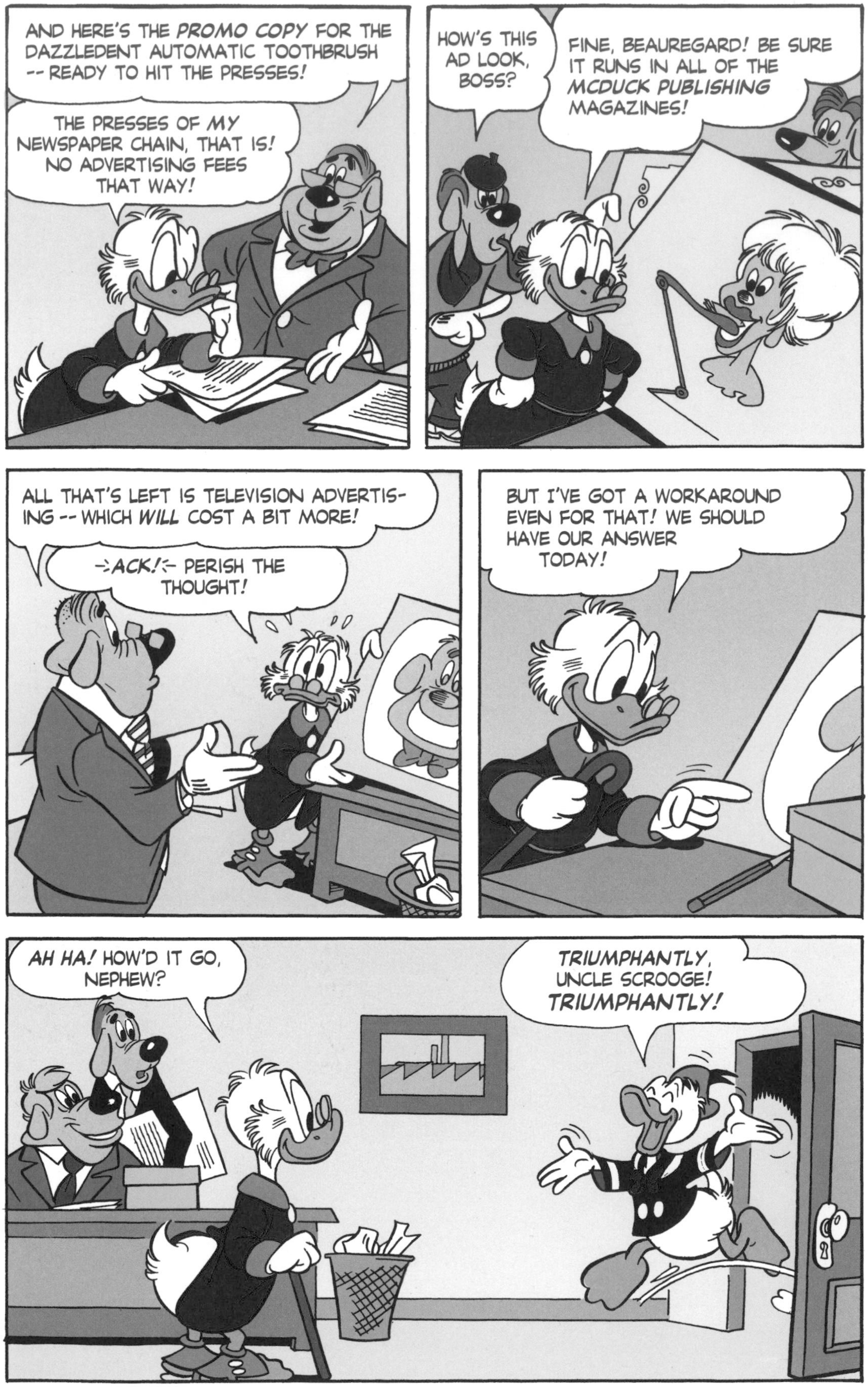
AND HERE'S THE *PROMO COPY* FOR THE DAZZLEDENT AUTOMATIC TOOTHBRUSH -- READY TO HIT THE PRESSES!
THE PRESSES OF *MY* NEWSPAPER CHAIN, THAT IS! NO ADVERTISING FEES THAT WAY!
HOW'S THIS AD LOOK, BOSS?
FINE, BEAUREGARD! BE SURE IT RUNS IN ALL OF THE *McDUCK PUBLISHING* MAGAZINES!
ALL THAT'S LEFT IS TELEVISION ADVERTISING -- WHICH *WILL* COST A BIT MORE!
ACK! PERISH THE THOUGHT!
BUT I'VE GOT A WORKAROUND EVEN FOR THAT! WE SHOULD HAVE OUR ANSWER TODAY!
AH HA! HOW'D IT GO, NEPHEW?
TRIUMPHANTLY, UNCLE SCROOGE! ***TRIUMPHANTLY!***

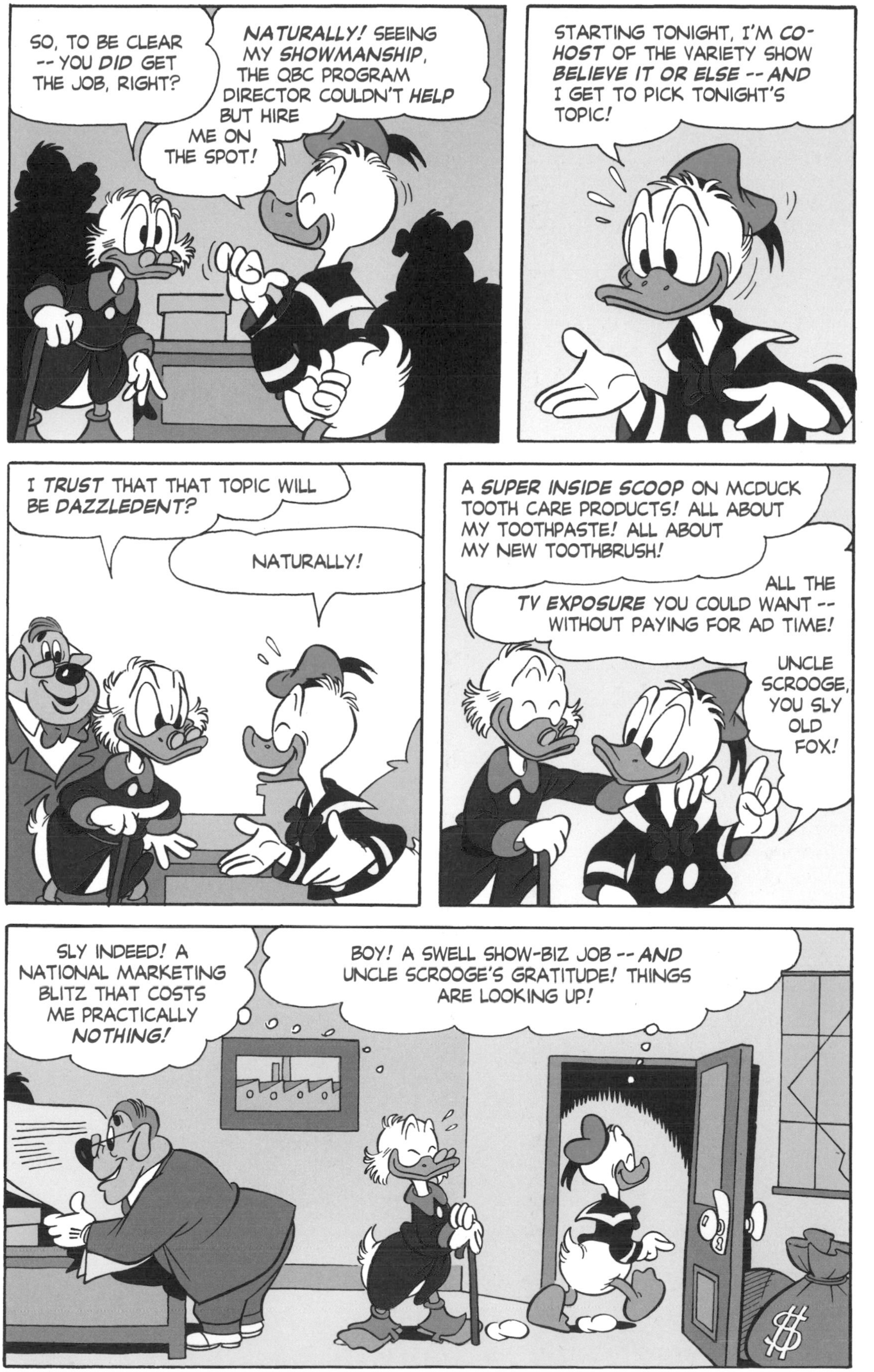
SO, TO BE CLEAR -- YOU *DID* GET THE JOB, RIGHT?
NATURALLY! SEEING MY *SHOWMANSHIP*, THE QBC PROGRAM DIRECTOR COULDN'T *HELP* BUT HIRE ME ON THE SPOT!
STARTING TONIGHT, I'M *CO-HOST* OF THE VARIETY SHOW *BELIEVE IT OR ELSE -- AND* I GET TO PICK TONIGHT'S TOPIC!
I *TRUST* THAT THAT TOPIC WILL BE *DAZZLEDENT?*
NATURALLY!
A *SUPER INSIDE SCOOP* ON MCDUCK TOOTH CARE PRODUCTS! ALL ABOUT MY TOOTHPASTE! ALL ABOUT MY NEW TOOTHBRUSH!
ALL THE *TV EXPOSURE* YOU COULD WANT -- WITHOUT PAYING FOR AD TIME!
UNCLE SCROOGE, YOU SLY OLD FOX!
SLY INDEED! A NATIONAL MARKETING BLITZ THAT COSTS ME PRACTICALLY *NOTHING!*
BOY! A SWELL SHOW-BIZ JOB -- *AND* UNCLE SCROOGE'S GRATITUDE! THINGS ARE LOOKING UP!

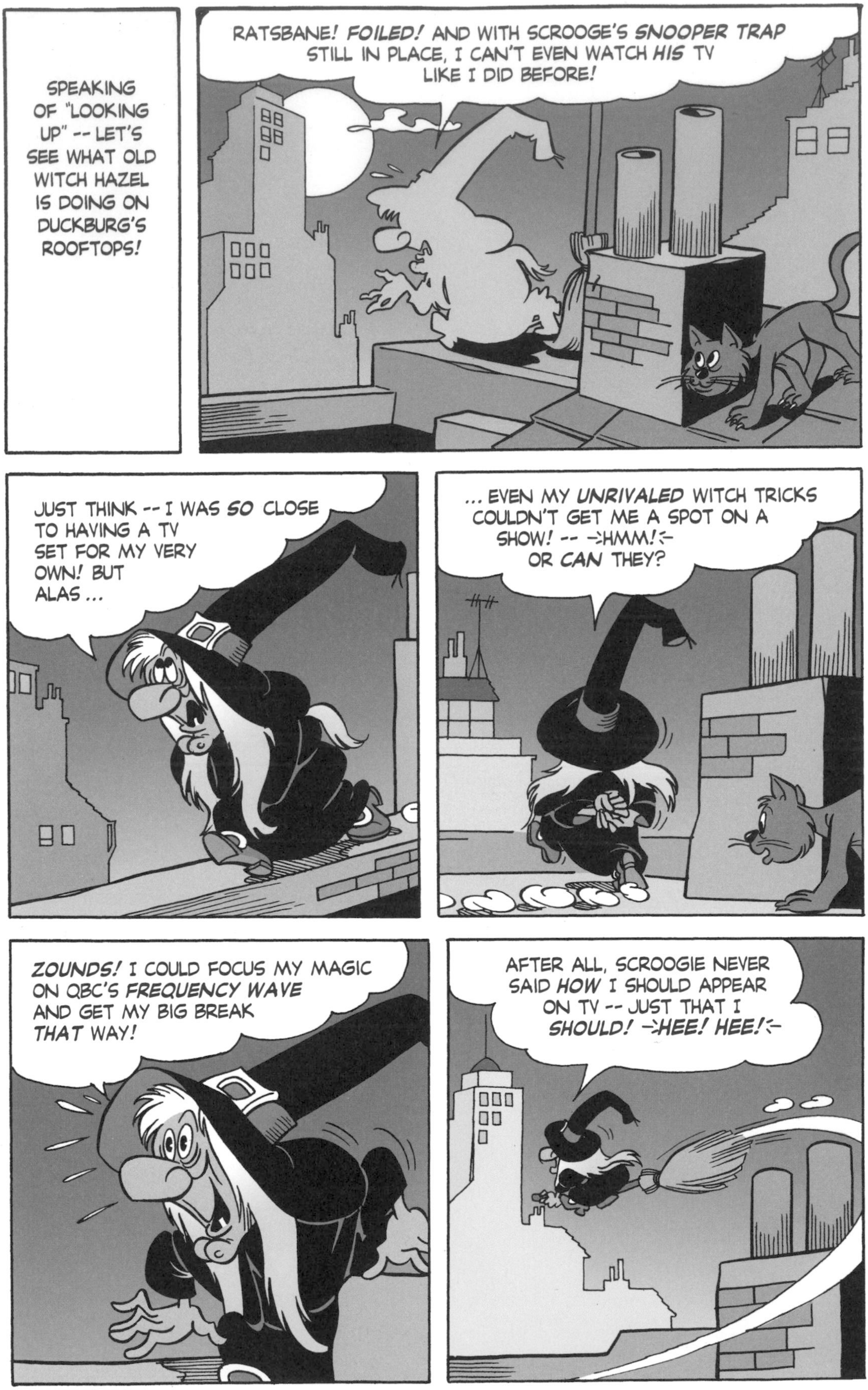
SPEAKING OF "LOOKING UP" -- LET'S SEE WHAT OLD WITCH HAZEL IS DOING ON DUCKBURG'S ROOFTOPS!
RATSBANE! FOILED! AND WITH SCROOGE'S SNOOPER TRAP STILL IN PLACE, I CAN'T EVEN WATCH HIS TV LIKE I DID BEFORE!
JUST THINK -- I WAS SO CLOSE TO HAVING A TV SET FOR MY VERY OWN! BUT ALAS ...
... EVEN MY UNRIVALED WITCH TRICKS COULDN'T GET ME A SPOT ON A SHOW! -- HMM! OR CAN THEY?
ZOUNDS! I COULD FOCUS MY MAGIC ON QBC'S FREQUENCY WAVE AND GET MY BIG BREAK THAT WAY!
AFTER ALL, SCROOGIE NEVER SAID HOW I SHOULD APPEAR ON TV -- JUST THAT I SHOULD! HEE! HEE!

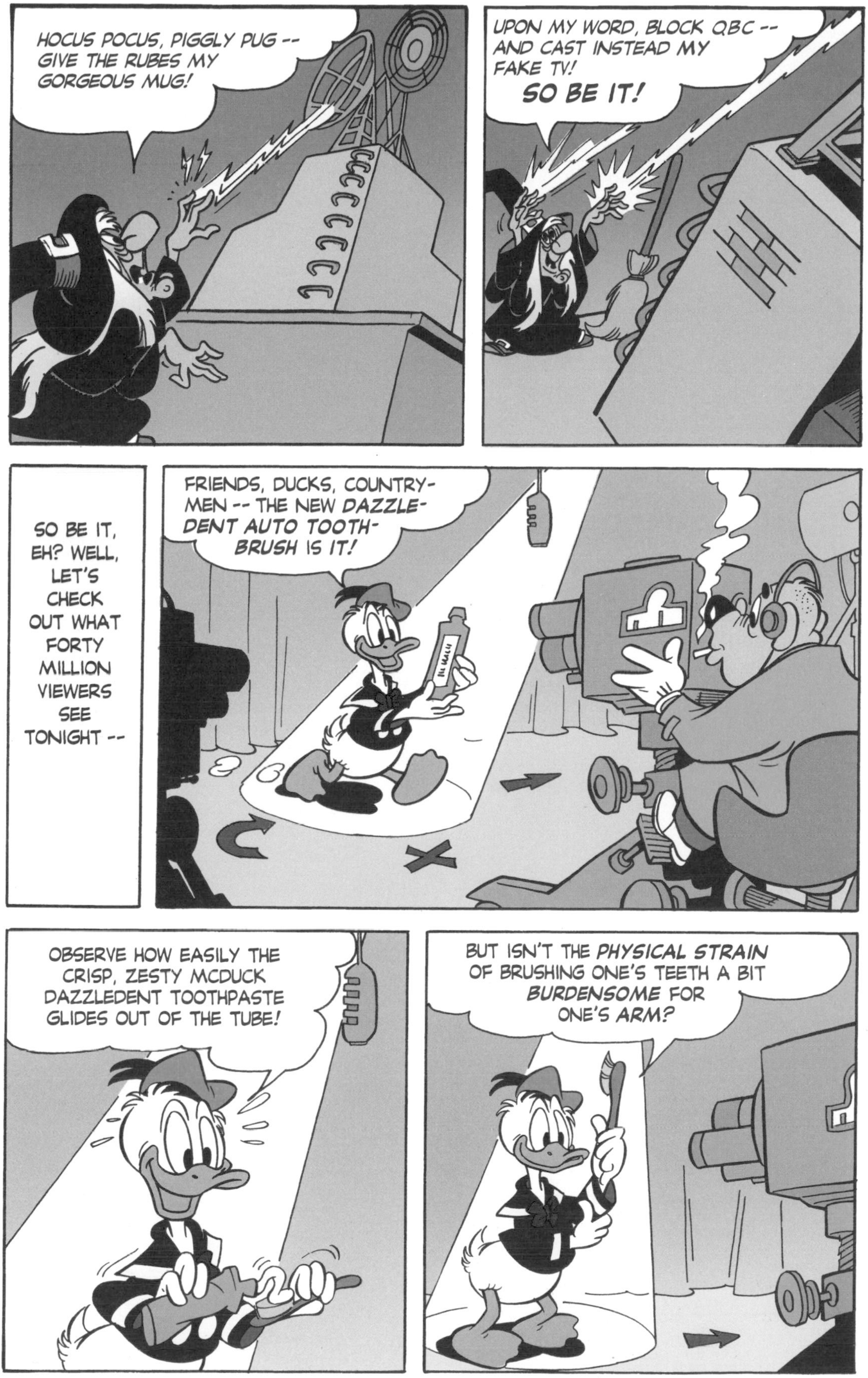

HOCUS POCUS, PIGGLY PUG -- GIVE THE RUBES MY GORGEOUS MUG!
UPON MY WORD, BLOCK QBC -- AND CAST INSTEAD MY FAKE TV!
SO BE IT!
SO BE IT, EH? WELL, LET'S CHECK OUT WHAT FORTY MILLION VIEWERS SEE TONIGHT --
FRIENDS, DUCKS, COUNTRYMEN -- THE NEW DAZZLEDENT AUTO TOOTHBRUSH IS IT!
OBSERVE HOW EASILY THE CRISP, ZESTY MCDUCK DAZZLEDENT TOOTHPASTE GLIDES OUT OF THE TUBE!
BUT ISN'T THE PHYSICAL STRAIN OF BRUSHING ONE'S TEETH A BIT BURDENSOME FOR ONE'S ARM?

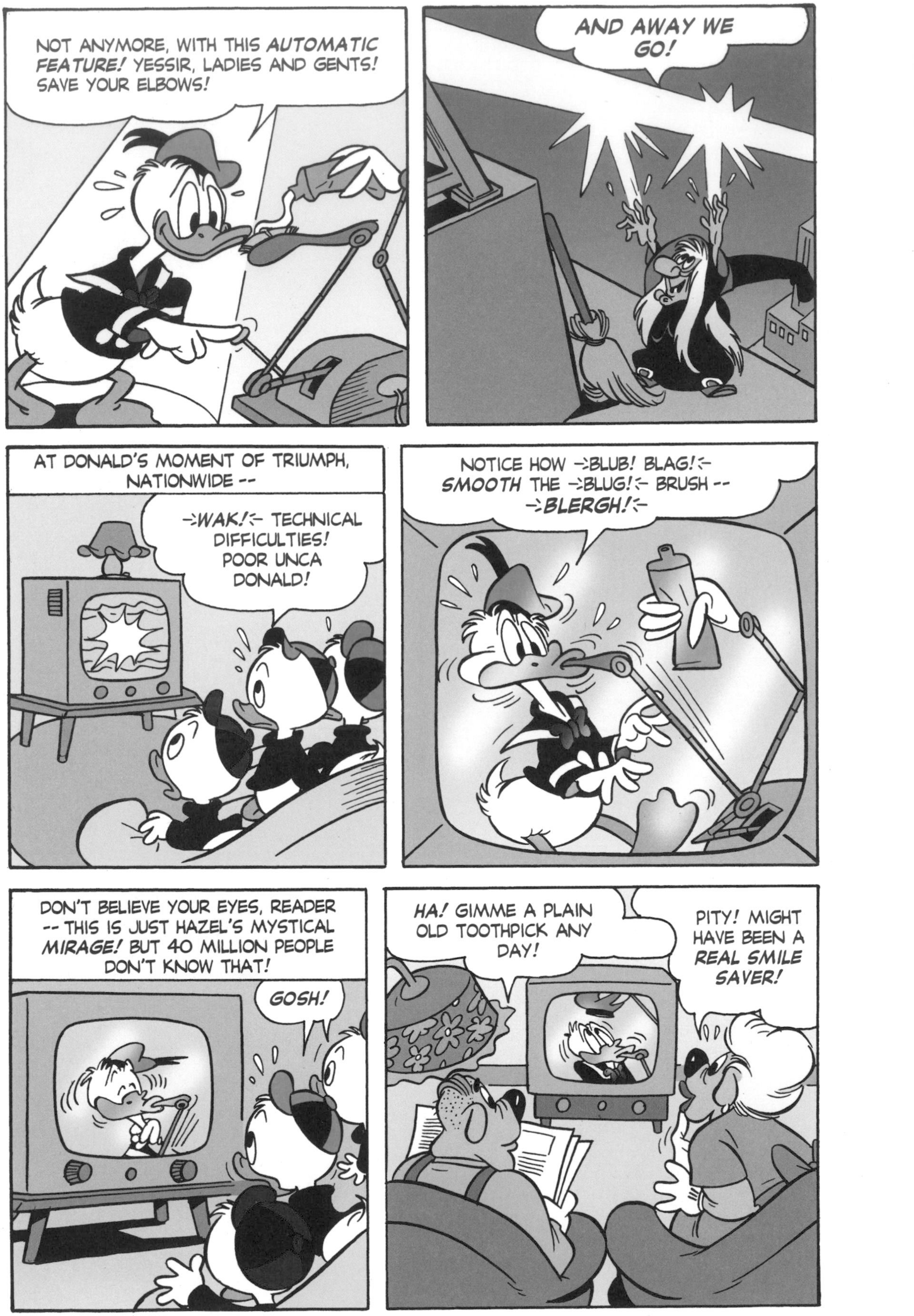
NOT ANYMORE, WITH THIS *AUTOMATIC FEATURE!* YESSIR, LADIES AND GENTS! SAVE YOUR ELBOWS!
AND AWAY WE GO!
AT DONALD'S MOMENT OF TRIUMPH, NATIONWIDE --
WAK! TECHNICAL DIFFICULTIES! POOR UNCA DONALD!
NOTICE HOW *BLUB! BLAG!* *SMOOTH* THE *BLUG!* BRUSH -- *BLERGH!*
DON'T BELIEVE YOUR EYES, READER -- THIS IS JUST HAZEL'S MYSTICAL *MIRAGE!* BUT 40 MILLION PEOPLE DON'T KNOW THAT!
GOSH!
HA! GIMME A PLAIN OLD TOOTHPICK ANY DAY!
PITY! MIGHT HAVE BEEN A *REAL SMILE SAVER!*

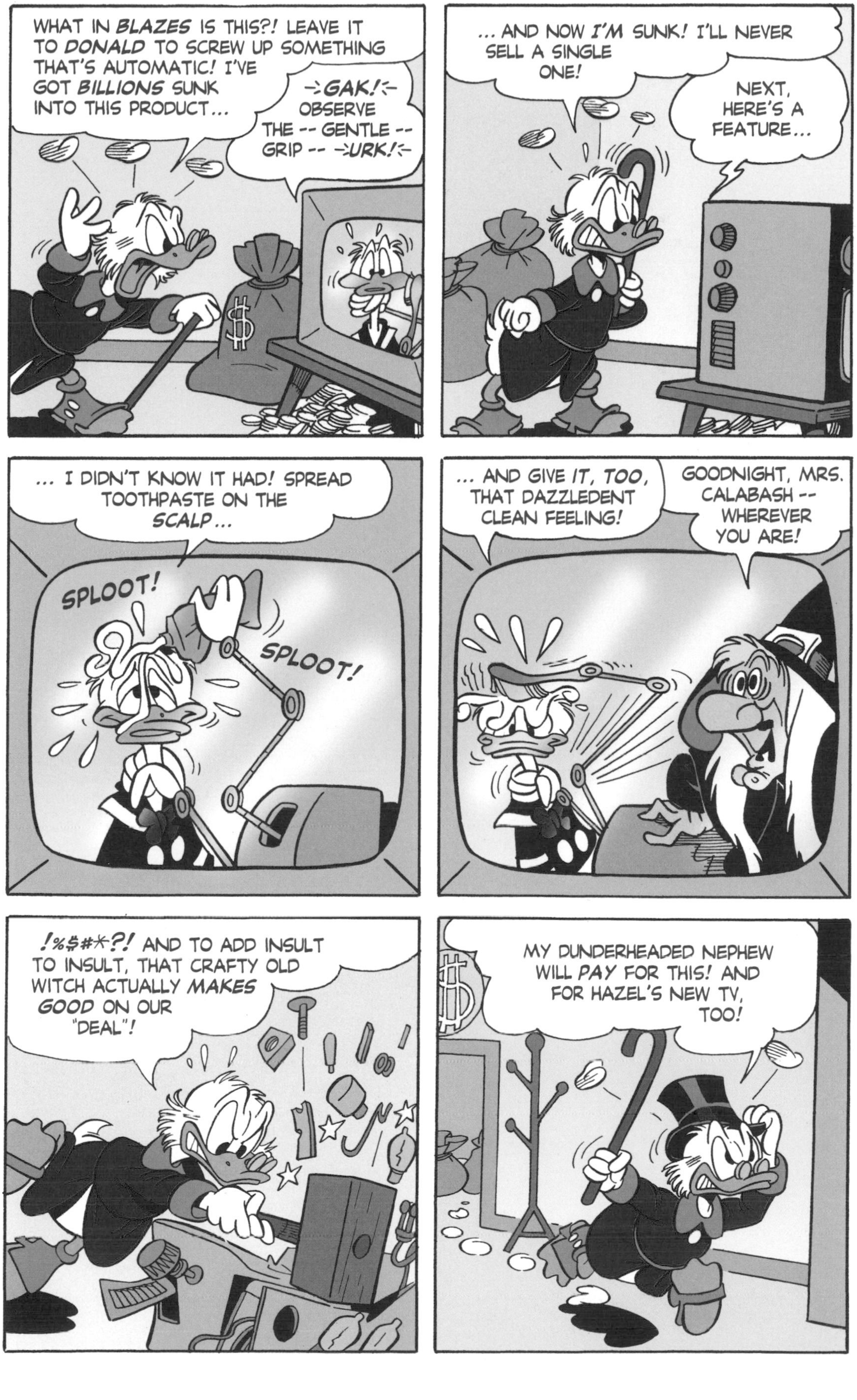
WHAT IN BLAZES IS THIS?! LEAVE IT TO DONALD TO SCREW UP SOMETHING THAT'S AUTOMATIC! I'VE GOT BILLIONS SUNK INTO THIS PRODUCT...
GAK! OBSERVE THE -- GENTLE -- GRIP -- URK!
... AND NOW I'M SUNK! I'LL NEVER SELL A SINGLE ONE!
NEXT, HERE'S A FEATURE...
... I DIDN'T KNOW IT HAD! SPREAD TOOTHPASTE ON THE SCALP...
SPLOOT!
SPLOOT!
... AND GIVE IT, TOO, THAT DAZZLEDENT CLEAN FEELING!
GOODNIGHT, MRS. CALABASH -- WHEREVER YOU ARE!
!%$#*?! AND TO ADD INSULT TO INSULT, THAT CRAFTY OLD WITCH ACTUALLY MAKES GOOD ON OUR "DEAL"!
MY DUNDERHEADED NEPHEW WILL PAY FOR THIS! AND FOR HAZEL'S NEW TV, TOO!

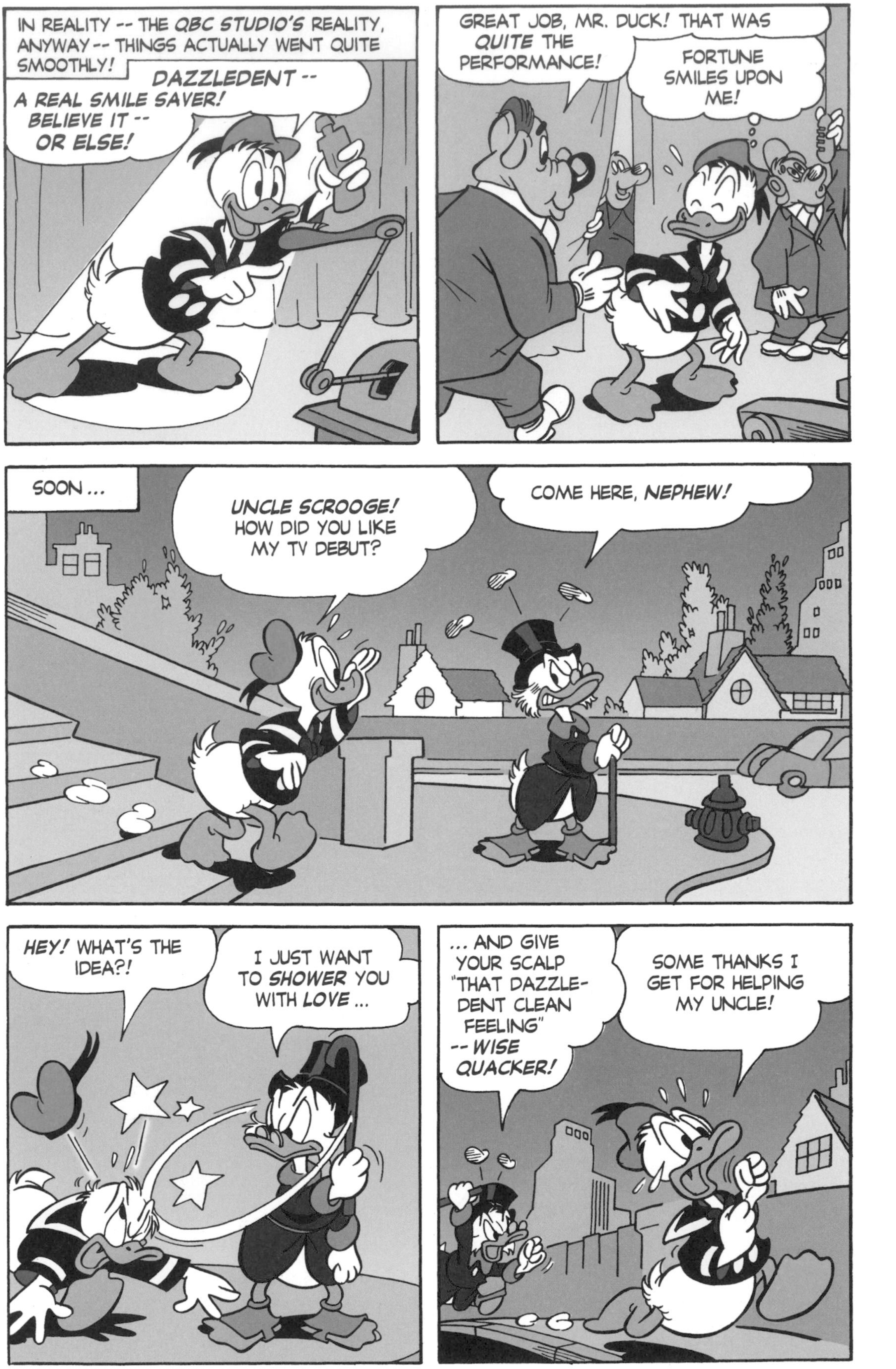

IN REALITY -- THE QBC STUDIO'S REALITY, ANYWAY -- THINGS ACTUALLY WENT QUITE SMOOTHLY!
DAZZLEDENT -- A REAL SMILE SAVER! BELIEVE IT -- OR ELSE!
GREAT JOB, MR. DUCK! THAT WAS QUITE THE PERFORMANCE!
FORTUNE SMILES UPON ME!
SOON ...
UNCLE SCROOGE! HOW DID YOU LIKE MY TV DEBUT?
COME HERE, NEPHEW!
HEY! WHAT'S THE IDEA?!
I JUST WANT TO SHOWER YOU WITH LOVE ...
... AND GIVE YOUR SCALP "THAT DAZZLE-DENT CLEAN FEELING" -- WISE QUACKER!
SOME THANKS I GET FOR HELPING MY UNCLE!

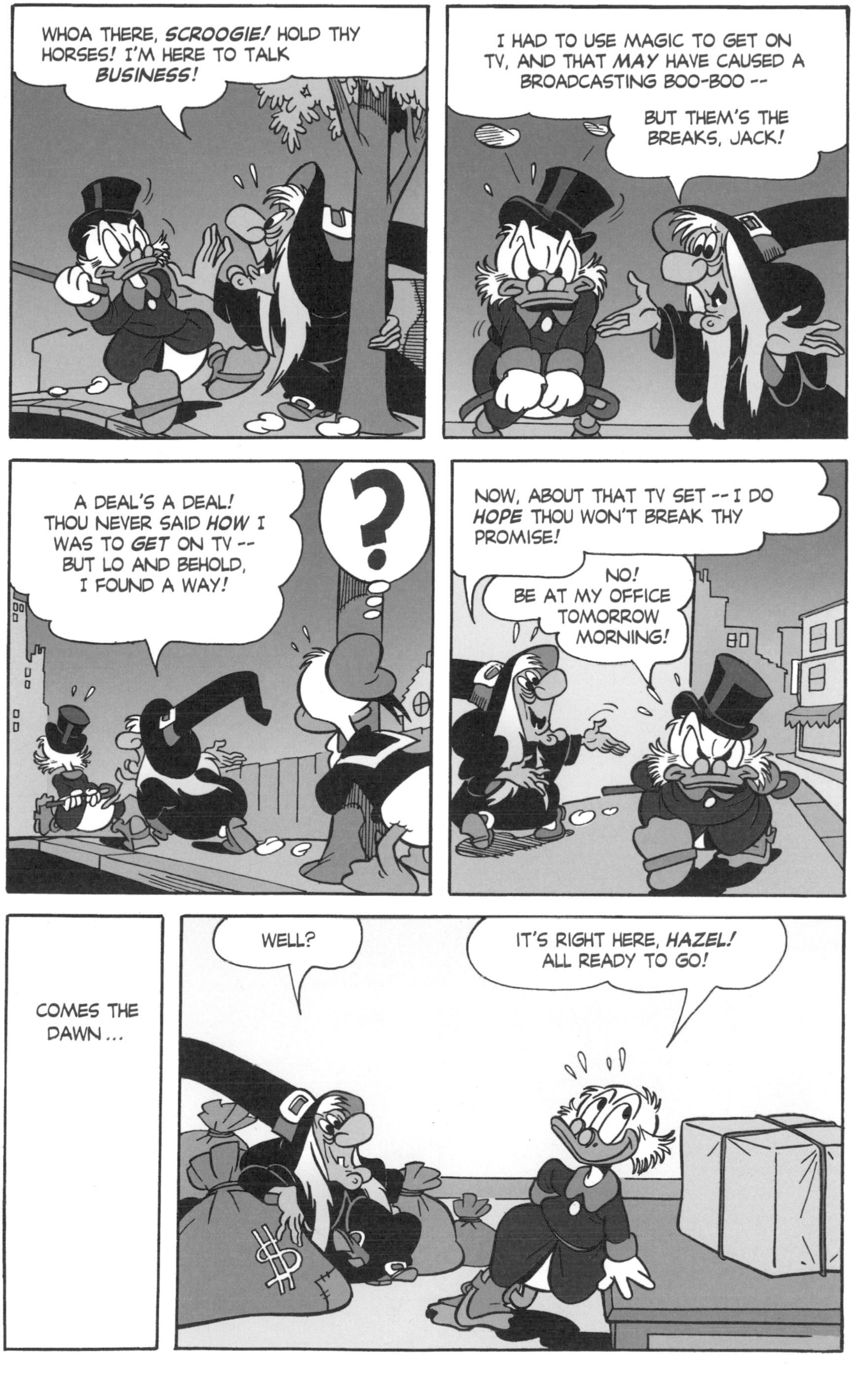
WHOA THERE, SCROOGIE! HOLD THY HORSES! I'M HERE TO TALK BUSINESS!
I HAD TO USE MAGIC TO GET ON TV, AND THAT MAY HAVE CAUSED A BROADCASTING BOO-BOO --
BUT THEM'S THE BREAKS, JACK!
A DEAL'S A DEAL! THOU NEVER SAID HOW I WAS TO GET ON TV -- BUT LO AND BEHOLD, I FOUND A WAY!
?
NOW, ABOUT THAT TV SET -- I DO HOPE THOU WON'T BREAK THY PROMISE!
NO! BE AT MY OFFICE TOMORROW MORNING!
COMES THE DAWN...
WELL?
IT'S RIGHT HERE, HAZEL! ALL READY TO GO!

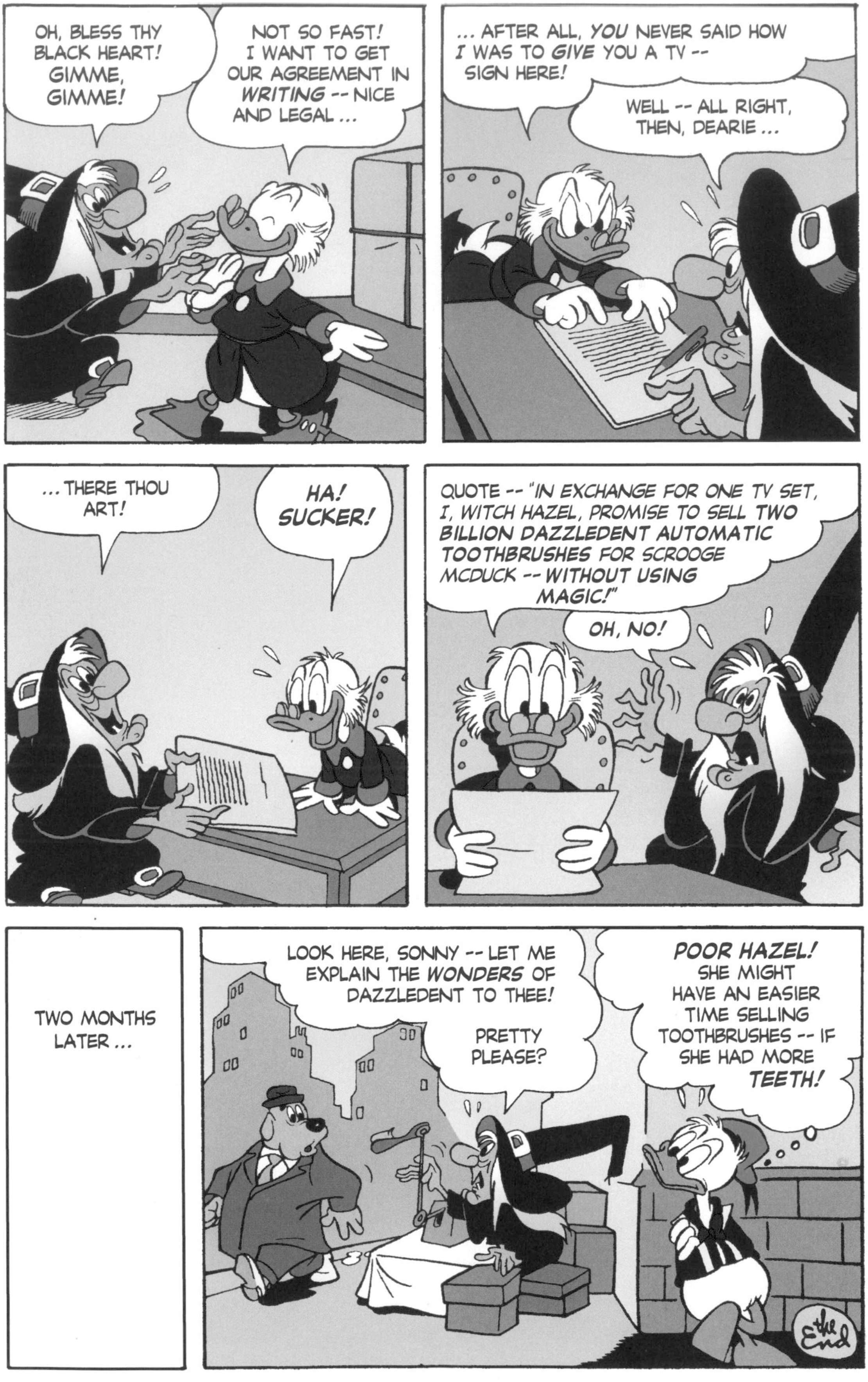
OH, BLESS THY BLACK HEART! GIMME, GIMME!
NOT SO FAST! I WANT TO GET OUR AGREEMENT IN WRITING -- NICE AND LEGAL ...
... AFTER ALL, YOU NEVER SAID HOW I WAS TO GIVE YOU A TV -- SIGN HERE!
WELL -- ALL RIGHT, THEN, DEARIE ...
... THERE THOU ART!
HA! SUCKER!
QUOTE -- "IN EXCHANGE FOR ONE TV SET, I, WITCH HAZEL, PROMISE TO SELL TWO BILLION DAZZLEDENT AUTOMATIC TOOTHBRUSHES FOR SCROOGE MCDUCK -- WITHOUT USING MAGIC!"
OH, NO!
TWO MONTHS LATER ...
LOOK HERE, SONNY -- LET ME EXPLAIN THE WONDERS OF DAZZLEDENT TO THEE!
PRETTY PLEASE?
POOR HAZEL! SHE MIGHT HAVE AN EASIER TIME SELLING TOOTHBRUSHES -- IF SHE HAD MORE TEETH!
the End

Luciano Bottaro

by ARMANDO BOTTO

Disney comics have remained hugely popular in Italy since their debut in the 1930s. That they have managed to retain their success can largely be credited to a handful of talented artists and writers who grew up reading the classic Mickey Mouse and Donald Duck stories by Floyd Gottfredson and Carl Barks and devoted most of their lives to re-creating the same kind of magic in new stories of their own. (In Italy, Mickey is "Topolino," and Donald is "Paperino.")

Luciano Bottaro (1931–2006) is one of those greats: his career spanned more than 54 years, during which he drew — and often wrote — a number of highly regarded adventures, featuring both the Mouse and the Duck families of characters. Not content to stop there, Bottaro also produced an impressive amount of non-Disney comics of the same high quality.

Luciano Bottaro was born in 1931 in Rapallo, a seaside town in northwest Italy. In 1949, he abandoned his studies and tried his luck in the flourishing Italian comics trade, presenting his rough but promising creations to a number of different publishers. He signed his first contract in 1951 with the Genovese publisher Giovanni De Leo, for whom Bottaro produced a set of stories featuring *Aroldo the Buccaneer*, a pirate involved in bizarre, surreal adventures.

That same year, Bottaro contacted Mario Gentilini, editor of *Topolino*, Italy's monthly all-Disney comic book, which had gotten its start reprinting Disney material from America's Dell Comics line. *Topolino's* publisher, the Milan-based powerhouse Mondadori, was preparing to move *Topolino* to a twice-monthly schedule in 1952.

Gentilini was hiring Italian artists because he needed to double his output of Disney comics pages. The number of Disney pages being produced in the United States was simply not enough to fill the Italian publisher's new needs. (Ultimately, *Topolino* would prove popular enough to become a weekly.)

Bottaro became one of the first "Italian Disneys," and together with other masters like Giovan Battista Carpi, Romano Scarpa, Guido Martina, and Bottaro's longtime collaborator, Carlo Chendi, they produced a huge body of Disney comics, most of which, to this day, still has not been seen in the U.S.

Luciano Bottaro in 2006. Image courtesy Paolo Castagno.

The first Disney story drawn by Bottaro hit the newsstands in July 1952. "Donald Duck's Honorific" ("Paperino e le onorificenze") detailed Donald's exhaustive search for a title of nobility. It was scripted by Alberto Testa. But Bottaro was also a prolific writer himself, and he soon started producing his own Disney scripts, making his debut as a writer in January 1954 with "Modern Art Mayhem" ("Paperino e l'arte moderna"), a spoof of contemporary art.

Bottaro also became active outside of the Disney universe with his own creations. The most important was *Pepito*, a series about a young pirate. Created in 1952, it proved especially popular in France, holding down its own comic book title from 1954 to 1972. In order to keep up with a demanding schedule for multiple publishers, Bottaro put together a group of collaborators from his region. Thus the "Rapallo School" was born, nurturing comics creators who would also become Disney regulars — including Giorgio Rebuffi, Guido Scala, and Chendi.

In one of their first team-ups, Bottaro and Chendi decided to use the lovably eccentric Witch Hazel, a Disney character created for animation just a few years earlier — and simultaneously introduced into comics by the American Disney Master, Carl Barks (*Walt Disney's Donald Duck: "Trick or Treat*," Fantagraphics Books 2015).

In April 1956, the funny old crone was the protagonist of Bottaro's and Chendi's "The Super Sucker Spell" ("Paperino e l'aspirapolvere fatato"), in which Hazel punishes Uncle Scrooge for his stinginess by hexing a vacuum cleaner — and causing it to make Scrooge's money disappear!

Chendi and Bottaro brought Hazel back in 1958 in a completely different context. "Dr. Donaldus Faust, M.D." ("Il Dottor Paperus") was one of the so-called "Great Parodies," set-piece stories in which the Ducks and Mice took leading roles in new versions of literary classics. In this case, Donald portrayed Faust, made famous by Marlowe and Goethe. Hazel fit perfectly into a story based on the supernatural.

But Bottaro's most definitive portrayal of Witch Hazel came in 1960. In "The Washed-Up Witch" ("Pippo e la fattucchiera"), Hazel meets Goofy, who — eccentric though he may be — definitely does *not* believe in witches and magic. Hazel tries everything to convince him, but thanks to a comedic series of unlucky breaks, every attempt is a flop. This very funny story was a great success — so much so that Goofy and Hazel's interactions became an ongoing theme in Italian Disney productions exploited by Bottaro — alone or with Chendi — in 11 more adventures in the years that followed.

The final Bottaro-drawn story to appear in *Topolino*, "Goofy and the Witch-Way Crown" ("Pippo e la corona delle streghe," 2005), brought the cycle of stories to a delicate and moving finale.

Bottaro drew more than 100 stories for Italian Disney comic books in the 1950s and 1960s. Standouts included a spectacular run of "Great Parodies," including spoofs of Alexandre Dumas's *The Count of Monte Cristo*, Homer's *Iliad*, Robert Louis Stevenson's *Treasure Island*, and Edmond Rostand's *Cyrano de Bergerac*. At 60 to 80 pages, the "Great Parodies" were longer than more typical Italian comics stories and so were serialized in two or three weekly installments.

In 1968, in the story "Tycoonraker! or From Zantaf with Lumps!" ("Paperino missione Zantaf"), Bottaro and Chendi introduced Dr. Zantaf, an eccentric, snake-loving mad scientist who still pops up in Italian Disney Duck adventures to this day.

"Tycoonraker!" also featured Donald's first appearance as an agent of the MIA (McDuck Intelligence Agency), Uncle Scrooge's private spy organization, which also continues its cloak-and-dagger mission into the present day in an ongoing series of stories by other authors.

Bottaro's work with Mondadori slowed in the 1970s. During that period and throughout the 1980s, he devoted more of his time to comics characters created by himself and his Rapallo School colleagues — among them, the humanized mushroom *Pon Pon*, the psychedelic *King of Spades* (*Re di Picche*), the bear-and-trapper duo *Whisky & Gogo*, and the Canadian Mountie, *Baldo*.

In 1981, Bottaro also devoted himself to a comics version of Collodi's original *Pinocchio*, serialized in the weekly magazine *Il Giornalino*.

But Bottaro was not entirely absent from Disney during this period. From 1978 to 1985, he drew all the illustrations for four sticker albums published by Panini: *Mickey Story*, *Donald Story*, *Goofy Olympique*, and *Disney Show* — the first two of which commemorated Mickey's and Donald's life stories with numerous tributes to vintage comics and cartoons.

In the 1990s, Bottaro returned to producing new Disney comics on a regular basis. By now, the artist's style — already bouncy and cutting-edge — had become even more original. His stories featured plotlines that allowed for near-psychedelic deformations of characters' shapes. Bottaro had definitely achieved the status as a master of comic art — in 1996, he received the prestigious Yellow Kid Award, in recognition of his lifetime career in comics.

Luciano Bottaro passed away in 2006, after a long illness that took its toll on his output in his final years. Nevertheless, he remained active until the end — working on the development of a new series that would have featured the Disney Ducks in the 17th century, in Bottaro's beloved pirate setting.

Bottaro's Disney output amounts to more than 150 stories, for a total of about 5,000 pages. His non-Disney comics are much more difficult to catalogue, as they appeared in a number of different publications — some of them obscure — over the span of half a century.

In 2008, the city of Rapallo honored its native son by naming a town square after him. Even if we can't track down all of his creative works, it is easy to find Piazzetta Luciano Bottaro, a spot at which he will always be remembered.